HER LAST RACE

KIM SCHAUMBURG

Black Rose Writing
www.blackrosewriting.com

ISBN: 978-1-61296-024-1

PUBLISHED BY BLACK ROSE WRITING

www.blackrosewriting.com

Printed in the United States of America

Her Last Race is printed in Book Antiqua

For the Horses, who have no voice and no choice

&

To Dad

Acknowledgments

First off, my apologies to everyone I'm going to forget to thank. This book took me so long to write that any appreciation oversights are due to my bad memory and poor record keeping, not ingratitude.

My sincere thanks to the following people: To my readers, Joni Dannis, Marie Coro, John and Mary Douglas, Cheryl Force, Darek and Jane Grant, Judy Harrison, Bernadette Henzi, Carol Hoover, and Denny and Jan Prichard for their observations and encouragement. To Sydelle Kramer, for taking the time to critique my manuscript back when it wasn't an easy read. To William Brown, for his wonderfully encouraging letter that I treasure. To Paul Littleton and Beverly Pedersen, for their excellent last minute help. To my friend Virginia Young, for all her reminders to never give up. To my late grandmother, Bobbie Beeler, for her unconditional love and encouragement and for sharing written memories of my mother's early childhood, which became the diary excerpts. To my late grandparents, John and Jean Schaumburg, for all their love and support over the years. To the late Thoroughbred trainer and real life cowboy, R.G. Pierce, for sharing some of his old-school horse trainer know-how and for giving me a chance to ride at a time when women jockeys were not popular. To Dr. Elliot Simpkins DVM, for his expertise with the novel's veterinary details; hopefully, I managed to get things right. To Waverly Fitzgerald, for her excellent critique. To my agents, Fran Pardi and Anita Melograna, for believing and for all their hard work. To my editors, Phyllis Hatefield and Irene Wanner, for teaching me how to write, with a special thanks to Irene for her racetrack insight, honesty, and inspiration over the years.

Peninsula Park, San Mateo, California
November 1993

Gray, everywhere gray, dark but not dark, morning yet not light, a time when things took on shape and shadowy form but no detail. A murky silhouette of horses and riders. The snap of a whip, the ebb and flow of hoof beats, the choo-choo blows of exertion as if horses were steam engines.

From atop a black gelding that stood with his muscled rump perpendicular to the chain-link backstretch fence on Peninsula Park's main racetrack, Rachel Nottingham, a Thoroughbred horse trainer, followed two of her charges as they finished a predawn workout. On the far side of the track, the pair sailed toward the finish, head and head, an ambiguous projectile. The trainer killed the splithand on her stopwatch as the horses galloped past the wire but continued to clock them another furlong, until they reached the seven-eighth's pole. She checked the time, then slipped the stopwatch into her jacket pocket. Her mount twitched an ear and shifted his weight off one hip.

At this early hour, the racetrack was busy. Joggers owned the perimeter, some backtracking to warm up or exit the track, others trotting a mile or more, all traveling clockwise, while gallopers, traveling counterclockwise, occupied the middle lane with the inside rail reserved for the fastest. There were horses who galloped with classic form, necks bowed and pulling against themselves, while others carried their heads stiffly higher and fought to go as they pleased. Exercise riders crouched in the irons, straining to keep their high-strung mounts in check, reins crossed along serrated-rubber strips and held firmly at the base of the withers. If dressage horses embodied the ultimate in communication between horse and rider, racehorses represented the opposite extreme.

Rachel was, therefore, not alarmed when a horse backtracking along the outside fence bolted toward her two workers as they galloped out. Near misses were commonplace. And with daylight yet sparse, she was too far away to clearly see what happened.

"Shit," she said, when only one of the pair exited the turn, an iron-jawed colt with a blaze like a bald-faced heifer. Rachel reined her ponyhorse hard right and loped into the flow of traffic, all the while glancing over her shoulder to gauge the approach of the colt with bad brakes. His white face closed in. The jockey steered to Rachel's outside. She gunned her mount and snagged the colt by the left rein before he shot past, eased both horses to a trot, then a walk. Unwrapping a strap from her saddle horn, she slipped the length of leather through the colt's snaffle ring bit and he reared and bounced against the pony, kicked out with both hind feet and cantered in place, a flesh-and-blood rocking horse. With a firm but gentle hand, Rachel cocked his head to her knee, angling his rump and catty heels away from her pony. After a brief pause to face the inside rail, she turned and loped both horses along the outside fence toward the gap.

"What the hell happened?" she asked the jockey.

He turned his head away to spit. "Horse on the outside fence bolted into us, coming outta the turn."

"Vanderford's mare go down?"

"Yeah."

"Shit."

Rachel slowed her pony to a walk at the gap and led the colt off the track and onto the broad stretch of sand there. One of the outriders had closed the chain-link entry gate. The red light signaling a loose horse was flashing atop the clocker's stand, a tiny raised fortress of white with green trim, not much bigger than an outhouse, which bordered the track between entrance and exit. The clocker called out to her, wanting to know the names of the two horses that his colleagues in the upper reaches of the grandstand had just clocked five-eighths.

Ignoring the man, she passed the colt to a groom who was waiting to lead him to the barn, then wheeled her pony and sent him back onto the track in a fast trot. The clocker's voice cut the air as she hung a left at the exit and galloped past.

"Track's closed, Nottingham. And no galloping the wrong way or you'll be paying a visit to the stewards again."

Rachel glared at the clocker as she rode by, then gunned her pony. He was blowing hard when she pulled him up on the clubhouse turn. Her other worker, a chestnut mare, had risen and was standing in the middle of the track just past the three-quarter pole with the jockey at her head, the kid—some apprentice whose name Rachel could never recall—looking pale beneath a face full of dirt but otherwise undamaged. The horse that had caused the accident was nowhere in sight and presumably had been caught by one of the outriders, while the gallop boy sat slumped on the ground by the outside fence, moaning about his ankle. Rachel regarded the young man a moment, decided he would live, then dismounted and went to her horse.

The mare was holding up her left foreleg, her hoof and pastern bent forward at an unnatural angle. Rachel muttered a profanity and turned away. The track veterinarian, who had driven up in a shiny Ford Bronco, stepped from his vehicle without a word and examined the mare's leg, then turned to Rachel.

"I don't need to tell you it's bad," the vet said. "She have any value as a broodmare?"

"She's a cheap claimer with no breeding," Rachel said.

"It's not compound fractured, so there's always a chance of saving her. Probably cost a small fortune, though."

"And she'd be good for what?"

"Your barn mascot?" he said, cracking a smile.

Rachel frowned.

The vet cleared his throat. "Seriously, I'd have to see X-rays to be certain, but I've treated worse. There's a decent chance she'll heal up if you splint the leg, providing she doesn't founder or colic."

Rachel remounted her pony. The morning was growing lighter and mist formed above dewy ground, a wispy haze that hugged the earth, then thinned and vanished as it rose.

"Put her down," she said, and galloped away.

~

Two days later, Rachel flew to Los Angeles and attended a Thoroughbred yearling auction at Hollywood Park. After inspecting horses all afternoon and most of the evening, she had selected fourteen for serious consideration from the 154 consigned to be sold. At nine the next morning, hip 1 was led in nickering and trembling. The auctioneer's call crackled from loudspeakers to charge the atmosphere with a quick fire chant of numbers and rhetoric, seven-eighths factual with a dash of bullshit lest anyone doubt he was really a salesman. He oversaw the action at center stage from an elevated, polished wood stand that resembled a judge's bench. Black cast-iron horse-head posts and two strands of thick gold rope enclosed the ring. Bid spotters in tuxedos patrolled a narrow walkway along the front row. Overhead screens displayed the hip number and current price. By ten-fifteen, the sale arena's amphitheater was three-quarters filled.

Rachel had no interest in any of the first dozen or so yearlings and sat smoking a cigarette in the third row, long legs stretched out, her boots propped onto the armrest of an empty seat in the preceding row. An African bush hat rested just above her dark eyebrows. A khaki jacket and pants with a leopard-spotted silk shirt completed her outfit. When someone tapped her from behind, she took a drag and glanced over her shoulder. Two men were standing there.

"Security, madam. There's no smoking," the one told her.

"Management's ordered us to escort you from the premises," the other said.

Rachel yanked her feet from the armrest and pitched forward, crushing the cigarette in an empty coffee cup on the floor while at the same time exhaling a lungful of smoke. She quickly straightened, twisted around in her seat, and flashed the two security officers a smile, then noticed that they lacked uniforms and looked suspiciously like a couple of frat boys. Her expression went cold as they struggled to hold straight faces.

"Reno McAllister sends his regards," the one said.

"He's sick of choking on your secondhand smoke and wants you to shove that cigarette up your ass," the other said.

The pair burst into laughter.

Rachel stared at the young men until they were quite through, and then turned back around. Reno McAllister could just go to hell, she thought. She'd come to buy horses, not play games with her rival. J.K. Vanderford, her biggest client who owned several dozen horses in training, sat to her right, Seth Marten, another wealthy client, to her left. Since returning home to northern California ten years ago with eight horses and a reputation as an up-and-coming trainer on the tough New York circuit, her stable had grown to seventy-plus head and she'd captured the last five training titles at Peninsula Park, the Bay Area's super track. She hadn't set out to win any congeniality awards.

The bidding on hip 12 proceeded at a crawl for several minutes before the hammer finally fell and the electronic board flashed sold. The yearling was calf-kneed, a serious conformation fault in which the forelegs appear to bend back at the knees. He had sold too high, Rachel decided, but the agent consigning the colt was noted for bidding up the price. An accepted if not admirable practice. Hip 12 was led from the ring. A worker, armed with a shovel, rushed out to clear away any road apples. Rachel was thumbing through her sale catalog, when J.K. Vanderford elbowed her arm.

"Everybody's always gunning for the top dog," he said.

She grinned. "'Top dog' isn't the canine term I'm accustomed to hearing."

"I don't imagine," he said, with a straight face that contradicted several nasal snorts.

"Thanks for the support, J.K."

"You were any nicer, I'd have to find a new trainer."

"I'm not all that nice."

He ran a finger over a silver mustache that resembled a steel wire brush. "I was kidding. Tell me again about my chestnut mare that had to be put down."

Rachel looked at Vanderford. When one of his horses lost a race, he would shrug and have a gin and tonic, such conduct having earned him the distinction of being her most pleasant client.

"Her leg was a mess," she said.

"Beyond repair, I take it?"

"No sense throwing good money after bad."

"I see. Well, if the wife asks, be sure and mention the astronomical odds of saving her. She was rather fond of the mare."

"These horses aren't pets, J.K."

"No, of course not."

"Mare win three races this year, so I feel bad as anyone. You'll be letting me claim a replacement, I assume?"

"Possibly," he said. "In the spring."

Rachel rolled her lips under and out. "Reno McAllister keeps buying all my decent horses, I'll be down to two ponies and a goat by then."

"Relax. Meet's only a month old and you're already six wins up on Reno."

"He's not just pilfering my claimers, in case you haven't heard."

Like most public trainers with large stables, the majority of Rachel's horses competed in claiming races, which comprised six or seven of the nine events on an average Peninsula Park card and formed the bottom of horse racing's class pyramid. In her opinion, claiming races imparted a modicum of fairness into an unfair world by helping to ensure that horses of similar ability competed together. Of course, the system rewarded trainers, such as herself, but she refused to apologize or feel guilty for being competent. If a trainer couldn't take the heat, he or she needed to get the fuck away from the stove because claimers were an indigestible soup of training challenges.

In human terms, she likened the sport's recruitment of Thoroughbreds to that of drafting every available kid, even those who flunked P.E. in high school, had attention deficit disorder, sociopath issues, or were accident prone, and then turning them into professional athletes. Cheap claimers were the toughest to train, horses who were afflicted with physical and mental limitations, plus any number of injuries, both chronic and not. And a $5,000 claimer ran for about half the purse money of a $50,000 horse but cost the same to train. Although, they cost ten times less to buy, which was why she usually had her clients claim the $50,000 horses.

Presently, none of her clients was willing to risk fifty grand for her to purchase a claimer of uncertain soundness, knowing that after the race, alive or dead, they owned the horse. Only last year, she'd lost a $10,000 claimer that was worth the money, but the owners were quite pleased to have gotten a win check and ten thousand upon hearing that their former horse, who was a temperamental sort, had reared in the test barn after the race, hit his head and died. With episodes like that, it was no wonder clients had a tendency to view claiming as a crapshoot, a guessing game, a pin-the-tail-on-the-donkey affair. Checkers as opposed to chess.

But Rachel knew better and spent almost as much time watching her own horses train as she did everyone else's because the claiming game was played twenty-four seven and most of the contestants were professional amateurs who regularly entered animals over their heads or jumped in to halter horses without doing their homework. And then they whined and cried foul if they actually ran a horse where it had a shot to win and another trainer claimed it, as though claiming was a hypothetical concept and the horse hadn't really been up for sale. Which, in Rachel's book of training sins, smacked of the top no-no: falling in love with one's horses.

She fully expected to lose horses via claims. What had her concerned was the exodus of her allowance and stakes horses, her most valuable stock that ran for larger purses and changed hands only by conventional transactions.

"Don't tell me you're still moping over Speedmeister Slew?" Vanderford asked.

"Colt was the top two-year old on the West Coast," she said. "Hell no, I'm real pleased you sold him to my toughest rival."

"A man receives a phenomenal offer, he'd be a fool to turn it down. Besides, Reno's client sent the colt to Santa Anita."

"Yeah, at least McAllister doesn't get to train the best damn colt I've ever developed."

Vanderford slapped her between the shoulder blades. "I've the utmost confidence you'll find me another Speedmeister today."

Rachel just rolled her eyes.

She knew damn well that *that* was the goal of everyone sitting in the amphitheater who intended to make a bid. Each year horsemen throughout the country attended Thoroughbred yearling sales with dreams of buying the big horse, be it a winner of prestigious races coast-to-coast or merely a local champion. Her expectations were more realistic. Namely, she hoped her two-year olds could run fast enough to win races, even if only at the cheapest competitive level, because talent was not a given. Training a two-year old up to a race was an expensive, often disappointing, proposition. She'd watched her father spend countless painstaking hours on worthless two-year-olds in the seven-foot, solid-board fence that enclosed the family ranch's round pen. Her father drove the yearlings like a coachman without a buggy, walking behind them, a line in each hand, teaching them to guide to the bit. Or broke them, sometimes getting bucked off. Or stood in the center like a circus ringmaster while a riderless horse galloped round and round, then changed directions at the flick of the whip to work the other way. "If you're going to do something, do it right," he'd drilled into her head. They had got by, she and he, just barely, doing everything themselves.

The memory of it made her crave a peanut butter and marmalade sandwich. Or a smoke. Beside her, J.K. and his grown son were trading ribald comments like old fishing buddies. Rachel took out a cigarette and wondered where she'd now be if her father hadn't died and left her at twenty-three with the family's central California ranch mortgaged to the hilt. They'd seldom talked, let alone laughed or joked, so she suspected he wouldn't have been sitting by her side. She put the cigarette between her lips and raised a lighter. Then Seth Marten slammed his left fist against her armrest.

Her heart was pounding as she calmly gathered the cigarette and lighter from her lap and returned them to her purse. Marten seemed unaware that he'd startled her. Pushing fifty, his dark hair looked vacuum-able and lent him a distinct resemblance to one of the Three Stooges. At the thought, Rachel managed a smile.

"Yes, Seth?"

"I like this fifteen," he said. "He's a royally bred son-of-a-bitch."

"Colt's bigger than the Hindenburg," she said, and thumbed to hip 15 in her sale catalog, pointing to a word in parentheses beneath his name. "And it's a cribber. Most would rather suck air than eat."

"This one obviously prefers eating," he said.

Rachel sighed. A single horse might teach her entire barn the nervous habit of clamping teeth onto objects — doors, gates, buckets, whatever — and sucking air with a disgusting grunt. The conventional method of dissuasion, the crib strap, a leather and metal contraption fastened around the offender's throat-latch, making it unpleasant to swallow air, was marginally effective at best. A collar spiked with nails struck her as a more effective option. Worn inverted. But, of course, she should have told Marten to buy hip 15. He always did the opposite of what she advised. Instead, she pointed to the dam's produce record, which revealed that the colt's ten siblings had earned a grand total of five-hundred-and-eighty dollars. Before Marten could think to argue, the hammer fell.

Hip 16 sold next. Hip 17 balked outside the ring until two of the largest handlers locked arms behind the colt and packed him in. Bidding started. When Seth Marten poked her arm and told her to buy hip 17, she nodded absently and searched her purse for ibuprofen. Finding none, she lit a cigarette, took several quick puffs, and jammed the rest into her empty coffee cup before anyone noticed. Hip 17 was slightly sickle-hocked, a confirmation defect of the hind legs. He was also a bright bay with four white socks. Besides pedigree, Seth Marten based his choices on important physical attributes such as color.

She glanced at the classy, long-legged colt and nodded to a bid spotter. Sickle hocks were not the worst conformation fault. No horse was perfect. Marten was capable of worse selections, much worse. But as high as she bid, someone always went higher. At $26,000, Marten dropped out and left the stands to get a cocktail. Hip 17 sold for $26,500 and a black-gloved handler led in hip 18, a muscular, long-hipped, dark bay grandson of Northern Dancer.

Rachel shifted to the edge of her seat, all business. Without question, hip 18 was her favorite yearling in the sale, her opinion bolstered when the colt entered the ring and calmly surveyed the crowd like a stakes winner posing for a track photographer. A sign of heart and class, she hoped, intangibles that could turn a mediocre animal into a winner and a gifted one into a champion, attributes more vital to a Thoroughbred than physical perfection, unknowable until a horse actually raced. How many millions, she wondered, had been wasted on royally bred, physically superior horses that *wouldn't* run a lick. Morning glories that wilted or imploded in the paddock and spit the bit or choked in a race. How many hours, days, years had horsemen spent searching for a foolproof heart and class gauge. She added another minute to that total, then the auctioneer switched into high gear. The bidding began at $3,000, jumped in increments of $500, rapidly climbed to $20,500, and hung. The reserve price, Rachel decided. She nodded to one of the bid spotters and the auctioneer's call rose another notch.

"Give me twentyone, twenyonetwenyonetwenyone..." he chanted. When a bid spotter waved, the auctioneer slowed.

"Do I have twenty-one, Bill? Okay, gi'me twenyonefive twenyonefiftwenyonefiftwenyonefif...."

She looked around to see who was bidding against her but couldn't tell. With no intention of letting the colt's consigner jack up the price, she waited until the last moment, then nodded, the slightest dip of her chin. Bidding was a subtle art.

The auctioneer resumed his spiel at $22,000. And swiftly drew a counter bid. Rachel watched the spotters and saw that the competition was seated in her immediate area. She glanced about. The auctioneer's chant wound down and he commenced his hard-sell routine, carrying on about the colt's superior conformation and black-type pedigree, citing numerous stakes winners. He raised his gavel and hesitated, looking Rachel's way. She touched a finger to her cheek. The auctioneer caught the gesture and upped his chant.

In seconds, one of the bid spotters pointed at someone behind her and the auctioneer's call jumped from $23,000 to $23,500. Rachel looked over her shoulder and spotted a familiar white Stetson. Reno McAllister, her Peninsula Park rival. To his right sat a yuppie-looking kid in a Seattle Mariners baseball cap, while to his left, was an older man in an Arabic headdress and three-piece suit. Both appeared short next to Reno in his ten-gallon special. McAllister was six feet, she guessed, maybe six-one. Broad-shouldered and lean. A horseman, not a businessman trainer.

Rachel kept staring until her rival noticed. With a swift nod of his head, he tipped his hat and smiled. She smiled back, a flash of white that was more a show of teeth, then she turned and waved wildly at the auctioneer. They traded bids until $85,000, but she would go no higher and dropped out.

"Damn," Rachel said aloud, as McAllister signed the acknowledgment-of-purchase form for hip 18. She brooded for all of about ten seconds before grabbing the sale catalog to recheck her picks.

Next to her, Vanderford whistled softly. "Eighty-five thousand. Never seen you go that high to win a bidding duel."

"I was upping the price. Breeder's a friend of mine."

"Like hell."

"Okay, I'm lying." She nudged him in the ribs. "You loan me a few million and I'll fix Reno."

"He's divorced and the same age as you. Be simpler if you married him."

"Oh sure, J.K. Last year, the guy sent me a sympathy card on Valentine's Day and bought me a Shirley Temple in the Turf Club after I hung a halter on one of his top claimers. I can take a hint."

"Women are always getting love and hate mixed up."

"Men are always getting love and sex mixed up."

Vanderford chuckled. "I think you're letting Reno get under your skin. Unless he's recently won the lottery, he won't be badgering you the entire evening."

"Yeah," she said. "Nobody's that foolish."

Seth Marten returned to his seat a few minutes later with a martini in hand. She calmly tried to talk him out of buying hip 22, a splay-footed, cow-hocked disaster, but Marten insisted she bid on the yearling. Needless to say, she was pleasantly surprised when McAllister outbid her again. While Marten grumbled about losing the next Triple Crown winner, Rachel ripped out a blank page from the back of her sale catalog and scribbled a note. She passed the folded piece of paper to a woman in the row behind her, who passed it to someone else, who handed it to Reno McAllister. He opened the note, which read: "Violets are blue, Roses are white, Twenty-two's legs are one helluva sight."

Rachel watched as he crumpled the paper in a fist. Clearly, her rival had no sense of humor.

~

Things grew progressively worse after hip 22. Each decent horse that Rachel bid on, McAllister bid higher. And he bought no more lemons. Although she *had* attempted to provoke him into buying another crooked-legged thing but almost got stuck with the filly herself. By hip 150 or so, Marten and Vanderford had grown restless, not to mention cranky. Rachel decided Reno was prepared to buy every quality yearling in the sale to keep her and her clients from obtaining even one. She couldn't believe anyone would be crazy enough to spend the money required to pull off such a stunt. Horse racing was in a decline. Increased pressure from lottery and casino wagering was taking a large hunk of the American public's gambling dollars, but crazy or not, Rachel had no intention of leaving Hollywood Park without a single horse. To that end, she had Vanderford and Marten watch the remainder of the sale from the bar, while she moved to a seat in the back row of McAllister's section, out of his sight. Twice he stood and scanned the amphitheater in search of her, she presumed, and she had ducked until he sat back down. By the end of the sale, she'd purchased eight yearlings.

Rachel filled out the paperwork and arranged for the horses to be vanned to Oceanstead Farm, a training facility southwest of Peninsula Park where they would be boarded, then broken to ride come December. Afterward, she waited outside the sales pavilion with Vanderford and his wife, while their son fetched a rental car. Rachel was smoking a cigarette when she heard the steady beat of boots approaching from behind. When she turned and found herself face to face with Reno McAllister, the rest of the world ceased to exist.

Rachel threw down her cigarette and ground it into the pavement.

She hated this thing that he did to her. The way he monopolized her attention and sent her stomach into a tailspin. Without looking at him, she knew every aspect of his face—the straight nose that jutted with character from the well-proportioned face; the hair grown an inch or so longer than shirt collar; the scarred cleft on the chin; the slight space between otherwise respectable front teeth; the confident smile; the intense, somewhat close-set dark brown eyes, hooded by a curved swatch of lighter brows. The details that formed the whole of the man who was her enemy.

This was how it was between enemies, she gathered, and if

none of her other foes evoked quite the same emotional response, neither were they as formidable.

"Rachel," he said, in the slow deliberate manner of a gunslinger sizing up his opponent.

She skipped the pleasantries and got right to the business of outdrawing him. "You buy every yearling foaled in the world this year, you'll win the Kentucky Derby by default in two years, not to mention the Preakness and the Belmont."

McAllister winked. "My bidding hand got a cramp."

"Course, you'll look rather foolish. Not to mention incompetent."

"I believe you just did."

"Personally, I'm into out-training the competition."

"Lucky thing you always seem to have twice as many runners to work with."

She scoffed. "Was I just lucky I win all those races last year, and the year before that, and the year before that, and the previous year, and the one before that?"

"You can train some," he said, with the barest dip of his chin.

"Buying me out of business is one classy strategy."

"*That* from the queen of classy tactics."

She planted hands on hips. "I beg your pardon, but I don't do anything worse than the men."

McAllister whipped off his hat and slapped it against his thigh. "Oh, I think you've done plenty worse, lady."

"Go to hell," she spat.

The Vanderfords' son had pulled up in a rental sedan. She slipped into the backseat beside Mrs. Vanderford and moved to slam the door, but McAllister grabbed the handle and won the resulting tug-of-war.

"Dammit," Rachel hissed. "You're starting to piss me off."

He put a hand on the roof and leaned over. "We're not through talking yet, lady."

"Quit calling me lady."

"No problem. Sow fits you better."

"Screw you, mister."

"Come to think of it, calling you a sow is an insult to pigs. A sow takes good care of her young."

Rachel glared at him with confidence. "The ones she doesn't accidentally squash."

He smirked. "Maybe some tequila would refresh your memory."

The slightest pause from Rachel. "So that's where we're going," she said, and flashed a sarcastic smile at the Vanderfords before turning back to her rival. "I confess, I overindulged and embarrassed myself the other night. Satisfied?"

"Don't forget that secret you shared."

"I don't recall saying anything," she said, inching toward the center of the back seat in a subtle retreat.

McAllister's mouth twitched up at the corners. "Yeah, I'd imagine not, after ten tequila shooters."

"Nine."

"The bit about being a mother?"

"Oh, that." She blew off his accusation with a burst of laughter. "For crissakes, most of the backside thinks I'm a mother-something-or-other. You've been listening to too much gossip."

Reno McAllister looked hard at her face. "A friend of mine's an acquaintance of your aunt's in Los Angeles. Monica Warner, I believe."

Rachel froze. Then she pursed her lips and stared back without blinking. "It's nobody's goddamn business."

McAllister released the door.

She slammed it and the car pulled away, leaving him on the curb.

The Vanderford family mentioned nothing of the exchange. No one spoke at all. When they hit the freeway Rachel opened her handbag and took out a pack of cigarettes, then remembered that the mere sight of the Marlboro Man in a magazine was enough to make J.K.'s wife carsick. Mrs. Vanderford eyed her from the opposite side of the backseat like a socialite advocate for the American Cancer Society. Rachel put away the cigarettes. Her short-sleeved silk shirt clung to her skin, the car's air conditioner having yet to cool the vehicle. She rubbed a hand over the back of her neck and twisted her head from side to side with the stiffness of a woman who hadn't looked over her shoulder in years. The mystery of what her aunt, Monica Warner, might have told Reno McAllister's friend ticked away in Rachel's mind like a time bomb. The car rolled on. She stared out the window at the urban monotony flanking West Century Boulevard and focused on horses and racing until that diversion tactic finally failed and the silence drove her to speak.

"He's lying," she announced. "I have no children."

J.K. nodded. His son turned on the radio and cranked the volume.

Mrs. Vanderford patted Rachel on the shoulder. "It's okay," she said. "We didn't hire you to be a babysitter."

~

They passed the remainder of the short drive to Los Angeles International Airport in silence. Vanderford dropped his wife and son and their luggage at the terminal and asked Rachel to ride along while he returned the rental car. She hesitated, then got in front and shut the door.

"Rachel?"

"Yes, J.K.?"

"Whatever possessed you to get into this heartbreaking business?"

"I suppose it's in my blood, my father being a trainer."

"And?"

"Is this about that other thing? Because I'll admit I had too much to drink in public and that was stupid of me, but I just want to forget the whole goddamn episode," she reeled off in a single breath.

"Not at all," he said, looking at her. "I'm simply curious to know why you do what you do."

"Oh." Rachel thought a moment and decided to make light

of the situation. "Would you believe, when I was a kid, the class bully told me, 'Girls was only good for doing it.' Judging from the way he spit the words at my feet, I knew it was nothing I wanted to build a career around."

Vanderford smiled. "And?"

She thought again. "There's something wondrous about a trainer and a horse working toward a common goal, the way a horse who's won arches its neck and prances back to the barn full of pride, knowing full well it finished first, which all normal people would swear was bullshit and every racetracker knows is the truth."

"Here I thought you did it for the money."

Silence, then Rachel abruptly tossed back her head and laughed.

"Totally, J.K. I was pulling your legs and your arms too," she lied. On the grounds that it was nobody's business if winning races moved a part of her nothing else seemed to reach.

Westover Meadows, Portland, Oregon December 1993

The buzzer rang with an ear-aching loudness. A jockey who looked as if he had forgotten to eat in several weeks hocked a loogie with a rattling snort, while another waiting by the door whistled "Taps," then someone told the whistler to shut the fuck up and everyone started for the indoor paddock where the horses were being saddled. Along the way one of the shorter jockeys teased the lone woman riding the race.

"What's a nice girl like you doing in a place like this, Stringbean?"

Nikki Summers stopped. Technically, as long as she made weight it didn't matter that she was five-foot-seven, but she still felt like decking anybody who called her Slim, Stretch, Too-tall, or Stringbean. Especially Stringbean. She opened her mouth to call him a munchkin.

"Hell if I know—Mike," she said, standing with her knees slightly bent to pretend that she wasn't taller than everyone else in boots and silks. With a smile and some quick footwork, she slipped past a rider who raised his whip to engage her in a mock sword fight, then she dashed ahead to the number nine stall as her mount, Sunrise Flame, kicked out with both hind feet, leaving fresh gashes on a gray wall already battered by hundreds of hooves. A sharp crack echoed through the paddock.

Trainer Winchester Cannon snapped his fingers. "Move that sonofabitch's ass."

The colt's groom, a toothpick of a man who looked to have slept in his rumpled overalls, muttered to himself then tugged on the reins and led Sunrise Flame a few steps forward. The gangly red chestnut stood big-eyed and trembling, fear steaming from his thin winter coat. Nikki reached out to stroke his neck, but Winchester Cannon grabbed her arm and pulled her aside.

"Give 'im an easy trip. Colt needs a race," Cannon said, releasing her arm. A straw cowboy hat rode low on his forehead and there was no manure on his lizard-skin boots.

Nikki gave a nod. "Yes, sir."

The trainer grunted. "Stay outta trouble and teach 'im to run."

"Okay," she said, now nodding briskly. She had never ridden a horse for Winchester Cannon and did not particularly respect him as a horseman, but she wanted to do a good job for the track's leading trainer, which entailed following instructions, since Sunrise Flame stood no chance of winning.

Saturday's seventh race, a six-furlong allowance contest for two-year-old colts and geldings, had drawn some of the best young horses on the grounds. As a maiden—a non-winner—among previous winners, Nikki's mount was accorded a three-pound weight advantage that she knew wouldn't help much in his first start. He needed another month of training and would have benefited from additional schooling in the gate as well, but Winchester Cannon hadn't been interested in hearing her training tips.

Horses and their grooms circled the sand walking ring that surrounded the saddling stalls, which were set in the center like a wheel of cheese cut into fourteen wedges. Cannon walked to the concrete and chain-link fence enclosing the paddock and spoke to a bald man in a navy blue sport coat on the other side. Sunrise Flame's owner. While Cannon was gone, Nikki gazed out at the spectators, scrunched up her nose and shook her head, not wanting people to waste their hard-earned money on a colt who wasn't fit enough to win. Several bettors nodded in silent comprehension.

Shortly, the paddock judge called for riders up. When her turn came, Cannon gave Nikki a boost and she eased onto her two-pound saddle and tied a smooth, double-overhand knot in the reins as the groom led Sunrise Flame to the track. More than 3,000 fans watched from behind the glass-enclosed grandstand of Oregon's largest Thoroughbred racetrack that second week of December. Snow was falling and the animals blew out foggy puffs in the cool air. The field loped to the backstretch and slowed to a walk. Nikki hoped people would bet quickly, but the parimutuel handle went nowhere fast and the post parade dragged on. Sunrise Flame jogged in place, his red coat lathered with sweat.

At the outrider's call, the horses trotted into line and headed down the three-quarter chute and behind the starting gate. The first four loaded in order. Nikki lowered her goggles.

"Two back," someone on the gate crew shouted.

The second to last colt was led in, the doors shut behind him.

"One back!"

The number ten colt loaded halfway and balked. Two members of the gate crew got behind the horse, locked hands and herded him in, then slammed the back doors. The shudder of metal reverberated throughout the steel structure. Sunrise Flame, who had loaded without incident, reared. An assistant starter perched on a narrow ledge along the left side of the stall worked to ease the colt down, while Nikki sat tight with a finger hold of mane, ready to break if he descended or bail off if he flipped over backward. The instant his front hooves touched the ground, the bell rang and the field exploded from the gate.

Sunrise Flame broke cleanly and charged for the lead, but Nikki eased him back and let the speed go on, for leading start to finish would be hard on an unfit horse. When the first sand from the front-runners hit the colt, he threw his head skyward and climbed, reaching up instead of out to escape the hail of stinging sand. Nikki played with the reins, gave and took with the bit, transmitting calm through the lines. Her mount relaxed. His stride lengthened. Down the backstretch Sunrise Flame settled into eighth position, ten lengths off the leaders, on the outside and clear of tight quarters in compliance with Cannon's orders.

The pack raced into the far turn, the number three and six

horses showing the way with the four sandwiched between them a half-neck slower. When the six switched onto its left lead, it dropped down sharply to the rail and squeezed the four, leaving the colt nowhere to run. The jock on the four squalled, rose in his irons, and threw his weight against the reins to check his mount. Too late. The hole slammed in his face and front hooves clipped hind heels with a click-click of metal on metal.

Down went the four.

The fallen horse toppled and crashed to the track with the jockey tucked in a ball and rolling. A second animal, unable to avoid the accident, tumbled to the ground and his rider flew through the air. Horses ducked in and out and slammed into one another to avoid the pileup. Nikki took in the scene, frame by frame, as if she had a slow-motion camera in her head, then Sunrise Flame shot past the two downed horses and jockeys.

If all the others fell, she might win, Nikki thought, right before her mount tried to bolt to the outside fence where the running appeared safer. The fence grew rapidly larger. Large enough to reach out and touch. She noted this adrenalin moment with horrified composure, using finesse and muscle, plus a firm smack of her whip to convince the colt to return to the center of the track. They headed out of the far turn running sixth. At the top of the stretch Sunrise Flame began to tire so Nikki let him coast home under no pressure, crossing the line a dozen lengths behind the winner. The colt pulled up quickly, his sides heaving. He was still gasping for air when she trotted him back to meet his groom and a valet along the concrete wall that bordered the grandstand. Winchester Cannon and the colt's owner were waiting for her outside the door to the Jockeys' Room.

"What happened?" Cannon asked.

"Two horses fell," Nikki managed to say before he cut her off.

"What about down the stretch? Don't you know how to use a whip?"

"Colt got real tired."

"Idea's to win, Summers."

Nikki's eyes widened. "You told me to give him an easy out."

"Don't feed me a bunch of phony-ass excuses, girl."

"But the colt's exhausted," she said, her deep voice cracking into a higher pitch.

"She probably thinks a whip's a fashion accessory. Like carrying a purse," Sunrise Flame's owner told Cannon, then ripped up a handful of parimutuel tickets for her to see.

The trainer stepped closer and got right in her face. "Colt woulda won if you'd stomped his ass."

His breath reeked of booze and onions. Too dumbfounded to say anything, she wiped his spit off her forehead with a sleeve of her silks and decided to talk with Cannon in the morning, when his head had cleared. A guard opened the door to the Jockeys' Room and ushered her past the two men.

"You're a loser, little girl," the colt's owner shouted.

That was the last thing Nikki heard before the door slammed shut.

~

Inside the Jockeys' Room, she removed her colors and threw them in the dirty silks barrel, then stalked past the scale, past the open entry to the men's dressing area, and into the women's room. She closed the door with a bang and rounded a corner in two strides, crammed her gloves into a tight ball and chucked them at a row of shelves on the wall. The gloves ricocheted to the floor at her feet. The women's room was about as big as a bread box.

"Told you Cannon chewed her ass out," jockey Rita Marshall said to another rider, Kris Nelson.

Marshall, a sunken-eyed, nineteen-year-old with a dragon tattoo on her arm, was slouched on a lumpy couch, her long dark-brown hair in need of a comb or scissors. Nelson, a short muscular girl with a warm smile, sat on the opposite end of the couch, eating popcorn. The attention of both women drifted between Nikki's face and the television set suspended from the ceiling above the room's only toilet stall. A replay of Sunrise Flame's race was just finishing.

"Least you made the course," Kris said. "That's better than Ralph and Juan. They okay?"

Nikki removed a lightweight protective vest and pulled off her helmet and goggles. "I think so. They were counting their fingers in the starter's car."

"What'd Cannon say?" Kris asked. "I saw the big turd waiting for you."

"He wasn't real happy with my ride," Nikki said.

Kris rose from the couch. "Knowing Cannon, he probably expected you to hop off and carry the colt. Don't take it personal. That prick hates everyone."

"Shoulda carved him a new asshole," Rita quipped.

Kris smirked at Rita. "The horse or Cannon?"

Rita gave Kris the finger. "The horse, pinhead. Leading trainer finally rides a girl and it's Nikki. Fuck that shit. I win twice as many races."

"Colt's a rank bugger." Kris again. "He needed a jock who can ride."

"Fuck you, bitch."

"Screw you, cunt."

Nikki cut in. "Be nice. You two'll feel awful if one of you goes out and gets killed today."

Kris and Rita paused briefly, then resumed trading insults.

"Right," Nikki said to herself, removing a knapsack from one of six open locker boxes on the opposite wall. Each was filled with goggles, white nylon riding pants, waterproof mud pants and jackets, T-shirts and turtlenecks, leotards and beige stretch leggings, rubber bands, helmets, gloves, plastic wrap, duct tape, spray cans of furniture polish—for cleaning goggles—perfume, deodorant, hairbrushes, blow dryers, makeup, et cetera. Her box was a tidy jumble with everything shoved aside to make room for a stack of clean clothes and polished boots that the valets delivered before the first race.

"You ask me, it sucks," Kris said, pulling a faded blue,

number-five cover over her helmet in preparation for the next race. "Cannon gets you to do all the work and give the horse an out, then cans your ass. Sure as shit, he'll put a boy on when the horse has a shot."

Nikki shrugged. "I never expected to ride the colt. I thought Cannon would just pay me for galloping."

"Send him a bill. The guy's a parasite," Kris said. "I've seen you in the three-quarter chute almost every morning on that screwy chestnut, loping in figure-eights and spending thirty minutes on him."

"Colt did take some extra time," Nikki said. "Wasn't like I could just hop on and gallop him a mile."

Rita reached over and grabbed a handful of Kris' popcorn. "Tell Cannon to fuck off and die. That's what I told this trainer in Sacramento after he screamed at me for wiping out his horse. Like, I never even rode the fucking race."

Kris gave Rita a dirty look. "I heard Cannon's first name used to be something like Dick or Poindexter, but he changed it to Winchester—same as the gun company, 'cause it sounds catchy with Cannon."

"He should've named himself Loose," Nikki said.

Everyone laughed but her. She sat down on the bunk bed crammed against the wall between the couch and the boxes. The rusted frame creaked with her weight. She was always careful to avoid the lower bunk if the top one was occupied, having no intention of becoming the only jockey in the history of horse racing to be crushed by a collapsing bed. She opened a text on organic chemistry. For the past six years, Nikki had been dividing her time between the track and Northwest Pacific College. Between morning galloping and evening racing, she took classes and was just fifteen credits shy of her B.S. degree in zoology. Of course, racetrackers really howled when they heard she was majoring in bullshit. Whenever she mentioned her dream of becoming a veterinarian, people looked at her cross-eyed and asked why she was wasting her time riding horses in circles. Because she loved the rush of almost getting killed several times a day, she would answer, grinning. And the horses, she'd add more seriously. After ten years of buying into this line, she almost believed it.

~

Twenty-five minutes later, she was jogging in place when the buzzer sounded, calling riders to the paddock. At Westover Meadows, there were eleven races Wednesday through Friday evenings, and twelve on Saturday and Sunday afternoons, the emphasis being on quantity not quality. Her mount, King Donican, a ten-year old winner of more than $100,000, circled the walking ring with the other $2500 claimers, his ears pricked and his black tail cutting the air with a whish and a snap. He'd started out as a bullheaded two-year old who threw nearly every exercise rider on the track. Back then, trainer Matt Wilcox believed women were liable to break into little pieces when they hit the ground and initially refused to let Nikki try the colt. That she'd shown up at Wilcox's barn wearing a helmet with a green cover hadn't scored any points in her favor. When the trainer finally ran out of options and gave her a shot, she let King Donican think he was in charge and he allowed her to stay on board, although they *had* taken a short detour across the infield. Eight years and twenty-two wins later, she had learned to expect the unexpected from the gelding.

Matt was leaning against the six-foot partition between saddling stalls, his head even with the top board, his sights focused on the steady parade of horse legs. A straw cowboy hat concealed part of his face and all of his receding hairline.

"You know how to ride the old man, so I'll keep my mouth shut," he said.

Nikki rolled her eyes. "That'd be a first."

"How'd you like to muck stalls in the morning, gal?"

"Would I still have to gallop?"

The trainer just smiled.

"Donnie's really strutting his stuff," Nikki said. "Feeling like a stakes horse again."

"That's ex-stakes horse. There's not a nag among this bunch

I'd pay twenty-five hundred for, including Donnie."

"*Matt.*"

He pushed the hat up his forehead. "I like the horse, don't get me wrong, but there's the dollars and cents of the matter. Running for an eighteen-hundred-dollar purse, a man purt near has to win every race just to break even. I'd drop King in for a grand if the racing secretary'd write a claimer that cheap."

"*Matt.*"

"Anyhow, the old fellow's stiff ankles ought to like the soft going. Warm him up good. I walked him at the barn but you know how peggy he gets anymore."

She nodded.

King Donican had suffered a minor chip fracture in one of his sesamoid bones a couple of years ago and wore supportive racing bandages on all four legs with protective patches under his hind ankles to prevent him from running-down and burning his fetlocks, as sore horses were prone to do. Donnie would turn eleven on March 6, though the official birthday of all Thoroughbreds born in the northern hemisphere was the first day in January.

Nikki remembered seeing a horse foaled for the first time, the mare, a pretty bay with big doe-eyes, sniffing the slimy heap in the straw as if she had expelled a foreign thing of suspicious origin, the colt rising wobbly, the mare looking at him as though he were some other horse's foal. It was the mare's first and she had refused to let him nurse, so the colt was raised on a bottle and turned out smallish and timid and won no races. Nikki had been eighteen and rubbing horses on a ranch in eastern Oregon, where the owner had hired her for room, board, and fifty dollars a week. He never asked where she came from and she'd never said. He also cheated her out of a month's pay, she recalled.

Presently, the paddock judge's voice echoed throughout the paddock and the horses were returned to their stalls. Nikki fastened her helmet strap. Matt wished her good luck, legged her up, and she and King Donican were led to the track by Matt's assistant trainer, head groom, and wife, Susan.

"Summers! You cocksucking noodle-armed bow-wow, the idea's to win!"

Nikki's head whipped around. Sometimes the names got so bad she didn't know what they were calling her.

"Hey, beaner," the same voice shouted at Angel Gomez on the nine horse. "Try not to fall off, you gutless wienie."

Nikki picked out the heckler from among the few patrons who'd ventured outside for a closer inspection of the post parade. The man's clothing reeked of affluence, his vocabulary of effluence. She was debating whether or not a jockey had an ethical right to spit at total strangers who bet their money foolishly, when another man along the fence caught her attention. Winchester Cannon. He glared at her as she rode past and deliberately dropped his focus to King Donican's legs. When she looked back, Cannon was gone.

The post parade moved past the winner's circle with racehorses and lead ponies alike spooking and shying and snorting at three human-sized plastic beer bottles standing beside the track's manager and the director of publicity in a promotional stunt for a beverage company. King Donican was one of the few who walked quietly past, although he did give the beer bottles an extra-long look. The remainder of the post parade passed rapidly, and then the horses were in the gate. One minute and fourteen seconds later the race was over. King Donican came flying at the wire but ended up a head short and finished second under a strong hand-ride from Nikki.

She let him stand a minute to catch his breath after pulling up. She stroked his neck and told him he had done well and wondered if they might have won if she'd moved him sooner or slipped through along the rail. First paid $1600 more than the $800 for second, and the Wilcoxes needed new tires and brakes for their pickup. A degree in veterinary medicine wasn't free either. The winning jock mount paid $240, but for finishing second Nikki would earn only about thirty-five dollars after paying her valet and agent.

When she rode King Donican back to be unsaddled, he trotted straight to the winner's circle and waited to have his overgirth removed for the photo. Meanwhile, the real winner of the race pulled up alongside.

"Donnie, I think we finished second," Nikki whispered, tapping him with her heels.

The old gelding did not move.

She clucked softly, whispering louder, "Come on, get going. We lost."

He planted his feet and refused to budge. Nikki slipped her toes from the irons and urged him onward with her long legs and a few mild slaps on the neck. This tactic proved unsuccessful as well, so she finally dismounted and led King Donican to where Matt, Susan, and a valet stood laughing

Matt was laughing hardest. "What in the heck you doing, gal? You finished second, you know."

"Donnie thinks he won."

"Next time."

"Yeah," Nikki said. "Next time."

Then she pulled off her tack, turned, and spotted Winchester Cannon standing along the fence behind them. Matt, who had also spotted Cannon, scowled at her with one eye squeezed shut—a not quite subtle reminder of the importance of keeping one's mouth shut in a business where horses changed hands as quickly as the drop of a slip of paper into a wooden claiming box. Nikki bowed her head, weighed out, and returned to the Jockeys' Room. Claiming a ten-year-old gelding would be irrational, she told herself, and counted the rational trainers she knew on the fingers of a single hand.

After a shower, she changed into jeans, a ski sweater, and high-top sneakers, blow-dried her shoulder-length blond hair, stuck on a Giants baseball cap, and headed to the clubhouse, ascending a flight of stairs two at a time. Halfway up, Kurt Kaiser, an agent for several of the track's top riders blocked her path. His gaze lingered on her chest before rising to her face. Nikki folded her arms and considered staring at his crotch, but didn't think she could keep from laughing. Kaiser coughed and shifted his weight.

"Nice try on King Donican, but you might've won if you'd

cracked him a time or two."

Nikki exhaled loudly. "Donnie tries his hardest. I don't need to beat him up."

"Don't get all bent out of shape," Kaiser said. "I'm only trying to give you some constructive criticism."

"How come whenever I win on a horse that's been getting whipped to death by other jocks and running up the track, people never say the horse won because I didn't hit it?"

The agent scratched his peach-fuzz goatee. "Maybe not all horses run from the whip."

She took that as an apology. Kaiser worked for some of her competitors and was not to be trusted, but compared to most jockey agents he was practically a Boy Scout.

"You wanted me for something specific?" she asked, gazing beyond him as though in a big hurry.

"I liked the story about you in *The Oregon Thoroughbred Review.*"

"I was the only girl in the room when the writer showed up."

"Give yourself some credit."

"Well, I haven't killed anyone yet," Nikki said, realizing that to her fellow jocks, ability wasn't measured in how many trips a rider made to the winner's circle but whether or not he or she could make the course without crippling anyone in the process.

"You've improved a ton. I remember when you showed up wearing a green helmet."

"Believe it or not, Kurt, I sort of grew up around horses," she said, neglecting to divulge one minor detail: only until the age of five.

He grinned. "What, plastic ones? I never saw anyone fall off so many different ways."

She drew a sharp breath, then made herself exhale calmly. "That's because the only horses trainers would let me gallop were crazy ones that everyone else was afraid to get on."

"Yeah, I'm surprised you didn't kill yourself."

"What was it you wanted?"

"Here," he said, and handed her a copy of the magazine. "Thought you might want one to send to your parents."

She took the magazine and tried not to think of *who* she wouldn't be sending it to.

"Hello? Anyone home?" Kaiser had leaned to within inches of the tip of her nose and was making a goofy face with his mouth in a twisted grin.

Nikki drew back a step. "Sorry. My head's in California."

"California here she comes, right back where she started from," he sang. "Someone told me you're from Beverly Hills."

"I'm from Stockton," she said quickly.

"You're from some two-bit farm town? Heard your family's loaded."

She laughed. "Would I be driving an old beater?"

"Bet they disowned you for hanging out at this seedy hole."

"And vice versa." Nikki bit her lip. She started to step around Kaiser.

"Wait a second," he said. "What about having dinner later?"

"I've got to go to the barn and take care of King Donican."

"Let one of Wilcox's grooms do it."

"I like taking care of him."

"Normal jocks just ride the horses."

"Maybe I'm not normal." Nikki managed a small smile and started upstairs to the clubhouse before the agent had a chance to reply. Her smile did not linger.

She wished men would let women do the asking out. She fancied herself better at handling rejection than administering it. Who was she kidding? She would just never ask anyone out. Before starting college, she'd dated her share of guys and had made a few spur-of-the-moment decisions, none of which resulted in any permanent mistakes, thanks to latex. Men gave her claustrophobia. She felt no attraction to women either. She liked people, wanted to feel something deeper for them, but seemed unable to scale the wall that existed between herself and the rest of the world. Anymore, she wasn't even sure whether scaling it involved a ladder or dynamite.

Nikki entered the bar and searched for her agent's bouffant blond hair. Tanya Lindsey was chatting at a table with three middle-aged gentlemen. Nikki pulled up a chair.

"My driver's license is in my car, but I'll be twenty-nine in July," she said to the waiter who asked to see her identification, then squinted and pointed to the faint wrinkles around her eyes and mouth.

The waiter shook his head.

Tanya came to the rescue. "Look, pal, she's only five years younger than me. Bring us another round and an orange juice for babycakes." The agent then turned to the men. "Like I'm always telling my rider here, booze breaks down muscle tissue and she can't afford to lose any muscle."

The men broke into laughter. "Why, Nikki," one said, "you'd need to be strong as a bull ox to pack home those bums your agent here's been hustling for you." He patted her on the head as the trio rose to go to the parimutuel windows.

Tanya Lindsey stirred the ice in a Bloody Mary and watched the men leave. "I spoke with Winchester Cannon a while ago. He's not riding you back on Sunrise Flame."

Nikki strummed her slender, callused fingers on the table top. "I kinda got that impression. Sorry."

"Winchester let me keep the call on Sunrise. For Warren. Only because you spent so much time galloping the colt." Tanya also hustled book for two other riders, Warren Zielinski and apprentice Skip Howe.

Nikki blinked hard. "He's riding Warren?"

Tanya took no notice. "I'll split my percentage with you, if the colt ever wins."

Half of twenty-five percent of ten percent of the win purse came out to about a dollar by Nikki's estimate, but she did appreciate the offer. She gazed out the glass windows. The horses in the eleventh race broke together and finished apart in staggered disarray. When the cheering faded, she opened her mouth to ask her agent how she had managed to convince Cannon to ride Warren, then Nikki decided what was done was done and to hell with it. Her agent was lying. Nikki could always tell by the way Tanya started talking faster than an auctioneer. Women played the dog-eat-dog game as lethally as men, only instead of sticking a knife in your heart, a woman would have you humanely destroyed.

At the thought, she changed her mind about saying nothing. "Hey, I didn't just fall off the pumpkin wagon. Cannon was using me to straighten out his problem horse."

"That's turnip truck," Tanya said.

"Pumpkins, turnips, whatever. You knew Cannon was only riding me once, when the colt had no shot, then switching to Warren. Don't lie."

After glancing around to see that no one was listening, Tanya leaned closer and lowered her voice. "You got a jock mount out of the deal, didn't ya?"

"Yeah, twenty-five bucks for fifty hours' work comes out to fifty cents an hour." Using her palm as an imaginary calculator, Nikki punched in figures. "Wow, my financial worries are solved."

"Don't be flip. Winchester Cannon win seventy-two races last season and Warren's on the verge of stardom. For the past seven years I've worked my ass off and you always finish near the bottom in the rider standings. You were lucky to ride a single horse for a big barn like Cannon's."

"But Tanya, college tuition is expensive. If he goes around bad-mouthing my ride on Sunrise Flame, it'll cost me mounts."

"Listen, I'd no idea Winchester would blame the loss on you. It's like I've told you about five thousand times before, if ya rode more aggressively, you'd hear a lot less shit from trainers."

"Cannon told me to go easy on the colt. I'm sick of hearing I ought to whip more." Nikki considered firing her agent but figured she could do worse.

Tanya cuffed her lightly on the head. "Watch the other riders. Their arms don't stop whacking 'til they cross the wire."

"If I were a horse and some fool starting smacking my butt, I'd think what's the use of trying hard if I'm going to get punished anyway?" Nikki said.

Her agent shrugged. "If I were a horse I'd be one of those circus horses with feathers and jewels and long slim legs." She was shorter than Nikki but lived in three-inch heels.

"So you're a circus horse. Swell, Tanya. Pretend you've been abducted by racetrack gypsies and they've entered you in the third at Timbuktu Downs."

"Fake hitting them. I don't give a crap, just make it look good. Owners want their money's worth."

"Shoemaker and Cauthen didn't beat their mounts to death."

"And they were on horses like John Henry and Confirmed."

"Affirmed," Nikki corrected.

"Call him Twiddledum if you want. I'm only saying *that* horse could outrun anything you ride at this little ass pit." Tanya finished her drink and started on the celery stick.

"It's all relative," Nikki said. "The tenth at Westover Meadows isn't the Kentucky Derby."

Her agent flagged a waiter and ordered another Bloody Mary. "I wish you'd start wearing makeup. And lose that black helmet cover and the black chaps you wear mornings. Trainers don't want a Hell's Angel chick for a jockey."

Nikki stood to leave.

Tanya wasn't through. "Lee Roy Cobb says he'll ride ya on a winner, you go out on a date with his grandson Bubba."

"You're kidding, right?"

"Gives new meaning to the racetrack term, hustling mounts." Tanya almost managed a smile but her sense of humor was drier than cracker crumbs.

"I'd rather empty bedpans," Nikki said.

Now the agent did smile. "Bubba's got big hands and feet."

"I'm not even gonna comment on that one, Tanya."

"Seriously, I'll make it up to you," she said, and fiddled with one of her five earrings. "For all the work you did on Sunrise Flame."

Nikki nodded. She wasn't so foolish as to believe such a promise yet wanted to think her agent would keep her word.

~

Nikki left the grandstand and drove to the backside to take over the job of cooling out King Donican, stopping the hot walker about every ten minutes to give Donnie a few gulps of water. After half an hour, he was done drinking, so she put him in his clean stall. When the gelding had finished rolling, she filled two neoprene boots the length of hip waders with crushed ice from the Wilcox's ice machine and strapped them on his forelegs. Next she fixed his evening feed. Two gallons of rolled oats, a half of barley, plus flaxseed, electrolytes, vitamins, molasses, a dozen chopped carrots, and an apple. She mixed the grain with hot water and hung it in the stall's front corner, and Donnie picked out the carrots and apple and ate them first. When she tossed on his night blanket, he paused to pin his ears. He did not appreciate blankets and ripped them to shreds unless she coated them with a mixture of hot sauce and mild liquid soap.

After thirty minutes, the ice boots came off. She dried King Donican's wet forelegs, cleaned his feet, packed them with mud and Epsom salts, and brushed him, then doctored his hind fetlocks—where he'd run-down and burnt off hair and flesh—using hydrogen peroxide to clean blood, sand, and dirt from his raw flesh before applying an anti-bacterial ointment. She checked his bad ankle for swelling or heat, but both front legs felt tight and cold, although they *had* just come out of ice. She did them up in a drawing poultice, smoothing thick, cool, medicated goop over his ankles and tendons to the knees, covering the poultice with a sheet of damp cotton and a layer of plastic wrap. A thick cotton standing bandage and a thin outer wrap held everything in place, while duct tape went over each of the Velcro straps, because Donnie liked to play with Velcro.

And he wasn't very good at putting his bandages back on.

~

In an hour, Nikki was in her studio apartment, sitting at the laminated wood desk she had bought for almost nothing at a yard sale. She ate a green salad buried under honey mustard dressing and too many corn chips, then read the magazine that Kurt Kaiser had given her, skipping the article about herself. After finishing, she glanced around the room. A thick layer of dust coated a set of ten-pound barbells in the corner. Her career win pictures—over two hundred in all—covered three walls, but she knew top jockeys in California and New York won more races in a single year. Another wall held enlargements of King Donican's four stakes victories. Albeit minor stakes with purses less than ten thousand dollars, but her only stakes victories, her only big wins.

In the beginning, she had lifted weights, run stairs, practiced whipping on bales of straw and studied hundreds of race replays. Ballet classes from age seven until seventeen had strengthened her legs and stomach, but that was years ago. Monica Warner, the aunt who raised Nikki, had wanted her to dance professionally, but she'd had other ideas. Years of criticism throttled her love for dancing. In fact, she couldn't recall ever having done *anything* well enough to genuinely please her aunt. To be fair, both of Monica's real children had been hard-pressed to do anything right, either, although with their who-gives-a-crap mentalities, it wasn't like they'd actually tried.

Sometimes Nikki wished she could not give a crap, too.

But if she'd been cursed with an obedience gene, it eventually mutated. After graduating from high school, she gave Aunt Monica the equivalent of a bronzed finger by changing her last name from Warner to Summers, an appropriately rebellious choice considering her maternal grandfather's surname had been Winters. Then Nikki packed her things and headed north to become a jockey.

She hadn't seen her aunt since. Ten years later, none of

Nikki's relatives had ever shown up to watch her ride a single race. Her aunt sent a card each birthday and Christmas, along with a perfunctory letter, which Nikki gathered was meant to make her feel guilty. At first, she'd always called to say thank you, but the conversations had ended badly with Aunt Monica —who possessed the tact of a land mine—trying to coerce Nikki into a change of careers. Now she just sent reciprocal cards.

On the bright side, ballet had come in handy. With balance born of pointe shoes and pirouettes, she'd only fallen off one hundred times instead of two hundred. Her aunt, Nikki knew, would not be impressed. Nor her mother, Rachel Nottingham, Northern California's most successful Thoroughbred trainer the past five years, a woman who had once publicly referred to a jockey as "a goddamn gnome." Following a win. Nikki liked to think she'd taken after her father, whoever he was.

She closed her eyes and imagined her aunt looking smaller and less formidable with the passage of time. A diet-crazed socialite with her manicured nails and too tight Ralph Lauren jeans, glass of wine in her hand, some rare vintage that she could identify nose plugged and blindfolded. She saw her mother next, standing in the doorway in baggy faded denims and a Santa Anita T-shirt, nervously glancing over her shoulder like a wild creature poised on the brink of fleeing. Nikki had been six. She'd lain in bed and listened while the rumble of her mother's pickup faded in the distance. Nikki thought nothing could ever hurt as badly. She'd been wrong.

Peninsula Park
December 1993

The home stretch and finish line on the west side of the main racetrack caught the sun's first light, illuminating horses and riders as they emerged from the shadow that still darkened the backstretch. Rachel was waiting on her pony for jockey Jim Bruner when he pulled up after a workout. She took hold of the filly's bridle and lit into Bruner.

"I said not to hit her."

"Only tapped her."

"Filly's wound up like an eight-day clock. I'd better not find any welts on her."

"Lazy bitch was cheatin', same as she does afternoons."

"I'll ride someone else on her."

"Have at it. Let some other jock wear out his fuckin' arm."

Rachel scowled at Bruner. The jockey closed his mouth and pressed a finger the length of his thin colorless lips. She considered the points in his favor and came up with two. He was a competent rider and good looking—for whatever *that* was worth. It took her considerably longer to add up all his negative qualities. They rode off the track without speaking. At her barn, Bruner sprang from the irons and strutted off like a bantam rooster, fringe on his leather leggings swinging in time with his step. Rachel passed the filly to her assistant trainer.

"Cool her out by hand," she told Sam Monsen, a gangly kid with a short-cropped haircut reminiscent of a badly shorn sheep. He wasn't terribly bright, nor was he blessed with horse sense—a combination that she worried would someday result in an unfortunate accident—but he was dependable and kept his mouth shut. There was nothing worse than a mouthy assistant trainer, as she could attest.

The filly was washing out badly, sweat running down her muscled neck, chest, and flanks. She leaped through the air and danced at Sam's side and Rachel's assistant danced his own awkward steps to keep his feet from being smashed. Aluminum shod hooves clapped the pavement.

"Sam," she shouted. "Don't cripple her."

Her assistant's walk stiffened. He glanced back and nodded, cringing as the filly tromped on his foot.

~

Three hours later, Jim Bruner met his agent outside the Peninsula Park race office, a white building trimmed dark green, the size of a small house with a neat lawn in front and flanked by row upon row of dark green barns. Almost nine, the racing secretary's entry updates were being broadcast via intercom throughout the backside like a theme song for the late morning bustle. The slap of the screen door closing provided a frequent if erratic beat.

"Just spoke to Nottingham," the agent said, as the intercom went silent. "She says you're off her horses." He reached up and loosened his tie. Droplets of perspiration shone on his forehead.

Bruner shrugged. His gaze followed a gallop girl in tight jeans as she hurried between barns.

The agent cleared his throat. "Said you screwed up."

Bruner continued to stare at the girl. "Big shittin' deal."

The agent jammed a condition book—listing the projected upcoming races—into his suit jacket. "Nottingham practically owns this joint," he said. "Whoever rides her barn is on top, so it's a huge shitting deal."

Bruner yawned. "Reno's breathing down her ass. I'll ride for him."

"McAllister wouldn't name you on a pot-bellied-pig." The agent removed a silk handkerchief from a breast pocket and wiped his forehead. "Listen, I don't care if she's fucking Medusa, treat her with respect."

"Fuckin' who?"

"Forget it. Go find Nottingham and apologize."

"I'm not kissing her ass," Bruner said, and shoved a wad of chew in his mouth. "That's your job."

"Which I've been doing for the past thirty minutes with no luck. It's you she wants to see grovel, so get going."

"I'll go in the morning."

"Go now."

Bruner stared at his agent. He spit out a mouthful of tobacco juice, gave a nod and a salute, then sauntered toward barn twenty-eight and the forty stalls filled with the horses Rachel Nottingham trained.

He found her patrolling the shed row, clipboard and pen in hand, the dictator of detail, checking shoes, checking legs, checking everything. She ignored him. He apologized. She gave a big huff and stopped. She was busy. Come pleading another time. Like five-thirty tomorrow morning. She had a groom with an injured shoulder and Bruner's presence on the end of a pitchfork would speed her routine considerably. He hadn't mucked a fuckin' stall in years. One of her Mexicans could dump his shit cart. Better yet, he'd make her nerdy blonde assistant haul the poop to the pile.

She swept past him without a glance and went after her pony. Tossing the reins over the animal's head, she sprang into the saddle and rudely informed him that she had just given two of his mounts to another jockey. Two of *his* paychecks. Jim Bruner grumbled as he watched her ride away. She sat a horse pretty. Straight but not stiff. And smooth, never bouncing around like a sack a shit. Never came close to losing her black cowboy hat unless it was windy. His sights dropped to her hips and he shook his head. Nottingham wasn't no forty-seven. Whoever told him that was full of shit or had her mixed up with some other broad. She wasn't half-bad, he had to admit, nice ass...and she could train 'bout as well as the top men trainers he'd ridden for. The best were cold.

~

With a touch of her heels, Rachel urged her pony into a fast walk and left Jim Bruner standing in the road between barns. She dismounted on the lawn outside the race office and dropped the reins over her pony's head and to the grass, since he was trained to stand ground-tied and would stay put until she returned—providing no one walked past shaking a bucket of oats. She strode up a short flight of stairs and inside.

Entries were closed, but the draw—for post positions—had yet to start and the room was packed. Trainers and agents and officials were arguing over the eligibility of a horse in the sixth race and had squared off on their respective sides of a counter that extended the length of the room. The racing secretary, who ran the show—approving horses for stalls at the track and writing the races—was hunched mumbling over a computer, checking data to determine whether a horse met the conditions of the race in which it had been entered. His assistants were similarly engaged. Trainers and agents muttered amongst themselves, the shorter ones leaning against the counter, the taller ones pressing closer from behind, though this apparent act of courtesy was purely accidental.

"Colt was haltered twenty-eight days ago for twenty thousand, so he can't run back for that price 'til he's out of jail," the racing secretary said, stepping over to the counter. "Rule clearly states that a newly claimed horse shall run at a twenty-five-percent higher price for thirty days. Forty-eight hours from now, when this race card runs, will be day thirty. Colt's ineligible to run for twenty thousand 'til day thirty-one, which means he's a no go, which leaves the race with only five head, which makes it a goner. Sixth race is off," he announced. "Sub-race two in the book goes with nine head."

One of the agents pounded a fist on the counter. "Nottingham'll switch that colt of hers out of the allowance race and into the sixth."

"Like hell I will," she shouted back.

The agent blew her a kiss. "My boy rides the favorite. We need a win. Give me a break, Rachel baby."

"Kiss my ass, Lenny," she said, then waited for the whistles and wisecracks to subside. "I rode that boy of yours on a short-priced filly last month. Got her in more trouble than a rat in a maze. Kid can't ride his way out of a wet paper bag."

The occupants of the room burst into another round of teasing.

"Rachel's having a hot flash."

"She's right, Lenny. Your jock's a half-wit."

"Hey, Rachel, you can kiss my ass anytime."

"What's the matter, Nottingham? Afraid Reno'll lead away another one of your horses?"

"Mix her a Tequila shooter, she'll run the colt at the bottom."

She glared at all of them though at no one in particular. The group gazed back, several of the men whispering amongst themselves like the offense in a huddle.

"Colt just win for thirty-two thousand," she announced. "I'm not running him back for twenty."

Lenny the agent gave her an ear-to-ear smile. "Better stick to whiskey. Tequila can make a person go goofy."

She scratched the side of her face with her middle finger. He blew her another kiss. The group at the counter went back to arguing.

"You can do better than that," said a trainer by the name of Bo Drake.

Rachel gave him a long look. "I'm getting shy in my old age."

"I'd have told him to kiss Reno McAllister's ass."

"Go ahead." She folded her arms. "I'm listening."

Drake clucked like a chicken. "I only have two horses to lose so I'd like to stay on Reno's good side. It's just the first week in December and you've already had nine horses claimed, eight of them by McAllister. Unbelievable."

"Nine sonofabitching pay horses. Didn't own a one. Who are you, Drake, my press agent?"

"I try to keep informed," he said, tipping an English-style tweed cap.

Rachel exhaled heavily, blowing through the bangs of shoulder length, reddish-brown hair that went as it pleased in defiance of mousse and hair spray. McAllister would have gotten all nine, but there were multiple claims dropped in for one, a bay with bad knees, and he lost the shake for the mare. Rachel wished he'd gotten stuck with it. Of the eight he had haltered, six were worth the money. A trainer couldn't run animals for more than they were worth just to keep them from being claimed and hope to ever win a race. On the other hand, no trainer could afford to lose good horses, especially with the economy slow and clients reluctant to buy replacements. With McAllister trailing her by only three wins and armed with an arsenal of millionaire clients, she didn't dare drop a horse in class to steal a race.

Beside her, Drake rattled off the names of six of her former top allowance and stakes runners that, as everyone within earshot knew, McAllister had recently bought outright from her clients. Rachel listened for about ten seconds, then turned her back on Drake. He snapped his fingers and told her that she needed to find another rich man to marry. She opted to swallow her pride, but it refused to stay down.

"Drop dead, Drake," she shouted back, and headed out of the race office.

It was a short walk to the backside cafeteria so she left her pony behind on the lawn, his eyes closed, asleep in the sunshine. She figured to have a cup of coffee and return in time to catch the tail end of the draw. Cries pierced the air as she reached the kitchen.

"Loose horse," several voices shouted.

"Clear the gap," someone else called out.

The kitchen was located on the north side of the gap, adjacent to the half-mile pole. From where Rachel stood, just outside the door, she had an unobstructed view of horses walking on and off the track, their riders glancing about nervously, the outrider swinging shut the exit gate. The entrance was already securely fastened, the red light atop the clocker's stand flashing. She glanced at her watch and smiled. Nine-fifty-two. Time for Reno McAllister's free-spirited gray filly. This would be the sixth morning of the past seven that Rachel had seen the gray two-year old running loose without a rider. McAllister always sent the filly out right before ten o'clock, when the main track and the smaller training track closed for galloping and fewer horses were about for an ill-broke thing to bother. Rachel lit a cigarette and waited for the entertainment to begin.

The clapping of hooves on pavement grew louder, then from nowhere a gray streak of a filly shot down a road from the south barn area and galloped straight toward the entrance to the main racetrack. All around people stood watching. No one jumped in her path waving their arms and shouting. No one tried to stop her at all. Everyone stayed put in a safe spot until she had thundered past. The filly's hoof-beats turned silent as she crossed onto the sand at the top of the gap. Long stirrups on her empty saddle bounced wildly, the irons hitting her belly, which didn't seem to faze her in the least. She slowed to a lope, pricked her ears, and zeroed in on the six-foot chain-link gates with none of the witless, eyes-rolled-back-in-her-head mentality of a panicked horse. Upon seeing both entrance and exit to the track were shut, she calmly broke to a trot and turned in a wide circle. Her tail stuck straight up and streamed behind her like a gray silk flag.

The day before, the filly had galloped through the open gates and onto the track, engaging the two outriders in a game of catch-me-if-you-can and kicking at anyone else who got in her way. Now, Rachel stepped closer to the security of the bleachers. The filly, seemingly content to play hard to get, easily dodged the dozen or so people who lunged for her bridle. She kept up the chase for about a minute and fired four explosive kicks that whistled through the air. The pursuers on foot backed off and left the loose filly to the gap outrider and his clever strawberry roan pony, which soon cornered her against the exit gate. They eyed one another, the roan and the gray, then the outrider drove his mount forward and sideways and reached for the gray's bridle. The situation appeared in hand.

But the filly spun and started kicking like a mule, jumping back and into the roan with every shot, the pony scurrying to escape her heels, the filly firing away with both barrels until the two horses reached the center of the gap. Then she bolted toward the closed exit gate in a full gallop. Rachel winced. She had seen horses run headlong into fences or barns or even cars, many ending up DOS—dead on the spot. But there was no time to intervene. She bit her lip and watched the filly bear down on the six-foot obstacle without breaking stride or slowing.

A split-second before impact, the gray launched her body skyward and leaped over the gate. She cleared it with room to spare, landed cleanly, wheeled right, and galloped into the flow of what little traffic yet remained on the track, bounding along, tail up, ears pricked, scattering everything in her path. A second outrider left her post at the quarter pole and closed in from the opposite direction, putting the two horses on a collision course. Rachel climbed the steps of the trainer's stand for a better view. The oncoming outrider slowed, wheeled her pony around, and galloped off in the same direction as the riderless gray, herding her into the rail as they drew even but, when the outrider attempted to snag the filly's reins, she burst ahead and put ten lengths between them. Just that quick.

Rachel punched her stopwatch an instant before the gray flew past the three-furlong pole, followed the horse to the six-furlong marker and snapped off. She read the time and let out a whistle. The filly had sizzled five-eighths of a mile without a jockey's urging in: 57 flat. Rachel checked her stopwatch again. The main hand was frozen on fifty-seven seconds. She couldn't recall having seen a horse work five furlongs that fast with a rider, let alone without one.

Second time around, the outriders caught the filly and passed her to a stocky, bow-legged kid, who was McAllister's assistant trainer. Reno rode up shortly on a sweaty buckskin pony and escorted the pair across the gap, where they disappeared into the second barn on the north side of the road. Rachel started after them. Common sense told her to cut and run. The gray could flat fly but was an outlaw and damn good at making a fool out of a trainer who was no fool. Rachel kept walking. Anything he could train, she could train better.

She met up with McAllister as he rode back toward the track. He in his customary Lee blue jeans and white Stetson. She wondered if Reno realized this gray of his was a regular rocket or if he was just too busy with his string of class runners to bother with a problem horse, talent be damned. Rachel stepped in front of his pony and he reined to a halt. She looked up at him. A nervousness fluttered in her stomach, not quite butterflies but possibly moths. They hadn't spoken since the auction at Hollywood Park.

"That gray cow you've got isn't worth twenty cents a pound, but my nephew wants a jumper," she said, as though doing him a great big favor.

Reno pushed his high-crowned Stetson up his forehead. "I'd sooner give the filly away than have her kill some kid."

"My nephew's no kid," Rachel said. "He's a professional bullrider."

"Thought he wanted a jumper."

"*Ex*-bullrider. I'd think you'd be delighted to saddle me with a half-a-ton a trouble."

"I bet you don't even have a nephew."

Rachel locked her gaze onto McAllister's face and made a spur-of-the-moment decision to either defuse or detonate the worry that he had planted in her mind at the auction at Hollywood Park. She had fought a mental tug-of-war the past few weeks. Her need to know what he knew, versus her desire to forget.

"I bet *you* don't have any friend who knows my aunt," Rachel practically shouted.

He gave her a hard look. She threw him the same.

"Don't tempt me, lady. You don't want to go there today."

"You're waving an empty gun, mister."

"It's loaded. I simply don't fancy shooting a woman in the

heart."

She scoffed. "I'm wearing my bulletproof vest."

"Mood I'm in, I'm afraid I might aim for your mouth."

At a loss for an immediate comeback, she glared at him—wondering perhaps, if she had come on a bit strong. She could tell he was bluffing. Her mother's sister, Monica Warner, hadn't told Reno McAllister's alleged acquaintance anything or he would've gone for the kill by now. Reno was easier to read than the Sunday comics. He had nothing on her that she hadn't heard before. Innuendoes based on gossip and secondhand accounts, her own drunken babblings. And whatever the unscrupulous felt like saying, whenever.

"Are we through?" he said. "Because I've got better things to do."

She recalled her original business. "Gray filly's not worth a quarter."

"Probably less. Now if you'll move, please."

Rachel stood her ground, having known all along that he would never sell her a horse outright.

He asked her to move again, this time without the please.

She planted her feet. Of course, he could have simply reined his mount around her, but as with previous confrontations, she realized there would be a clear winner and loser. Reno McAllister was not the conceding type. On the other hand, she could have been the one who stepped aside, but Rachel was curious to discover if he would actually knock her over. After about a minute, he made a constipated face as if to convey that she was a huge pain in the ass, then touched heels to his pony, reined hard right and left her behind, the apparent victor of their little game of chicken. Not feeling the least victorious, she watched him ride off in the direction of the race office before going after her cup of coffee.

The kitchen was the same as Peninsula Park's other official buildings, white with green trim. Inside were stacks of trays and a shiny stainless steel counter, tables and chairs everywhere, neither fancy nor comfortable but practical and mostly clean, especially in contrast to the white linoleum floor smeared dirt brown from the daily onslaught of hundreds of filthy boots, no matter how often the help mopped. Abstract horses painted in shades of red, blue, and yellow raced across otherwise plain walls.

More than a few heads turned when Rachel entered. She went straight to the crowded counter and got a cup of coffee to go, adding considerable milk and sugar. On her way out, she ran into Dr. Billy Cortez, Reno McAllister's new veterinarian. Just crashed right into him.

"Morning," Cortez said as he reached out to steady her.

Rachel brushed aside his hand. "Do you mind?"

Cortez laughed. "You're like stepping in front of a train."

"I'm in a hurry," Rachel snapped, then studied his face. She already knew of him. Newcomers were five-star fodder for the racetrack's gossip hogs and to her, gossip was simply information to be gathered and evaluated. She was well aware that Cortez was single and in his late twenties. And tall, lean, and muscled like the classic image of a Thoroughbred, though she had never seen a horse with a buzz cut or an emerald stud earring.

"Relax," he said. "You're too uptight."

"For your information, I'm training forty here and thirty more out at Oceanstead Farm. I'm busy."

"Me, too." Cortez gestured to the fresh blood splattering the sleeves of his denim shirt. "Care to take a break and catch a basketball game tomorrow?"

Her mouth dropped open. She always expected the unexpected but this one buried her like a Swiss avalanche. "I'm very busy."

"It's a Tuesday. No racing. I've got great seats."

At once she smelled a two-legged rat. "Did McAllister put you up to this?"

Cortez grinned. "No way."

"Yeah, right."

"Honest."

Her eyes narrowed. "I have this rule about not mixing business and pleasure."

"From what I've seen," he said, "you have a penchant for breaking rules."

"Not my own."

"All work and no play's a bummer."

"Only if you hate your job."

"That a yes?"

She shot a glance toward the race office, then looked him over, her gaze pausing briefly on his crotch. He was certainly easy on the eyes, the most drooled over hunk on the grounds from what she had seen and heard. And not the marrying type, which suited her fine. She hadn't been on a date in over a year and wasn't getting any younger. And Dr. Cortez was Reno McAllister's veterinarian. A detail that cried out for exploitation. However, she made a habit of ignoring other people's opinions about horses and would be the first to admit that brain-picking was not her area of expertise. Nonetheless, the possibilities jumped out at her like wishes from a genie's bottle. The man was a veterinarian, not some uneducated racetrack boob. But McAllister was no dummy either, she recalled, and the smell of rat came to her again, a foul sensation that brought her to her senses.

"Some other time," Rachel said and hurried off.

~

At the first opportunity to slip away that afternoon, she drove to San Bruno and visited her long-time friend, Pepper Roswell. Eighty-one, he lived by himself in a flat-roofed studio apartment in need of paint, on a block landscaped with half-dead junipers and brown grass. She stopped by about once a month to check on him, bringing DMSO for his sore joints or a homemade burrito from the backside vendors. He answered the doorbell in seconds, greeting her with a wide porcelain smile. Age had robbed him of several inches, reducing him to her height, about five-eight. His eyes still reflected a sharp mind, but his face was a spider web of veins and arteries. And the thick dark hair—flecked gray—which had earned him the nickname Pepper was all but gone. Jokingly, she once called him Baldy but he had acted hurt and she hadn't teased him about his hair since.

Rachel purposely showed up in the late afternoon so as not to interrupt his line-up of daytime soap operas. This was what happened when a person didn't have a life, she assumed. Years ago, Pepper had been one of the top trainers in northern California. Shortly after she had moved to New York, he was ruled off for life, permanently losing his license for running a horse with a fractured knee in order to have the horse claimed. She remembered him calling to tell her the news.

The colt was a three-year old coming off a long lay-up. Well-bred, he had shown much promise as a two-year old but pulled up lame with a chipped knee after his only race. His owner, an elderly woman, depleted her meager savings to pay the training bills. Pepper stopped charging her altogether when he realized she was practically broke. After all, the colt was working strongly and figured to cover his bills and earn the woman a small nest egg. He finished second for a twenty thousand dollar claiming tag in his first race as a three-year old. He was sitting on a win.

But a few days later, the colt's good knee came up hot and swollen. X-rays revealed a minor fracture. With the prospect of another year on the sidelines, Pepper decided to enter the colt right back for sixteen-thousand, a drop in class intended to convey the pretense of a crafty trainer stealing a win. If everything went as planned, the colt would be claimed and his elderly owner would have money in the bank and be rid of an expensive headache. Pepper gave the colt extra painkillers and froze the knee, using a liquid freeze in conjunction with an ice boot for several hours beforehand. He told the jockey to pull up after leaving the gate. When the bell rang, the colt broke hard and snapped the fractured leg all but off. Unable to rise, he was destroyed where he had fallen by the state veterinarian. Luckily, he had been claimed, but the new owners cried foul as the replay showed the jockey standing in the irons and pulling on the reins when the doors to the gate opened. Eventually, the jockey got scared and talked. So ended Pepper Roswell's training career.

Rachel had groomed horses and ponied for Pepper at the old racetrack south of San Francisco that predated Peninsula Park. She remembered the year distinctly. She'd been twenty-three and her father had recently died. With no disrespect intended to her father who'd taught her everything about horses, Pepper was the one who taught her about racing and winning. The tricks of the trade, the cowboy secrets, the things trainers had better do lest their horses be claimed by horsemen willing to do them. From Pepper, she learned when and where to enter a horse. How to get a horse running good and keep it good. To be unpredictable, creative, sly. Mostly, she learned from watching, although based on the number of times Pepper had chewed her out, he'd taken her education to heart. She had shown up at his barn, broke and in search of work with a child in tow, her illegitimate daughter, whom she'd passed off as a relative's kid. For that white lie and associated fibs, Rachel owned more excuses than a high-priced defense attorney and would admit with a clear conscience to believing every one.

The sixties were remembered for hippies and free love, but in Rachel's reality, mainstream society had been unsympathetic to women who bore children out of wedlock. She had watched others, ostracized in high school before dropping out, raising bastard kids on welfare, working part time at the local drive-in or grocery store while searching for a Prince Charming to save the day, only to discover that men were, generally, not into raising some other guy's kid. Luckily, she'd already graduated from high school, although nothing else about her predicament ever struck her as lucky. A living human being had grown in her body, yet she'd given birth to an alien creature sent to screw up her life? Why hadn't she felt all loving and motherly like women were supposed to feel?

With her 20/20 hindsight, the answer seemed obvious: raised by a man on a ranch among men after her mother was killed in an accident, there had been no one to teach her all the maternal stuff she somehow lacked. Although the ranch hands *had* taught her how to smoke and cuss. Which, as she recalled, were not useful mothering skills. At least not the smoking. In any case, she was living proof the world's expectation that women excel at motherhood based on instinct and on-the-job training was a pile of crap. But Rachel refused to take full credit for her failure, not when there were more family accolades to dole out.

Upon learning she was pregnant, her father had about ruptured her eardrums with his "her-life-was-officially-over" tirade. For crissakes, you'd have thought she'd robbed a bank. When she inquired about an abortion, he'd told her no — underscored by the use of a profanity — then he grounded her for six months. She'd been shocked to hear *him* cuss. The ranch hands cussed enough to compile an English/Spanish dictionary of obscenities but not her father, ever faithful to his religious upbringing. He'd been raised a Southern Baptist in South Dakota. His parents had come to California to visit every year for a week at Christmas. Rachel would never forget when she was seven or eight and inquired about their dog's balls — politely referring to them as the little round fuzzy things attached to Fido's butt — and her grandmother, Olive, washed her mouth out with soap. Literally, grabbed a bar of Ivory and jammed it repeatedly into her mouth with such force that it took a toothpick to extract the soap wedged between her teeth. That was the last anatomy question Rachel ever asked her grandparents.

Unbelievably, they'd managed to raise five children who wanted nothing to do with them. The sixth, her father, married an atheist. That, based on ranch hand gossip and her grandparent's snide comments, as Rachel's memory of a woman she could no longer picture in her head was unreliable at best. What she *did* recall with the clarity of Russian vodka, was attending church every week from the age of five. From her observations all those Sundays, she came to believe that people inherently possessed a certain degree of goodness that was not necessarily amplified by stepping into a place of worship, which, to the contrary, had a way of exposing —

among other immoralities—hypocrisy, intolerance, and greed in those whose sole motivation was eternal life. She'd long since come to terms with the fact that she had gotten screwed in the goodness department.

All the more reason she should've begged her father to let some stable, wealthy, loving married couple adopt her kid, but *that* hadn't happened. Not with her 20/400 foresight. But even if she could've predicted how badly things went, her father had been adamant that she take responsibility for her mistake. So he shipped her off to Aunt Monica in Los Angeles until after the baby was born. When Rachel returned home, he had her tell anyone who asked that the kid belonged to a relative who'd died in childbirth. Sometimes after drinking too much, she squeezed her eyes shut and strained to see the world from her father's boots, but his perspective felt blurry and out-of-focus and not just because she was plastered. Warm memories of her father had been frostbitten by her grasp of a cold truth: upholding a moral facade had been more important to him than his daughter's welfare.

But, to be fair, the only perspective she could decipher with certainty was her own: Her father's shame had caused her to emotionally detach. She hadn't bonded with her daughter.

Plus there was the matter of her personal mantra that he'd pounded into her head for as long as she could remember: "If you're going to do something, do it right." Because she'd perceived no solution that would allow a single woman to succeed on *her* perfectionist terms at both motherhood and a career, and because she possessed no talent at the former, she had chosen the unthinkable choice, knowing full well that society would view her as a monster of sorts, which is why she'd only ever told one person the truth. Pepper would take her secret to the grave. That was the thing she admired most about him.

"So," she said, after they'd finished discussing all the most recent racetrack news. "Think you're up to doing me a little favor?"

He aimed the remote control at the television until the

picture disappeared. "Something illegal, I hope."

She rolled her eyes. "Pepper."

"Ain't weaving any baskets, that's all I'm saying."

"I need you to buy a filly from a rival trainer. Naturally, he won't sell her to me."

"Reno McAllister?"

"How'd you know?"

"I still keep tabs on the ponies. This Reno fellow looks to be a horseman and not some businessman clown, but I know a trick or three myself."

She smiled. "You'll show him, all right, Pepper."

"Be my pleasure to buy this horse for you," he said, lighting a cigar.

He offered her one and she thanked him and lit up, then they settled on a plan. A time, his transportation and tender. Something about his facial expression or his manner of speaking or maybe the fact that she knew his exact age gave her cause for concern.

"McAllister thinks he's got the dirt on me," she said.

"And he never breaks any rules?"

"Not that kind of dirt."

"Oh," the old man said. "Yeah, I heard you tied one on at some fancy new hangout over by Coyote Point."

"Pepper, it was clear back in October."

"I ain't exactly the first one to hear any hot news."

She ran her hands over her face and to her lap.

"Well?" he said.

"Tequila hit me like truth serum."

"I swore off that stinking tequila years ago. Swear the damn worm gave me the trots for a week."

"I didn't eat any worms. Least not any that got digested."

"The boys said you had a little diarrhea of the mouth, too."

She made an effort to laugh. "More like memory flatulence."

"Flat what?"

"A memory fart."

He nodded. "People don't put much stock in the ramblings

of a drunk."

"So I had a few drinks."

"Damn-near passed out, from what I heard."

"Yeah, well, nobody's perfect. Anyway, only you and the relatives know—about *her*," Rachel said. "I don't need to tell you it'd be embarrassing as hell if word got out I have a kid, let alone one I didn't raise." She glanced down. "Not to mention the uproar it would cause if she shows up wanting to ride my horses. Clients hear I've got a daughter who's a jockey, I stand to lose business."

"You know, my memory ain't what it used to be."

Rachel glanced up. "I figured as much, Pepper. No more tequila for me."

"Pretty wicked stuff."

"Did a number on my head."

"And stomach."

"Right."

She thought they would leave it at that, but Pepper drew on his cigar and looked her over with a cramped expression that portended a heartfelt talk. She crushed her own cigar in a plastic ashtray and eyed the door.

"Ever consider making up with her?" he said.

Rachel stood. "You know how I feel."

"Sit your butt back down. We're *gonna* talk."

She wrung her hands and sat down with a lurch. "I'll rot in hell before I let you saddle me with a guilt trip."

"Need my butt tanned for not saying something years ago. When you first moved back."

"It wouldn't have changed anything."

"You don't do nothin' half-assed, I'll say that for you."

"I was no good for her."

"Ain't her name Nicole?"

"I *know* her name. I named her, goddammit."

"Probably explains why she changed it."

"Nice. That really makes my day, Pepper."

"Don't go gettin' your dander up. I'm just saying she takes after her mother."

Rachel blew a breath through her bangs. "I kept my ex's name after the divorce because my career was starting to take off. I didn't just change it for the hell of it."

Pepper gave a snort. "Same difference. And what's this about her being a jock?"

"I told you that."

"You did not."

"Did, too. About ten years ago, after she ran off to the track and my goddamn aunt called and chewed out *my* ass over the whole situation."

"When's the last time you talked to her?"

"Three, maybe four years ago. Monica would sooner forgive Hitler."

"Your *daughter*."

Rachel sighed heavily. "I don't know—a dozen years. She called me in New York. Charles didn't know about her."

"You didn't tell your husband you had a kid?"

"Men don't want women with kids."

"Well, yeah."

"Maybe sometimes I wish I'd done things differently, okay?"

"From what I saw, you were a darn good mother."

Rachel drummed her fingers on the arm of the chaise lounge. "Evidently, *she* didn't think so. When I'd come back to see her, she'd run off and hide. Or cry."

"She's no kid anymore."

"Why do you presume she wants anything to do with me?"

"For crissakes, Rachel, you're her *mother*."

The silence was a deafening roar that threatened to devour any excuse she might make. She stopped drumming her fingers and stared across the room without expression. The second hand on her wristwatch went around, then around again.

She rose to leave.

Pepper clucked his tongue in disgust. "Should've known talking wouldn't do no good."

Rachel was halfway across the room before she stopped and slowly turned back. Mostly regret was a surface wound, a superficial scar, hardly noticeable, except on those rare occasions that it ached from within like an old broken bone in the cold. She rubbed her hands over her upper arms and shivered.

"Shutting that door was the hardest thing I've ever done in my life," she said. "I don't think I could open it again, even if I wanted to."

Westover Meadows
December 1993

Sunday morning the temperature rose above freezing. Driven by a blustery east wind, sheets of rain battered the racetrack, the water overflowing backside drainage ditches and running out of places to go. Nikki shivered. The sky was still dark when she dashed under the cover of Winchester Cannon's barn.

She spotted him at the far end of his shed row, yelling at his assistant trainer while grooms scurried about in the background. She lengthened her step. The trainer could walk all over his barn crew, because to them a job was a job and Cannon paid decently. She, however, was not on his payroll.

"Good morning, Mr. Cannon," Nikki said, and made herself smile, remembering that she'd promised her agent to be courteous.

"What do *you* want?" The trainer peered at her with bloodshot eyes. Stubble the color of paprika dusted his face.

"About yesterday."

"Ya cost me a race, Summers, you're off the horse." He bowled past her and stomped down the shed row.

"I did not, sir, cost you the race," Nikki called out to the back of his head. She jogged after him. "You told me to take care of the colt and not to worry about winning. Remember?"

Winchester Cannon lurched to a halt then swung around. Up and down the shed row, his crew paused to watch. Even the horses seemed to be looking. A queasiness filled Nikki's stomach as it occurred to her that people with red hair—and hangovers—often had short tempers, but she held her head high and stood her ground.

"You knew the colt wasn't fit enough to win," she said.

For a second, the trainer's expression softened, then his lips pursed shut. "He lost, that's all I know. Now scat."

Nikki didn't move. "Warren couldn't make it this morning, so I'm catching his gallopers. My agent told me you had a horse for him to breeze?"

"I'll get someone else."

"Fine by me," she said, then decided to hell with courtesy. "Mister, you couldn't train a goose to shit."

Silence gripped the shed row like a bad cramp. Nobody dared smile, let alone grin. Down the line a horse pawed its stall door with a bang. Another sneezed. A muffled snicker escaped one of the grooms, which had a domino effect and soon four other grooms, two gallop boys, and the assistant trainer were cracking up. Cannon whipped his head toward the sound. Which was like flipping the off switch on a laugh track, and his help disappeared into stalls and tack rooms. Cannon returned his focus to Nikki. With the physique of a Sumo wrestler, or at least the abdomen, the trainer's significant belly engulfed his belt buckle, testing the durability of a pin-striped western shirt. She figured it was probably time to leave.

"Get out of my barn, Summers," he bellowed, getting right in her face. "Out of my barn."

Nikki took a hurried step backwards, then another, moving out from under the shed row and into the rain. The trainer followed. The Wilcox's horses were stabled in the neighboring barn, but the short stretch of ground between the two structures lay under several inches of water due to a broken pipe and a clogged runoff drain. In the process of repairing the pipe a maintenance crew had dug a ditch somewhere nearby and Nikki wasn't sure if they had refilled the trench. She hesitated at the edge of a miniature lake.

"Get out." Cannon raised his arms. "Out!"

In order to maintain some semblance of pride, Nikki fought an urge to break and run. From behind, in the light from the barn, she caught a glimpse of pooled water boiling with rainfall. She took a long step backward, careful to ease her toe down and touch solid ground before transferring her weight. Cannon followed.

"And stay out," he was saying as his boot splashed the surface with a loud kerplunk and he dropped into three feet of chilly, brown water.

Nikki's mouth fell open. Uh-oh, she thought, they hadn't filled the ditch yet. She reached out to the trainer, but he was bellowing and floundering and slapped away her hand. The ditch caved in several times before he managed to crawl free. With water pouring from his pants, he stumbled over to her and his left hand formed a fist and the fist rose, past his belly, past his chest to eye level. Her eyes.

Nikki bolted through the wind and rain and under the cover of the Wilcox's barn. After skidding to a stop, she ducked among the bales of timothy and alfalfa that were stacked to the roof along the outside of the shed row, opposite the stalls. She leaned against the hay and let her heartbeat slow to normal. She had grown up thinking that adults matured beyond childhood hurts and could therefore look back on the past unemotionally. Nikki hoped to become an adult before she hit thirty.

After peeking to make certain that neither Winchester Cannon nor the Wilcoxes nor their grooms were in the shed row, she ducked out of the hay and walked to the other end of the barn. King Donican and Captain Fuzzy, a two-year old colt with more winter hair than a Siberian Husky, occupied the last two stalls. Both Donnie and Fuzzy were bright bays with no white markings, but the old gelding was a bit taller at sixteen hands. And rangier, an amalgamation of long. Long legs, back, neck, long flat muscles, long stride. Personality-wise, he had serious Dennis the Menace tendencies and was obstinate yet never rude. At least not to her. Donnie lived to win, but he was a prize fighter who reserved his game face for game day. As for Fuzzy, he just wanted to have fun. A stayer built like a sprinter, he was an eager to please kid with bulky, menacing quarter horsey muscles buried under his thick reddish coat and silly demeanor. Nope, she had no problem telling the two geldings apart.

When she'd first started working with horses they had all looked alike to her—within the basic color groups. Her very first task had been to brush a colt named Mickey described only as "the parrot-mouthed bay" by the farm's manager as he pointed down an excruciatingly long shed row at some indefinite stall. After finding eight bay colts in the first ten stalls and ascertaining that none possessed a beak or talked, she tried calling Mickey by name and soon had eight bay heads staring curiously out of their stalls. This had not been helpful. In the end, she'd guessed, picking the one with the biggest ears, and of course, had brushed the barn's ponyhorse.

Since then, her perception had evolved considerably, at least where horses were concerned. More than she could've ever predicted, considering she'd never experienced a horse crazy stage like many young girls did, although she figured her present circumstances qualified her as a late bloomer in that regard. Nikki reached the end of the shed row, gave Donnie and Fuzzy a pat on the neck, then went about removing grain tubs and night blankets. Fuzzy was not particular about where he slept. Come morning, his red blanket was often a gross shade of green and starched with manure. Next, she took off Donnie's bandages. After hosing the mud poultice from his front legs, she returned him to his stall and gathered the wraps, a purple one, a red one, and two blue. She set the colorful pile on a bale of straw by the blankets and went to the tack room that doubled as an office.

The room was warm and muggy and reeked with the odor of drying rain sheets and saddle towels, a blend of sweat, dirt, and manure that was so pungent, she felt an urge to breathe through her mouth but didn't, for fear of tasting the smell. Matt was seated at a small desk crammed into a back corner of the cluttered room, his lanky frame hunched over the Sunday paper. Susan, his wife of fourteen years, was at a saddle rack in the opposite corner changing a worn set of stirrup leathers. She carried ten extra pounds on her hips, but her figure bore the firmness of a woman who could buck one-hundred-pound bales of timothy hay. Matt swung his chair around to greet Nikki. She plugged her nose.

"What's the matter? Can't take a little stinky laundry?" he asked.

"Yuk. You're never doing my laundry."

Matt glanced at the puddle that was forming at her feet. "From the looks of you, I don't need to," he said, chuckling. His smile was a mosaic of coffee-stained teeth, too-white caps, and gold crowns, a reminder of years spent riding bulls. Marriage ended that short career twenty-five years ago, and he had been a horse trainer ever since.

Nikki removed her helmet and set it on the floor in front of a space heater. The cover was an original. Solid black, she had stitched a scarf-like piece along the back to keep the rain from running down her neck, which Susan claimed made her look like a female version of Lawrence of Arabia. Or Darth Vader, according to Tanya.

"Now, honey," Susan said. "Don't start in teasing poor Nikki to death, or I'll stick your jeans in the machine with Fuzzy's blanket."

"She oughta be grateful I'm not tracking any horses in this weather."

Susan's mouth opened in mock surprise. "That's what you always say, then you stand around at the gap, gabbing with all the moronic trainers who'd send one out to gallop in a hurricane." She turned to Nikki. "By nine, Matt'll be running around like a rooster with his head cut off, throwing tack on three or four horses at once."

"I sure won't," he said to his wife. "But if I change my mind, I expect my gallop girl's not gonna melt."

"Pretty hard, holding tough horses in a downpour," Nikki said. "You know how slippery the reins get."

"Better not let anything run off, gal."

Nikki grinned. "Cut my pay."

Susan frowned at Matt. "If we paid her to gallop, she wouldn't have to risk her neck on goofball horses to cover her college tuition. Like that thing she rode for Winchester Cannon yesterday."

"No trainers 'round this poorhouse pay jocks to gallop, Suzy. That's why she's riding ninety percent of my barn."

"*Your* barn?"

"*Our* barn. I warned her Cannon's a no-account son-of-a-buck." Matt turned to Nikki, who stood with one hand on the door handle. "Can't you use a little common sense, gal, and steer clear of users like Winchester and their cull stock?"

"I'm not afraid to get on the bad ones," she blurted.

Both Wilcoxes nodded patiently.

"You ride your share of idiots, that's a fact," Matt said. "You're tough as a pine knot and one heck of a roller. Maybe I'll start having you get on that nickel bolting jughead I've been paying a two-hundred-pound gallop boy to keep between the rails."

Susan frowned again, then walked over to Nikki and gently manipulated her left arm for Matt to see.

"She's also broken her collarbone, four ribs, and a hand, honey. And in case you haven't noticed, ever since she pinched that nerve in her neck a few years back, this arm doesn't work quite right."

"It works okay," Nikki said, wiggling free.

"I'll be glad when you have your degree and get out of this godforsaken business," Susan said.

Nikki avoided eye contact with either of the Wilcoxes.

"I may hold off on vet school and ride at Peninsula Park for awhile," she said.

Husband and wife traded unsmiling glances.

"Awful tough down south, gal. Thought you still had about a dozen flaws to iron out?"

"I'll probably be ready by summer."

"I was you, I'd concentrate on studying," Susan said. "Not many jockeys get accepted to vet school at Washington State University."

Tilting his coffee cup to nearly vertical, Matt swallowed the last drop. "Not *any* others, I'm aware of."

"I'm going to California first," Nikki said.

"The sooner you get that doctor degree, the sooner you can come back and do my vet work."

"Maybe I don't want to be a racetrack vet," Nikki said.

Matt shuffled through a pile of paperwork. "Since I give you your start, I get free vitamin shots, Lasix shots, and cortisoning of knees and ankles. And worming. And teeth."

Susan scowled at her husband and then turned back to Nikki. "Your mother's in California, isn't she?"

Nikki sighed. "Yeah."

"You two still not talking?"

"Yeah."

"How long's it been now, forever?"

"About."

"You should break the ice and make up."

Nikki made herself smile. "I'd need to enlist the Coast Guard's help."

"She *is* your mother," Susan said.

"She's pretty busy."

"Too busy for her daughter?"

"Apparently."

"Well, that stinks."

"Just because I'm her daughter doesn't mean she has to like me."

The rattling hum of the space heater was the lone sound in the room. Nikki stared at her boots. She wanted to take back the words but it was too late. To possess the truth was bad enough, but to say it aloud for others to hear gave virtual meaning to the word humiliation. Nikki glanced at both Wilcoxes and saw the curiosity in their expressions, but she couldn't bring herself to tell them the details. She thought about people starving in Third World countries and her troubles seemed trivial.

Matt ended the silence. "What do you mean you don't want to be a racetrack vet, gal? I was countin' on saving big bucks."

Susan aimed a rolled polo bandage at his head.

He ducked and the wrap bounced off the wall. "I'm

kidding. I'll pay her. Some."

Nikki seized the opportunity to change topics. "Donnie didn't clean up his dinner, Matt. He's hurting."

"Did you put bute in his feed? That'll stop him from eatin'." The permitted painkiller and anti-inflammatory drug, phenylbutazone, tasted bitter.

She shook her head. "I never give him any bute for three days after a race, so we can see what's going on with his legs."

"It's just that old trick ankle of his, gal."

"I think it's something else. He ran down worse than ever." Nikki paused. "You don't think Winchester Cannon would claim Donnie, do you?"

Matt puffed up his chest and made a show of laughing. "Nobody in their right mind'd claim a ten-year old."

"Since when is sanity a prerequisite for a trainer's license?" Nikki said.

This time Susan cut loose with a burst of laughter.

"Well, ladies, last time I looked, my name was still on King's registration papers. I'd love to get twenty-five hundred for the sore old bugger."

"But *Matt*, Donnie's earned his retirement," Nikki said. "He's made you over a hundred grand."

"Yeah, honey," Susan said. "It's not Donnie's fault you insisted on reinvesting most of it in slow horses."

" *We've* already got a five-acre field full of senior citizens *we* should've canned long ago," Matt said.

"Honey, be nice. Donnie's part of the family."

"You know darn well he'll end up a freeloader at the Wilcox retirement home, but not before he wins a few more races."

" *Matt*, why can't you just retire Donnie now?" Nikki said.

"The darned horse's sitting on a win. Winchester Cannon may not know which end the poop drops out, but I guarantee he won't touch King with a ten-foot pole."

Nikki twisted her mouth into a frown. "That's because even a blind man can see he's sore."

"His bad ankle's a tad arthritic. Paint some DMSO on those

legs of his. And while you're at it, stick some on your bruised face."

She wrinkled her nose. Matt thought DMSO—dimethyl sulfoxide—a clear liquid drug with an oil-like texture, could cure anything. She didn't share his assessment and had no intention of smelling like metallic garlic the rest of the day.

"Put King back on bute tonight," he added. "Three pills."

"Matt's right," Susan said. "Donnie takes care of himself."

"Not when the bell rings," Nikki said. "He'd run through a brick wall to reach the finish line first."

~

The rain didn't let up. At eight-thirty that morning she rode a gelding from the track in a downpour, the horse plodding along with a wet and stringy tail tucked between his legs and his long ears drooping to either side of his head. She slid off at the horse's barn, untacked him, and jogged down the shed row squishing and dripping in her leaky raingear. She exercised six more horses for six different trainers before the outrider finally locked the gate at ten. Some of these trainers would ride her on a horse and some would pay her or already had, while others would do neither. That was how things worked at Westover Meadows.

After dismounting her last horse, Nikki lowered her head and dashed between barns and under another shed row. Rain pounded the metal roof overhead, but she detected the faint sound of hooves banging wood. She sprinted toward the stall of a cast horse. Inside, a chubby brown filly lay pinned against the back wall, unable to rise and thrashing wildly, the boards shaking under her onslaught.

Nikki glanced up and down the empty shed row, shouting, "Cast horse."

When no one answered, she ducked into the stall and grabbed hold of the panicked filly's halter and inched her away from the wall. The filly churned and kicked with her eyes rolled back until she had room to extend her front legs and prop herself up. With a loud grunt, she struggled to her feet and took several deep breaths. Then she gave a squeal of delight or rage or whatever and leaped into the air, bucking and kicking. Nikki made a dive for the door and somersaulted into the shed row.

"Hey, dummy, wasn't my fault you got stuck," she said to the filly, then found a hose and washed the mud off the seat of her pants. Wetter than ever, she continued to the Wilcox's barn.

With no trackers that morning, all their horses had already been walked but King Donican. It was raining too hard to put him on the hot walker, so Nikki hand-walked him under the shed row with water streaming off the roof. Because Donnie's right foreleg felt hot and slightly filled to her, she led him slowly and he gimped along like a car with one semi flat tire. They made four laps of the barn while one of two grooms mucked the stall. When he had finished, she put Donnie in, hung his hay bag, and strapped ice boots on his front legs, then saw to Captain Fuzzy.

Fuzzy stood in the doorway with his nostrils completely submerged, gurgling away in a water bucket hung outside his stall. A sizable puddle had formed on the ground below. He paused when she called his name and rubbed his dripping muzzle across her face like a thousand-pound puppy. She snapped him to a rubber tie and brushed him, picked and greased his feet with a hoof product, and rubbed his legs with liniment.

King Donican nickered when she emerged from the stall. He followed her progress with one ear cocked forward, the other at half-mast, a tuft of fluffy hair sprouting from each. He blew out loudly, then gripped his stall guard in his teeth and shook until she had ducked inside. The grooms were doling out lunch, their blue jeans wet from the knees down, grimy with straw dust. A couple of high school dropouts, eighteen and twenty, they were too big to be jocks or gallop boys, too aimless to work normal jobs, and had no book smarts but enough common sense to keep from getting killed. They moved from stall to stall, one manning a wheelbarrow, the other an empty coffee can, dispensing rolled oats and sweet feed.

Donnie chewed each mouthful thoroughly while Nikki brushed his bright bay coat. Next door, Fuzzy attacked his feed tub. The colt didn't eat; he inhaled. As she was cleaning Donnie's hooves, he stretched his head around, unfastened a Velcro flap, and jammed his nose into one of her jacket pockets. Next, he rummaged through the plastic box that held her grooming things. The straw was soon littered with dollar bills, tissues, brushes, bottles, and a rub rag.

"Donnie!"

The old gelding pricked his ears and gave her a big-eyed look of innocence with a plastic bottle hanging from his lips. She shook a finger at him and he dropped the container.

Around ten-thirty, Nikki went home to shower, eat, and change her clothes, then she returned to Westover Meadows. Before reporting to the Jockeys' Room for Sunday's races, she went by the Wilcox's barn to pick up her whip. No one else was around, only the horses. Right away Nikki noticed that King Donican's bottom door was open, the same door she'd closed herself less than an hour ago. Donnie had been known to fiddle with the latch, so she walked down the deserted shed row and peeked over his stall guard. He nickered. One of his front bandages was missing. The sheet cotton and plastic wrap still covered the leg but the outer bandages were scattered among the straw. She went inside and gathered the mess and saw that the tape stuck over the Velcro strap had been neatly ripped, not gummed by a horse's teeth.

Nikki wheeled at the sound of creaking timbers.

A glance out the door revealed no one. The shed row was empty. She cocked her head and listened. Rain trickled on the roof and a gusty wind rattled plywood sheets nailed over open windows along the wall enclosing the shed row.

After rewrapping Donnie's bandage, she ducked out of his stall, unlocked the tack room, and stepped inside. The door swung shut, leaving her in total darkness. She groped for the light switch dangling from a string at the center of the room. Something brushed her face. She flung an arm in that direction and leaped away, punching the air, then another object hit her on the nose and another grazed her neck before she managed to snag the light cord.

The room was empty.

Polos, stall wraps, and a wet cotton lead rope hung drying from a length of baling wire strung between walls—all swaying from her blows. She cussed her reaction and grabbed her whip. Outside, a horse nickered, followed by the fading thud of footsteps.

Nikki dashed out the door and caught a glimpse of a denim-clad leg running from the barn at the opposite end. She sprinted the length of the shed row and over the washrack to the edge of the massive puddle between the Wilcox's and Winchester Cannon's barns. Across the way, Cannon stood in his shed row. Even from a distance, she spotted the up-and-down motion of his shoulders and belly. The trainer was out of breath.

~

By eight that evening, Nikki had taken a hot bath and sat cross-legged on her bed in a nightie—i.e., an extra-large T-shirt—reading Beryl Markham's *West with the Night.* When the phone rang, she ignored it momentarily—expecting a summons to show up early for work in the morning—but the caller was her cousin, Brad Warner. His deep raspy voice reminded her that he was no longer a kid.

Brad had been ten and Nikki almost six when she'd showed up on his family's doorstep in Beverly Hills, accompanied by Rachel. Nikki's memories of Rachel were of a mother who seldom spoke to her, a dark shadow in the Warner's vast house, restless and quick to mouthoff to Aunt Monica. Nikki hardly remembered seeing Rachel the month before she'd split. Mondays and Tuesdays were the only days Rachel showed up for dinner. Weekends, she came and went in the dark. Then she was gone.

Monica had kindly insisted Nikki stay with the Warners

until Rachel got her act together in San Francisco or wherever she was headed. At first, Rachel visited every couple of weeks, but after a few months, she showed up less and less. She always had some excuse about having to work and not being able to get away, then she hit the road for New York. After a year, Rachel flew back for Nikki's eighth birthday. A surprise visit.

Aunt Monica had been livid. About ten seconds after Rachel walked through the door, Monica gave her an ultimatum: stay and find a real job or stay the hell away. Rachel told her to drop dead. Things had gotten wild after that. Nikki raced outside and climbed into Monica's favorite Japanese maple, breaking several prime branches in the process. Brad's little sister, Tiffany, recognizing an opportunity to kiss up to the adults, had busted her arm in an unsuccessful attempt to haul Nikki to the ground. A cat fight ensued between Rachel and Monica, a shouting, shrieking, slapping, extremely distressing debacle that resulted in the neighbors calling the police. With all the commotion, Nikki refused to come down from the maple tree. Rachel had begged and pleaded, but Nikki pouted with the resolve of a mule. She spent the night in that tree. Her mother returned to New York alone.

After that, Brad had been Nikki's savior of sorts, the ever-smiling big brother who could always cheer her up—be it sticking jellybeans up his nose or sharing his copies of *Playgirl*, although she was too embarrassed to spend more than a few seconds looking at photos of naked men hung like horses. Nikki hadn't seen her cousin since the day she'd packed her things and headed for the racetrack. They'd kept in touch, but Brad hadn't called her in more than a year and she had grown tired of always being the one who made the effort.

"Hey, how's it going, stranger?" he asked.

"Brad?"

"Just wanted to say hi. Make sure you're alive."

"Wow. Good to hear from you."

"Yeah, you know I care even when I don't call."

"Same here. So how's it going?"

"Great. You?"

"Fine."

"Winning lots of races?"

"No."

"Heard from Monica, lately?"

"Not since her last pleasant letter at Christmas."

"I bet she's been planning to call you."

Nikki sighed into the receiver. "Oh, so that's it. Monica's guilt tripping in her old age."

"You could give her a call, you know."

"She put you up to this?"

"Be the bigger person, Nicole."

"That's Nikki."

"Oh yeah, I forgot. But if you're waiting for Mom to apologize—good fucking luck."

Nikki realized then, with some remorse, that she didn't give a damn about Aunt Monica, nor had she *ever* felt any connection to the woman. "I'm sure as hell not apologizing for refusing to let her run my life," she said.

"Don't be such a snot."

"Monica's not *my* mother."

"That would be *Rachel*, the hard-wired bulletproof narcissistic piece-of-work."

"Can we drop it, Brad?"

"I'm getting even for those times you borrowed my razors to shave your legs."

"You're even."

"Seriously, you know Mom has had it with the whole racetrack thing and your crazy-ass determination to follow..."

Nikki cut him off, having concluded that Aunt Monica probably didn't give a damn about her either. "Have you introduced Monica to any of your boyfriends yet?"

"You know Mom's policy, smart ass."

"Yeah, like the army's. Lie."

"That's don't ask, don't tell."

"Why can't she be that way with me?"

"You need to get over it, Nicole. You're too smart to piss

your life away trying to win over Mommie Rachel with your expertise among short people who beat on horses."

"Thanks, Brad. That's real nice." In Nikki's estimation, there was no pleasing any of the women in her family, although she would give Monica credit for being around to offer criticism.

"Have 'Rot in Hell Mom' tattooed on your ass and leave it at that," he said.

"You're taking Monica's side against me?"

"Hello. She's my mother."

"Yeah. I know."

"Hey, I'd be a serious bad seed if I didn't stick up for her once in awhile."

"Yeah, I get it. Listen, thanks for calling but I need to go study."

"Oh sure, blow me off."

"What did you expect?"

"Want some advice?"

"No."

"Rachel doesn't give a fuck. Move on."

"Take care, Brad."

"Sure, be that way. Don't let me stop you from being a loser."

"I won't," she said.

~

Nikki slammed down the phone and lay on her bed. The anger that fueled her ambitions flickered to life and she pounded her fist against the mattress, vowing her relatives would need some real strong onions to ever make her cry. The last time Monica had called, about four years back, Nikki had gotten so mad, she'd kicked the bed frame and broken a toe. She had won three races the next day. At the moment, Nikki felt an urge to practice her whipping on the side of the bed. She rose as far as a sitting position, then lost the urge and strained hard to recall her early childhood with Rachel and compile a list of bad memories versus good, in hopes the bad might this once prevail and kill what little expectation of a happy reunion yet remained in her heart. Nikki no longer wanted a mother for the sake of being mothered. She'd been without one so long that even imagining such a thing seemed laughable. It was a matter of proving her own worth. A matter of allocating blame.

But being reminded of the maple tree incident and how she'd acted like a selfish brat hadn't helped her cause on that last count. Nikki lay back down with her guilty conscience and stared at the ceiling. There should be a statute of limitations on childhood mistakes, she thought. And adult ones. Her current status as a mediocre rider at a third-rate track led her to worry that Brad was right about her being a loser. She wondered if she had rashly let anger dictate the direction of her life.

Two years after Rachel left for New York, Monica told Nikki that Rachel had been killed in a training accident at Belmont Park. Nikki was ten. She'd hidden under the bed and cried and cried, believing that her absentee mother, now supposedly deceased, had intended to eventually return. Monica's white lie might never have been exposed if Rachel hadn't become a hotshot horse trainer.

At the age of sixteen, Nikki's love for reading subjected her to the truth. She was thumbing through a women's magazine while waiting for a dentist appointment and came across an article about a successful New York Thoroughbred trainer named Rachel Nottingham. Nikki, who wanted nothing to do with horses or racing since her mother had been killed, started to turn the page but was drawn to a photograph of a smiling Nottingham with her arm around a smiling jockey. After gaping at the photo for several minutes, Nikki read the article. Nottingham, daughter of the late Jeremiah Winters, a respected northern California horseman, had set a New York record for wins by a woman trainer. The story called her the most courageous lady in racing and went on to discuss her recent divorce, stating that her marriage was just one of the sacrifices she had made for her career. The article failed to mention any daughter.

A dozen years later, Nikki was still dismayed to find that the discovery of her mother's rebirth had hurt worse than her death.

Peninsula Park
December 1993

By the middle of December, Rachel's lead in the trainer's standings had shrunk to a single win. Late on a Friday morning, she walked down a road between barn rows with her assistant trainer at her side, Sam jogging every few steps to keep up. A halter and shank swung in his hand. The main racetrack and the smaller five-eighths-mile training track had closed a half-hour earlier and tractors towing harrows now renovated both ovals, plowing under thousands of hoof prints to leave the surfaces even and lightly grooved. Most of the 2,000 Thoroughbreds stabled on the grounds had been galloped or walked and were back in their stalls.

Rachel stopped outside the end barn nearest the gap and surveyed the shed row. Shiny royal-blue placards, emblazoned with a bright yellow horseshoe and the initials R.M., hung outside each of forty stalls just beyond the outstretched necks— and teeth—of bored or curious occupants. A gallop boy was cleaning saddles on the wash-rack. His jacket and leather leggings were the same blue and yellow, along with buckets, manure carts, saddle towels, polos, and blankets. Rachel's own stall placards were silver with a black thunderbolt edged in sapphire blue. Clients expected a first-class operation.

Sam was looking at her.

She pushed her hat down in front. "I'm getting a cup of coffee. Pick up the filly. Reno balks, tell him I bought her fair and square."

Rachel handed her assistant a copy of the bill of sale, then hurried toward the cafeteria. After buying coffee, she waited outside, blowing and sipping at the paper cup until Sam led the new horse from Reno McAllister's barn and headed toward her own. Rachel followed, mulling over how she planned to win more races. She caught up to Sam and told him she was having a plot of grass laid behind the barn and would list daily which horses were to graze. She told him to see that each horse received a half-gallon of chopped carrots in their evening feed every day, rather than at the grooms' discretion. She told him that happy horses won more races.

Barn 28 was the first of three situated along a high concrete wall topped with razor wire that marked the northern perimeter. Behind the barn, hot horses in blue blankets and black polo bandages were being hand-walked around a sand ring until they cooled out, along with horses scheduled to walk that morning. Other less valuable or less fractious animals circled a mechanical hot walker—a revolving maypole topped by four metal arms with rubber ties, the arms extending outward at 90 degree angles, hypothetically, far enough to prevent kicking battles, although Rachel had seen plenty of those.

She stopped at an empty stall at the end of the shed row, where Sam had led in the new occupant. The filly poked her head out and gazed around as though she owned the place. Rachel liked what she saw.

Lucifera was a light gray dappled with darker splotches the size and shape of saucers. Her mane and tail were a pale silver, the latter nearly brushing the ground, the former pulled short to about four inches in racehorse fashion with a bridle-path clipped along her poll. Her face was finely chiseled and intelligent. Her neck was long, her shoulder flat and sloping. She was packing good weight—neither fat nor whippet thin— and was surprisingly well-muscled for a horse that had never raced. She had short cannon bones, clean tendons, and large flat knees, neither calf-kneed nor buck-kneed but perfectly aligned. Her pasterns sloped in an appropriate angle and she was not pigeon-toed or splay-footed. Her hind legs were straight, her hocks correct. A short and strong back complemented a deep girth, a powerful chest, a long hip and strong hindquarters. Her feet were proportionately sized with plenty of heel, an important consideration, as Rachel believed problems often started with the feet and worked upward. Stepping back, she took in the whole picture. Except for long, rather mulish ears, Lucifera possessed nearly perfect conformation. In combination with her unusual color, she was the most strikingly beautiful horse Rachel had ever seen.

Rachel planned to have her veterinarian examine the gray filly to make certain no physical abnormality or hidden injury was responsible for her obnoxious behavior. And like all new horses to the barn, she would be given a worming and a blood test. Reno McAllister was not the type of trainer who neglected the basics, Rachel knew, but she felt compelled to follow her usual routine step by step, just in case. She took hold of the filly's halter and slipped two fingers into the side of her mouth to see if her teeth needed floating. To prevent painful mouth sores, at least once a year the sharp edges caused by uneven wear from chewing were filed by a veterinarian, using a rasp-like instrument.

Rachel felt smooth teeth on both sides. Lucifera, with her long ears halfway between pinned and pricked, did her best to be uncooperative, slinging her head from side to side. Rachel withdrew her hand and wiped it dry on the filly's neck. Lucifera snapped at her arm and ended up with a mouthful of jacket sleeve. A short tussle ensued. Rachel jerked free with a huff and headed to the other side of the barn.

Halfway there she sensed someone treading in her footsteps and looked over her shoulder, expecting to see a groom, but instead she found herself nose to nose with Lucifera. They both froze in their tracks. Oh so slowly, Rachel reached for the chin ring on the gray filly's halter. Lucifera snorted and flung up her head. Rachel lunged for the halter, missing, as the filly wheeled with a sassy grunt and kicked out with both hind feet. Hooves slashed the air.

But Rachel leaped clear, having anticipated the double-barreled attack. She shouted to Sam and her other help, then sprinted down the hard-packed dirt of the shed row and rounded the corner in time to see Lucifera's dappled rump disappear at the other end. The filly had crawled under her stall gate, Rachel realized, angry at herself for not installing a full-length screen. She cut back in the opposite direction and nearly ran into two of her grooms. Darting around them, she shouted commands in Spanish and both men raced to head off Lucifera, but the gray filly trotted out of the shed row and onto the road. Rachel dashed in pursuit, following the trail of chaos. She sprinted past a barn whose wash line of wet saddle towels and bandages lay scattered in the dirt. The grooms shook their fists and the trainer shouted unpleasant things, calling the filly a fleabag and Rachel an old bag. She didn't stop to chat. Up ahead, Lucifera was heading toward Reno McAllister's barn like a homing pigeon. The filly stopped long enough to peer down the shed row before her gray rump trotted inside and disappeared.

One of the most basic unwritten rules among racetrackers is that a trainer's barn is like private property, trespassers unwelcome. Rachel skidded to a stop at the edge of McAllister's shed row. She glanced left and right, saw the coast was clear, and resumed the chase. She was rushing down the east side shed row in a fast walk, so as not to frighten the horses, when from behind a hand snagged her by the wrist. Rachel lurched to a halt and wheeled on the rebound with her left arm flying to strike something solid. Reno McAllister's head, as it turned out.

He cussed loudly. She jerked free of his hold, then raised her fists and drew her right knee to waist level, thigh taut as a bowstring, her foot the arrow. There she stood, poised like an actor in a bad martial arts film. Her blow had dislodged McAllister's Stetson, exposing thick sandy brown hair, graying at the temples, which shot to hell her belief that men who always wore hats were bald. He rubbed his chin and appeared to contemplate walking away.

"What are you doing?" he said instead.

Rachel let out the breath she'd been holding and lowered her hands and leg. "You ought to learn some goddamn manners."

"You might try staying out of my barn."

"Well, excuse me but I lost a horse."

McAllister rocked back on his heels and laughed. "Does Lucifera make you wish you'd stolen something useful, like maybe some of my clients?"

"I bought her honestly and you know it," Rachel said, then hiked up her chaps, which had conspired with her jeans to migrate in opposite directions.

He stopped laughing. "I sold her to a kindly old gentleman, you've obviously corrupted."

"How many of my horses have *you* connived to steal?" She thrust a hand in her rival's face and was counting names on fingers, when his assistant trainer walked around the corner with Lucifera. Sam stumbled onto the scene then, huffing and puffing, to snap a shank on the filly's halter and lead her from the barn. With McAllister's attention diverted, Rachel stuck her thumbs in her front pants pockets and inconspicuously tried to rearrange her jeans.

He saw and cracked a smile. "Lady, you're a real charmer in more ways than one."

Her face reddened. "My underwear feels like it needs to be surgically extracted."

"Maybe they can find your conscience while they're at it."

"Go to hell, Mister."

"Have fun with the filly," he said. "You two deserve each other."

Rachel sucked a breath through her teeth, then wheeled and stomped off.

~

In a past life, Reno McAllister envisioned himself living out West either as a renegade cattle thief who robbed the rich and gave to the poor or as a sheriff who rode into town and wiped out the bad guys, which led him to believe he'd watched too many old movies. His real life seemed dull by comparison. He had grown up on five acres near Red Bluff in northern

California, the third of four children. He had a sister named Shasta, and two brothers, Carson and Elko. His parents had owned a successful construction company and took the family on regular vacations, bought each of their children a horse, and stressed the importance of hard work. They'd given him no cause to ever end up in a shrink's office.

High school found him in Lee jeans and a black Stetson. He chewed Copenhagen, drank Coors, and hung around with a group of guys known as the cowboys. He let the fuzz above his upper lip grow, thinking he looked cool. Not that girls had been the least interested in dating a scrawny punk routinely mistaken for an eighth grader until his senior year, an outsider who shunned football and baseball in favor of rodeos.

How he had loved bronc riding. Bareback broncs, saddle broncs, and calf roping, after he'd grown taller and stronger. A bum shoulder had prevented him from pursuing a professional career. In college, he discovered horse racing and spent much of his free time at tracks in Sacramento, Stockton, Pleasanton, and the Bay Area, watching and learning. After graduating he got married and worked as a civil engineer long enough to buy a house and accumulate some savings, then decided life was too short to spend it doing something he viewed with indifference. At thirty, he'd quit to become a horse trainer.

Lean times followed as he learned his new trade. His wife divorced him inside of a year, which hurt like hell until he realized that she cared more for material things and had done him a favor. On the mend, he married again, doing so out of loneliness, rather than love. Two years later, they parted on good terms and he had never come close to marrying since. Women seemed to find him attractive, and he enjoyed women but treated his girlfriends respectfully at arm's length. The distinction between sex and love fell into sharp focus under his twenty-thirty vision. He didn't foresee getting married again, not at forty-six. Not with racing to occupy the majority of his time.

Yet, Rachel Nottingham intrigued him in the manner that lions and tigers and bears intrigued him, a beautiful, dangerous creature his big-game-hunter side found desirable. He chalked up her allure to the male curse of wanting what he couldn't have. Or shouldn't have. Like a man mortified to discover a secret craving for something taboo, he added her name to the list of things that were bad for him. Snuff, beer, whiskey, fast cars, television game shows, poker, bacon, pork ribs, red meat, mayonnaise, butter, chocolate-covered cashews, cheese cake, and Rachel Nottingham.

She personified the classic Thoroughbred trainer, gifted with horse sense, deceitfully crafty, dedicated to perfection, obsessed with winning, hard nosed, and a touch cruel. From a professional standpoint, she had his complete respect. On a personal level, his early impressions of Nottingham had been formed by credible gossip. When she'd arrived on the scene about ten years ago, the hot New York trainer returning home from the big league, a rumor began circulating that she had abandoned a child. At the time, he passed that story off as the sort of jealous rumor people fabricated about successful and ambitious women. His first encounter with her came soon after, when a 2-1 favorite he trained had been beaten badly by her 10-1 shot. He recalled congratulating her and would never forget how she'd looked him in the eyes dead-on and said, "Trainers like you make my job easy."

He had since dedicated himself to making her eat those words. No easy accomplishment, he'd discovered after years of failed efforts. He originally likened his plight to that of a small business trying to keep pace with a corporation, but his recent procurement of big-money clients had shown him what a superior horseman she really was. Two months into the meet and he'd expected to be a half-dozen wins in front of her, not one behind. This year, he had resolved to go all out to win the training title. To that end, he overreacted to the news that she had downed a few too many tequila shooters and publicly bragged about having a daughter. Other competitors had let the matter drop, Reno gathered, out of empathy and because they saw no advantage in using it against her, not in a sport that embraced toughness. He, however, had hired a private detective to exhume her skeletons.

And discovered that she did, indeed, have a grown daughter. He felt about seven-eighths ashamed of what he'd done, but he had done it and there was no going back. He began to worry that, subconsciously, he had acted on his vague attraction to her. From an ethical perspective, this seemed the preferable scenario. As for what it said of his taste in women, he had to wonder.

Whatever the case, it seemed they *did* have something in common. With the deceptive purchase of the filly, Lucifera, Rachel had proven equally skilled at drawing a not quite straight battle line. He and she both understood that pride was the least of the spoils up for grabs. The winner of the trainer's title attracted clients like shit drew flies, and while that was not a pretty analogy, Reno believed it an appropriate one. Sometimes, when he was half asleep, his thoughts drifted to an idealistic place from his youth where winning mattered only for the satisfaction of winning, then he would awaken and feel the sink hole in the pit of his stomach and be reminded that pride was nothing more than a windfall. If the sport continued on its present course, he envisioned a day when trainers behaved worse than a pack of cur dogs. Already, he felt his own focus zeroing in on Rachel's throat, recalling the look on her face when he'd slapped her with a solid dose of humility at the Hollywood Park Fall Yearling Sale. For a split-second, he'd detected a glimmer of fear in her eyes upon hearing that he knew she had a daughter. If Rachel was superwoman, he had discovered her kryptonite. His guilty conscience be damned.

~

Rachel went directly to her office after leaving Reno McAllister's barn. She dropped into a padded swivel chair and swung around to a quartersawn oak desk, grabbed cigarettes and a pencil, then began marking potential claims in the afternoon's copy of the *Daily Racing Form*. The room was the size of a blue-carpeted stall and was neat and clean, except for the top of the desk. Glass-framed, 8 x 12 inch win photos accented white walls, along with a Chippendales calendar and a San Francisco Ballet poster of the Black Swan. Rachel started as someone knocked on the door. For an instant, she imagined Reno McAllister had followed her and was standing outside in the shed row. She lit up and sat staring at the door.

"Track security! Come out with your hands above your head and the cigarette in plain sight."

"Very funny, Virginia," Rachel shouted. She drew deeply on the smoke and exhaled with a sigh toward the door.

A petite woman in a bright yellow sweat suit stepped inside. "That's Ginny. And if I'd been a guard, you'd be paying another fine."

Virginia Hammond wore her hair in a lightly layered, frosted blond bob. Her features were as delicate as a China doll's, though her face appeared overly smooth for a woman in her late sixties, suggesting plastic surgery. In the two years that Rachel had trained for Hammond, she'd never been so impolite as to ask.

"If you weren't a client, I'd ban you from my barn." Rachel aimed another lungful of smoke across the room.

Virginia fanned a hand through the air. "You really should stop smoking those dreadful weeds. If I could stop, anyone can."

"Are you here for something specific?"

"Lunch."

"Oh," Rachel said, unable to recall having agreed to such a thing.

Virginia had proven impervious to the fundamental rule of not mixing business and friendship, which meant she frequently asked nosy questions. Worse yet, she owned just two cheap claimers. Rachel could think of more enjoyable ways to spend her lunch hour but knew better than to offend a client.

"How does brown-bagging it sound? I brought sandwiches, iced tea, and cocoanut-pecan pie from that wonderful deli on the corner." Virginia plunked a paper sack onto the desk and began removing the food.

"I'll gain ten pounds off the fumes alone," Rachel said, unwrapping a roast beef and Swiss cheese sandwich.

"You could use ten pounds."

"Yeah, on my chest."

"Speaking of boobs, that Reno McAllister's playing with a stacked deck," Virginia said.

"I'm taking steps to even the score." Rachel pursed her lips to keep from smiling. She pictured Lucifera winning stakes races but kept the vision to herself.

"You've robbed a bank?"

"Very funny."

"So?"

"Billy Cortez, McAllister's vet, asked me on a date." Now Rachel smiled fully. But her humor passed over Virginia's head like a weather balloon.

"I certainly hope there's not a hell, dear."

Rachel's smile faded. "Believe it or not, I do have principles, but no matter how gracefully I fall on my ass the world's not gonna stop and pick me up."

"I would."

"Yeah, right."

"I most certainly would."

Rachel took a bite of her sandwich. Chewed and swallowed. "Well, you shouldn't."

"And why not?"

"I'm way too heavy."

"Piffle. You're slim as a fashion model."

"That's not what I meant."

Virginia paused a moment. "*Oh.*"

There was a stretch of silence and both women concentrated on their food. Barn noises seeped through the walls—a horse popping its lips, a nicker, the scraping of teeth on a bucket.

"I just bought a filly out of McAllister's barn," Rachel said, jump-starting the conversation on a less personal note.

"Reno sold you a horse?"

"Not exactly. I got my old friend Pepper Roswell to buy her

for me."

"Oh?"

"Lucifera, that's her registered name. Her dam was a multiple stakes winner and her sire earned over a million."

"Is she pretty?"

"Pretty? Well, I suppose, but beauty's irrelevant unless you consider the relationship between function and form."

"Want to run that by me again?"

"Virginia," Rachel said, her deep voice jumping higher. "This filly has a ton of raw ability. I think she's a runner."

"That's Ginny. Why'd they sell her then?"

"Can't keep a rider on her back. Filly's a notorious rogue. Four white socks and a white nose, cut off its hide and feed it to the crows. Four gray socks and a gray nose, sell it to Rachel and she'll turn it into a — nothing positive rhymes with nose."

"Rose?"

"Roses have thorns."

"You're certainly very good with bad horses, dear."

She winked at Virginia. "The horses are easy. Training their owners is the trick."

~

After Virginia had gone, Rachel sat alone in her office. She finished marking a training chart and lay her head on the desk. Years ago, her father had refused to run a sore horse on an illegal painkiller that was passing undetected in post-race test samples. The horse finished far back. Her father sold the animal after the race for practically nothing and it won its next start by five lengths for another trainer. Her father once told her that winning wasn't everything, that there was no shame in losing. She thought this would probably be true in a fairytale land where honesty trumped deceit, unfairness was illegal, and money grew on trees. As her father's sole offspring, she'd admired his integrity but placed greater importance on real world matters like making a decent living, plus there were achievements to be considered. After she was dead and gone, the details that made her an individual would soon be forgotten. Her memory would live on in her deeds alone, provided she accomplished something worth remembering. Rachel lifted her head, then picked up the receiver and dialed her bank. Nobody remembered losers.

~

Before leaving, she stopped by Lucifera's stall, the filly now secured behind a full screen-gate with an extra latch. Rachel had trained rogues before, the nastiest of outlaws, and learned early on that winning every battle did not always transform a horse into a winner on the racetrack. Sometimes an occasional draw proved wiser and more profitable. Diplomacy was the key, not brute force. Never let a horse figure out it was the physically superior species, though the gray filly appeared to have been born with this knowledge. Was that why her breeders named her Lucifera, Rachel wondered, because she was the devil? Or perhaps the name was due to her tendency to escape—Loose-ifera? Registration information, including sex, color, markings, and name choices, were sent to the Jockey Club after the birth of a foal, so if a weanling had a distinct personality, it often received an appropriate name. Rachel had known her share of horses officially tagged with unpleasant adjectives—Mean Old Bill, Crazy Nannie, Slow Motion Moe, and so on. Most lived up to their calling. In all her years as a trainer, she had encountered few truly unmanageable horses, and the majority of those were jug-headed dirtbags who were not worth the effort.

"You *will* win a race," Rachel told the filly before leaving.

Lucifera squeezed her eyes shut and yawned.

~

In the morning, the gray filly walked from her stall dead lame with heat in her right front hoof. X-rays revealed no fractures to the coffin bone, and pictures of her pastern bones and ankle were clean as well. Rachel ordered the groom to soak the foot in Epsom salts and hot water every morning, then pack the sole with a drawing poultice. After a week, a farrier cut out an abscess. After another week, Lucifera was ready to resume training, but she turned up lame again, this time with a hot left forefoot and the whole process started over.

Christmas came and went. In Rachel's opinion, the holidays were a gigantic pain in the ass but—knowing others did not share her opinion—she gave her help monetary bonuses and her clients each a box of fancy chocolates, then showed up at the Vanderford's annual Christmas party with a bottle of expensive Napa Valley wine and a fresh-baked apple pie purchased from a local bakery as her culinary skills consisted of a talent for microwaving frozen dinners.

The Vanderford's party was mostly a family affair with dozens of relatives, including a slew of youngsters, tons of presents, a tree, all the usual trimmings times ten, and Rachel. This year was no different. Attending another family's holiday celebration was not something she looked forward to, but the Vanderfords were genuinely nice people who meant well, so Rachel always came with a smile. The past four years, she'd endured the affair with minimal mental anguish over not having any relatives of her own to celebrate with—who didn't detest her. But not this year. After watching one of J.K.'s little tow-headed granddaughters bounce up and down for what seemed like an hour on her new rocking horse, Rachel felt an unexpected urge to cry and went home early. She sat in the dark and drank vodka and cranberry juice and studied a video of race reruns recorded off a cable channel, all the while reminding herself how much it would suck to have relatives butting into her life, telling her how to run her business, to quit smoking, to drink less, whom to date, what to drive, where to live, and on and on. Later, she fell asleep watching *It's a Wonderful Life.*

The Monday after Christmas, she sent her first set of horses out to exercise when the track opened at five-thirty, as she did every morning. A pair of two-year olds, fit and on the muscle, two bundles of nervous energy. They needed to race, but Peninsula Park was swamped with cheap colts and fillies, which meant at least a month between starts. During the interim, Rachel sought to keep the youngsters from tearing themselves and the barn apart without over training them. She told her gallop boys to jog them two miles.

She believed in lots of jogging. Trotting offered a less stressful exercise routine between workouts or races. It kept the young horses from falling into the go-go-go habit every time they set foot on the track, while at the same time strengthened their bodies without causing undue stress. Too many people trained their two-year-olds hard and fast, a method that made no allowances for immature bones, thus ruining many youngsters, in particular, late-developing ones. Hurry a horse and it'll find a way to make you wait, as she had learned the hard way, more than once.

By six, Rachel had completed her rounds—checking feed tubs for uneaten grain, inspecting legs for soundness, taking the temperatures of half her forty head, with Sam catching the other half. She had just emerged from the tack room when officers from the Department of Immigration and Naturalization stormed her barn.

The shed row erupted in a blur of motion as her grooms and hotwalkers scattered like flushed pheasants with I.N.S. officers in rapid pursuit. All of Rachel's dozen grooms and four hotwalkers were from Mexico or Central America. Five were illegal immigrants. When the dust cleared, three were carted off to a government van for the initial leg of a free return-trip home, along with four others who possessed green cards but panicked and bolted with their countrymen. Rachel argued diplomatically with the authorities for several minutes, to no avail, and then threw a fit, demanding to know if all the other trainers at the track who employed Mexican immigrants—in other words, practically all the other trainers at the track—were going to have their barns raided. In the end, the flustered officer in charge escorted the four men to their tack rooms where they revealed proof of legal residency.

After all was said and done, she stood outside her barn and waited until the Immigration van drove off. The uproar had attracted a crowd of onlookers—other trainers, jockeys, jockey agents, gallop boys, owners—eager to snicker at her plight, but they scattered when she told them to go jump in the infield lake. With that, she returned to work. At five minutes to ten, she watched her last tracker gallop and escorted the colt back to the barn, dismounted her pony, grabbed a pitchfork, and cleaned stalls herself. At ten, trainer Opal O'Reilly kindly sent one of her grooms over to help, and he ended up cleaning eight stalls, which was as many as two grooms would normally clean.

The trainer dropped by around noon and talked with Rachel in the shed row. O'Reilly had recently dyed her gunmetal gray hair jet black and wore it in a blocky, Cleopatra cut. Red Converse high-top basketball sneakers, baggy jeans, and a Budweiser T-shirt completed her look, which Rachel couldn't begin to label. She made a mental note to hire a fashion consultant if she made it past seventy.

"Thanks for the groom, Opal. I owe you one."

"I plan to run a colt in that maiden allowance race next Saturday. You're not figuring on entering that thing of yours that's run three straight seconds, are you?"

Rachel nodded.

O'Reilly cuffed her on the arm. "Shit, honey, you and Reno aren't leaving a whole lot of meat on the bones. Rest of us have got to win a race now and then, too."

Rachel rubbed her arm. "I suppose I could skip that race."

O'Reilly stared at her with squinty-eyed suspicion. "For real?"

"Just don't be dunning me down the road."

"Wouldn't think of it, Nottingham."

"Anyone else get raided?"

"Nope."

"So I was the only one?"

"Yup."

"Shit." Rachel thrust her pitchfork into a bale of straw,

glanced about for security guards, then lit a cigarette and held out the pack.

O'Reilly took one. "Heard it was a riot. Those boys from the I.N.S. are better than the Keystone Cops."

"It wasn't funny, the peckerheads."

"Don't get your tits in a twist."

Rachel glanced at her chest. "Like *that* could happen."

"Your grooms'll come sneaking back in a day or two," O'Reilly said.

"Yeah, I'm hoping." Rachel took a long drag, then abruptly threw down the butt and ground it into the shed row. "I'll bet you a thousand bucks McAllister ratted on me to Immigration."

"He is mighty unhappy you duped him outta the gray hurricane."

"I bought her fair and square."

"With ol' Pepper Roswell, who's not even supposed to be allowed on the grounds."

Rachel grinned. "Told the guard he was my grandfather. Nobody recognizes poor Pepper anymore."

"Reno sure didn't. He swallowed Pepper's bit about buying bucking stock for the rodeo faster than a man eatin' raw oysters."

"Like I always say, 'don't get mad, get even.'"

"Too bad you have to train that gray demon."

Rachel stopped grinning. "Yeah, for someone who was hoodwinked, McAllister seemed pretty pleased to see her go."

O'Reilly cleared her throat with an air of importance. "Pleased as rum-spiked punch. He's only sore on account of his assistant trainer told him you was scoping out his horses."

"What?"

"Word's out you got desperate and stooped to snooping."

"That's bullshit."

"I know. I saw you chasing the filly."

Rachel kicked the air. "No wonder everyone's been giving me uglier looks than usual. I'd crawl buck naked over broken glass before I'd sneak into another trainer's barn to check out their horses."

"Bet a lotta folks would pay money to see that."

"Opal."

"I've been sticking up for you, if it's any comfort."

"Not much, but thanks anyway. I'll admit, I do what I have to do sometimes. Okay, all the time, but sneaking into someone else's barn, that's just slimy."

"Hell, honey, don't get mad, get even."

"Oh, I intend to," Rachel said, and made straight for her office in a running walk.

~

The first thing she did was remove a compact from her purse and check her makeup. Besides too many wrinkles, the mirror revealed smudged eyeliner and faded lipstick. She touched up both, brushed her hair and gave it a shot of spray, then placed a daub of perfume on her throat—an exotic French brand that would linger for days, weathering any number of baths and showers if she failed to use restraint. After a final glance in the mirror, she rose from her desk—along with her uncertain strategy—and went in search of Dr. Billy Cortez, Reno McAllister's veterinarian.

She made a beeline for the backside cafeteria, guessing where she might find Cortez at noon. Sure enough, she spotted him at a table with a chubby blond whose makeup application fell into the category of war paint and a pig-tailed brunette wearing a Madonna tank top. Both were gazing at him in dreamy-eyed adoration, while he concentrated on a plate of semi-burnt biscuits and pasty gravy like a man who hadn't eaten in days. Rachel stepped into line at the counter, checking her reflection in a shiny cylindrical coffee pot. She bought a candy bar and a Coke, then returned a loud hello to a jockey who nodded at her as he walked past. Cortez looked up from his plate. Rachel caught his eye. She glanced at the door, letting her gaze linger there, before leaving him with a trace of a smile to wait outside in full view of the cafeteria windows. When she saw him rise and start her way, she popped a breath mint into her mouth and strolled to a discreet location along the outside fence of the main track. He joined her there.

She apologized for interrupting his lunch date. He smiled. Strong, white toothpaste commercial teeth. The two girls in the kitchen followed him everywhere, he explained, a couple of high school dropouts who groomed horses. Nice kids. If they didn't stop drooling over him he was going to start eating his lunch elsewhere. Rachel said she couldn't help him at lunch but knew of an excellent place he could have dinner in private. Her condominium. Not one for minor details, she neglected to mention that she couldn't cook.

"Why the change of heart?" he asked.

"Even geniuses make mistakes," she told him with a not quite serious smile.

His confident one revealed that he was conceited enough to believe she'd fallen for him. She didn't one-hundred percent rule out the possibility. Time and again, her head had failed to overrule her hormones when it came to picking men, so her rival's young buck of a veterinarian seemed right up her alley. Cortez had one of those round, firm dancer's asses that reminded her how much she adored the ballet. The venerable War Memorial Opera House, the dancers like Thoroughbreds, long-legged, lithe, sleekly muscled, a melding of music, motion, and drama. She gave him her address and was walking back to her barn, when she found herself recalling her one other date with a vet. Rachel kicked a paper cup in her path, a swift kick delivered in stride that sent it flying with a hollow pop.

Her first year in New York, she had owned and trained a fledgling stable of three horses, worked two jobs seven days a week, and lived on saltine crackers and tuna fish in a cramped and dusty tack room. She had been unable to afford a veterinarian yet couldn't afford not to have one if she wished to keep her trio of cripples patched together and on their toes. The three horses ended up winning eleven races. New York was where the term dog-eat-dog originated, she'd discovered, a city in perpetual motion, too crowded to slow down, too busy to lend a hand if a person happened to trip or fall under the weight of their dreams. Or maybe she had just met the wrong people. She struggled to draw forth a happy memory from those eleven wins, but recalled only the cheap motel and how Dr. Bryant's breath smelled of peppermint gum and garlic and how she had closed her eyes and wished she were somewhere else. Thereafter, she had paid her vets by check.

At her barn, Rachel went inside the office and locked the door. She sat at her desk, took off a sport watch with a thick black band, and gazed at the underside of her wrist, at the two-inch razor scar there. A thin pink slash, guilt deep and as fine as the line between survival and getting even.

Westover Meadows
January 1994

Nikki had spent most of Christmas day peeling potatoes and chopping onions. Westover Meadows had been closed for racing. She'd received about a half-dozen dinner invitations but felt uncomfortable at other people's family gatherings, as she always migrated to deserted corners unless she got drunk, in which case she ended up the center of attention and could never remember why. Instead, she volunteered to cook at a local shelter for the homeless, along with Matty and Hank, two racetrack veterinarians who also had no special place to be. Afterward, the three of them went to a Chinese restaurant and porked out. The following morning, Nikki weighed 118 pounds on the scale at her apartment, four pounds heavier than normal. She galloped ten head, jogged a mile in a scuba wetsuit, and fasted all day. Nonetheless, by post time that evening she could tack no lighter than 117, leaving her two pounds overweight on one of her mounts.

Nikki lived on raw vegetables, orange juice, and nonfat yogurt for the next few days, but on New Year's Eve, she went to dinner with a college friend and consumed way too much pizza and champagne. On New Year's Day, her pants popped. Her mount ducked out sharply leaving the gate in Saturday's seventh race, and all five snaps let loose. Pop, pop, pop, pop, pop. Nikki felt the wind rushing over her bare thighs and worried that she would get tangled up in her pants and fall off. She envisioned her picture in *The National Enquirer* and experienced a flood of panic.

The day was warm for January and Nikki wore nothing but bikini underwear, so she crouched lower to keep her nylon jockey pants from slipping down. After a half mile she began to tire. When the time came to flatten over her mount's withers and drive to the finish, she had been in that position since the start and her legs were burning with fatigue. With a half-furlong to go, no chance of finishing in the money, and no desire to flash the grandstand, Nikki raised in the irons and held up her pants.

Tanya Lindsey was furious. The agent cornered Nikki in the jockeys' parking lot after the last race.

"Do you have any idea how bad you looked?" she said, more of an accusation than a question.

Nikki kept walking toward her car. "My pants were coming off. I didn't want everyone in the grandstand to see my undies."

"Nobody cares about seeing you butt-assed naked if they've bet their money."

"Sure, you're sitting in the grandstand with your pants on. The horse was running nowhere." Keys in hand, Nikki longed to leap inside her old Nissan 300 SX and drive home, but Tanya had positioned herself in front of the driver's door.

"I'm a salesperson and you're my product. Why can't you be like other jocks?"

"I don't know."

"Why'd ya have to tell the trainer you got tired? You're supposed to say the bloody horse got tired."

"I did get tired," Nikki said.

"Trainers don't want to hear the truth."

"Some do."

Tanya scoffed. "Which reminds me, Winchester still hasn't forgiven me for your pushing him in that ditch."

Nikki looked up. "I *didn't* push him. And he must not be that mad. I see Warren's riding Sunrise Flame tomorrow."

"He'll win, too," Tanya said, then went into her fast-talking routine. "No offense, but the colt has a start under his belt and Warren fits a big lazy colt a little better than you. Besides, you're on one for Matt in the race. Captain Fuzzy have a shot?"

A smile formed in Nikki's mind. "He's a big lazy colt who's never started," she said.

Tanya yawned. "Don't forget, you have to tack twelve on Friday."

"Maybe on the moon."

"Tell the clerk of scales you're, you know...retaining water."

"I can only have my period so many times per month, Tanya."

"The clerk of scales is a pushover. Sweet talk him."

"I can't do one hundred-and-twelve unless I cut off an arm."

"Go on a frigging diet, *please.*"

Nikki promised to try. She went home and sprinted the three flights of stairs to the top floor of her apartment building and down again ten times, until she was gasping to catch her breath. Then she did fifty sit-ups, twenty-three push-ups, and wiped the dust from her ten-pound barbells but found that she was too tired to lift the weights once she had dug them out of her bedroom closet. She had almost talked herself into a change of jobs, when she envisioned her mother hearing the news. Something stronger than pride refused to let Nikki give Rachel Nottingham the satisfaction of thinking she'd given birth to a loser *and* a quitter.

But beyond that, Nikki failed to summon any newfound enthusiasm for working out. Instead, she ate an apple, a granola bar, and a glass of nonfat milk for dinner, then fell asleep while studying. Her winter quarter classes started Tuesday.

~

Steam rose in the cold air when she slid the saddle from King Donican's back after an easy mile gallop the following morning. Donnie was sweating heavily. Nikki hosed the sand from his legs and sponged them with warm water and disinfectant, then wrung out the sponge and wiped his head and body.

"Told you to give him a brisk gallop," Matt said. "Didn't you see me waving you on?"

She'd seen him all right. Hanging out of the backside trainers' stand, flailing his arms. "Donnie's sore."

Matt blanketed the gelding and put him on the hot walker. "He dead lame?"

"No, but his right ankle's been hot since his last race."

"Next you're going to tell me Winchester Cannon whacked his leg."

"He took off the bandage."

"Donnie got to playing and ripped it off himself."

"I saw Cannon running from the barn."

"You caught a glimpse of someone hightailing it out of my shed row and thought it was Cannon 'cause you spotted him puffing like a broken-winded horse."

"It was him."

"Gal, the man's a hundred pounds overweight and a chain smoker. He gets pooped just standing."

"Who else would sneak into Donnie's stall and check him out?" Nikki didn't wait for Matt to reply. "Last night, one of the other jocks told me Cannon talked Sunrise Flame's owner into claiming Donnie, saying he'd be worth twice as much without me riding him."

"Even if Cannon's foolhardy enough to claim a horse after seeing a mud poultice on its leg, he'd never claim one that's just turned eleven and has to win a race each year to stay eligible."

"Donnie won five last year. He may be old but he gets the job done." Nikki folded her arms and gazed at the rafters. Cobwebs hung everywhere, wispy strands encrusted with dust, the envy of any respectable haunted house.

"Donnie's sitting on a win. I'm not turning down a sure thousand bucks."

"But, Matt."

"I'm not laying-up an eleven-year old, for crissakes. He'll hold together for one more race."

"Let me buy him," she said.

"You know a jock can't own a racing horse."

"Twenty-five hundred plus the thousand he'd earn for winning."

"He's not for sale. Not with what you've been saving for school. Someday I'll give you the darned horse."

Nikki rolled her lips under, then out. "If Donnie feels the least sore, I'm easing him."

Matt slapped her on the back. "Fair enough, gal. Win or lose, it'll be Donnie's last race.

~

At five minutes past noon, Nikki dashed into the Jockeys' Room with a knapsack full of books slung over her shoulder.

"Summers, unless you call in late, jockeys are to report to the room before noon, not *after* noon," the clerk of scales said, every white hair in place beneath his short-brimmed, Dick Tracy hat.

Nikki glanced at the large electric clock on the wall, then checked the time on her wrist watch and saw that it was forty minutes slow. "Oops. I didn't have a quarter for a call?"

He pretended to frown. "Going to do fourteen today?"

"If I hold my breath. Maybe."

"No more excuses. You finally got your hot box."

Nikki waved a fist in the air and bounced in place, her sneakers squeaking on the linoleum. "The one I've been bugging management to buy for the past five years. Yes!"

She rushed inside the women's room and inspected the hot box. Bright yellow, the second-hand portable sauna was crammed into a corner by the couch, looking like a giant lemon with a hole at the top. Unfortunately, it smelled like moldy stinky socks and not a lemon. Nikki hoped her weight was okay.

She had just finished changing into her riding clothes to find out, when Rita walked in with her stomach bulging as though she was pregnant. Rita made straight for the toilet. Upon finding the stall had been locked from the inside, she muttered obscenities and pounded a fist on the door. Behind her, the couch was littered with soda pop cans, sandwich wrappers, an Oreos package, and a large potato chip bag, all empty. Rita turned to Nikki.

"Bitches locked me out of the can and I need to flip for the first."

"Well, least you won't have to pack any lead." Nikki's humor was wasted on Rita.

"Just crawl under and open it," she said.

There was about a foot of clearance between the bottom of the stall door and the threadbare carpet below, Nikki estimated. The filthy threadbare carpet.

"Open the fucking door," Rita repeated.

Nikki scrunched up her nose. "I'm not crawling under there."

Rita made a gagging noise. "I'll puke in Nelson's new boots."

"Okay, okay. Hold your horses," Nikki said, then climbed onto the sink countertop and over the partition and into the toilet stall, where she unfastened the latch and rushed to vacate the premises, colliding in the doorway with Kris Nelson and another jockey, Brenda Zimmerman. Before Nikki had a chance to explain, the sound of Rita barfing sent the three of them on their way in a hurry.

The main room was crowded. One tall rider was clad in only a towel, his body gleaming with sweat, skin as pale as something grown in a dark closet, skin stretched over bones, a walking skeleton. Nikki stepped in line for the scale. The device appeared big enough to weigh an elephant and accurate enough to weigh a flea. By the rules, a jockey was allowed to ride seven pounds heavy, providing the excess was reported to the clerk of scales an hour before the first race; however, trainers and owners didn't like their horses packing overweight jockeys. Every so often, one of the heavier jocks would jam a spit wad under the scale and everyone would weigh as much as a pound lighter until the wad was discovered. Once or twice, in an emergency, Nikki had resorted to the spit wad trick herself. No one ever suspected. But usually she just pleaded with the clerk of scales because at Westover Meadows, jockeys hardly ever received a hundred-dollar fine for not making their declared weight.

She was thinking that *that* was a good thing or she'd probably end up in debt, when Max, her valet, emerged from the men's room with an armload of saddles, pads, and girths.

"Woman," he said to her, "you got balls big as watermelons, pushing Cannon in that ditch."

"Pushed? I heard she decked him." Mel Hinshaw, at fifty-nine one of the senior riders at Westover Meadows, did a boxer's shuffle, fists jabbing the air. "It's the blond bomber. Put up your dukes, Slim."

"The gossip mill around this place must be fueled by nuclear bullshit," Nikki said, punching Hinshaw lightly on the shoulder as he danced past.

She hadn't eaten since dinner and her stomach felt the size of a dried apricot, so she slipped into the Jockeys' Room kitchen and emerged with a tuna fish sandwich. When her turn came to weigh for the second race, she picked up the sandwich along with her saddle and girth and stepped on the scale. The needle stopped a hair over 114 and a half. Since jockeys were allowed a half-pound leeway, she raced into the women's room and returned braless beneath her turtleneck. Now the needle jumped to 150 pounds. She turned and saw a grinning Joe Garcia, the leading rider at Westover Meadows, kneeling behind her with a towel wrapped around his waist and dripping wet from a shower.

"No food for you, sweetheart," he said, then removed his finger from the scale and the needle bounced down and stopped on exactly 114 and a half.

Nikki faked a swipe at Garcia's towel, purposely missing by a wide margin.

He leaped back, a hand flying to his waist. "Ah, ah, ah. No peeking."

"Yeah, I wouldn't want to strain my eyes."

His grin widened. "Thanks for breezing that horse for me the other day. I melt in the rain."

She smiled. "I didn't know lard melted in cold water."

"So where are we going on our date tonight, sweetheart?"

"Nowhere."

"Got yourself a college boy, I bet." He pinched her on the forearm.

She rolled her eyes. "You've fallen on your head once too often."

"You're breaking my heart, beautiful."

"You need glasses."

He blew her a kiss and disappeared inside the men's room.

Nikki felt herself blushing and rushed to put her tack in the number eight box on the far wall.

A valet poked her in the back from behind. "Hey, Dolly," he teased. "You weigh without your boobholder, you have to ride without it."

"I will when the guys who weigh without their shirts ride shirtless," she said, then folded her arms tightly to her chest and ducked inside the women's room before her face turned any redder.

Her mount in the second race, Captain Fuzzy, was listed at long odds. No one had ever been on his back but Nikki and — as per the Wilcox's instructions—she never let Fuzzy record any official morning workout times better than average. Only she and Matt and Susan knew the colt was capable of going faster. That was the beauty of predawn training at a racetrack too cheap to turn on the lights. Like all jockeys, Nikki was allowed to bet on her own mounts but figured she'd jinx the colt if she did. Matt, though, planned to bet a thousand to win on Fuzzy. Nikki stretched and put on her silks, then sat on the couch with her eyes closed, envisioning alternative strategies in case the race failed to go as planned. She tried to forget about the money until the buzzer summoned riders to the paddock.

Sunrise Flame led by five lengths at the head of the stretch, with Captain Fuzzy running sixth and stuck in traffic. At the eighth pole, Nikki aimed Fuzzy toward a crack of daylight between rumps, and the colt switched gears and shot through the hole. He won by a length, pulling away, while Sunrise Flame stopped badly and finished last. Nikki, who was not given to spontaneous emotional outbursts, whispered a yeehaw. She flashed Winchester Cannon a smile from the winner's circle.

~

Thursday dawned cold and clear, the sky a vivid shade of blue and completely cloudless. By nine-thirty, Nikki hopped off her last galloper. As she was removing the horse's bridle, the gelding flung its head and bopped her on the nose, a blow that hurt like hell but drew no blood. She hung up the tack and stood blinking hard and rubbing her nose for about a minute, then hurried off to take care of Donnie and Fuzzy, jogging along with her head tipped sideways and one eye closed, studying her profile. All bone and sharp angles, her nose looked as straight as ever. She'd always hoped to break it in the line of duty and have a plastic surgeon give her a new one, but she had smacked her nose solidly on numerous occasions with no such luck. She was cleaning dirt and boogers from King Donican's, when Tanya poked her head into the stall.

"I've been hunting for you for the past hour. Backside P.A. system's gone hoarse again."

"Very punny," Nikki said, twisting her head around. Donnie rubbed his soft muzzle against her cheek, his long face slightly dished in the manner of the breed's Arabian forebears, his warm breath grassy sweet. She scratched him behind an ear and ducked under his stall guard and into the shed row.

"Don't you love the smell of horses?"

Tanya gagged. "Stinks up clothing like cigarette smoke, only worse. Listen, Bill White's had a horse tacked for the past thirty minutes. Hustle over and see if you can catch it before the track closes."

Nikki made no move to go. "Bill White feeds moldy hay. His stalls are filthy. I'm not getting on a horse for the guy."

Her agent stuck fur-lined mittens on her hips. "I don't care if he feeds them Crackerjacks and beds them on nails. He wins races."

"Last year, I worked a two-year old for him. Remember?"

"Not exactly."

"Filly traveled like she was galloping over hot coals, and after dismounting, I noticed she was unshod. Mr. White spits out a mouthful of tobacco juice, then drawls, 'I don't put shoes on 'em 'til they shows me they can run.'"

"He said that?"

"Uh-huh."

"No wonder all his horses are sore."

"Yeah, that pretty much explains it."

In the back ground, Donnie began popping his lips while Fuzzy gurgled bubbles in his water bucket. Tanya glanced at the horses, then at her watch.

"Forget it. You won't make the track before it closes." She pulled up her fur-lined hood. "Who you want to ride in Thursday's second? Wilcox's mare, the one that spit the bit and puked last time, or Kenny Albright's two-to-one shot?"

"Wilcox's."

Tanya gave her the once-over, then took out a condition book and marked the appropriate race. "Captain Fuzzy ran big. Nice win."

They slapped palms.

"You've done a lot of work on Matt's colt, so I'm not taking my cut. It makes up for Sunrise Flame."

Nikki thanked her agent. "I heard Warren got canned. Wasn't his fault Sunrise Flame ran last."

"Easy come, easy go. Winchester Cannon couldn't train a bunny to eat carrots."

"He's a dandy, all right."

"That reminds me," Tanya said, frowning. "Winchester told me he has a surprise in store for you."

"A surprise?"

"Probably plans to toilet-paper your car or something. That man is just the world's worst sport."

~

King Donican was entered in the seventh race on Saturday. That same afternoon, Cindy Ansell, an apprentice, made her first trip to the winner's circle. Neither Kris, Rita, nor Nikki had ridden the fifth race, and they squeezed onto the couch in the women's room and watched the television, cheering Cindy on. Afterward, Nikki blocked Rita's plan to carry out the long-standing initiation rite among male jockeys, following their maiden win, to have a certain area of their anatomy painted with black boot polish.

"Forget it. We're not doing *that.* We'll throw buckets of cold water on her instead."

"Bastards painted me," Rita said. "That black shit itched and wouldn't come off for a week."

"Did you try bathing?" Kris asked.

"Be nice, you two," Nikki said, then the three of them, armed with cold water, joined Joe, Warren, Mel, and a half dozen other riders gathered outside the entrance to the Jockeys' Room to douse one very excited nineteen-year-old apprentice, who was smiling the type of smile that made face muscles ache.

When the women returned to the room, Rita was wetter than Cindy. Someone was a lousy aim with a bucket. Both were shivering, so Nikki knelt by the electric wall heater and fiddled with the manual control. A thump from her fist started it working. Kris informed everyone that the fastest way to get warm was to stand at the entrance to the men's room, which was heated to around eighty degrees. A side benefit of this, according to Kris, was that she had seen most of the guys naked and knew who was hung. For sharing that pertinent bit of information she received one Bronx cheer and two pillows to the head, plus they had to endure Rita reciting the names and bedroom prowess of the jockeys she'd laid. All seventeen.

~

Less than an hour later, King Donican kicked up his heels at the grandstand and burst into a springy trot beside his lead pony, the old gelding showing no signs of pain or soreness in his right foreleg. From Nikki's perspective, Donnie understood winning. Not the economics, not the glory, but the finish line, the plain and simple act of reaching the wire before his fellows, and not because he felt the slash of the whip or was duped by a mechanical rabbit. Nikki believed the competitive fervor of a Thoroughbred was passed from generation to generation with a vigor that had intensified through the centuries since the first English mares were mated with Arabian stallions. She believed some Thoroughbreds bore memories of their ancestors, victories from Newmarket to northern Africa, racing across the desert sands with their Bedouin masters, racing until they dropped if asked. She also believed other horses possessed no instinct or desire to win races whatsoever.

An assistant starter loaded King Donican, then left to steady a ranker entrant. Nikki cocked Donnie's head to the left and he stood quietly.

"One back," the gate crew shouted.

She straightened Donnie's head and felt his muscles gather and tighten. The back doors were slammed behind the last horse to load, the flag went up...then the five horse reared. Up and over he went, a thousand-plus pounds smashing against the tailgate, smashing Mel Hinshaw. The jockey hung upside down, pinned from the knees with his arms dangling limply and his fingertips brushing the ground. The gate crew was quick to free him. One man popped the tailgate and two others swept Mel to safety while his mount toppled out backward, struggled to his feet, and was caught. The remainder of the field was unloaded and returned to their pony riders. The horse that had flipped was scratched from the race and returned to the paddock. Jockeys dismounted, as required, given the prospect of a long delay.

Several riders and assistant starters wandered behind the gate and watched the ambulance attendants cut off Mel's boot and bloody sock. His foot was twisted grotesquely. He moaned and passed out. Most everyone turned away. Nobody needed reminding that the starting gate was solid steel, equally capable of crushing jockeys, the gate crew, or horses, a structure stronger than a jail cell in Nikki's opinion. And though collectively larger, each numbered stall was about the size of a phone booth, if there were phone booths for horses.

"Ruins the fun, doesn't it," Kris said to Nikki.

"Kind of," she said. "You nervous?"

"You?"

Nikki glanced around. "A little."

"Me, too. Any jock who says he's never scared is either crazy or lying."

"Or on drugs."

"That makes me feel better."

"Yeah, right."

They both smiled, if only barely.

Medics loaded Mel onto a stretcher and into an ambulance, and the vehicle drove away, minus flashing lights and siren. The jockeys remounted and the horses were reloaded. King Donican broke from the gate alertly and settled into the middle of the pack, his stride long and smooth and effortless. With a quarter mile to go, Nikki angled him to the outside and they charged for home. At the sixteenth pole, they drew even with the leader. Head and head, the two horses raced for home with Donnie thrusting his nose under the wire first, the winner by a whisker.

He slowed on his own after crossing the finish and pulled up lame before the turn.

Not severely, but he was favoring his right foreleg. Nikki stroked his neck, told him he'd gone out a champ, and let him take his time to walk back to the grandstand. A large group was huddled in the winner's circle with hands stuffed into the pockets of heavy winter coats and heads bowed like so many mourners at a funeral service. Susan Wilcox held Donnie while a valet removed the overgirth, then she led the gelding forward without a word of excited chatter, without saying anything at all.

"Now entering the winner's enclosure is King Donican and jockey Nikki Summers," the track announcer said. "King Donican races for Matt and Susan Wilcox, trained by Matt Wilcox. The running time was one minute twelve-and-two."

The cold weather kept all but a few fans confined to the grandstand. Sparse clapping. A gleeful cry. A handful of tickets waved in the air. After smiling for the photo, Nikki glanced around and noticed that no one else was smiling. She shot the Wilcoxes each a questioning glance. They looked away. She sprang from the saddle and Matt limply shook her hand and Susan hugged her with her free arm, then blinked back tears as a valet snapped a red claim tag to King Donican's bridle.

Nikki squeezed her hands into tight fists. She wanted to snatch the reins free and leap aboard Donnie bareback to gallop away from the dreary reality of Westover Meadows and the sport that seemed to care for money and only money, but she just stood with no emotion on her face, watching him go. Watching as one of Winchester Cannon's grooms led him from the paddock and across the infield. Watching until Donnie's black tail disappeared from sight.

Peninsula Park
January 1994

The last week of January, Rachel entered the main stable gate an hour earlier than usual and flashed the guard her license. A thin layer of frost covered the ground. The smell of cedar from wood-chip hot walker rings blended with the pungent odor of cooking oats. A rooster crowed. Another answered. She stuffed her hands into the pockets of a fleece-lined jacket and walked faster, her shadow growing and shrinking as she passed under a floodlight. She hung a left when the road branched. Two grooms were heading into the restroom across from the gap, two murky shapes moving through the shadows and into the bright glare at the entrance before disappearing inside. She passed the kitchen, which was still dark at four a.m., as were the adjoining laundry room, two tack shops, and the chaplain's office. Beyond the row of buildings, eucalyptus trees lined the backstretch fence like an eerie black forest. The entire stable area would awaken shortly.

Rachel slipped inside her barn without hitting the lights and rushed down the darkened shed row toward her office, frowning as she passed a vacant stall along the way. Reno McAllister had claimed the former occupant the previous afternoon. The gelding had been worth ten thousand, so she ran him for ten, won the race, but lost the horse. Stalls were like gold at Peninsula Park. She would have to claim a replacement or haul a horse in from the farm before the stall was assigned to someone else. After unlocking her office, Rachel took a small jar of black shoe polish from her desk and hurried to the other side of the barn.

A trainer seldom acquired two horses that looked exactly alike but she found herself with just that in a pair of dark brown three-year old colts, the two nearly identical but for a white star. Appearance was all they shared. One was well-bred and slow, while the other possessed the pedigree of a plow horse but could flat fly. Naturally, she owned the snail.

Rachel went inside the fast colt's stall, haltered him, and rubbed the shoe polish into the white hair on his forehead until the star vanished. She admired her handiwork in the dim light. The fast colt would pass for the slow one as long as no one checked his lip tattoo. Which usually only happened at the receiving barn and in the paddock before the horses were saddled for a race. She could tell the two apart because she knew them well, but the clockers or anyone else would be unlikely to notice, seeing as they had yet to notice for previous mandatory official workouts.

The slow colt, Northern Windsor, was entered in his first race on Thursday, a maiden $25,000 claiming contest, although he was a full-brother to a filly who had earned a half-million dollars. Such breeding merited maiden allowance company. A well-bred horse was too valuable to risk losing by way of a claim, if the horse could run at all. By dropping Northern Windsor into a claiming race, his initial start, Rachel hoped her peers might be duped into believing she was out to steal a win and halter him. She simply needed one more quick move from the colt to arouse interest. A quick move from a colt incapable of working faster than average.

When Sam arrived, Rachel told him to have the fast colt ready to work as soon as the track opened. She trusted her assistant trainer to dutifully do as instructed. He would ask no questions about the blackened star, understanding that this was one of her secret deals, understanding that the less he knew, the better. Sam definitely wasn't the sharpest implement on the backside, but she treasured his ability to keep his mouth shut.

After walking to the kitchen for coffee, Rachel returned at quarter to six with a seldom-used apprentice jockey. Her regular jockey, Jim Bruner, stood waiting in the shed row. He popped a bale of straw with his whip and spit out a mouthful of chew in the direction of the younger rider. When she informed Bruner that his services were not needed at the moment—unless he cared to muck stalls again—he spit in her direction, then strutted off. It came as no surprise to Rachel that the lesson she'd tried to teach him a few months back had failed to downsize his ego. How she wished horses would run of their own volition like greyhounds.

A vision of riderless racehorses lackadaisically chasing a mechanical carrot brought her back to reality, and she went after her pony while Sam brought out the fast colt to work and legged up the apprentice. She usually had the lighter of her two gallop boys, Clint—another faithful employee—work both dark-brown colts, reality being that a secret was not long a secret if too many people knew. Now she was counting on the apprentice to spread the word. Rachel told the kid to take a strong hold of the colt and breeze him an easy five-eighths, knowing he was iron-jawed and bullheaded, knowing the harder the kid pulled, the swifter his mount would go. The clockers caught the fast dark-brown colt—masquerading as his slower look-alike—in 59 2/5, the quickest five-eighths-of-a-mile of the morning, a bullet work, which would be indicated by a black dot next to his time in the *Daily Racing Form*. Afterward, as Rachel and her pony jogged past the trainer's stand with the colt, she spotted McAllister leaning against the rail, stopwatch in hand. It was all she could do to keep from smiling.

Back at her barn, the apprentice dismounted and removed the saddle and the bridle. A groom held up a bucket of lukewarm water for the blowing colt to drink, but the bridle had left sweat marks along his poll and behind his ears, giving him an itch worse than his thirst. Before the apprentice could slip out of reach, the fast dark-brown colt rubbed his head on the sleeve of the kid's red jacket, leaving behind a streak of black shoe polish.

~

By three-thirty the same afternoon, the guard on duty raised the electric barrier at the main stable gate and Rachel drove her silver Ferrari Testarossa into the Peninsula Park backside. The car was reputed to be capable of 180 mph, though the fastest she had dared was 145 on the Bayshore Freeway at three in the morning. Now Rachel parked by her barn and supervised the afternoon chores because her help worked harder when she was around to crack the whip. Horses were creatures of habit and if a meal was ten minutes late, they voiced their displeasure by nickering or kicking the walls or pawing. She was checking the progress of a finicky eater when she heard one of her least favorite clients, Seth Marten, shouting her name. She trained ten horses for Marten, but he went through trainers like Henry the Eighth had gone through wives.

Marten's voice grew louder.

Rachel ran a hand over the back of her neck and forced her facial muscles to form a pleasant expression, then ducked under the screen-gate and into the shed row. "Seth, what a nice surprise. Didn't expect to see you on a Monday afternoon."

"When's my big two-year old colt scheduled to work again?"

She made a show of frowning. "Do you remember that boy you insisted breeze him last Saturday, the one you slipped a fifty and told to see how fast the colt could run? He bucked the colt's shins," she said, pausing to allow her knowledge of his deception to sink in. "Young horses' bones strengthen in response to exercise. If asked to do too much too soon, the attachment of the periosteum to the cannon bone can be torn, resulting in micro-fractures as bone shears off. You're lucky the colt didn't blow a knee or ankle. He wasn't ready to go full tilt."

"Don't patronize me," Marten said. "I know what bucked shins are. So train him easier."

"Colt needs to be blistered and turned out." In her opinion, a liquid chemical burn was the quickest and surest treatment. Blistering produced inflammation, which supposedly promoted healing but more importantly, forced impatient owners to give their animals at least a few months' rest.

"My training bill's already exceeding the national debt. I

need to win races."

"About your training bill—"

Marten cut her off. "I want you to claim a horse from Reno McAllister on Thursday. Mare's name is Youwho Molly."

"Youwho Molly's sore and nutty," Rachel said. "Everybody knows that."

"Maybe it's escaped your notice, but McAllister has haltered three of my top claimers along with half your barn."

"I've noticed," she said.

"He's about to blow you away in the trainer standings."

"I'm still one win ahead, in case it's escaped *your* notice. Be a cold day in hell before McAllister can out train me."

"I'm beginning to think bullshitting's your primary talent."

She ground her teeth. "I'll claim Youwho Molly, Seth. Just don't forget who tried to talk you out of it."

"After the mare's won three in a row for me, don't *you* forget who picked her out." He glared at Rachel.

And she at him. "It's your money, speaking of which, I've been carrying your training bill for three months."

"I'll write you a check before I go." With his toupee noticeably askew, Marten walked off.

To the other side of the barn, Rachel assumed, but at the end of the shed row, he neglected to round the corner and instead headed away without paying her. She would've given a thousand bucks for a big gust of wind.

~

The following morning, after she finished her work at the barn, she drove back to her condominium in the hills above San Mateo for a shower and a change of clothes. Mondays and Tuesdays were dark days—no racing—at Peninsula Park, and she was meeting client Virginia Hammond for lunch at the Oakdale Country Club in Burlingame. The spacious dining room was an eyeful of contemporary opulence with massive wood beams, an oak tongue-and groove ceiling, a slate floor, a granite-topped bar and hearth, a grand piano, and walls adorned with large black and white photographs of the Golden Gate Bridge, Alcatraz Island, Fisherman's Wharf and other local landmarks. Among the many patrons were several of Peninsula Park's most distinguished Thoroughbred owners, most dressed for golf. Virginia was wearing tennis whites. Rachel, who never had time for golf or tennis and who deemed January too cold for such activities anyway, wore knee-high Cossack boots, black slacks, and a burgundy tunic. The maitre d' commented that she looked suitably prepared to conquer Siberia.

"What about this horse of yours who's favored to win on Thursday?" Virginia asked, when they were through eating. "Northern Windsor."

"Save your money," Rachel said, lowering her voice.

"So you don't like his chances," Virginia said, too loudly.

Rachel went to shushing. "No. Not particularly. First time starters are unpredictable."

"*The Daily Racing Form* has him picked as the heavy favorite. He does have some impressive workouts."

"Sometimes the clockers get horses mixed up," Rachel whispered.

Virginia's expression lit up like a Vegas casino. "Knowing the heavy favorite definitely won't win, we could make a killing at the windows."

Rachel cringed. "I didn't say *that.*"

"Then I should bet a little something on him?"

"No. Can we leave it?"

Virginia responded with a dainty grumble. "What's that rumor I heard about Reno sending you a present the other day?"

"He sent me a butterfly net."

"And whatever compelled him to do that?"

"Gray filly I bought from him, Lucifera, got loose and terrorized the barn area." Rachel reached for a sourdough roll and began tearing it into little hunks on her empty plate.

"At least she has a beautiful name. Race horse names are usually so incredibly inane. Did you really send him a toilet seat in retaliation?"

"You bet. He's so goddamn full of shit."

Virginia frowned. "You two go at it like the Hatfields and McCoys."

"He sicked Immigration on me."

"The biddies in the Turf Club mentioned something about that."

"What else did they have to say?"

"The usual tittle-tattle about how you're a jump ahead of other trainers in the hop department."

"The hottest dope won't turn a poorly trained horse into a winner. Quality feed, vitamins, and a conditioning program that fits each horse's personality are the keys," Rachel said, like a trainer lecturing at a public seminar. She judiciously neglected to mention hormones and steroids.

After listening patiently, Virginia cut to the juicy Turf Club gossip. "They also said Reno's assistant trainer caught you in a stall taking off a horse's bandages to inspect its legs."

Rachel slapped her thigh. "Why that lying s.o.b. That's it. I'm sending him an enema thingamajigger."

"Lovely," Virginia said. "I'm sure Reno will appreciate it."

"He'll probably think it's a turkey baster. Anyway it's nicer than the box of chocolate-dipped dog turds that Al Chadwick sent Vic Donner after he claimed Al's favorite horse. Vic's wife almost ate one. Now that's disgusting. To get even, Vic had her bake some laxative-filled brownies. Compared to those trainers, McAllister and I are practically best friends."

"Piffle. I expect he'll be sending you a bomb one of these days."

"Maybe when he finds out how I fff...foiled his plan to pick my brain," Rachel said, changing her original choice of verbs.

Across the table, Virginia's tapered eyebrows climbed her forehead.

Rachel exhaled out her nose. "Excuse me, but you're making me feel like a little kid."

"I am nearly old enough to be your mother."

"You're my client."

"Perhaps you should try acting like an adult."

"I do what I have to do to stay sane."

"I'd say all you horse trainers are a bit *insane*."

"I'm under a lot of pressure, Virginia."

"Ginny."

"Listen," Rachel said, running her tongue over her teeth. "I like you and I value your business and we can talk horses over lunch or at the track or wherever, but we're not friends."

"Of course not, dear."

"You're my client."

"I'm your client," Virginia said, with an agreeable lilt. "Does your mother know what a hard-boiled daughter she raised?"

Rachel stared at the ceiling long enough to count fourteen boards, then took a deep breath and let it out slowly. "No. She died when I was five."

"How?" Virginia asked, after a respectful pause.

"Hauling a load of horses. I was asleep on her lap, then everything went upside down."

"I'm sorry. What an awful thing for a child to go through."

Rachel's face went blank, a window with the blinds drawn. "It was a long time ago."

~

After the accident, the memory of her mother had lost its fine edges and became a blurred picture of dark blotches and warmth, splattered with pain, fading, until all of it was too confusing to consider. So Rachel made no attempt. Not then, not now. But she found that her childhood memories grew less hazy beyond the age of five. On the drive home from the country club, she recalled with mild amusement the time she went searching for bullfrogs by the creek that crossed her father's ranch and came across a nest of baby garter snakes.

She filled a tin box with a swarming mound and gave the box and a crayon-colored card to her new nanny. The lady smiled politely, accepting the present, then lifted the lid and threw the box to the ceiling. Snakes went flying in umpteen directions. She shot out the front door ten minutes later, still screaming hysterically, a hastily packed suitcase in each hand. After she drove off, Rachel crawled out from beneath the kitchen table and gathered up her little friends, a task that took more than an hour, and even then one remained at large. She wondered if the lady would have liked frogs better, although none of the three previous nannies had. They'd claimed Rachel was a difficult child and had sought employment elsewhere, which was fine by Rachel because she hated being bossed around by women trying to act like her mother.

Rachel didn't remember much about the accident except that it had taken her mother's life. And her brother's too. Sometimes in the middle of the night, she had woken crying from a bad dream and heard the padding of her father's slippers on the hardwood floor outside her bedroom and saw a crack of light beneath the door. He never came in and offered words of comfort or a hug, but knowing he was out there made her feel better. And time passed, until not having a mother didn't matter anymore. Photographs revealed her mother had been pretty, but pictures were only paper and held none of her essence. Then more time passed and the nightmares stopped. Rachel had dreamed so many bad dreams that the past became a dream and soon, she didn't know what was real and what wasn't, or whether she'd ever had a mother or not. She welcomed the chores her father gave her, before and after school and on weekends. Horses had given her something to do besides mourn or feel sorry for herself. Something to focus on.

One night, she'd listened from her bedroom as a ranch hand knocked on the door and informed her father that a mare was about to foal. Rachel snuck out to the barn to watch. Her father and the hired man stooped under a lantern hung in the doorway, washing their hands in a bucket of warm soapy water. The mare lay on her side, grunting and groaning. From her perch in the loft, Rachel watched her father drop to his stomach and gently work a hand into the mare's vulva and attempt to extract the baby. For more than an hour, he struggled to help her give birth to an abnormally large foal, before he declared the baby dead and went about the grisly task of trying to save the mother. The foal ended up in pieces, strewn in a bloody pile on the fresh straw. The mare had lived. After sending the hired man back to bed, her father daubed at his eyes with a rag. Rachel figured he'd gotten dirt in them, because her father never cried.

He sometimes made her cry, though. Hidden in her bedroom closet with a pillow crammed over her head, crying alone. She had tried hard not to goof up, but her father was strict. Mostly he yelled but occasionally she suffered a few swats from his leather belt. If she ever actually pleased him she was never certain. Once he had patted her on the head after she caught a high-strung yearling that jumped a fence, then she'd gone and ruined the moment by bragging that she could talk to horses, which earned her a stern lecture on the evils of lying.

Unbeknownst to her father, she actually *had* spent a lot of time talking to horses. They'd lived on two hundred acres southeast of Stockton, California, about ten miles from the nearest town with a grocery store and gas station on a grassy plain cut by a shallow creek, mountains to the east, hills to the west, and few neighbors let alone ones having children her age. Mostly she had played with her palomino Quarter Horse, Pete. He'd patiently abided peacock feathers tied to his forelock and tail when she pretended to be Geronimo, and the aluminum foil armor that she strapped on him during her Joan of Arc phase, but she had to bribe him with carrots for her Annie Oakley routine. Even then, he'd fidgeted unhappily as she sat on his back and fired a .22 rifle at tin cans. The day she appeared with a plastic sword, a la Alexander the Great, Pete had rubbed his head against her face, his way of saying that he was happy to masquerade as Bucephalus or any other historical horse that had lived before the onset of firearms.

Besides Pete, Rachel held daily conversations with many of

her father's mares and colts and fillies, though no words were exchanged. She was also good friends with the ranch's stallion, whom the help feared for his vicious outbursts. Rachel would spend hours in the stud's stall, scratching his mane at the roots where his skin was dry and itchy, while he wiggled his nose and made happy little grunt noises. On days that he ignored her arrival, she let him be. He was one horse she'd never argued with.

If her father still doubted that she could talk to horses, he kept the thought to himself after hearing what happened one Saturday night when he was away racing. He had left Rachel under the supervision of the latest nanny, Mary, who proceeded to throw a kegger party. Rachel spent the evening holed up in her room until the gathering moved outside. She trailed everybody to the corral next to the barn and watched from the shadows as Mary led Pete from his stall and swung aboard minus a saddle and bridle, hollering a slurred "giddyup" each time she raised her legs to thump him in the ribs. Pete didn't budge. With a look of big-eyed confusion, he gazed over his shoulder at the young woman on his back, as if seeing a problem bigger than he could solve, until a sharp whistle from Rachel sent him bursting ahead. Mary shot in the opposite direction just as fast. She landed hard but was drunkenly limber and did not get hurt. After sobering up some, she chased Rachel down and was in the process of yanking her hair out by handfuls when her father came home and sent nanny number sixteen packing.

Not long after that, Rachel rode Pete out to check a section of fence in the remotest part of the ranch. She started back at a lope, then flattened her body against Pete's mane and sent him into a gallop so brisk that the rush of the wind made her eyes water.

She never learned why he fell.

Whether he stepped in a hole or just took a bad step, without warning, Rachel barreled head first into the ground, then everything went black. When she came to, Pete was standing overhead, nudging her, his velvety nose bloodied and dirty. She stroked his face, slowly sat up, and noticed that his left front fetlock was twisted in an odd direction, like a leg belonging to Gumby's horse. Her father, who must have seen her fall, appeared shortly. As he carried her toward the house, one of the hired men dashed past them with a rifle in hand. She saw him stop beside Pete before a crack like thunder cast her into darkness again.

Rachel realized that she hadn't thought about Pete in years. A few months shy of her thirteenth birthday, she had started exercising her father's racing stock and lost all desire to get another saddle horse of her own. She'd been too busy to play anymore.

~

When Rachel's last horse returned from the track on Wednesday morning, she sent her assistant to saddle Lucifera, whose abscessed feet had fully healed. Ten minutes later, Sam came running.

"The gray filly...I think you better come see." Sam stared at his sneakers. "We can't get her up."

Rachel hurried to Lucifera's stall and found the filly lying motionless in the straw. "I know she ate up last night. She's not rolling or sweating, so we can rule out colic. Come on, gentlemen, no excuses."

Sam and a groom traded futile glances.

"Oh, hell, I'll do it myself." Rachel unsnapped the full screen gate and went inside. "Up, pretty babe, get up," she said, in a gentle, high-pitched voice.

Lucifera pinned back her ears.

Rachel clucked softly, then tapped Lucifera's rump with a boot toe.

The filly yawned. A lazy yawn that seemed to take a great deal of effort as she squeezed her eyes shut and opened her mouth wide, then wider, exposing all her yellowish-white teeth.

Rachel waved her arms and whooped and hollered, "Yah,

yah, up sow, up!"

Lucifera opened her eyes with a sigh.

Rachel swung the chain end of a lead shank at hip level in a slow circle. "Last chance, filly."

Lucifera pinned her ears and snapped her teeth but still made no effort to rise.

"Fine. We'll do it the hard way," Rachel said, then whipped Lucifera across the flank, a single whack that launched the filly to her feet, teeth bared and charging. Rachel ducked out of the stall in a hurry. From the safety of the shed row she pressed her face to the screen, stepping back as Lucifera's teeth raked the metal.

"Retake her temperature," Rachel told Sam, and went after a cotton lead rope.

The entire barn had registered normal readings five hours earlier, but she would feel foolish if the filly came up sick after training. Sam was lifting the gray's tail to insert the thermometer, when Rachel returned. Lucifera pinned her ears flat. Rachel shouted at Sam, but too late. The filly cow-kicked him in the crotch and he doubled over, groaning in pain. Rachel helped him from the stall, then threaded a lead shank through the side rings of Lucifera's halter and in one quick motion slipped the chain under the filly's upper lip and snug to her gums—the lip chain a method of humane restraint.

"Maybe she's got ear mites," Sam said, from where he stood hunched, pale and shaken, in the doorway.

Rachel probed inside one of Lucifera's ears. "There's nothing in her ears. Nothing in her head, for that matter."

With several swift jerks on the shank, she guided the gray's rump into the corner. While she held the lip chain snug in one hand, she inserted the battery-operated thermometer before the filly knew what had happened. When the thermometer beeped, Rachel grabbed a handful of gray tail and pulled, throwing Lucifera's weight onto her near hind leg to prevent her from cow kicking. Rachel snatched the thermometer and slipped clear. The filly slashed out with a hoof but caught only air.

Several of Rachel's grooms had stopped working and

gathered outside the stall to watch. Intent on giving them a get-the-hell-busy look, she released the lip chain and turned her back on Lucifera. Just that quick the filly nipped her on the butt. Rachel spun with a yelp and raised a hand to deliver a solid smack to the gray's head, but the giggling from the shed row changed her mind. Shouting orders, she slipped from the stall and shooed her help back to work.

Lucifera's temperature was a normal 100 degrees. Rachel saddled the filly herself and mounted her pony. Clint, her best gallop boy, led Lucifera onto the road beside her barn and passed the cotton lead rope to Rachel, stepping clear as she snubbed it to the saddle horn. She managed only one wrap before Lucifera reared. Rachel reacted instantly to urge her mount into the filly — knocking her off balance — then she threw a very short dally that left the gray's chin anchored against the horn.

And so Lucifera dumped no riders that morning, though Rachel never turned loose of the dally. Instead, she dragged the filly three laps of the training track with Lucifera bucking, grunting, propping, squealing, sucking back, rearing, fighting every foot of the way, but at least the gallop boy had stayed on. Rachel swore to tow the filly a thousand laps, if that's what it took.

She stopped outside Lucifera's stall before leaving that morning. After glancing up and down the shed row to see that nobody was listening, she called the filly in a soft voice. And Lucifera answered, the clack, clack of her teeth snapping the air. Rachel tried again, then gave up and headed to the parking lot. The filly was having none of her kindness. Horses didn't like Rachel much. They used to, and she them, but no more. About the third or fourth time she watched a horse break off a leg, something inside her had gone dead. Now she looked at horses and saw only running machines — conformation, disposition, breeding, soundness, class, heart — the parts that equaled the whole that raced into the winner's circle, though she never forgot they were individuals who talked through their actions.

as to

Horses yawned, they stretched, they coughed and grunted. Their stomachs growled, their tempers flared, they became arthritic, they died of cancer and heart attacks. Some were sweet and naive, others mean and despicable. Lucifera seemed to despise Rachel. One lash with a chain shank and she had made an instant and probable lifetime enemy, for horses never forget. Later, in her office, Rachel thought about training and how she knew every trick in the book and some that weren't in any book. Whether or not Lucifera liked her was irrelevant.

~

On the walk to the parking lot, Rachel made an impulsive decision to take a longer route and cut past McAllister's barn. Dr. Cortez's red, extended-cab Chevy pickup truck was parked in the road out front. As luck would have it, the two men emerged from the shed row and went to the pickup, although she reserved judgment whether it was good luck or bad. While they talked, Cortez filled a syringe with a milky white substance that she recognized as an antibiotic. They both looked surprised when Rachel walked up from behind.

"Gentlemen," she said, sarcastically.

McAllister glanced over his shoulder as though to make certain that none of his horses was in sight. Cortez eyed her uneasily. She folded her arms, watching with an amused smile as he overfilled the syringe, the plunger popped out, and the contents dribbled onto his shoe.

Their date had been a glorious disaster. Things had started out promising enough. She'd anticipated having to endure a boring conversation about snowboarding or rap music while they got suitably inebriated, but Cortez had talked about his fishing trips in British Columbia to places such as Rivers Inlet, Tsuniah Lake, Hakai, and Nootka Island, remote green country, far different from her black-and-white contentious world. When they'd finally dispensed with the pre-sex chatter and began kissing on the couch, he was wild, almost frantic in his rush to satisfy himself. She categorized him as a certain type—

young, confident, successful, well-endowed—who believed he need only show up. Sex was one department in which she regarded men to be basically untrainable, her best efforts wasted, as they were quick to revert to what felt best.

After approximately one minute, she had grown annoyed and shoved him off the couch. He'd climbed to his feet, zipped his pants, and apologized. On the way to the door, he started talking about the track, asking questions, pumping her about her barn—as if he'd suddenly recalled his primary agenda.

Rachel got angry all over again just thinking about it. Presently, she was deriving a small measure of revenge watching Cortez use a tissue to smear the antibiotic on his tan leather desert boot into a messy dark stain speckled with white flecks. Her head shot up at the sound of a guttural growl, and she glanced around, thinking someone had snuck in a dog, until McAllister cleared his throat again.

She gave a little laugh. "Thought I heard a big dog, but it's just you."

"I thought the same thing when you walked up," McAllister said, not laughing.

She acknowledged he'd one-upped her with a tight-lipped smile, then lit into him. "Did you really suppose I'd be so enraptured by your vet that I'd tell him about my horses?"

His face registered a blank. "Lady, I don't have the slightest idea what you're talking about."

"Don't bullshit me. I know damn well you two are in cahoots."

Now McAllister got it. He turned to Cortez and started to grin. "You went out with *her*?"

The vet—who had been rapidly shaking his head at Rachel in an apparent plea for her silence—rose from wiping his shoe. "*She* asked *me* out."

"He asked me out first," Rachel said.

"So you went on a date with her?" McAllister repeated with a bigger grin.

Cortez retrieved a fresh syringe from the back of his truck and shoved the needle through the rubber stopper of the antibiotic bottle. "She is kinda hot."

"For a woman her age," McAllister said.

Rachel exhaled hard out her nose and considered her rival's face, his apparent amusement in particular. Her pride began to smolder, then burn out of control. She smirked at Cortez. "For a big horse, you were one helluva a quick ride, Billy."

McAllister stopped grinning. He looked at Rachel, then at Cortez. "What's she talking about?"

The vet held up his hands, syringe and all. "I don't know."

"You slept with her?"

"No."

"On the first date, for crapsakes?"

"No."

"And she'd lie about *that?*"

"Apparently," Cortez said, and hastily began filling the syringe.

"*No,*" Rachel said.

McAllister made a face like he'd bitten into something rotten. "Apparently?"

"No, I would not lie about that." Rachel again.

McAllister gave a huff. "Someone's sure lying."

"Like it's any of your business, mister."

"If you've sunk your claws into my vet, I want to know so I can hire a new one."

Rachel eyed McAllister, imagining where she'd like to hit him. Before she could think up an obnoxious reply, anxiety or opportunity or both seemingly elbowed Cortez in the ribs.

"Okay, I told a white lie," he announced, with the minimal facial motion of an assertively frank man.

McAllister and Rachel turned to stare at him.

"Hey, gentlemen don't kiss and tell," the vet said next.

Now Rachel wanted to hit Cortez.

"You better start telling," McAllister said to his vet, "if you'd like to keep your job."

Cortez hesitated for about a millisecond, then bent closer and spoke out the corner of his mouth, like someone sharing a regrettable secret. "I admit, we had sex, but we never discussed your horses."

Rachel digested his response with a scowl and was about to tell Cortez that she didn't need any help lying, when McAllister cast her a final look of disgust and headed into his barn. The inferno inside her died and went cold. If she'd had a rational objective for dating Cortez, she couldn't say what, although she felt reasonably certain that coming across as a slut hadn't figured into her plan. The vet was rummaging through drawers in the back of his truck. She went over to him.

"You went out with me just for the sex?"

"Hey, I'm a guy." His toothpaste commercial smile, brash, smug, but more innocent than guilty.

She regarded his expression a moment, then sighed. "Why'd you have to go asking about my horses?"

"I was trying to save face after you stomped my ego."

"Getting turned down by a woman my age must have been excruciating."

"Yeah, so thanks for the bragging rights." He patted his rock-hard, six-pack of a stomach.

"Only reason I went out with you, numbnuts, was to irritate Reno."

"Like he cares who you screw?"

"Shut up," she told him. "Just shut the hell up."

~

The following morning, Rachel's stable veterinarian, Conrad Steele, stopped by the barn with the results of Lucifera's X-rays and blood samples, which had uncovered no physical problem to explain her obnoxious behavior. After he left, Rachel walked over to Virginia, who had been waiting in the background, talking to a fat two-year old nicknamed Hoover for her proficiency at sucking straw through a muzzle worn to prevent her from eating her bedding. Needless to say, the muzzle had not been a success.

"I'm always amazed at how many horses are named

Sonafabitch," Virginia said.

"You've been spending too much time at the gap."

"I like being where the excitement is."

"Your timing's impeccable."

Rachel swung aboard her ponyhorse and Sam led out Lucifera. This time Rachel dallied the rope around the saddle horn *before* snapping onto the filly's halter, then the gallop boy was legged-up and they started toward the training track with Virginia and Sam trailing on foot.

Halfway there, Lucifera exploded.

The filly leaped backwards, threw her weight against the rope, and fought like a rabid animal. She grunted with rage. She whipped her head wildly and pawed the air with her front hooves, sharp jabs that struck nothing. Rachel gripped the dallied rope tightly—held it above the saddle horn so as not to lose any fingers or a thumb—and shouted at her help to get after the filly before the rope's snap broke. Sam waved his arms and hollered while Clint whipped her across the flank, which only maddened her further. Rachel shouted for them to stop. At once, Lucifera quit struggling. Without delay, Rachel urged her pony forward and dragged the filly to the track, her aluminum shoes screeching against the pavement and sparks flying. They had not gone far when she sat on her haunches and keeled over. Clint leaped clear. For several seconds, Lucifera hung suspended from the saddle horn by the dally, then Rachel released the rope and eased her to the pavement where she lay in a heap, eyelids closed and not moving.

"Get her up," Rachel told her help.

Sam and Clint were already huddled over Lucifera's inert form.

"She's dead," Virginia nearly screamed.

"I think Mrs. Hammond's right," Sam said.

Rachel tugged her hat down in front. Cussing in a loud whisper, she swung off her pony and took a closer look at Lucifera's head. An eyelid fluttered, then opened, and the filly peeked around before shutting the eye. Rachel lifted a foot to give the gray a swift kick in the chest but caught a glimpse of

Virginia in the background, her mouth wide open in a silent shriek. Rachel stomped the ground instead. And told Sam and Clint to coax the filly to her feet, then remounted her pony and observed their progress, which was nil. They sweet talked, pushed, pulled, clucked, and even begged, but Lucifera played dead with stubborn resolve. As a last resort, Rachel had them remove the tack. Freed of saddle and bridle, Lucifera jumped to her feet with a squeal and a kick. Rachel directed Sam to lead the filly onto the training track and pass her off on the run. He nodded and started ahead.

A crowd of curious onlookers trailed them. Lucifera plodded onto the five-eighths training oval like someone's old milk cow with Sam leading her clockwise along the outside fence, all the while looking over his shoulder to gauge Rachel's approach. When she touched heels to her pony and closed in from behind, Sam started to run, while at his side, the filly broke into a trot to keep pace. He passed Rachel the shank as she drew even and ducked out of the way, ever wary of Lucifera's heels.

But Lucifera was too busy pinning her ears and ringing her tail at Rachel to fire a kick Sam's way. Up and down the filly's tail snapped. Rachel whipped the rope twice round the saddle horn and gunned her pony, who shot ahead. With no chance to balk, Lucifera was forced to gallop alongside, her stride stiff and crow-hoppy, a reluctant dog on a leash, until quick as a rattlesnake, she hammered her teeth against Rachel's right hand. Rachel doubled over in pain. Seeing she was momentarily vulnerable, the filly flipped her head and smacked Rachel on the nose. She swayed in the saddle and started to black out. Blood ran off her chin and into her lap, but somehow she managed to fight her dizziness and keep both her mount and the filly under control for three laps with Lucifera straining against the rope every stride.

Afterward, Virginia swore Rachel's nose was broken. Upon accompanying her to the women's bathroom, Virginia insisted on daubing up the blood with a wet paper towel. Rachel, who couldn't remember the last time anyone had shown her such kindness, explained that she had broken her almost-straight nose once before and knew it was not presently broken.

"Thanks, *Ginny,*" she said, as they walked back to the barn. The older woman just smiled.

Westover Meadows
February 1994

Nikki parked her car in the unlit field on the north side of the racetrack and crept among rusty, beat-up horse trailers to the chain link fence enclosing the barn area. Clouds blotted out the stars and a sliver of moon. After glancing around, she scaled the fence, careful to ease over the three strands of barbed wire on top without snagging her jeans, then dropped to the ground on the other side and dashed among the shadows. It was after eleven. All lights were off in Winchester Cannon's shed row, but one horse sensed her arrival and nickered, a deep, rumbling sound. Nikki unlatched his door and slipped under the stall chains and went inside. King Donican gently butted her face.

In the month since Cannon claimed Donnie, Nikki had snuck in to visit the gelding eight times, climbing the fence after ten o'clock since the main stable gate was locked to vehicles at ten and Winchester Cannon always drove inside to check his horses.

"Shhhhh, buddy. Don't wake up the other prisoners," she whispered, then opened a bag of carrots.

Nikki was trying to pry Donnie's nose out of the carrot bag, when she heard a rattling noise and froze. Down the line, a horse banged a feed tub. A second paced about, rustling straw. Another exhaled with a rippling sigh. She crept to the door and scanned the darkness, while behind her Donnie chomped the last of the carrots with a steady munching that sounded much louder than she ever remembered possible.

"Shhhhh, buddy. Can't you chew any quieter?"

He couldn't. Nikki put an arm over his neck and waited until he swallowed the last mouthful, then listened a few minutes longer but heard only horse sounds and the ebbing thump of her own heartbeat. Convinced she had imagined the noise, she stuffed the paper carrot sack into her jacket and went about scratching Donnie's itchy spots using a mane comb. She was happy to admit he seemed well cared for. His hay bag held fresh timothy, his stall was deep with clean yellow straw, his water bucket full, his forelegs wrapped neatly in bandages—two of the same color, no less.

Nikki gave Donnie a hug good-bye, latched the stall door, and snuck across the hot walker ring and over the fence like a cat burglar. She had been watching for Donnie on the track each morning but saw him only once, being ponied without a rider. He hadn't recorded an official workout nor started a race in the month since being claimed. A few weeks ago, she had called Donnie's new owner about buying him, but he'd told her to talk to Winchester Cannon. Twice, she had offered Cannon twenty-five hundred for Donnie. The first time, the trainer licked his chapped lips and appeared to consider her offer before he said, "I aim to win a race with the horse, Summers. Take a hike up Mt. Hood."

The second time, he'd simply walked away without answering.

~

Cold spells usually meant fewer horses to exercise at Westover Meadows. Lots of standing around time, lots of teeth-chattering time for jockeys and exercise riders. Three days earlier, the wet sand track had frozen to the consistency of Interstate 5. Most horsemen on the backside kept their stock in the barn rather than chance injury on the hard surface, but trainers soon grew restless with no break of the Arctic front in sight. Their horses had become four-legged kegs of dynamite that twitched and trembled in anticipation of the slightest excuse to explode, bucking and bolting around hot walkers, scattering icy chunks of wood chips and dirt in all directions. By day four of the cold spell, trainers who had been hesitant to send horses out to exercise started doing so.

Nikki galloped her first horse before daylight. She jogged the colt out the six-furlong chute, rising up and down in the saddle to post in rhythm with his trot, then standing in the irons when he broke into a gallop. She crossed the reins and held them firmly at the base of the animal's neck, and he bowed his head, galloped into the bit, and pulled against himself. Her fingers and toes ached from the cold, despite her thin gloves and thick socks.

In the inky darkness, neither horse nor rider saw the frozen ridge left by the tractors where the chute ended and the racetrack began. The colt stumbled and fell to his knees. Nikki managed to latch onto his neck as she was catapulted from the saddle. Facing backwards with her left foot still in the stirrup iron, she clung to the colt's side while he took off like his tail was on fire, hooves rattling over the hard surface. Too busy to be afraid, in one swift motion, she kicked up and over and swung back onto the saddle, then raised her leg to retrieve the right iron. Without warning or cause the colt propped, slamming on the brakes faster than a bad driver. Nikki sailed over his head for good this time.

"Thank God the horse didn't get hurt. You okay?" Tanya asked her, two hours later.

"Yeah. I rolled." Actually, Nikki had bounced in a forwardly manner.

"Don't get on anything else this morning," her agent said. "Go home and rest. You're riding six tonight."

"I'm fine, Tanya, honest. I still have a bunch to gallop."

Snow was falling. A thin veil of delicate flakes floated downward and clung to the bare, dry pavement. Nikki and her agent walked down the road between barns, Tanya flashing a smile to every trainer and owner they passed along the way.

"Management's cutting purses," she said.

"Guess they had no choice," Nikki said. "Handle and attendance are way down."

"Horses at the bottom will be running for fifteen hundred now."

"I heard. The winner'll barely make enough to pay a month's keep."

With a mirror deftly extracted from a purse the size of a grocery bag, Tanya checked her lipstick. "Twenty percent of a winning jock mount will almost feed me for two days if I skip lunch. They're cutting races, too."

"Races?"

"Three from each card to be replaced by simulcasts."

"Three every card?"

"Every mutherfucking one."

Nikki slapped a hand against her hip. "I know a percentage of any simulcast handle goes into purses for live races, but fewer races means less money for the horsemen. That just sucks."

"Management doesn't give a shit," Tanya said. "They make the same and don't have to bother with the horses."

"Where are the simulcasts coming from?" Nikki asked.

The cold air had turned Tanya's cheeks hot pink and she dusted them with a beige rouge as they walked. "California."

Nikki slowed. "Hollywood Park?"

Tanya shook her head. "Peninsula Park."

At the mention of her mother's domain, Nikki stopped in her tracks and regarded the bleak barn area that appeared no less bleaker under a scant layer of fresh snow.

Tanya tapped her on the arm. "You don't look so hot, kid. Go home."

Nikki kept staring at the snow. "I intend to. After this meet's over."

Tanya leaned closer, lowering her voice. "Were you wearing your helmet when you fell off?"

~

"Sure you're okay, gal?"

"Positive."

Matt paused from saddling a horse to study Nikki's face. She had left Tanya and walked directly to the Wilcox's barn.

135

"Look awfully pale to me," Susan said. "One of these times you're going to fall on your head and forget everything you've learned in college."

Matt sucked in a long breath and forced it out with a rush. "She says she's fine, Suzy. We got to get these horses tracked." He stomped down the shed row after his pony.

"Sorry," Susan said. "Matt's under a ton of pressure, what with slow-paying clients and bills stacking up."

"He shouldn't have blown the twenty-five hundred he got for Donnie claiming that sore mare of Cannon's," Nikki said, and fastened her helmet.

"Money doesn't just burn a hole in Matt's pocket, it incinerates his whole damn leg," Susan said. "Especially when it comes to getting even."

"Too bad you had to turn her out. No tires or brakes for your truck?"

"No new furnace, either. Just another four-legged mouth to feed." Susan led the next horse to gallop from the barn and gave Nikki a leg up.

She exercised horses until the track closed, then groomed Captain Fuzzy and stepped inside the tack room. She sat down on an empty ten-gallon plastic bucket and tipped her head from side to side but failed to alleviate the kink in her neck. The space heater had broken earlier and the tack room felt colder than a frozen food locker. A draft seeped in through a crack along the doorjamb. The east wind, which blew down the Columbia River and off the mountains and right through Westover Meadows, could find its way into anything—down jackets, long underwear, barns, the cafeteria, just anything. Susan, with her stout frame buried under several layers of clothing, stood eating a chocolate-glazed donut. Matt, in a scruffy blue parka zipped to his chin, sat at his desk doing paperwork. A powdered-sugar mustache dusted his thin upper lip.

"Want one?" he asked Nikki, pointing to a box of donuts.

"No thanks," she said. "Donuts give me heartburn."

"Don't be feeding any of these to that darned colt. With my

luck, he'll get colicky and croak."

Captain Fuzzy had won his second race two weeks ago, and Matt was treating him like the next Secretariat. Nikki refrained from mentioning that she'd already given Fuzzy two maple bars. She picked at her short nails cut to the quick, leaving nowhere for dirt to hide.

"Thirty days are up and Donnie's out of jail, so Cannon's free to run him for twenty-five hundred again."

Susan stopped chewing. Matt kept scribbling in his notebook.

Nikki stood. "You're planning to claim him back, right?"

Matt put down his pen and looked up. "Can't do it. Sorry, gal."

"Then I'll claim him myself."

"We've hacked this trail before. Not with money you need for college."

"I've already paid winter quarter's tuition and March's rent, plus I've taken an extra job, assisting one of the vets on his farm rounds. I won't have to move into a tent under the freeway anytime soon."

Matt rubbed his chin. "Meet's over in two-and-a-half months. Winchester'll be giving the old bugger away come April."

Nikki glanced from Matt to Susan. "Donnie's my friend. Maybe I can't save every doomed horse at the track, but I can save one."

"We could see to his keep," Susan said, massaging Matt's neck. "Donnie *was* our meal ticket during some lean years, honey."

He chuckled and shook his head. "Okay, you two win."

Nikki couldn't stop smiling and didn't try. In minutes, the honking of a horn sent her dashing out the door and onto the passenger seat of a Dodge truck belonging to the veterinarian who had offered her a part-time job. Dr. Montana talked about navicular disease, laminitis, and sail boarding on the Columbia during the drive to Bluemeadow Training Center. Nikki rested her head against the window and listened. For two hours she hurried from barn to barn consulting trainers, holding horses, scrubbing joints to be cortisoned, and doing whatever else was needed, then they drove back to Westover Meadows and she dashed off to school for her three o'clock class. Whenever Nikki felt too tired to go on, she closed her eyes and saw King Donican in Winchester Cannon's barn.

~

Toward the end of February, Nikki, Kris, Brenda, and Rita squeezed onto the couch in the women's room to watch the tenth race rerun from the previous day. At the eighth pole, Rita's mount suddenly veered in and bounced off the inside rail. Launched airborne, she straddled the hollow steel pipe and rode it for about twenty yards before tumbling onto the infield. Except for what the medics discreetly described as a rug burn in the vicinity of her crotch, she had survived unhurt. Nikki and Kris struggled to keep from laughing.

"You want my opinion, if you don't have an I.Q. of at least fifty, they ought to confiscate your jock's license," Kris said.

"Nobody asked you, cunt face," Rita said. "Shit happens."

Kris burst into laughter. "Yeah, but why does it always happen to you?"

Rita took out a pack of cigarettes and everyone groaned in unison. She lit up and exhaled in Kris's face, which started Brenda coughing.

Nikki waved a hand through the smoke. "You're the only one of us who smokes, Rita, so do you think you could please do it outside from now on?"

"I'll use the can," she said with a smirk, and promptly did.

Smoke drifted over the stall door and throughout the room. Kris twisted her fists together as if breaking a neck. Brenda put an imaginary gun to her head, pulled the trigger, and toppled over sideways. Cigarette smoke nauseated Nikki, so she went out to check her weight, getting in line behind jockey Willie Redfield. When his turn came, he stepped onto the scale and dropped his towel.

"There's a soldier in the grass, with a bullet up his ass, take it out take it out, like a good girl scout," he sang, showing her a profile view of an arrogant smile, among other things.

Nikki covered her eyes.

Her valet, Max, who made Willie Redfield look like an elf, grabbed the towel from the floor and popped the jockey's naked butt. "Cover up, you pimple-assed pipsqueak."

At the sound of a snap and a yelp, Nikki giggled.

"Fuck you, Max." The naked jockey snatched back the towel and wrapped it around his waist.

"Watch your mouth, Redfield," the clerk of scales said.

Nikki uncovered her eyes. "Yeah, Willie, I'm embarrassed."

"Like she never cusses," he said.

"I never sing naked in public, that's for sure."

"Snotty cow with her college books." Redfield stomped away.

Nikki flashed a grin at her valet and the clerk of scales. "Now we know who won't be posing for *Playgirl*," she said, and ducked back inside the women's room.

Brenda and Rita had gone to ride the first race, leaving Kris behind. Nikki recounted what Redfield had done.

"He did that to me once, too," Kris said. "Willie thinks he's hung like Moby Dick."

"More like Flipper."

"The guy ought to be gelded."

"Better yet, make him wear a stud ring."

"What's that?"

"It's a whatchamacallit you put on a stallion's thingamabob, so he can't you know...entertain himself all the time and get worn out," Nikki explained.

"Probably be easier to set him up with Rita."

"She's already been there, done that."

"Oh yeah, I forgot," Kris said. "So when you going out with Joe Garcia?"

A copy of the day's racing form lay on the couch. Nikki picked it up and started to read. "Joe's nice."

"And leading rider, and a major hunk. Short, dark, and

handsome." Kris put a hand over her heart and sighed dreamily.

Nikki rolled up the paper and batted Kris over the head. "I'm not giving any of the guys around here bragging rights."

"Oh, my gawd, she's never done it."

"Yeah, I have."

Kris started laughing so hard she snorted. "I can see the headlines after the autopsy. Virgin jockey dies in race."

Nikki rolled her eyes. "Only if the coroner's farsighted."

"You need a man."

"Horses are less trouble."

"You know what they say about Catherine the Great and boy horses?"

"Very funny," Nikki said, chucking a pillow at Kris. "I'm not that desperate."

"Have faith, Summers. Prince Charming's out there somewhere."

"Yeah, and with my luck I'll end up with a toad. Like my mother." Nikki flopped onto the bottom bunk and attempted to forget that her perspective of half the population had been distorted in childhood. It was, however, rather unforgettable.

~

She couldn't remember his name. Trivial details went in one ear and out the other of a six-year old's head. What she remembered was the shouting, the slapping, the punching, not often in the beginning, then more and more. Blood and bruises, sometimes blood, always bruises, big and black and lumpy, turning purple before fading to yellowish. Mostly, Nikki had listened from her bedroom. She could still hear the hollow thud of his fist hitting her mother's breastbone, his angry voice but not the words. They lived with him for about a year. A way too long year. In Nikki's opinion, an hour was too long to be around this man who had come into their lives and taken over. She started first grade, finished first grade. She spent a lot of time at the baby sitter's apartment and sometimes didn't see her mother for days. Near the last, Rachel began to change. She hardly talked. She would avert her eyes whenever she did speak, as if talking to herself. When the end finally came, Nikki lay in bed listening until she couldn't stand to hear her mother being hit a second longer, then she tried to help and had gotten thrown across the room. She'd lifted her head dizzily and felt something warm trickling down her chin. Her mother had wiped away the blood while crying and scolding her at the same time. After that, they moved in with the Warners.

Uncle Ned and Aunt Monica had engaged in their own brand of combat before they'd divorced, though mouth-to-mouth not hand-to-hand. Nikki had listened to fouler things, but never had she heard any crueler remarks than the ones her aunt and uncle dished out. Nikki spent more than one night lying awake with a pillow crammed over her head.

By the time she was old enough to care, thoughts of marriage made her panicky. She equated a long-term relationship with being locked in a cage at the zoo with a member of an incompatible species. Her aunt had decided that there was a problem after Nikki turned down a date from the quarterback of her high school football team, so Monica sent sixteen-year old Nikki to a psychologist twice a month for a year. Talking was okay, she discovered. Especially to a stranger paid to hear her troubles, which left her feeling like less of a burden for bothering someone. She even understood that the idea was to fix herself and not the past. Her problem was as obvious as a clogged drain, yet she could not have felt more helpless to repair the damage had someone stuck a wrench and a snake in her hands. How could she love someone else if she didn't love herself? And how could she love herself if her own mother hadn't loved her?

~

Several days later, Nikki rode a horse for an unfamiliar trainer whose horses were not stabled at Westover Meadows. She greeted him in the paddock with a handshake. He belched.

Even in the cool air, she could smell the booze. His orders were simple: Win. And don't fall off. When it came time to leg her up, he goosed her butt and Nikki jumped so high, she about flew off the other side. During the post parade her mount exhibited the enthusiasm of a draft horse and loaded reluctantly into the gate, then the bell rang and the unthinkable happened.

The doors didn't open.

Horses reared and lunged and bounced off the inside of the steel structure. The starting gate shook. Nikki's horse took a step backward and cranked his head around to give her an aggrieved look. A minute passed. Then, without warning, the doors suddenly burst open and the field was away in uneven order, her mount lumbering out only after a slap on the rump from one of the gate crew. Dead last, they trailed the pack by a sixteenth of a mile, but on the second turn, they hugged the rail and slipped past two stragglers. At the head of the lane, she clucked to the horse, then flagged him with her whip, figuring they had a shot to run fifth or better, and at the very least, earn the owner the cost of a losing jock mount. By the eighth pole, she had Rita boxed in behind a wall of horses and in trouble.

"Let me out! I'm going down," Rita screamed.

She was standing in her stirrups, sawing on the reins, but her iron-jawed mount was going onward, hole or not. Nikki angled her own mount toward the outside and gave Rita room. Her horse charged through the opening and won the race. Nikki finished third.

Back in the women's room, Rita thanked her. "I owe you one," she said, before heading out the door for the next race.

"Fat chance," Kris said. "Rita owes everyone."

"C'est la vie," Nikki said, and went to the sink and ran hot water over her numb hands.

"Say what?" Brenda wanted to know.

Nikki grimaced as the feeling slowly returned to her fingers. "C'est la vie. That's life."

"It means 'tough shit' in French," Kris explained.

~

Before the night was over, Nikki won the feature race on Captain Fuzzy, the colt's third straight win. Tanya Lindsey called the Jockeys' Room and left word for Nikki to meet her upstairs in the clubhouse after she finished riding. Nikki found her agent sitting alone at the bar and slid onto a neighboring stool. A half dozen video monitors blazed brightly overhead, the odds for the ninth race glowing white on royal blue screens. Nikki hadn't won many feature races and anticipated kudos from her agent.

"Captain Fuzzy ran big." Tanya made a toast to Fuzzy and raised her martini glass. "Course, he might not have won if the favorite hadn't drawn the ten hole. Outside post going a flat mile's the kiss of death."

"He'd have won," Nikki said. "Colt's got a decent shot of taking the Westover Meadows Derby."

"With over a hundred grand up for grabs, you can bet some decent colts will ship up from California. Fuzzy," Tanya said, with a slight wrinkling of her nose, "hasn't beaten anything but the locals."

"Maybe not, but he's undefeated and tonight's win came against allowance company. The top colts at the track." Nikki was puzzled by her agent's lack of enthusiasm and decided Tanya had consumed one too many.

Tanya nodded impatiently. "Considerate of you to let Rita out in the seventh race."

"I had no shot to win," Nikki said.

"All you had to do was mind your own business and hold a straight course. If Rita runs over horses and goes down, that's her problem."

"You know I couldn't do that, Tanya."

"How I know." She stirred her drink and watched the olive sink. "The trainer just got through with me. Swore you cost him the race."

"The gate malfunction cost him the win."

"You were still going to finish second if you hadn't let Rita through."

"And what if other horses went down and Rita wasn't the only jock to get hurt? Both Warren and Skip were riding trailers."

"I don't care to argue," Tanya said.

"Me, neither," Nikki said.

"Listen, you'd be better off hustling your own book. You don't need an agent."

"But, Tanya..."

"I'm sorry. You're not a money-making proposition. I've got to invest my time in Warren and Skip."

Nikki looked about quickly, skimming faces in the room, searching for an ally to come to her defense. No one did. "But you've always been my agent," she finally said.

"I think very highly of you as a person."

"But?"

"There's just no nice way to put it. You're a lousy ass kisser."

The bell rang for the tenth race, a simulcast from Peninsula Park. Nikki sat staring at her hands and Tanya sat drinking her drink and the race ran on the video monitors. The winning jockey, owner, and trainer were announced. Jim Bruner, J.K. Vanderford, and Rachel Nottingham.

Nikki's head whipped toward the nearest monitor. The Peninsula Park tote board showed the order of finish in the race, followed by a brief shot of the winner's circle crowded with smiling faces, the jockey, the owners. A close-up of Rachel. With only magazine and racing form photographs to supplement her childhood memories, Nikki gaped at the attractive woman on the screen, shocked at seeing her mother come to life.

Tanya banged her glass down.

Nikki started badly and almost fell from the stool. "Thanks for everything, Tanya. I'll leave your check in the race office."

Having lost all desire to beg and plead with her agent, Nikki made for the exit. On the walk to the parking lot she concentrated on the money to be saved by hustling her own book. Money, always money, and to hell with loyalty, to hell with friends, to hell with family. She zipped her jacket to the collar, pumped her fists, and whispered a curse word, but her anger proved false and gave way readily. She stuck her hands in her pockets, shivering as the night air accosted her without mercy.

"To hell with Tanya," Nikki said aloud to the darkness and resigned herself to being her own agent.

She got in her car and started the engine. The steering wheel was cold, and she switched from hand to hand until the heater kicked in. She had called her mother about a dozen times after finding out that Rachel was alive and prospering in New York. Only once had Rachel spoken to her. And then just long enough to say that she regretted what had happened, but that she was no longer a mother and to stay out of her life. Nikki wrote letters next — apologizing for being a difficult child. Her letters went unanswered.

After a few minutes, she made herself stop thinking about it and turned on the radio. The Beatles were singing "Oh bla-dy oh bla-da, life goes on...." With her voice jumping from flat to falsetto, she joined in loudly and cried all the way home.

Peninsula Park
February 1994

Northern Windsor, Rachel's slow dark-brown colt, ran last by an eighth of a mile in Thursday's second race, though officially, he beat the horse that pulled up on the backstretch and failed to finish. Northern Windsor was the first horse to gallop back. A valet snapped a round bright red claim tag onto the colt's bridle, he was unsaddled and led to the paddock. From a window table in the Turf Club, Rachel let out a whoop, then watched as a liver chestnut colt entered the winner's circle. After the photo, he also received a red claim tag. His trainer, Belinda Davenport, gestured furiously with her hands as she spoke with the clerk of scales, which Rachel interpreted as a good sign that the colt was a worthwhile claim. Having sold the caboose and bought the engine, she gave another whoop and hurried downstairs to oversee the exchange of horses.

The paddock—a circular saddling arena and walking ring surrounded by a semicircular amphitheater of tiered concrete that rose sharply upward to accommodate several dozen rows of polished wood benches—occupied the ground-level southwest corner of the grandstand. Fans clutching racing forms, programs, and beers peered down with winning expectations, while yet more people lined the rail above the open tunnel pathway leading outside to the racetrack. A guard blocked the stairs that intersected the tunnel, halting the flow of patrons crossing from north to south grandstand until the claimed horses had passed inside.

Rachel went to the owner's platform in the center of the paddock, all the while careful not to trip or bend over too far in heels and a short tight dress as she was accustomed to pants and boots. She watched Northern Windsor's groom remove the colt's bridle and Reno McAllister's assistant trainer slip on a halter and lead the horse away. The winner came in next, blowing and prancing, trailed by Sam with a halter and shank in one hand. The crowd had thinned between races but was beginning to grow in anticipation of the next field to be saddled. Rachel glanced around for her rival, a swift stomp of a high-heel pump the only indication that she had failed to spot him. She was still looking when trainer Belinda Davenport marched over.

Davenport's cheeks were flushed hot pink and matched her lipstick. Black stretch jeans as tight as leotards exposed cellulite dimples on the ample hips of a figure more teapot than hourglass. An innocently girlish face camouflaged a cutthroat disposition. Rachel avoided Belinda whenever possible.

Early on as a trainer, Rachel had naively believed that the sport's few female participants would stick together. The exact opposite proved closer to the truth. Women trainers stood apart and selfishly defended their place in the male hierarchy as though only so many of their sex would be tolerated. At Peninsula Park, the sole woman trainer of any distinction who would speak to her on friendly terms was Opal O'Reilly. Of course, none of the men trainers were especially chummy with her either.

"What happened to Northern Windsor? Didn't run up to his last work, did he?" Davenport said.

Rachel twisted her mouth in a flippant smile. "He had a migraine."

"Horse shit. That bullet work wasn't his."

"Clockers thought so."

"Screw the clockers." Davenport pointed a long manicured nail in Rachel's face. "That boy you rode was shooting off his mouth after he dismounted, saying you hosed him. Claims the colt wasn't the same one he worked in fifty-nine the other morning."

She shrugged. "Average jockey's about as perceptive as an earthworm."

"Boy's got a red jacket stained with black shoe polish to

prove it."

"Like you'd give a shit if I hadn't just claimed the best colt in your barn."

Davenport's nose crimped up. "I hope Reno kicks your ass."

Rachel flicked a piece of horse hair off her dress sleeve. "Even if he does, I'm still ahead of *you*."

~

Peninsula Park was one of the few racetracks in the country showing gains in attendance and handle. In addition to quality horse racing, no one would go home hungry with the Eclipse, a three-star Turf Club restaurant atop the grandstand, the Ascot Court, a family restaurant on the main level, and numerous fast-food stands on the floors in between. There was a free nursery and daycare center for children and a video arcade and fun center for older kids, teenagers, and bored adults. The York Lounge provided big-screen coverage of alternative sporting events such as football, baseball, and basketball. A handicapping league, consisting of more than two hundred teams from throughout northern California, vied for daily and seasonal monetary awards. An upper-level boutique sold designer-label Peninsula Park jackets, T-shirts, and other chic clothes. Lower-level shops offered more affordable souvenirs. Peninsula Park had something for everyone.

At the entrance to the Turf Club—an upscale viewing and dining area restricted to members only with money being the sole criterion—Rachel nodded to the guard and went inside. Bypassing parimutuel windows, she headed for the Newmarket Pub, a long narrow room of brass, dark leather, and burnished wood, where the replay of the third race was running on video monitors. Rachel stopped to watch. After the winner crossed the wire, she felt someone staring and turned to find Reno McAllister eying her from a stool at the bar. Her first thought was to leave. She'd been avoiding him since Billy Cortez spread the word that she was a great lay, although had anyone else besides McAllister—or Ginny—asked, Rachel would've admitted to enjoying the notoriety. It was nobody's business that she'd done nothing racier than kiss the young hunk of a vet—and eyeball his large package, which he'd proudly removed from his pants of his own accord—before she booted him onto the floor and out the door. At forty-seven, she saw the matter as a second chance to appreciate all the whistles and flirtatious comments she'd taken for granted in her youth. Leave it to McAllister to rain indignity on her feel-good parade.

"What are you looking at?" she said, and tugged at the hem of her short black Chanel, aware that the dress stood out among the suits, slacks, and jeans of her fellow trainers.

"Not what you're thinking," he said. "I'm guessing you're either on the prowl for another boy-toy or making a liar out of that sportswriter who made a nasty comment about you in his last column."

"He claimed I purchased my wardrobe from Indiana Jones, Buffalo Bill, and Captain Hook."

"More like Linda Lovelace."

Rachel tugged at her hem again. "Are you through?"

"You plan on sticking around if I'm not?"

"Long enough to congratulate you on claiming the soundest horse in my barn."

McAllister slid off his stool. "And the slowest, no doubt."

"Absolutely."

"Colt I clocked in fifty-nine and change the other morning had a considerably shorter tail," he said. "You in the habit of running horses with hair extensions?"

She gave a little shrug. "I really don't care to discuss it."

"Discuss this then. What were you thinking of, dallying Lucifera?" He reached for Rachel's nose but stopped just short of touching the blackish-purple bruise that she'd attempted to hide beneath makeup.

She pushed away his hand. "I've been getting her around the track. That's more than you can claim."

"You're going to end up in the hospital, you don't start using common sense where that gray outlaw's concerned."

149

"Like you give a damn," she said. "Lucifera *will* get her picture taken."

"Sure, she will," he said. "Only horse to ever end up in a police lineup."

"I can't wait to see your ego implode when I win a race with her."

"Your problem, lady, is you can't imagine caring about anyone but yourself."

"And you're just so goddamn considerate. Spreading rumors that slander me, you big hypocrite."

McAllister looked her in the eyes with the intensity of a pit bull. "You did a pretty fair job of that yourself."

Rachel lofted her head higher. "And you're what—a virgin?"

His mouth fell open, followed by a short pause, then a change of topics. "You snuck into one of my stalls."

"*I did not,*" she hissed through gritted teeth to keep from shouting.

"My assistant swears you did."

"He's a liar. I didn't peek in any of your goddamn stalls."

"And you never lie."

"I'd lie to you in a heartbeat if it involved respectable gamesmanship, but not about this."

He cocked his head to one side, as if to see her from a different angle. "You're telling the truth?"

She met his gaze unblinking. "Yes."

"Oh," McAllister mumbled, then abruptly tipped his Stetson with an exaggerated waggle of a hand, dispelling any notion that he might apologize. "My mistake, lady. Stay the hell out of my barn and we won't have this problem again."

"Count on it," she said.

"I am."

He cut for the other side of the room and pulled up a chair beside an attractive brunette. Rachel set out in the opposite direction at a brisk clip with her stomach in what felt like an unrecoverable tailspin. At the far end of the bar, she ordered a straight shot, dispatched the whiskey in a single gulp, and slammed the glass down. Then she ordered another.

~

Rachel went directly to the Turf Club's exclusive restaurant, the Eclipse, and was seated at a table by herself. The alcohol had coated her raw nerves with ambivalence and shifted her perspective away from Reno McAllister. She ordered a cup of smoked salmon chowder with fresh-baked crackers and thumbed through a condition book, marking future races. Soon thereafter, she was joined by three of her clients, Larry Parker, the owner of Peninsula Park, his wife, Natasha, and Margot Tate. The fiftyish Parker and the much younger Natasha always looked as if they'd stepped out of a tanning salon, while Tate bore an eerie resemblance to Cruella de Ville with her angularly pointed features and exotic collection of fur coats. Parker noted the frustrations of betting on morning glories, horses such as Northern Windsor, who worked like a runner but wilted under the pressure of competition. Rachel attempted to steer the conversation in another direction but the man was relentless.

"Yes, Northern Windsor was a real mystery," she fibbed. "All that talent and no heart."

"I lost a bundle on him," the track's owner said.

"I don't think the colt liked the surface. Bottom's too hard. When the rain hits, they're going to be hauling horses off by the truckload." A genuine concern of Rachel's.

Larry Parker ignored her complaint. "You know, I heard your friend Mrs. Hammond cashed a wad on the winner." He dealt her an unfriendly look. "Strange she didn't bet on Northern Windsor."

Rachel glanced at her watch. "That Virginia, she's devised a very scientific handicapping system. Bets on anything with pink silks."

The group laughed politely.

Rachel changed the subject. "Your big three-year old filly's training well," she told the Parkers.

"I take it she'll be ready to run soon?" Larry asked.

"I'm aiming for the end of the month."

He looked at his wife. "Natasha and I want you to ride a girl on the filly."

"You know I'm not crazy about riding women," Rachel said, stirring her soup.

"Yes, I've noticed," Natasha Parker said. "You're as chauvinistic as the men trainers around here."

Rachel stopped stirring. "Excuse me?"

"Not only do you not ride women jockeys, but you don't have any women exercise riders or grooms in your employment, either."

"I admit, I do have more confidence in men where physical skill is involved."

Natasha Parker frowned deeply. "What women lack in strength, they make up for with finesse. A jockey can't beat a win out of a horse."

Not wishing to argue, Rachel resorted to a witty comeback. "No, but judging from the way Northern Windsor ran today, they have to be strong enough to carry some of my horses to the wire."

Neither of the Parkers looked amused.

"Put a girl on the filly when she runs," Larry said.

As the owners of Peninsula Park, they were important clients of Rachel's. She dumped the crackers into her soup and methodically sank them with her spoon. "It's your horse," she said.

Natasha pushed her chair away from the table and rose, her husband doing likewise. "I think you'll be pleasantly surprised."

Rachael forced a smile.

Arm in arm, the Parkers headed off to bet the next race.

After they had gone, Margot Tate pushed bifocals down her nose to examine Rachel's short black dress. "Are you making a fashion statement or did you simply tire of wearing pants?"

~

Rachel left the Eclipse fifteen minutes before the fifth race, took an elevator to the next level, and made her way to a narrow corridor housing private boxes. Stopping at the fourth door down, she stuck a key in the lock, found it was already open, and went inside. The room was the size of a small office and overlooked the racetrack at the finish line. Photographs of Man O' War and Ruffian hung on the walls along with a racetrack video monitor, a television, and an in-house phone for ordering food and beverages. A bright-blue Art Deco table by the window held a smoke filter and an ashtray. Ginny, who occupied one of four white leather and stainless steel Le Corbusier style chairs, lowered binoculars to her lap. Rachel tossed her purse on the table, sat down, and attempted to cross a leg without exposing herself.

"Now I *have* seen everything." Ginny burst into laughter.

"Never mind."

"It's a miracle you managed to saddle a horse without flashing the grandstand or breaking an ankle."

Rachel gave up being polite and undaintily crossed a leg. "I'm having a bad day, okay?"

"You've lost a slow horse and claimed a fast one. How can you possibly be having a bad day?"

"I don't *know.* Everyone's in my face. Belinda Davenport, the Parkers. McAllister."

"I heard Reno claimed your slow horse."

"Yeah."

"So why are you frowning, dear?"

"Let's just say I should stick to serving revenge cold."

"What?"

"Never mind." Rachel reached for her binoculars and observed the post parade. "Another client of mine, Seth Marten, insisted I drop in a claim for a mare of McAllister's named Youwho Molly, who'll be lucky to make the course next race."

"The vet will certainly scratch her," Ginny said. "Won't he?"

"I guarantee you he isn't about to scratch the even-money favorite if she makes it through the post parade without keeling over. Whoever hired a state vet by the name of Elmer has a morbid sense of humor."

Ginny was a moment in getting it. "Elmer...oh. Like the glue."

She fell quiet and they both concentrated on the action below until the race was over. Youwho Molly pulled up at the quarter pole, where the jockey sprang off and held the mare by the reins. Rachel muttered to herself. Sometimes, she hated to be right. She gathered her purse and took a final look out the window. The horse ambulance chugged past the finish wire on its way to the quarter pole, a green tractor towing a long, windowless silver trailer.

"You can save her, can't you?" Ginny asked.

"Operations are expensive. Marten will want the mare put down."

Ginny let out a mortified gasp. "But is it possible to save her?"

Rachel shrugged. "Well, maybe. But not practical."

For the next two minutes, she calmly recited the economics of the matter, only to be interrupted by Ginny's hysterical pleas to spare Youwho Molly. Rachel could've kicked herself for not lying. Ginny listened to nothing. The mare was calf-kneed, which meant each time a front leg bore the weight of her stride, the limb hyperextended, bowing back—a conformation defect that was susceptible to injury. Rachel was tempted to lay the blame on McAllister. No doubt, he'd had Youwho Molly's knee injected with cortisone a number of times in order to keep her racing, but Rachel couldn't bring herself to condemn him for doing what she herself had done before and would do again. Unquestionably, a cortisone injection into a joint, followed by continued racing stress, caused irreversible damage, but when one dealt with cheap horses, inherently unsound, artificial measures were necessary to prolong their limited racing lives.

Rachel rested her valuable stock if they got sore or injured, but with cheap claimers, the object was to win races and lose the animals. She had long since risen above starvation level, but remembered days past when a kind-hearted decision meant going hungry.

"Racing's a tough business, Ginny."

"Please don't give me the 'horses are bred to race, cattle are bred to be eaten' bit, again," she said, blowing her nose.

Rachel would admit to being desensitized to the horrors of the sport, but she was not inured to playing God. She stepped out the door, then stuck her head back inside. "I'll save her for a broodmare, okay?"

Ginny smiled. "You'll sleep better tonight. I know I will."

"Like Rip Van Winkle," Rachel said, closing the door.

~

The horse ambulance transported Youwho Molly to Rachel's barn, where Dr. Steele and an associate X-rayed the mare in the shed row and found she had slab-fractured her knee. An operation was required if she was to have any chance of survival. Rachel took the vet aside and had him give Youwho Molly a shot of strong painkiller for the time being, then instructed Sam to cool her out in her stall and hurried to the backside cafe where Seth Marten awaited her.

Rachel found him reading a copy of *The Wall Street Journal* and took a chair across the table. Marten tossed the paper aside and pounded his fist down. She took a deep breath and felt the hair on her arms stand on end. The crowded cafeteria went silent. There was hardly a head that hadn't turned to watch and listen.

"You've claimed the last broken down horse for me, Nottingham," he all but shouted.

The buzz of many voices both English and Spanish swept over the room. Rachel knew this day had been coming, the day he'd fire her as he fired all his trainers.

"You picked her out," she said, with equal intensity, and

155

removed an envelope from her purse and tossed it across the table. "There's your bill. I'm not carrying you any longer."

He stuffed the envelope and the newspaper into his suit jacket, then they walked to the race office, side by side, not speaking. Inside the race office, he wrote her a check for the $67,349 he owed for the past three months of training, and her ten percent share of the win, place, and show purses grossed by his seven head. Rachel put the check in her purse. When the racing secretary gave Marten his horses' registration papers, he bragged about getting his trainer's license and said he was shipping his stable to Santa Anita. Rachel requested that none of his horses leave her barn until his check cleared the bank. Legally, she could not hold the animals, but she didn't want any more money troubles. Before they parted, she advised him to have Youwho Molly euthanized. He agreed.

She drove home and an hour later, returned to the barn with her new three-quarter-ton black pickup and matching two-horse trailer. She informed Sam and her help that she was taking Youwho Molly to a private clinic for an operation, then had them load the injured mare and drove to the main stable gate, giving the guard her name on an out slip, as all arriving and departing horses had to be accounted for. Rachel continued to a nearby shopping mall and pulled into the deserted reaches of the parking lot. If she had Youwho Molly euthanized on the grounds, it would become public knowledge, and Rachel feared Ginny would hear about it. She lit a cigarette and waited for Dr. Steele.

~

Rachel didn't bother to go home and switch vehicles. In thirty minutes, she drove onto the southbound freeway. Reaching San Jose in forty-five, she pulled into a truck stop and parked among the semis, checked to see that the side and back doors of the trailer were locked, then went inside and ordered a Bloody Mary. A cowboy wannabe wearing a sterling silver belt buckle big as a searchlight sat down across from her with his eyes glazed in the way eyes get after several strong cocktails. The cowboy sat and talked about himself. About all the mechanical bulls he had ridden, how he had seen every John Wayne movie ever made at least twice, that his name was Wally and he was a tax accountant. She finished her second drink, ordered a third. He claimed to have watched her pull in and asked what she was hauling in the trailer. Rachel thought fast, but her brain wasn't presently in high-speed mode.

"Dead horse."

"No shit?"

"Yup."

"You married?"

"Nope."

"Kids?"

"Yeah. No."

"You want kids and don't have any, or you don't want 'em but you got 'em?"

Rachel rose swaying to her feet. "If you'll excuse me, I have to pee like a racehorse."

She walked cautiously to the ladies' room and on the way envisioned in her mind a crayon picture Nicole had drawn of a very boy horse going both one and two at the same time. Pee and poop. The horse in all his crayon glory was preserved in Rachel's head with photographic detail that both blew her away and frightened her, for she had no desire to spend hours or even a minute wondering what might have been when all she stood to gain from looking back was a sore neck. She washed her hands and then started toward the bar, taking short shuffling steps to keep her balance. San Francisco was not having one of its notorious earthquakes, she hoped, then cussed herself for drinking on an empty stomach.

Another stranger who was equally talkative soon took the cowboy's place, but Rachel wasn't listening and after a time he got the idea and let her be. She saw the horse picture again and cupped her hands over her face and sat in a darkness of her own making. Even with her eyes closed, she could still see that horse pissing and shitting.

~

Nicole's kindergarten teacher had scheduled a parent conference to discuss her progress in school, but all Rachel remembered was being shown *that* picture. The teacher laughed it off. She *had* asked the class to draw a horse *doing* something. Rachel, who would've given a kidney for an ounce of motherly instinct, recalled taking little comfort in the fact that Nicole hadn't depicted two horses doing *it*. Somewhere in the cavernous pit of Rachel's conscience she heard a voice, her own no less, saying that her success at the racetrack would never be enough to completely overshadow her one big failure. Getting pregnant in the first place was her biggest mistake.

By seventeen, she had grown to her full height of five feet eight inches. She was firm and slender from working on the ranch, had straight white teeth with a slight overbite, blue eyes the color of contact lenses, high cheekbones on an oval face she considered chubby, and full lips, which made her look temperamental unless she was smiling. As a teenager, Rachel hadn't given much thought to whether or not she was pretty.

And so she was shocked to be voted prom queen her senior year. She and the two princesses were crowned at a school function attended by parents and the student body. Rachel wore a brand-new red dress her father bought her for the occasion. She stood on stage with two other girls, the auditorium a solid mass of faces, then the winner was announced, a glittering tiara was placed on her head, the air erupted with clapping, and the ordeal was over. Her father had smiled nonstop for a week. Rachel wondered why he puffed up his chest over a silly honor awarded mostly on appearance, when other deeds she attacked with hard work and diligence went largely ignored. She worried that her holier-than-thou father believed a woman's only realistic option in life was to get married, and a girl with prom queen credentials would be more apt to nab a prize husband. Nowhere on her list of priorities could the word husband be found. Horses and racing engaged her from dawn to dusk. School was a formality, though she earned good marks, thinking it an advantage to be smart. She never made time to date in high school, but once kissed one of the ranch hands, just to see what the fuss was all about. Having someone else's slobbery tongue in her mouth made her want to puke. Needless to say, she had been slow in getting laid.

By the summer of her eighteenth year, Rachel had accepted additional responsibilities on the racing end of her father's operation and learned there was more to training horses than the horses. Her father had been one of the finest conditioners of Thoroughbreds on the West Coast but had garnered only respect and a good reputation. If honesty was the best policy, it was not a realistic one with a great many others cheating to get ahead. Unfortunately, her father's integrity kept them on the verge of bankruptcy. Once, on the sly, she paid a young backside ruffian fifty dollars to beat up a jockey who had been stiffing their horses race after race. Several other times, Rachel had lied to officials about what horse she was breezing, then told her father that the clockers had screwed up. She'd made up her mind early on not to let her father's weaknesses become her own.

That same winter, a full sister to one of the ranch broodmares won a major stakes race on the East Coast. Shortly thereafter, a man with money came calling to buy the mare and her yearling foal. Her father was away racing and had left her in charge of the matter. Rachel fixed her hair and wore makeup and a skirt, based on her newfound suspicion that being presentable never hurt. The buyer was movie-star handsome, but looks alone had never moved her before and it was something unseen, something forbidden about him, some imperceptible magnetism that had set loose her hormones with the rush of a stampede. Or maybe she'd just waited too long to have sex. In any case, she had opened the door and regarded the man with the same composed courtesy that she afforded all men and boys. And at once, felt very nervous, her face growing warm. He had looked on with an amused smile.

His name had been deleted from her memory years ago, but he bought the broodmare and her yearling. She couldn't remember the price or much else afterward, except that things got hot in a hurry and they did it on the living room couch.

Rachel never again saw or heard from the man. Months later she learned he was already married and had three kids. By then she'd lost her period, gained five pounds, and heaved every morning for three weeks straight. She wore a girdle and baggy shirts, hoping her father wouldn't notice until she found the courage to have a talk with him. Four months along, she owned up to being pregnant, although she'd refused to divulge the sperm donor's identity. Her father had been livid on both counts. And, of course, instead of letting her do something pertinent, he'd shipped her and a suitcase of clothes by bus to Los Angeles, where she stayed with her aunt and uncle until giving birth, then returned home with a baby belonging to a recently deceased cousin. Supposedly.

At the time, Rachel thought it seemed like a good idea. Better to tell a white lie than be known as white trash. Plus, she'd wanted to please her father. But, of course, there was no pleasing a man who saw the world as starkly black and white without the slightest contemplation of gray. How phony she'd felt, pretending to pray for forgiveness. If there was a God, surely he or she would value honesty more than devotion? It occurred to her again that the only thing she stood to gain from looking back was a sore neck and probably a headache, too, but the past continued to play in her head like a home movie directed by David Lynch.

Monica Warner had met her at the bus station with a smile, a hug, and a list of rules. Rachel's mother's baby sister was a socialite with a young son and daughter, a rich lawyer husband, and a mansion in Beverly Hills. With a swimming pool, an exercise room, air conditioning. A four-car garage with four vehicles, a wine cellar, a hot tub. And a bidet, which Rachel at first mistook for some sort of exotic but impractical drinking fountain. Fortunately, she hadn't been thirsty at the time. Anyhow, Monica bought Rachel expensive clothes and invited her to live at their home after the baby was born. Rachel, who up until a week ago never knew she even had an Aunt Monica, already missed the ranch. Fat and humiliated, she felt as powerless as a driver who'd spun out of control and was awaiting the crash.

In July of '65, she gave birth to a healthy baby girl. When Rachel's time finally came, the doctor decided she was narrow in the hips and took the baby by Caesarean section while Rachel lay there like a blob. A week later, she returned home to Stockton with her daughter, Nicole. Cousin Nicole, as Rachel's father was quick to point out.

The next four years were preserved in her mind with the clarity of crude oil. That motherhood could be a full-time career had never fully dawned on Rachel at this time, since living on the ranch allowed her the freedom to work *and* raise a child. A child who was quiet and less demanding than the horses. Rachel, who had never been much of a socializer, spent most evenings happily buried in books about veterinary science, equine feeding principles, training techniques, and so on while Nicole played with her toys or slept. Everything was going okay until Rachel's father took ill.

What started as sporadic intestinal pains grew progressively worse until he began passing blood and finally agreed to see a doctor. The verdict was colon cancer. Deaf to Rachel's pleas to rest, he trained the horses until he became too ill to get out of bed. To watch a parent die, to watch his body waste away and turn yellow and jaundiced, to see an intensely proud man wearing diapers, his spirit destroyed, was an experience she wouldn't have wished upon her worst enemy. Because her father hated hospitals, she kept him at home, hiring nurses to spare him the embarrassment of being cared for by his daughter. Between the horses and Nicole, Rachel already had plenty to do.

She was racing horses in San Francisco, hoping to make a dent in the stack of bills piled high on her desk, when her father died. One of the nurses phoned with the news, and Rachel hurried home. Halfway there, she pulled off the road and sat on the truck's bumper in the hot sun, in the gusty diesel wake of semis roaring past for twenty minutes before she could cry. And another hour before she could stop. Unlike a movie in which an incurable illness opened the emotional door of a heretofore unaffectionate parent, her father had stayed behind his walls to the end. She couldn't say if this was because they hadn't seen eye to eye on matters of the soul. All she knew with certainty was that he was her father and she had loved him. In the end, she was left with an unhappy feeling that she should've been the one to reach out.

Baggage, as it happened, was all he had left Rachel. Unbeknownst to her, he had mortgaged the ranch to the hilt. The bank took everything but two horses, a truck, and a two-horse trailer, which she'd hidden in the neighbor's barn. She and Nicole, two cats, a Quarter Horse pony and a yearling Thoroughbred colt had set out for the racetrack at San Francisco in an old rust-scarred pickup truck with their belongings, three bales of hay, and a sack of oats heaped in the bed. The real-life Beverly Hillbillies.

She should have suspected that's where they'd eventually end up.

~

The next morning at Peninsula Park, Rachel was greeted by seven empty stalls. She had awoken with a hangover and a sour taste in her mouth that was not exclusively due to forgetting to brush her teeth. Her answering machine was blinking in the darkness with unheard messages from the night before. She dragged herself out of bed and took a cold shower, while vowing to limit her alcohol intake to beer and wine. She was late getting to work.

Right after she left with Youwho Molly, a van had come for Seth Marten's horses, Sam explained. The driver and his helper possessed the registration papers and bills of sale for the seven head. They were big men. They spoke Spanish with a strange accent that Sam had trouble understanding. Out of desperation, he'd called the Stewards, and the three officials who oversaw the race meet were sympathetic but of no help. Marten's seven horses were loaded and the van rolled away, going to Oceanstead Farm for two others. There was nothing more to tell. Sam said that he had called her and left messages, his shoulders and face bunching in a sad shrug. Rachel listened without saying a word.

By nine-thirty, rain began to fall, hard and steadily, and she shifted in her saddle to inspect the dark clouds overhead. Exhaling heavily, her breath condensed in a fog. In the background, her help walked horses under cover of the shed row, while a set of gallopers on the rubber-matted washrack had the dirt hosed from their legs and the sweat sponged off, as it was too chilly for a full bath. Rachel zipped up her rain slicker, then rode down the shed row and shouted to Sam that she was ready for the last tracker. Her assistant brought out Lucifera.

With a mixture of rain and wet snow falling, Rachel ponied the filly and her gallop boy, Clint, two laps at a strong clip. The training track was empty of other horses, so Rachel decided to let Clint gallop Lucifera a mile on his own. After easing her black ponyhorse to a lope, Rachel unsnapped the cotton rope and Lucifera jerked free and spurted ahead as though intending to run off. Suddenly, she sucked back and ducked into the pony, laid against him hard and jammed Clint's left leg behind Rachel's right one. That done, Lucifera bolted.

The force of the impact combined with the swiftness of her acceleration locked Clint's and Rachel's legs. Rachel gunned her mount and tried to keep pace with the filly while struggling to free Clint, but Lucifera was too fast. The gallop boy's left leg stretched over the filly's rump, he clung briefly to the back of the saddle, then crashed to the ground. To avoid trampling Clint, Rachel swerved her pony hard to the rail as Lucifera sped away, kicking up wet sloppy sand in her wake.

Clint climbed to his feet, his body plastered with sand. Rachel galloped back and saw that he was unhurt, then attempted to head off Lucifera. The filly easily dodged her, as well as the outrider, plus Sam and Clint on foot, then bounded over the inside rail with two feet to spare and started grazing the infield grass.

"Shit," Rachel said, to no one at all. She tipped her hat to one side and let the water roll off.

It took almost an hour and a dozen people to catch Lucifera. By then, Rachel's pride had been eviscerated. She dismounted at the barn, passed her pony to a groom, shook off the heaviest drops, and went to her office. She hung her wet slicker and chaps on the wall above an electric heater. The refrigerator yielded a can of beer and one of tomato juice, then she rummaged through a desk drawer for a bottle of ibuprofen. Rachel drank her breakfast, leaned back in her chair, and stared at Seth Marten's sixty-six-thousand dollar check. She could sense the advent of trouble like animals sense a coming earthquake and braced for a whopper, but an hour passed before she reached for the phone and called Marten's bank to confirm her fears. He had closed all his accounts. The check was worthless.

The news came as no real surprise to Rachel, at least not since the moment she had seen those seven empty stalls. Determined to put all the day's unpleasantness behind her at once, she reached for a package from Reno McAllister that lay on the floor at her feet. She ripped off the paper and found a boxer's padded headgear. Her first impulse was to toss the thing into the trashcan, as she thought it preferable to get smacked on the nose again than be seen wearing armor when she ponied Lucifera. That she'd misread McAllister's drift, came to her next. Although, if he intended to verbally beat her up anytime soon, she thought earplugs would have been a more appropriate gift.

The morning was all but over before Sam found the courage to ask her if she knew that Reno had won the last two races the night before. She shook her head and went back to work. An hour later, Rachel halted dead in her tracks in the middle of the shed row, blindsided by the realization that for the first time in five years she was no longer the leading trainer at Peninsula Park.

Westover Meadows
March 1994

Trainer Marc Sampson spoke to a vet, a shoer, and a lady taking orders from one of the backside tack shops before he finally got to Nikki. The track closed in thirty minutes, yet she had spent most of the morning wearing holes in the bottoms of her boots, her third week without an agent. She smiled at Sampson. He gave her an impatient look. She compelled her lips to hold the smile and went about the uncomfortable task of selling herself.

"Need any help this morning?"

"I'm good, thanks. Already got all my horses out." The trainer hurried past.

She shifted a piece of butterscotch to the other side of her mouth and ran to catch up. "Marc, wait a sec. You put Warren on that bay filly I just won on. Why'd you take me off?"

The trainer kept walking. "Filly can win again, but she's in tough. Had to take my best shot."

"She hadn't run in the money 'til I rode her. You know I'll try hard."

He glanced back over his shoulder as though appraising her resolve, then stopped. "I heard you were having trouble making weight."

Nikki swallowed the butterscotch. "I'm tacking fourteen. Back in January I blew up a little but nothing major. Who told you that?"

"Your ex-agent."

"Tanya?"

"Said you couldn't do sixteen."

"Well, she's mistaken. Give me a chance on something. A longshot, a green maiden, your pet goat."

The trainer smiled and pushed away a playful pygmy goat

tied outside a stall. "My owners would string me up by the balls. You know how it is with owners and girl jocks."

"Yeah, I know how it is," she said. Fast talking wasn't her thing. Tanya would have bullshitted him out of a mount by now.

"Tough to make it without an agent," he said.

"Maybe so, but my loyal barns have stuck by me. I'll ride what I ride without a salesperson."

"By my estimation, half as many horses."

"It's only been a few weeks. I'll pick up new barns."

"Tell you what. I've got a two-year old colt with sore shins that no one wants to ride."

"Hurtin' bad?"

He rocked a hand back and forth in a gesture of so-so. "It's a jock mount. Colt can't run fast enough to breakdown."

Nikki glanced up at the clouds, at the cotton-candy puffs of white that blanketed the blue sky like a halcyon quilt, mocking a world that held little empathy for either the voiceless or the impoverished.

Sampson's face twitched impatiently. "Well?"

"Maybe you should turn the colt out for a rest," she said. "Give him a chance to heal."

The trainer told her she needed to find a new job, then walked off shaking his head. Nikki unwrapped another piece of butterscotch and went to the next barn.

~

Near the middle of March, wet flakes of snow hit the ground and melted following the last race on a Thursday night. Nikki shuffled in place to keep warm. After a final look around, she stuck a bag of carrots under her jacket, scaled the north fence, and slipped into Winchester Cannon's deserted barn. King Donican greeted her with his usual rumbling nicker. She unhooked the latch and tried to swing the door open but it wouldn't move. She ran her fingers along the edge of the wooden frame until she felt the cold hard steel of a padlock.

Her heart raced. She glanced about but spotted nothing in the darkness, then Donnie began tapping the toe of his hoof against the bottom of the door. Shushing him, she climbed into the stall, fed him the bag of carrots, and stood listening. The noise began as one of many obscure barn sounds and grew louder. Footsteps.

"Got to run, buddy," she whispered in Donnie's ear.

By the time Nikki had one leg over the door, a large someone was closing in. A dark hulking shape of a man. She dropped to the ground and a hand grabbed her arm, but she twisted free and sprinted down the shed row and out of the barn. She reached the edge of the stable area in seconds. Leaping onto the chain link fence, she scrambled as fast as a monkey to the top, flung a leg over the barbed wire and snagged her pants at the crotch. A voice bellowed in her wake and grew steadily louder. She tugged to get loose of the barb embedded in her jeans.

"Summers, I'll take a bullwhip to your ass!" Winchester Cannon was almost to the fence.

Nikki gave a huge yank to rip loose of the wire, lost her balance, and fell to the ground on the other side. She landed face down with a splat in wet and muddy grass and did not move.

"Summers, you hurt? Summers?" Cannon hollered.

She held her breath.

"Summers...Summers? I'm going after help." His footsteps started away.

Nikki raised her head with a jerk and scrambled to her feet. "Hey. I'm fine," she called out.

He walked back. "You didn't break anything?"

She stepped over to the fence, wearing a layer of grass and goop. "No."

"Lucky thing you lit in the mud," he said, then less kindly, "and on the other side. What've you been doing to that horse? I know this isn't the first time."

"Just feeding him carrots. I swear. Don't tell the stewards."

"Why shouldn't I?"

Her eyes narrowed in the darkness. "I know you were in the Wilcox's barn. You took off one of Donnie's bandages."

Cannon grunted. "Try and prove it."

She reached up to clutch the fence and pressed her face against the chain link wire. "Sell him to me. I'll give you twenty-five now and five hundred next month."

"I'm running him Sunday. Have Wilcox claim him back."

"Donnie pulled up sorer than ever after his last race. Don't run him."

"And look like a dumb son of a bitch for claiming him? Summers, the horse *will* win."

Nikki shook the fence. "I'll give you twenty-five plus the thousand he'd earn for winning. Please don't run him."

"He's not for sale," Winchester Cannon said, and walked away.

~

Nikki handed Matt a check for twenty-five hundred dollars the next morning, then reached for a broom and started to sweep the tack room. Matt folded the check in half and removed a leather wallet stained dark with use from his back pocket.

"I see there's a race in the book for Donnie on Sunday," he said. "They'll be starting the draw pretty soon, then we'll know for sure."

"Cannon's running him. Trust me."

"You don't know that for a fact, gal."

She swept a pile of dust out the door and told him about her midnight run-in with the trainer.

Matt threw his hands above his head like a hellfire preacher about to give a sermon. "Of all the jackass, harebrained things to do."

"I was just making sure Donnie was okay."

About then the door flew open so forcefully it hit the wall and in stomped Susan, out of breath and full of fury. "That bastard, Winchester Cannon. His fishing buddy, the racing secretary, hung up a special race for Donnie. Get this, it's for six-year olds and up, Oregon-breds only. It's so easy, I could win it."

Matt rubbed his chin. "You had four legs, I'd enter you."

"I'd as soon run as poor Donnie," Susan said.

"Yeah, he's real ouchy," Nikki said. "Yesterday I saw him limping off the track after a half-mile blowout."

There was a stretch of silence. Matt locked his hands behind his head and leaned back in his chair. "You women take the prize. Between the two of you, I don't know who's the biggest worrywart. I take that back. Suzy wins the blue ribbon for frettin'. The other day, I tried to flush a bee down the toilet but the pesky thing kept swimming back up. Before I could reach in there and squash the darned bug, Suzy rushes in and fishes it out. 'Poor Mr. Bumble,' she says. 'Bees are our little friends.' Somewhere out there, a bee's flying from flower to flower that was in my toilet. It'll be awhile before I spread any honey on my toast."

"You don't even like honey," Susan said.

Matt shook his head. "Not anymore."

Nikki stomped a foot. "I'm going to ask the stewards to scratch Donnie."

"Whoa," Matt said. "Don't go off half-cocked. I'm still claiming him for you come Sunday."

"Matt," Susan said, "the race is for *thirty-two*, not twenty-five."

Nobody spoke. Nikki felt her stomach growling, but for once didn't care if anyone heard. Matt reached into his back pocket and removed her check from his wallet and handed it back. She tore the paper in half, in half again, and dropped the pieces in the wastebasket.

"Sorry, gal. Who'd figure Winchester would run old King that high?"

Nikki just shrugged and turned away. A tightness gripped her throat, the grasp of something terrible to come that she had the power to prevent. She stared at the blinkers hanging from nails on the far wall, the equipment designed to keep a horse's attention on running. There were two sets of full cup, a French cup, a one-eyed, and clear goggles. She saw the bigger picture without obstruction, saw the course, the finish. She took out her checkbook and wrote the Wilcoxes a check for thirty-two hundred dollars.

Matt took it without saying a word.

~

Nikki spent the entire evening trying to figure out how to earn five hundred dollars in two days. By eleven o'clock, she concluded that her only possibilities were to rob a bank or become a prostitute. By midnight, she had eliminated the latter option. At twelve-thirty, she added numbers in her checkbook a third time and came up with a balance of $2,700 and change, for the third time. By one in the morning, she had begun to fantasize about stealing Donnie. She fell asleep in her clothes.

During the night, Nikki dreamed a strange disjointed dream. A horse cowered in the corner of a stall, blowing and trembling. A man was beating the horse. At each crack of the bullwhip the animal climbed the walls as if to escape, but there was no escaping the man. She begged him to stop, but he wouldn't, and when she grabbed his arm, he tossed her aside. Then the man and horse were gone and she was standing outside a corral watching a colt being ridden. The colt bucked off his rider and leaped the fence. She ran in pursuit, cornering the colt in a barn, only now he was no longer a horse but a young boy. She seized him by the shoulders and felt his arms tense. His eyes were wide with fear and tears glistened on his long lashes. She told him to go back, that it was hopeless to run away, for he could never be free and the best he could hope for was to win lots of races and always behave well and maybe someone would give him a good home in the end. She kissed him on the forehead and stepped away. He gazed at her wildly, as if he might bolt, but instead bowed his head and waited. She saw that he was crying even as he changed from boy to horse.

Nikki awoke at five in the morning. The dream lingered in her thoughts and before leaving for the racetrack, she phoned her aunt, Monica Warner. Nikki knew better than to underestimate the heartlessness of the women in the family but got her hopes up anyway.

Monica answered, sounding sleepy. "Hello?"

"Aunt Monica?"

"Yes."

"Hope I didn't wake you."

"Nicole?"

"Uh-huh."

"So. How have you been?"

"Fine. You?"

"I'm doing quite well, thank you, now that I've stopped worrying about you."

"I don't want you to worry about me, Aunt Monica."

"You've made *that* perfectly clear."

"What I meant is, I didn't become a jockey to hurt you."

"What is it you want, Nicole?"

"I need to borrow five-hundred dollars."

"What for?"

Nikki stared out her bedroom window. The apartment looked onto an empty lot overgrown with grass and blooming scotch broom, alder, bigleaf maple, and fir, an indistinct parcel of green dusted yellow in the suburban landscape. She came up with exactly four lies. A car, college tuition, down payment on a house, or a root canal.

"Well?" Monica said.

"A horse," Nikki said.

Monica laughed. "You've got to be kidding?"

"Please, Aunt Monica. If I don't claim him, he might win and then the bastard who trains him will run him again and Donnie's sore and he might not hold up. I promise I'll pay you back."

"Never."

"Donnie's my friend. I can't let anything happen to him."

"Why don't you call your mother and ask *her* for the money?"

Nikki hung up.

Thirty minutes later, her hand was trembling as she held the receiver to her ear, waiting for Rachel to answer her barn phone. She answered on the seventh ring. By that time, Nikki had changed her mind.

~

On Sunday, Nikki's mount in the third race took a step backward as the starter sprung the latch, and she finished last. An 11-1 shot, it was the shortest-priced horse she had ridden all week. She strode inside the women's room and kicked the dirty-clothes basket and it bounced off the wall and landed on Rita Johnson's head, littering her with an assortment of T-shirts, riding pants, and socks. Rita didn't move. She sat on the couch with a cigarette dangling from her lips, looking like a mannequin from an ugly hat shop. Nikki bent over for a closer look at Rita's eyes, then lifted the plastic basket from her head.

"You sure that's a cigarette you're smoking?"

Rita giggled.

Nikki walked out and checked the program, which was tacked page by page to a bulletin board in the main room, and saw that her mount in the ninth was a 50-1 shot. On the bright side, she was pleased to note that Rita was not scheduled to ride the race. She went to the kitchen and bought her a cup of coffee.

"Just remember, every trainer, owner, and motormouth in the grandstand's a critic, but you don't see them out there risking their necks," Kris was telling Cindy, the apprentice, when Nikki returned.

"Yeah, but this colt's a lugging-out mother."

"Cindy's got the heebie-jeebies," Brenda said.

"Sounds like something she caught from Rita." Kris and Brenda slapped palms.

Rita nodded and smiled. Nikki made Rita drink the coffee, hoping the caffeine would counteract whatever illegal substance she appeared to have ingested. The others kept talking.

"I hate riding horses who don't like to race," Cindy said.

"They've usually got physical problems," Brenda said.

"Like a set of registration papers that say Thoroughbred on 'em," Kris said.

"All people weren't born to be track stars, but all Thoroughbreds have to race. Bummer." Brenda again.

Kris wiped sand off her boots with a grayish-brown stained white rag. "Except in France, where they can work in the culinary industry."

Cindy was a little slow in digesting Kris' sarcasm. "Doing what? Oh."

The thought of eating horses turned Nikki's stomach. She climbed onto the top bunk and lay down but could not sleep. Later, her mount in the ninth race beat one horse. Afterward she showered and dressed, then joined the Wilcoxes at their favorite clubhouse table south of the finish line. The three of them sat staring in three different directions.

"Someday I'd like to have a ranch for old racehorses and orphaned children," Nikki said, after a few minutes. "A place for horses and kids that nobody wants."

Susan smiled and glanced nervously out the windows toward the paddock entrance.

"Better marry a billionaire," Matt said.

He finished a beer and ordered another. He bet fifty dollars on a sure thing in the tenth and lost. Susan sipped an orange soda and picked salt off a hot pretzel until the pretzel turned cold, then excused herself and went to the ladies' room. While she was gone Matt ate the pretzel, chewing methodically, as though eating a piece of chalk. When the eleventh race crossed the infield, he headed downstairs with a claim slip for King Donican in his pocket and Susan clinging to his side. All that remained was to drop the slip into the claim box outside the paddock fifteen minutes prior to post time. Nikki drummed her fingers on the table, then opened a racing form and read that King Donican's new jockey was noted favorably by four of five handicappers. Donnie was the even-money favorite. She pushed the form aside.

The Wilcoxes returned as the horses were coming onto the track. When the post parade galloped past, Matt studied King Donican through a pair of binoculars but didn't say anything about how he looked, and nobody asked. Nikki focused on the floor, on the alternating squares of black and white linoleum that reminded her of a chessboard. She decided the chairs were pawns and there were no other pieces. Her head shot up at the sound of the bell.

The field was off and running without mishap and remained tightly bunched down the backstretch. She watched the race on the nearest video monitor. When Donnie bobbled at the five-eighths pole and again at the half, she cupped her hands over her face and just listened. He lay third around the turn and into the stretch, then started to move. Nikki could feel her heart pounding.

"They're passing the sixteenth pole and that's Izzaboy and King Donican, head and head for the lead. Izzaboy and King Donican fighting it out. Now that's King Donican sticking a nose in front. Oh no," the announcer said, his voice faltering, "King Donican broke down."

Susan let out a clipped cry. Nikki dropped her hands from her face and saw Donnie crashing to the track with horses ducking around him. The gelding struggled to his feet. Minus the rider and dead last, he hobbled on three legs toward the finish line with the crowd cheering until he neared the wire, then the cheering stopped and the grandstand grew eerily quiet. Donnie's right front leg had snapped at the ankle. Below the break, his hoof and pastern swung loosely, connected only by skin.

Nikki sprinted down the stairwell and outside, shoved her way through the people crowded along the concrete retaining wall and bounded over and onto the racetrack. Donnie stood about ten feet short of the finish wire. He held his head high and gazed toward the horizon as if oblivious to the growing circle of people. Nikki pushed past the grave faces of track officials and grooms and up to the valet holding Donnie's bridle reins. She stooped over and cradled the gelding's broken leg at the knee, bearing the weight of it so he did not have to. The damage was considerable. She made herself look.

With machete-like precision, the flesh was laid open in a clean horizontal slash, bone exposed, blood dripping in a steady flow that pooled on the track and formed a grotesque red puddle.

She heard the tractor that pulled the horse ambulance rumble to life in the distance, then someone offered to switch places and hold Donnie's leg and she was stroking his face and telling him she was sorry, then Matt guided her aside and said he hadn't dropped in the claim. She just stared at him, waiting to hear that he was joking. He glanced down and repeated that he hadn't claimed Donnie. In the background, she saw the state veterinarian speaking with Winchester Cannon and Cannon nodding and the vet moving off. Nikki bolted for Cannon but Matt snagged her by the arm.

"Nothing you can do, gal."

"Let go, damn it." She threw her weight forward and struggled fiercely.

"I'm awful sorry about Donnie, but I'm not letting you blow your school money."

"Let me go, Matt. I'm going to buy him."

He grabbed hold of her other arm and turned her to face him. "The odds of a horse surviving a compound fracture are about a million to one. Infection's a given. You know that."

She stopped struggling. "I've seen horses with prosthetic limbs and they can trot and gallop and everything."

He looked away. "Susan's waiting in the truck."

"Matt, *please!*"

His grip relaxed and Nikki jerked free and spun around. The state vet was standing beside Donnie, the gelding glancing about nervously, his nostrils distended, breath labored. She called out his name. Donnie looked at her and hung his head, as if he was embarrassed to be standing on three legs in the middle of the track, shy of the finish wire, as if he was ashamed, then the vet reached into a jacket pocket and removed a syringe and needle, and the man holding the bridle reins lifted and steadied the gelding's head. Nikki could only watch as the needle penetrated his jugular and he collapsed in a heap to the track.

~

King Donican was buried the next morning. The Wilcoxes, with support from dozens of others, obtained permission from track officials to lay the gelding to rest in the infield. Nikki knew they'd done it for her. And yet she sensed they did it for themselves as well, to appease a lingering guilt over horses they had known or trained or owned or loved or just respected, who had died for the sport, then lay stiff and mangled in the horsemen's parking lot until the rendering truck came. It seemed the least they could do this once.

After the track closed for training, a crowd gathered in the infield and the body was towed on a sled by tractor and pushed into a gaping hole. A light drizzle fell. When the last shovels of dirt were packed down, the drizzle became a downpour and pelted the gathering. Everyone scattered. Walking briskly or running, they bowed their heads against the rain and returned to their barns or the cafeteria or went home. Nikki was the last to leave.

She stood alone with water dripping off her jacket collar and down the back of her neck and her boots sinking into the soft wet earth. She told Donnie she missed him and that she was sorry for letting him down and whispered a prayer of her own making. The rain fell harder. She wanted to cry but something inside her had gone numb. A flash of lightning ignited the sky to the north. She stepped over spongy grass to the tanbark infield pathway and to the edge of the track and slid the hollow pipe of the inside rail shut behind her, then walked quickly across the firm sand. Her bangs hung in wet strands, the rain streaming down her face. She thought about people who viewed Thoroughbreds as running machines, not living, breathing, walking, trotting, galloping, bucking, yawning, snorting, dynamic creatures. Commodities. Slow-witted things of instinct and trust and habit, domesticated and bred for centuries to win races. Not pets. Never friends. She kicked a lone horseshoe that lay in the road and the shoe went skittering across the wet pavement like a skipping stone. She saw now that she had no place in this world, that it was time to move on. How idealistic of her to think that by adhering to her own rules, she could play the game without culpability.

From overhead came the crack of thunder. For an instant, Nikki's imagination jumped into a darker place and there was her mother giving her the finger. Rachel, with her red hair looking as if she'd blow-dried it in a wind tunnel, and her delicate face chiseled out of some flesh-tone substance harder than diamond, just flipping her off.

Peninsula Park
March 1994

Rain fell heavily throughout the first week of the month, turning Peninsula Park's main track into a sloppy mess that was open to workers only, the inside rail blocked off with bright orange traffic cones to prevent the racing lane from becoming rutted and holey and dangerous. Dogs, the cones were called. Rachel found the name appropriate, because if the dogs were up, training was guaranteed to be a bitch. She put on her hat and headed out to track the morning's last galloper, Lucifera.

Classy horses usually didn't require the patience that the gray filly demanded, so Rachel was beginning to think Lucifera too common to amount to more than a cheap claimer. Her rational side advised her to sell Lucifera. She actually wrote an ad to post at one of the local hunter/jumper stables, before she experienced a pride attack that convinced her to toss the ad in the waste basket. Whoever came up with the cliché *pride is for fools* had never purchased a crazy gray filly from a highly competitive, somewhat attractive rival with a penchant for head games. In any case, Rachel saw herself stuck on the Lucifera train wreck until the end of the ride.

The day after scraping off Clint in the rain, the filly had come down with a fever. Following a round of antibiotics and two weeks' rest, Lucifera was set to resume training. When Dr. Steele stopped by the barn to give a number of vitamin shots and scope the lungs of a mare with a wind problem, Rachel had him give Lucifera a shot of tranquilizer in the neck muscle. Acepromazine was strictly a prohibited substance and could not be used for several days before a race, but Rachel had galloped a number of problem horses on the drug with excellent results. Even the wildest animals turned docile with a little relaxation medication.

Lucifera was saddled, then Sam walked her around the sand walking ring. After ten minutes, her gray head hung with droopy-eyed heaviness. Rachel had to smile. When she first began training, she had done minor vet work on her own string to save money and had accidentally given a horse eight cc's of tranquilizer instead of two. The gelding lay down and went to sleep for three solid days, got up with a yawn, and won his next race by five lengths. She sometimes wondered if that mistake wasn't worth repeating but with her present luck, figured she'd end up killing a horse.

Lucifera started out on the training track as gentle as a kid's pony. From the covered trainers' stand, Rachel watched as the filly loped along like a good thing for two laps before uncorking a wicked buck that drove Clint's face into the ground. Two jumps later, she got her long legs tangled and belly flopped.

Someone giggled. Someone else laughed unabashedly. Rachel felt her face growing hot and hurried from the crowded stand before the wisecracks started. Lucifera, now coated with sand and grayer than ever, staggered to her feet with her legs splayed wide behind and crossed in front, looking like a drunken giraffe.

The outrider caught the filly without a chase and Sam led her away, while Rachel waited by the track's entrance for Clint. The gallop boy hobbled over and spit a mouthful of blood, sand, and teeth at her feet. She sent him to the horsemen's dental clinic, then started for the barn. Reno McAllister called out to her from behind, but she kept right on walking.

"I gave her a nine-and-a-half, but what do I know about diving?" he shouted.

"I'm in no mood to hear any of your smart-ass comments," she shouted back, neither turning nor slowing.

His boots pounded the pavement in rapid succession until he arrived at her side, no more winded than a fit horse. She shot him a quick glance.

He grinned. "I could have told you tranquilizer wouldn't work."

"I don't have the slightest idea what you're talking about."

"Bullshit. Filly was practically snoring."

"Whatever. Why don't you make me out a list of things you've already tried?"

"No chance, lady. I'm getting a kick out of watching the filly make someone else look stupid."

Rachel stopped and wheeled to face him. "That was nice, by the way, convincing the stews to nullify your claim on Northern Windsor. Can't believe a bug boy's red jacket smudged with a little black shoe polish was all it took."

Reno gave her a sideways look. "I think Northern Windsor's getting beat by forty-three lengths played a small part in their decision."

"I hope the stews have noticed you're now riding the kid on half your barn," she said. "Talk about gratitude."

"You're just mad 'cause you got caught."

"I'm a little upset, all right. Second best isn't my style, Mr. Leading Trainer."

"Could've fooled me," he said.

She folded her arms. "You plan on rubbing my nose in *that* forever?"

"Probably."

"Figures."

"What'd you expect?"

Rachel reminded herself that she didn't care what he thought and moved to leave. Abruptly, she stopped. "I didn't really sleep with Cortez."

McAllister ran a finger the length of his jawbone. "So?"

She rolled her lips under and out. "When you asked Cortez if he'd went on a date with me, I wanted to wipe that fat grin off your face."

"You were trying to make me jealous?"

"Like hell."

"Wanting me to think you'd slept with my vet?"

"Like hell," she repeated, louder.

He rocked back on his heels. "Be nice, or I won't ask you out."

"In your dreams."

"Pleasurable nightmares."

She did a double take.

He gave a shrug and walked away mumbling to himself.

~

To fill empty stalls left in the wake of the Seth Marten fiasco, Rachel had hauled in seven horses from Oceanstead Farm, a privately owned, public training center where she kept some thirty head under the care of an assistant. Her former client had disappeared off the face of the earth. Lock, stock, and every asset. His wife claimed he skipped out to Argentina, his lawyer named Australia or Costa Rica as possible destinations, but Marten might have been on the moon for all the good it would do Rachel. Her money was gone. She didn't tell anyone what had happened. Even so, word of her misfortune spread more quickly than an exotic strain of the flu.

Near the middle of the month, she went to Hillsborough for dinner at client J.K. Vanderford's home. Afterward, she and J.K. talked in the living room. The Spanish style home was perched on a steep, oak-covered ridge that overlooked a broad ravine. Lights of other houses flickered at scattered intervals in the darkness below, and the rush of a creek swollen with the recent rain could be heard through an open window. J.K. retrieved a bottle of brandy from an antique mahogany liquor cabinet and poured Rachel a glass and one for himself. She sat down on a quilted suede ottoman, while J.K. took a seat on a matching couch.

"I see you've almost regained the lead in the trainers' standings," he said.

"Always nice to win five races in a week," she said.

"Too bad Reno won six."

She rose and went to the window. "I've got till August to catch him."

"Did anything else interesting happen while I was in Maui?"

"Same old crap. If horses were water, my barn would be a sieve, but I did buy a promising two-year-old colt. I could use a partner for the end that eats."

"How much was the colt?"

"Forty grand."

"Ouch," he said. "I thought you were broke."

She turned back to him. "Who told you that?"

"I hear things."

"Mostly bullshit, I'd say."

"Yes, I couldn't imagine you having a thing for a Reno McAllister."

Nervous laughter from Rachel. "Not in this lifetime."

J.K. winked. "Reno *is* a handsome fellow."

She gave him the once-over. "Any heart troubles I suffer will be from too much red meat, ice cream, and cigarettes, thank you."

"Or that gray filly of yours."

Rachel groaned.

"The horse from hell for the trainer from hell," J.K. said, pausing to wink at her again. "Bullshit or not, that filly's antics are the talk of the Turf Club."

"I'm selling her to a golf course in need of a lawnmower that fertilizes."

"You're kidding, right?"

"Actually, Lucifera is acting like a lady and hating every minute of it. Can't say I blame her."

"So you've straightened her out?"

"J.K., I could starch her and never get all the kinks out."

Rachel then explained her latest method of conquering the gray. She had resorted to an old cowboy trick. First, she tied a solid six-inch loop at one end of a stout cotton rope and ran the rope over the filly's withers and around her middle until the loop was hanging beneath her girth. She threaded the other end of the rope through the loop, running the end between Lucifera's forelegs, up her chest, and through the chin ring on her halter. Rachel mounted her pony and snubbed the filly to the saddle horn as before. Right away, Lucifera lunged back and tried to throw herself to the ground, but the rope around her girth tightened — much like having a choke-chain around her belly. A very surprised Lucifera had struggled for a few seconds, then froze straddle-legged with her neck stretched out like a mule's. She took a step toward the pony, the rope went slack, and the pressure about her girth relaxed. Then she exploded again. Three times, Lucifera tested the rope before giving in. The device had eliminated major disasters such as flipping, lying down, and running backward, but Lucifera remained headstrong and indomitable.

"What if the rope breaks when she's pitching a fit?"

"They'll find me and my pony in Sacramento, and Lucifera in the Pacific."

"Dumb question, sorry."

"Did I ever tell you about the time I roped a pig?"

"Not precisely, no."

"When I was a kid our neighbors had a field full of porkers."

"You didn't."

"Damn right. Roped one round the belly and I've got this pig and she's squealing bloody murder and my poor horse, Pete, he's about ready to croak."

"What did you do?"

"I released the dally and that piggie yanked me out of the saddle and dragged me through the filthiest stinking mud hole on the face of the planet."

"And why didn't you simply let go?"

"Father's best rope."

~

The next morning passed uneventfully until a new groom accidentally stuck Lucifera on the hot walker. The filly grabbed the rubber tie in her teeth and raced round and round, faster and faster, towing one other understandably panicked horse at a breakneck pace. Rachel tried to stop the pair, along with Sam and several grooms, but the machine and horses were moving too fast for anyone to snag either of the empty rubber ties without getting trampled in the process. They were attempting to calm Lucifera by shouting the word whoa, when the machine suddenly came apart. All four arms just clunked to the ground. While the one horse cowered trembling among the debris, Lucifera took off, towing a metal arm behind her like a fifteen-foot steel wrecking device until she zipped through a tight spot between the end of a concrete manure box and a support pole for the shed row roof. The walker arm got hung up. Lucifera hit the end of the rubber tie, came to an instantaneous stop, and flew backward as if launched from a slingshot into a huge mound of dirty straw. She emerged gray and green, and stayed filthy, because Rachel was so miffed that she had the filly returned to her stall without a bath.

At noon, Billy Cortez caught up to Rachel after she exited the kitchen with a cup of coffee. "I heard Hurricane Luci raised heck this morning," he said, grinning.

"It wasn't funny." Rachel reached up to pull down the brim of her hat, then remembered she wasn't wearing one.

"Least she didn't hurt anyone or kill herself."

"Yeah, if anyone kills her, it's going to be me."

"Filly okay?"

"Popped a splint." An appropriately descriptive phrase, for along the inside of Lucifera's left cannon bone, about three inches below her knee, was a hard, swollen lump, where the ligament binding the splint bone to her shin had been torn slightly. Rachel had seen complications develop before, but in most instances the lameness disappeared with rest and the leg was as good as new, though a harmless ossified lump would always remain.

"Going to blister the leg?"

She nodded. "I'm sending her out to the farm for sixty days. Why are we talking?"

"I haven't had a chance to thank you for getting my ass reamed by Reno," he said. "Almost lost my job."

"I told him nothing happened."

"Yeah, thanks for that, too. Luckily he's not a big talker so everyone on the backside still thinks I'm a stud." Cortez' made a subtle pumping motion with his hips.

Rachel removed the plastic lid from her cup. "Double standards suck."

"Yeah, that's a bummer you're a middle-aged slut."

"I'm definitely not as hot as you," she said, hurling her coffee at him.

~

An agent by the name of Kyote, an ex-jockey with the physique of a root beer barrel, cornered Rachel outside the race office early the next morning. His round face was all dimples, an entrepreneur of charm with more tricks up his sleeve than a pickpocket. Rachel had named one of his riders on a horse earlier that morning and stopped to talk.

"Better not spin me on Parker's filly," she said.

The agent patted a hand in the general vicinity of his groin area. "I'd sooner cut off a nut than screw the second leading trainer at…one of the top trainers in northern California."

"Listen, you goddamn little gnome, I'll castrate you myself, you don't ride the filly."

"You got first call, Rachel. My top boy, as promised."

"I better have."

"Although there's this little rumor going around that Parkers wanted a chick on their horse."

"Don't start, Kyote."

"This'll just take a minute." The agent shouted at a group of riders on the lawn, and a girl in a hot pink helmet sauntered over. He put a hand on her shoulder in a fatherly manner, then smiled at Rachel. "Meet my new jock. She killed 'em up north, so you got anything that needs the weight off, she can do ten easy."

Rachel stood with her lips parted, studying the girl's face. Her blue eyes, her pleasant features. A familiar face. Or perhaps not.

The girl extended a hand. "Becky Leonard."

Rachel blew out the breath she'd been holding. "You know I don't ride women, Kyote."

The girl, who was chomping on gum, popped a bubble with a crisp snap and withdrew her hand.

"I hear you," the agent said. "Men are stronger and tougher, but this chick's got a way with the ponies."

The girl popped another bubble. "You're a woman, but you don't ride women?"

"I like to win," Rachel said.

"Yeah, you're God's friggin' gift to horse racing," the girl said.

Rachel glared at the girl and she stared back with equal intensity.

The agent stepped between them. "I was just thinking you might give her a shot, Rachel. You know, seeing as I heard you got a daughter."

Rachel tensed, her posture as stiff as quarry in the crosshairs. "You heard wrong."

"*Hello*, lady," the girl said. "Everyone knows you dumped your kid."

"Everyone knows shit," Rachel said, and strode away muttering about people who had nothing better to do than mind her business. By the break, she had fired one of her grooms for saddling the wrong horse, yelled at the rest for various nitpicky mistakes, and chewed Sam out for no good reason whatsoever. She felt more than a little annoyed that she'd left the past behind, yet it managed to get right in her face without actually getting in her face at all. Taking her frustration out on others hadn't helped one bit, but it was irritating as hell to be reminded that the daughter she hadn't raised had become a jockey, of all things—like there weren't a million other careers *not* in the horse racing industry. Less dangerous jobs, for certain. Of course, she wished Nicole the best. Beyond that, Rachel didn't venture because that was a place she didn't belong and probably couldn't even find.

Instead, she downed the remains of a fourth cup of coffee and attributed her ugly mood to a case of hyper stimulated nerves. And spent the rest of the day reminding herself that after twenty years of practice, she knew how to forget.

~

Daylight faded in a pale blue sky, a full moon glowing through a lacework of pink and pinkish blue clouds. The horses in the evening's second race, a six furlong, maiden allowance contest for three-year old colts and geldings, entered the paddock. Trito, the fast dark-brown colt, opened at 40-1. Rachel ran a hand over her tailored suit jacket's breast pocket to feel a wad of fifty hundred-dollar bills. While the wisest horsemen and backstretch aficionados would have guessed that Trito's slow workouts in the *Racing Form* belonged to Northern Windsor, Rachel doubted they'd be willing to bet a fortune on the colt until they'd had a chance to see him run. It turned out she was right. She placed her bets at three different windows and Trito's odds stood at a respectable 12-1 with five minutes until post time. Rachel hurried upstairs to her box.

The room was too small to pace, so she made do with fidgeting from foot to foot and cracking her knuckles. Ginny arrived as the field was loading into the gate. She burst inside and slammed the door, unhappy that she had gotten shut out at the windows. Rachel explained how the owner had insisted she ride a jockey named Vinnie Valentino. She'd instructed Valentino to hustle the colt from the gate and lay near the pace. She told him not to hit Trito—even though she had entered the colt with a no-whip stipulation and the jockey was not carrying one—for she wanted to make it clear to him that the colt was timid and would tuck his tail and sulk if abused. Valentino had told her not to worry.

Trito broke cleanly and settled into third down the backstretch, two lengths off the leaders in the nine-horse field. He began to move after passing the three-eighth's pole. At the top of the stretch, he took the lead and was drawing away when Vinnie Valentino raised a hand and slapped the colt on the neck. Trito rang his tail, ducked left and right, hit the brakes. Four horses swept past. Valentino slapped Trito harder, five, ten, fifteen, twenty times before Rachel quit counting. The colt was barely galloping at the wire.

Rachel ran downstairs in record time and was waiting along the outside fence for Valentino when he dismounted. Without a word, she grabbed the kid by the collar of his silks and yanked him off his feet until only the tips of his toes brushed the ground. Then she let go and Valentino stumbled backward and fell on his butt.

"I told you not to hit him, you fucking idiot," she shouted.

Valentino had nothing to say. He scrambled up and darted toward the Jockeys' Room. Rachel was stomping through the winner's circle on her return to the grandstand, bumping anyone who failed to give her a wide enough berth, when the clerk of scales summoned her to the phone. The stewards, calling from their booth atop the grandstand, wanted to hear her version of the altercation they had just witnessed. She thought the jock was packing a twelve-volt battery, Rachel explained, heavy on the sarcasm.

The stewards were not amused. She was told to be in their office at eleven sharp the following morning. Her face was becoming an all too familiar sight, they went on to say. Perhaps they should purchase a wooden paddle laced with holes if she persisted in misbehaving. Rachel slammed the receiver down and went upstairs to the Newmarket Pub, found an empty table at the back of the room, ordered a shot of Scotch, and sat facing the wall. Heels clicked the floor like castanets, the sound growing louder, then Ginny sat down beside her, gasping to catch her breath. Rachel downed her whiskey, coughed, and ordered another. Ginny cleared her throat.

"Who were you talking to on the phone, dear?"

"The F.B.I."

"You've committed a felony?" Ginny put a hand over her heart and looked as if she might faint.

"F.B.I.," Rachel said, fumbling for a suitable f-word. "The

Fatheaded Board of Idiots."

"Who?"

"The stewards."

"You're in trouble again? A thousand for working a ringer in place of Northern Windsor, fifty for not wearing a helmet, one hundred for galloping the wrong way on the training track...." Ginny marked previous offenses on a napkin with an eyebrow pencil. "Pretty soon the track will be sponsoring a Rachel Nottingham Charity Purse and you'll be stabling your horses on Alcatraz Island."

Ginny was a real marvel at cheering up a situation, Rachel thought, and inhaled deeply on an unlit cigarette and studied a painting of Black Gold on the wall. In junior high, she'd read the Marguerite Henry story and knew the 1924 Kentucky Derby winner had sired but one foal, a colt who was struck and killed by lightning. She reached for her whiskey, but Ginny slid the glass to her side of the table and out of reach.

"Do you mind?" Rachel crushed her unlit cigarette in an ashtray.

Ginny looked on with a patient expression. "I'm a good listener."

"I don't know what you're talking about."

"If your conscience were any guiltier, it'd be on death row."

"Give me my drink back."

"No."

"Give it back. Please."

"No."

"Don't make me recite client/trainer boundaries, again."

"Piddle. I'm your friend and that's that."

"More like the booze police."

"As your friend, I'm obligated to tell you that you've got a problem."

Rachel blew a breath through her bangs.

"Talking helps," Ginny said.

Rachel blew another breath through her bangs. "A few months ago I got real drunk and announced to a roomful of people, predominantly racetrackers, that I'd had a child.

Satisfied?"

Ginny was nodding. "The tequila guzzling incident."

"You've heard?"

"The biddies in the Turf Club said you couldn't possibly be a mother."

Rachel allowed herself a quick grin. "I knew nobody'd believe me."

"Then it's true, dear?"

She glanced left, then right, then down. Swallowed hard. "It's not really my favorite topic."

"Can't imagine why."

"I thought I was doing the right thing."

"I'm a good listener," Ginny repeated.

Rachel fiddled with her nails. In her mind, she condensed the facts, starting when her father had died and she took a job grooming horses at the old racetrack, south of San Francisco that predated Peninsula Park. After six months of living in a dusty tack room, she started dating a bleach-blond rich boy, who moved her and Nicole into his ritzy Nob Hill apartment. Rachel considered omitting the parts where he'd slapped her around, except that she'd endured the abuse for her daughter's sake, which, she figured, basically cancelled out her bad judgment in the men department. Until the night Nicole became the object of his rage. From there on out, everything started to sound incriminating. Rachel ran her hands over her face.

"I don't even know what went wrong," she finally said.

"Sometimes, things just happen, dear."

Rachel motioned toward the whiskey. Ginny slid the shot glass across the table. Rachel tipped her head back and emptied the glass, took a breath through her teeth and waited for the burning in her throat to subside. The whiskey buzzed in her head and loosened all the locks to the doors to the room with the safe that held her emotional baggage. Her lips begin to quiver.

Ginny reached across the table and squeezed Rachel's hand. She bit her lip. Then she told Ginny the whole story.

Westover Meadows
April 1994

Nikki found a job waiting tables. By her fourth day at Fast Freddie's, a popular truck stop cafe, the odor of bacon and eggs had become nauseating. She paused long enough to pop a breath mint into her mouth, then delivered three breakfast specials. The racetrackers began to show up around ten-thirty. They requested to sit in her section and encouraged her to return to Westover Meadows, same as they had done each day since she'd left the track. Nikki couldn't honestly say whether she missed the faces or the horses or any of it.

She finished wiping and resetting a table as the hostess guided over another customer. Matt Wilcox tipped his straw hat and smiled. Nikki brought him a cup of coffee and tried to smile back, but her mouth refused to cooperate. Between working and studying, she'd kept to herself and hadn't seen either of the Wilcoxes in a week.

Matt blew on the coffee. "Can you spare ten minutes?"

The morning rush had waned and the restaurant was half empty. She slid into the booth across from him. "I have a break coming."

"Didn't think you were serious when you called and quit Monday afternoon."

"I was."

"You okay?"

"I'm fine. You and Susan?"

"We're gettin' by."

He took a drink of coffee. "What's done is done, gal. I feel bad as anyone."

Nikki ran her tongue along the inside of her cheek like a pitcher nursing a wad of chew. Her shaggy bangs, the color of wheat straw sprouting from darker roots, hung in her eyes. "The check would've bounced," she said. "I only have twenty-seven hundred dollars."

"I didn't come here to rub your nose in it."

She counted to ten in her head before answering. "It was my goddamn money and you had no right to decide whether I should or shouldn't have spent it. You had no right."

"You were making a foolish mistake. Suzy and I thought…"

"You had no right, Matt."

"I knew you were short," he said. "I'd have gotten stuck covering the difference, and I don't have money to spare."

Nikki propped an elbow on the table and cupped a hand to her forehead like a visor. "You know damn well I'd have paid you back."

He picked up his cup and swirled the coffee around and around. Took another drink. "You plan on staying mad forever?"

"I'm only mad at me."

"What for?"

"Doesn't matter."

"Sure it does, gal."

She lowered her hand and looked at him. "I worked there. I stood by and did nothing."

"Wasn't your fault. No one could've saved Donnie."

"That's just crap. That's how everyone at the racetrack appeases their guilty consciences."

"The odds of saving him were a million to one. You and I both know the vet won't put down a horse in front of the grandstand unless it's hurt awful bad."

"There was still a chance."

"Make that a billion to one. Would've cost a fortune to even try."

"I meant before the race," Nikki said, and stared out the window. "There's this person who has money, and she probably wouldn't have given me the time of day, let alone a dollar, but I was too proud to ask. Can we leave it?"

Matt finished his coffee. A woman shouted for her check and Nikki scooted from the booth. She delivered the bill, then filled water glasses before returning.

"Bet you're raking in a small fortune in tips," Matt said, grinning.

She eyed him balefully. "After they take out taxes, social security, and who-knows-what-else, I'll probably owe the restaurant money."

"The Westover Derby's in two weeks and Fuzzy stands a real decent shot. A hundred grand's a small fortune. I don't have to tell you we all could use it."

The hostess walked over and told her to get back to work.

Nikki slid from the booth. "I've decided the world's made up of three kinds of people—the fuckers, the fuckees, and those who live in mental hospitals."

Matt kneaded his chin between a thumb and forefinger. "Come back and ride Fuzzy in the Derby."

"Get some other jock."

"Colt thinks you're the greatest thing since blackstrap molasses."

"He'll run for anyone."

"He's gone off his feed since you left."

"Bull. Fuzzy's a garbage disposal."

"He *has* been awful quiet."

"Toss him some carrots."

"In a single race, you can make what it'd take six months to earn here. College ain't cheap."

"I'll scrimp by."

"Never figured you for a quitter, gal."

"I'm not quitting," she said. "I'm retiring."

Matt shrugged. "Same difference."

"I'm *not* a quitter."

"Could've fooled me."

Nikki glanced across the room to where the hostess and the manager had gathered to cast her malevolent looks. She unfastened her apron and laid it in a rumpled heap on the table. "I just want to make as much money as fast as I can and get out."

"Can't say I blame you."

"Don't expect me to go around smiling all the time."

"Wouldn't dream of it."

~

The next day, she galloped her first horse before daylight. By seven, the sun was shining brightly and Nikki had stripped to the cotton tank top she wore over her sport bra. Agent Kurt Kaiser fell in beside her as she was walking between barns. She folded her arms.

"Still thinking of riding at Peninsula Park?" he asked.

"No," she told him and meant it.

"That's where I'm heading, so if you need an agent..."

She cut him off. "I'm not going."

"We could have dinner at Fisherman's Wharf."

"No thanks," she said.

"Watch the sun set from the Golden Gate Bridge. Share an apartment. To cut expenses," he added, bobbing his eyebrows.

She stopped walking. "Kurt, if a disease were to come along and wipe out every male on the face of the earth but you, I'd become a lesbian."

"I'd be delirious. I could charge a stud fee."

"You're a creep."

Kaiser laughed. "I'm hurt."

"Yeah, I can tell. Are you on drugs or something?"

"I'm a little high, all right. Just got the call on a colt who'll be the big favorite in the Westover Meadows Derby. It's shipping up from Peninsula Park."

Nikki tensed from the inside out. "For who?"

"Rachel Nottingham. Top trainer in northern California. Wins everything."

"I know who she is," Nikki said, feeling as though her stomach had been pitched off a skyscraper.

The agent rubbed his hands. "When Nottingham saddles one, bet the farm."

"I don't have a farm."

"So bet a hundred."

Nikki swatted a yellow-jacket and the bug plunged to the ground like a shot fighter. "She flying up for the Derby?"

"Long as the horse comes, who the hell cares?"

~

Entries for the Westover Meadows Derby were drawn on Friday morning. Nikki went home after the races that evening and read Sunday's edition of the form while eating a package of red licorice. Captain Fuzzy was listed at odds of 10-1. Neither of the local favorites—Winchester Cannon's big colt, Klamath Mammoth, nor trainer Cliff Fernandez's charge, Simara—was the handicapper's choice. That distinction went to the California invader, Royal Master, who was shipping up from Rachel Nottingham's stable. Nikki studied the past performance charts, but the figures registered without significance, revealing no potential strategies whatsoever.

A clock on the kitchen wall clicked as the hands hit midnight. One of the top local riders, Troy Yarrow, was slated to ride Royal Master. To see another jockey's name next to her mother's entrant in the Westover Meadows Derby made Nikki feel strange inside, a mean-spirited sensation, emanating from an unfamiliar place in her heart that she envisioned as dank and completely lightless. She closed the form. Rachel's unsmiling photo graced the front page, the shot revealing a mixture of arrogance, ire, and beauty, which seemed to validate Nottingham's reputation throughout the racing world as a well-authenticated bitch.

Nikki stared at the photograph. From a physical standpoint, they were unquestionably mother and daughter, possessing similar blue eyes and high cheekbones, though Nikki saw herself as a much plainer replica. After a minute, she tossed the paper aside. She made a mental note to have her hair bleached again, then went to her desk and dug out a newspaper article from five years ago.

The article recounted how Rachel Nottingham had trained one of the top three-year old colts on the West Coast, until he broke a knee as the favorite in a prep race for the California Derby. Rumors abounded. The colt had been sore. She trained him too hard. She never should have run him. When his post-race blood sample tested for the permitted painkiller phenylbutazone at double the maximum allowed amount, it seemed to substantiate the gossip. Nottingham *knew* the colt was unsound. There was talk of fraud. One of her former grooms alleged the colt came up a wobbler a month before the fatal race. Wobbler disease affected the cervical spinal cord and vertebrae of horses and was marked by progressively worse coordination. The disease was sporadic, the cause unknown, and very few horses who contracted it ever recovered. The same groom swore Nottingham had the colt injected with cortisone several times to conceal the symptoms. The article accused her of making no effort to save the colt. He was sound enough to be loaded into the horse ambulance and driven to his barn, yet was destroyed by the trainer's veterinarian less than an hour after the race. The colt had been heavily insured and the three partners in ownership collected a half-million dollars. One was Nottingham.

Nikki returned the article to her desk, then went back to the kitchen table and handicapped the Derby with careful deliberation, concluding that Captain Fuzzy measured up with the California colt. For the first time, she really wanted to win the Westover Meadows Derby

~

On Saturday, she finished last in the third race, her lone mount on the card. Afterward, she tossed her saddle and girths to her valet, pulled off her helmet, and headed for the women's room. Smoke greeted her as she opened the door. Rita sat on the sink counter with a cigarette dangling from her lips, while Kris and Brenda occupied the couch, one reading a copy of *Penthouse*, the other a fashion magazine. Nikki threw her helmet into the sink with a loud bang.

"What the?" A startled Rita jumped from the counter.

Nikki walked over. "Stop smoking in here, okay?"

Rita took a drag and blew out forcefully in Nikki's face. "Make me."

The smoke caused her eyes to water and she blinked hard. "Why do you have to be a bitch?"

"Up yours."

Nikki didn't say a word. Instead, she wheeled and went out the door, returning in seconds with the bucket of water used to clean sand-encrusted whips after each race. She lifted the bucket and dumped the gritty gray liquid over Rita's head, drenching her, cigarette and all. Rita exploded with a wild swing toward Nikki's head that sent water spraying, but the blow missed by over a foot. Rita fired a second punch. Nikki ducked, then leaped into Rita, grabbed her around the neck and wrestled her to the floor. Rita scratched and clawed, but Nikki pinned her down with a knee to the stomach and drew back her right fist and took dead aim. At the last instant she let her arm go limp, got up as if Rita did not exist, and walked from the room.

~

Sunday dawned warmer still. The track was dry and fast, the sand heavily watered and firm. Nikki was scheduled to ride only the ninth and feature event, the Westover Meadows Derby, but arrived at the Jockeys' Room before the first race left the gate. The Derby was a handicap for three-year olds and the Racing Secretary had assigned weights, giving Captain Fuzzy 112 pounds. Matt and Susan claimed not to care if Fuzzy packed a few extra pounds, but Nikki wanted every advantage. She set the hot box to 300 degrees, filled the pan inside with water, put a clean towel over the seat, closed the door and threw another towel over the hole. After ten minutes, she stripped and climbed in, wrapping the towel on top around her neck before closing the door. She was starting to feel uncomfortably hot, when Kris walked into the room with a bag of fresh popcorn.

"How much you have to drop?" she asked.

"Four pounds."

"Does my eating bug you? I can go outside if it does."

"Naw," Nikki said. "I'm only thirsty."

"If Rita waltzes in popping a cold can of soda, I'll smack her for you."

"I'd appreciate it."

"No problem."

"Could you turn the temperature down to two hundred, please?"

"Sure." Kris did.

Nikki ran a hand over her stomach, feeling her skin slick and wet. She leaned her head against the towels and resigned herself to sitting in an oven. "Wish I was five inches shorter."

"No you don't," Kris said. "I'd kill to be taller than four-foot eleven."

"You're just the right size," Nikki said. "I'm always bumping my head on shed row roofs or galloping green horses with my knees in my face because there aren't enough holes in the stirrup leathers."

Kris grinned. "At least horses at Westover Meadows usually have plenty of mane to hang onto."

"Unless it rips out in your hand." Nikki lifted her head and shifted it to the other side. "On second thought, I wish I was five inches taller."

"You'd never make weight."

"Yeah."

In three hours, Nikki dropped the four pounds, getting out every twenty minutes to take a cold shower. She dressed and resumed watching the races from the top bunk, hoping to spot a bias in the track surface that might work to her advantage. Between races, she closed her eyes but didn't sleep. No one seemed to know whether or not Rachel Nottingham had flown up to saddle Royal Master. By late afternoon, Nikki ran out of people to ask.

The field for the Derby was led over from the stable area at five o'clock. Eight-thousand fans filled the grandstand at Westover Meadows. Spectators pressed into the concrete and chain link barrier surrounding the paddock and lined the fence along the track until hardly an empty patch of space was visible. The owners of horses in the race watched from a private area partitioned off exclusively for the Derby. Some were decked out in furs and three-piece suits with gold and diamond jewelry, while others were dressed in their best jeans and sport shirts.

The trainers saddled their charges, put on tongue ties, straightened saddle towels, tightened nosebands, adjusted bridles, and eyed the competition with an intensity meant to convey expertise. When the jockeys came in, the trainers greeted their riders with big handshakes and bigger smiles. Captain Fuzzy's stall was two down from Royal Master's and Nikki saw that the California colt reeked of class. From the snippet of white on the end of his nose to the tip of his long black tail, he was a finely tuned athlete. Nikki raised onto her tiptoes for a better view. A gangly young man with short-cropped blond hair stood talking to the colt's jockey. Rachel was nowhere to be seen.

Matt rapped his knuckles on Nikki's helmet. "Have you heard a word I've told you?"

"There's plenty of speed, so lay off the pace and make one run down the stretch," she said, repeating his instructions.

He gave her a long look. "That California horse can flat fly. Nottingham wouldn't have shipped him this far if he couldn't."

"So she can train a fast horse. Big deal." Nikki tapped her whip against her boot in a machine-gun beat.

Matt gave her another long look. His navy slacks and white shirt were neatly pressed, though the latter sported a green goober, care of Fuzzy. Susan, also suitably horsy in ruby red jeans and a Western shirt and vest, stroked the colt's neck and told him that he was the greatest thing on four legs.

The paddock judge called for riders up.

Matt slapped Nikki on the back. "Give it your best shot,

gal. That's all a man can ask."

"See you in the winner's circle," she said.

~

Twenty-one minutes later, the bell rang and the field for the
Westover Meadows Derby charged from the gate and past the
grandstand. Captain Fuzzy rated kindly and galloped into the
clubhouse turn lying fifth. Seven lengths ahead, Royal Master
and Klamath Mammoth led as a team. Nikki hoped they would
set rapid fractions and burn each other out.

As it happened, the pace was honest, if not quite blazing.
Midway around the far turn, the colt lying a length ahead of
Captain Fuzzy, Simara, felt the sting of the whip, rang his
chestnut tail, and stretched out for more ground. Nikki
followed. She lowered her body tight to Fuzzy's withers,
clucked, and he shifted gears and flew through a hole on the
rail in close pursuit. Klamath Mammoth puked at the quarter
pole. Simara and Katt Dancer sped past Winchester Cannon's
tiring colt and reduced the local favorite to a fading blur of
orange silks, then Simara was racing beside her and Royal
Master in front and nothing else mattered but winning—only
winning—beating Rachel Nottingham's horse, beating the most
famous, successful, talented, respected, unarguably despised
horsewoman in the country. Nikki's mother, the bitch. Nothing
else mattered.

Nikki shouted to Fuzzy and urged him onward with her
voice and pumped the reins along his neck in a furious but
ordered rhythm. The colt quickened stride. His hooves
skimmed the firm wet sand, his breath coming quicker. She
flagged him with her whip and hit him once and felt him
straining beneath her, then they drew away from Simara and
closed on the leader. An eighth of a mile remained. Fuzzy
flattened his ears and dug in. Stride by stride, he gained on
Royal Master, but the California colt fought to maintain an
advantage, with his jockey whipping right handed, then left,
then right, back humping, body twisting, the crack of leather

on glistening flesh muted by the roar from the grandstand when Fuzzy pulled alongside at the sixteenth pole.

The pair barreled the final half-furlong as one. Head and head, they battled, Captain Fuzzy on the inside, Royal Master on the outside, every tendon, every ligament, every bone, straining to reach the finish first. Nikki shouted to Fuzzy. Her thighs and calves burned with fatigue and her arms grew heavy until there was only Fuzzy, the other horse, and the wire. Fuzzy inching ahead in slow motion, sticking his nose in front. Fuzzy and the wire. The wire and nothing more.

A dozen strides from the finish, Royal Master drove his shoulder into Captain Fuzzy and bumped him hard. Fuzzy shoved back. Royal Master's jockey slashed his mount right handed, sawed on the inside rein, and forced the colt to lie on Fuzzy, crowding him into the rail. Nikki felt her boot scraping metal. She swung her whip high and knifed the crack of daylight between black manes, then with a flash of the photo finish camera the pair crossed under the wire. Fuzzy came up a head short. Nikki rose in the irons.

Right away, she spotted Royal Master's mouth, lathered with blood, frothy and pink, and without hesitation she laid into the colt's jockey, lashed his back, his ass, his helmet, struck him hard seven or eight times. She could never recall being so angry.

~

Captain Fuzzy and Royal Master reached the unsaddling area at the same time. As their respective grooms took hold of each horse, Nikki and the other jockey dismounted and charged toward one another. The valets were quick to restrain the furious pair. Nikki demanded to claim a foul and was escorted to the phone by the scale. The head steward informed her that she had earned a visit to his office first thing Wednesday morning for her display of poor sportsmanship after the race, then scolded her for losing her temper. Nikki slammed down the phone. The announcer broadcast her claim of foul and proclaimed Royal Master the unofficial winner of the race by a head. The colt's jockey remounted for the picture, while Susan led Fuzzy toward the test barn.

"Goldilocks fucked up," jockey Willie Redfield shouted as he weighed out.

One of the valets had to grab Nikki again. She almost smiled when the leading rider and perpetrator of jocks' room mischief, Joe Garcia, tripped Redfield as he stepped off the scale. Matt charged onto the track then, swearing he planned to sue if the California colt's number didn't come down. He told Nikki she'd done fine and not to worry. She waited with him by the scale and watched the celebration in the winner's circle— Rachel's smiling assistant trainer and her wealthy clients and their high-priced colt—and knew the race was a lost cause. Sure enough, it took less than a minute for the announcer to declare the claim of foul not allowed and the results of the race official. A record amount of money had been wagered to win on Royal Master. The infraction was hard to detect with certainty on the pan shot of the race, and the head-on replay was not shown. Nikki watched from the Jockeys' Room.

"You got screwed big time," Kris said, after the re-run had concluded.

Brenda's head bobbed in agreement. "The stewards are, like, legally blind."

Nikki stared at the floor as though plotting a new route to China. Kris and Brenda headed out early to ride the last race and gave Nikki her space. Alone in the room, her thoughts loomed vengeful and ugly. She made an effort to think about something else but could think of *nothing* else. In the span of a few short weeks, Rachel had come to represent everything Nikki despised about horse racing—the win-at-any-cost mentality, the inequities, the cruelty. She dropped to the floor and pressed her face into her knees.

After a few minutes, a copy of Sunday's form caught her attention. Someone had drawn a mustache over Rachel's photograph, a thick blue-ink slash of a handlebar mustache on her upper lip. Feeling sudden compassion for the mother she wanted to hate, Nikki grabbed the doodled over picture, spit on her fingertip, and gently tried to erase the marking, but the paper ripped. In a panic of sorts, she attempted to mend the tear by spitting directly on the paper, which had the opposite effect and created a hole where the lower half of her mother's face had been, leaving only the top of her head and eyes. Mortified, Nikki fell still.

She was staring vacantly at the paper, when something about her mother's mangled photo prompted a closer look. A squinting Nikki drew the paper nearer. In short order, she came to an unhappy conclusion, sprang to her feet, and crumpled the racing form, hurling it at the wastebasket on the other side of the room. The eyes in the photo were her own.

~

The stewards suspended Nikki for the final two weeks of the Westover Meadows race meeting. She did not appeal their ruling. True to his word, Matt had contested the Derby finish — as was his prerogative, being Captain Fuzzy's owner — and the case was scheduled to go before the Oregon State Racing Commission at the end of the month. When the meet ended, he asked her to accompany him and Susan and the horses to Canada for the summer or to stay behind and house-sit their farm and farm horses until September. Nikki considered her options. The Wilcoxes cornered her for an answer the next morning.

"You going or staying, gal?" Matt asked.

Nikki picked straw from a bandage she was rolling and didn't answer.

"All done riding?" Susan's long hair was tied back under a yellow bandanna and lime dusted the front of her jeans.

Nikki turned away.

"That a yes?" Susan asked.

Matt shook his head. "Suzy, when someone doesn't want to talk about something, can't you take a hint?"

"No. I mean yes, but..."

"Just drives you women nuts, don't it? Always having to know everyone's biggest secrets. Why, Suzy can recite my Uncle Hubert-from-Alberta's shoe size in her sleep."

Susan stuck out her tongue at Matt. "Fifteen double wide. How could I forget those surfboards?"

Nikki turned back around. "I'll watch the farm for you this summer, but first I'm going to California for a few days."

"How come?" Matt and Susan asked at the same time.

Looking at both of them and neither of them, Nikki explained her predicament. Her voice stuck in her throat and came out in pieces and sounded like someone else talking.

"When I was a kid, my mother left me with relatives. I haven't seen her in twenty years. She acts like I don't exist. Like she never had a daughter. I have some things to say to her, whether she wants to hear or not."

Nikki didn't tell them her mother was a horse trainer. She did not tell them her mother was Rachel Nottingham.

Peninsula Park
April 1994

Nikki drove more than eleven hours before she stopped in Redding, California, for something other than gasoline. She pulled into a deli, bought a cup of coffee and a chocolate-chip cookie, then stretched and walked back and forth along the front of the store until her butt quit aching. The air was hot and dry and crackled with insect chatter. Atop the roof, a crow cawed. A woman wearing knee-high English riding boots and hunt pants exited the deli, towing a young girl by the hand. Nikki flung the remains of her cookie at the bird, got back on the freeway, and drove south. Portland seemed like another lifetime.

A few hours later, "California, here I come, right back where I started from," was echoing in her head like some awful commercial ditty, over and above a Nirvana tape. Nikki turned up the volume. She drove across the Bay Bridge singing her own version of "Smells like Teen Spirit," with the Golden Gate Bridge rising like an apparition from the dusk haze of the western skyline. She continued past San Francisco and south on the Bayshore Freeway, reaching Peninsula Park in forty minutes. The parking lot was empty, the races over for the day.

Where her mother might be, Nikki had no idea, so she decided to put off confronting Rachel until morning and stopped at the first motel that displayed a vacancy sign—a cramped row of blistered pink units, replete with cockroaches, cigarette-burned furniture, and the all-pervading smell of curry. Nikki paid for a room and wrestled a suitcase from the trunk of her car. She paused to consider her riding tack, which she had thrown in as well, then cussed her foolishness and tucked the canvas duffel bag behind a spare tire and under a toolbox.

For the next hour, Nikki gazed blankly at an open veterinary textbook. When her stomach began to growl, she went in search of the nearest restaurant, walking for blocks along the four-lane thoroughfare by the motel before coming to a diner with a giant red-white-and-blue chicken on the roof. A waitress showed her to the counter, seating her at a stool next to a middle-aged woman in a neatly pressed polyester pantsuit.

The woman smiled. "Nice young lady such as yourself shouldn't be eating alone."

Nikki opened the menu. "I'm from Oregon."

"On vacation?"

"No."

"Staying long?"

"No, I've got school on Monday. I'm just here to see my mother." The words sounded strange to Nikki and her stomach did a flip flop. For an instant, she had no idea what she planned to say to Rachel or why she'd come at all, then the feeling passed.

The woman kept talking. "Your mother's very lucky."

Nikki looked up from the menu. "How's that?"

"She has a loving daughter who's traveled a long way to visit her."

"It's no big deal, really."

"Oh, but it is."

"But it's not, really."

"I haven't seen my daughter since she moved to New Zealand, over six years ago," the woman said.

Her face seemed to age with a sadness that deflated her entirely. Nikki wanted to say something but sat in silence while the stranger got up, paid her bill, and left the restaurant. Nikki wondered if Rachel ever felt saddened by what she'd done. Those who knowingly brought pain to others were often incapable of feeling sorry for anyone but themselves, so it stood to reason that if Rachel had any regrets, they were self-centered in nature. At any rate, Nikki doubted her mother had ever uttered the words lucky and daughter in the same sentence.

By the time Nikki's food came, she'd lost her appetite. She

ate a few bites of a turkey sandwich, then had it wrapped to go. She returned to her motel room and went to bed. A wind-up alarm clock ticked on the nightstand. She closed her eyes and anticipated lying awake, but fell asleep within minutes.

Sometime in the night, she awoke hot and sticky to toss the covers aside and sit up, sniffing as a drop of sweat rolled from the tip of her nose. The room was dark and had an ominous, claustrophobic feel that settled over her like a pine box. She assured herself she was no longer dreaming, though the dream had implanted itself in her head and she didn't see herself forgetting anytime soon. The gist of it was short and to the point. She had jumped off the Golden Gate Bridge. And felt herself falling, plunging through nothing, sprawling downward, waiting to hit water, expecting to hit water, never hitting anything, then she looked up and saw her mother at the rail looking down. Rachel was laughing.

~

At Peninsula Park, a farrier shod Lucifera in the shed row. The filly's popped splint had healed soundly and a small calcified lump on the inside of her left foreleg was all that remained of the injury. After returning from her lay-up at the farm, Lucifera had quickly re-established herself near the top of Rachel's worry list. Money occupied the top rung. She owed money for bills, needed money to claim horses, to buy horses, to win. In retrospect, she could see that her misfortune had begun last summer with the sale of the best colt in her barn, Speedmeister Slew, and had snowballed ever since. Her clients were hesitant to sink more money into a barn winning fewer races than usual, which had forced her to run horses over their heads to prevent them from being claimed, lest they not be replaced. But running horses for too high of a tag meant stiffer competition, fewer wins, and unhappy clients, who then threatened to take their business elsewhere. So she ran horses where they could win and lost them. Either way, she ended up with empty stalls.

The money that Seth Marten cheated her out of had

crippled her operating budget. At a time when she ought to be employing aggressive tactics, she was forced to play defensively, which kept her stuck in second place in the trainer standings. Only the memory of her father losing the family ranch kept her from mortgaging her half-million-dollar San Mateo condominium. She needed to find clients who would give her a long leash and lots of cash, but selling herself was an art she'd never quite mastered. She contemplated her options as she held Lucifera in the shed row. Something would come to her, Rachel felt confident, but nothing did, at least nothing practical or legal. The shoer clipped the nails of the filly's right front shoe with his nippers and tossed the shoe aside. He released her foot and slowly straightened, until he only vaguely resembled a hunchback. Rachel thought she should make an effort to pay attention.

"Leave plenty of heel," she told him. "You know how I hate long toes and short heels."

"Yeah, yeah. 'Long toes cripple sound horses and don't make 'em go no faster,'" he said.

"Just shoe the horse, please," she said.

He picked up Lucifera's right front hoof and proceeded to trim it. "Heard this filly's a dirty, rotten sow."

"I've trained worse."

The shoer reached for his rasp. "I bet not."

"I'm trying to stay positive."

"Bucks, huh?"

"Among other things."

"Get'cha a cowboy. These racetrack boys don't know shit about broncs."

"I'll train the horses around here, Leroy, if that's okay by you," she said.

The shoer inhaled with a rumbling snort and spit out a phlegm projectile that missed her boot toe by inches. With only the slightest crimping of her nose, she stepped on the spot and ground her boot into the shed row dirt, then took a closer look as the shoer cut away black tissue embedded in healthy white hoof where the abscess had been. It had fully healed, along with the abscess in Lucifera's left front foot. When the shoer finished, Rachel returned the filly to her stall and followed the sound of happy horse commotion to the other side of the barn. Ginny was feeding her two horses pieces of apples, and they were very actively vying for her attention.

"Dammit, Ginny, they're going to hurt themselves and stir up the rest of the barn," Rachel said.

"Next time, I'll have their grooms mix it into their grain, I promise," Ginny said, while holding up an empty plastic bag for the horses to see. "No more goodies. All gone."

The horses continued to paw and nicker.

Rachel groaned. "I need a drink."

"Whiskey isn't going to solve your problems."

"A soft drink, Ginny."

She eyed Rachel's cotton polo shirt, which was darker under her armpits. "Oh. You *have* worked up quite a sweat."

"Liquid humiliation. I broke Luci off from my pony, hoping to get a three-eighths breeze in her, but she stuck her toes in the ground and launched her rider a half-furlong from the wire. The boy went like a rocket in thirty-five and two."

"Oh, my. He okay?"

"Busted a collar bone."

"Jim Bruner?"

"No. Some struggling apprentice, desperate for a shot. I gave him one all right. A moon shot."

"I thought Luci was training at the farm?"

"She was, but I had to send a sick one out and needed a horse to fill the stall until I claim another. Stalls are tight. Leave one empty and by morning you'll have a horse in it. Someone else's."

"Perhaps you should wait until Reno McAllister has an empty stall, then sneak over in the middle of the night and put Luci in it."

Rachel's expression momentarily brightened. "That's a possibility. Yesterday she nailed a thick-necked gallop boy who looked capable of surviving a fall from the Empire State Building. I don't dare risk Clint or Jose anymore. Good help's *ten days*

too hard to find."

"I'm sure Luci will come around, dear."

"Yeah, maybe if I stack a case of dog food outside her stall."

Ginny shuddered. "What about hiring one of those animal psychiatrists," she said, totally serious.

"I'm not even going to comment on that one," Rachel said. "Think maybe I will get me a cowboy."

~

Nikki's alarm clock rang at four-thirty the following morning, but she was already up and dressed. At five-thirty, she showed her Oregon jockey's license to the guard at Peninsula Park's main stable gate. The guard made her sign in and gave her a guest pass, then explained that the licensing office of the California Horse Racing Board opened at eight and was located just north of the race office. She told him she didn't plan on staying. He advised her not to be galloping any horses without a California license and gave her Oregon one a last look. Recognition spread across his face.

"You're the jock that thumped on Nottingham's horse in that race up north."

"I whacked the jockey, not the horse," she said.

"Hell, you did. I've heard more than one trainer mention starting a collection to pay your fine."

"The stewards gave me five days instead."

"Time's money. Too bad you're not staying."

"How's that?"

"The leading trainer's main boy went down yesterday and broke his leg. He and Nottingham are big enemies. Bet Reno would ride you on a horse or two, seeing how he's short a jock." The guard chuckled at his accidental pun. "Short—jockey. Get it?"

Nikki listened without expression. "Which barn is Rachel Nottingham stabled in?"

"Barn twenty-eight," he said, shaking his head. "She'll never ride you. Nottingham never rides women."

"I wouldn't ride a horse for her for a million bucks," Nikki told the guard before walking away.

The sky was growing lighter and a world painted in shades of gray and black became gradually infused with color. She followed the white numbers stenciled on the end of each barn, which led her to the gap and past the kitchen and farther. She walked swiftly and gathered her grievances like someone collecting wood to stoke a fire until barn 28 came into view. At the sound of a long-ago familiar voice, she froze, watching as a dapple gray was led out from under a shed row and onto the road, followed by a woman in black chaps and a gaucho hat, who sat astride a black Western saddle adorned with silver on a black saddle horse. The anger in Nikki's heart flared briefly, more gas flame than wildfire, then died out altogether. She drew in a sharp breath.

This beautiful woman in black was her mother.

~

"There's no room for carelessness in a business where a person can do everything right and still have a hundred things go wrong," Rachel had told Sam a few minutes earlier.

Right before she'd mounted her ponyhorse without checking to see if the girth needed tightening.

Now she rode in from behind, dallied Lucifera, and started toward the training track to pony the riderless filly three miles in hopes of burning some of the energy that fueled her misbehavior. They had not gone far when the filly reared, sucked back, and slung herself from side to side. Anticipating such behavior, Rachel had dallied Lucifera to the saddle horn with a cotton rope around the filly's belly. When the rope tightened, Luci quit struggling and leaped into the pony, but not before Rachel's saddle had slipped lopsidedly to the right. She threw her weight into the left stirrup to compensate. Lucifera detected an advantage and lunged back again. In one swift motion, Rachel's saddle plunged beneath her pony.

~

Nikki tipped her head sideways and took in the entire scene. Her mother released the dally as she fell, and the gray raced off, the sound of her hooves clattering over the pavement. For several seconds, Rachel hung completely inverted beneath her pony, then she kicked free of the stirrups, rolled out from under the black horse, and climbed to her feet. The pony stood trembling. She stroked his neck and spoke to him gently, waving away her assistant trainer and four grooms. She worked quickly to unfasten the heavy saddle and hoist it back in place and re-cinch it, then punched the dents from her crumpled hat, brushed off the seat of her pants, and remounted. The loose horse was nowhere in sight. She turned her pony in a half-circle and rode off in the direction of the gap.

Nikki watched as her mother caught the gray in short order and ponied her three miles on the training track. After returning both horses to her barn, Rachel walked into the restroom across the way. Nikki followed. She paused outside the door to take a deep breath, then went inside. Rachel was leaning against the wall, head down, smoking. She glanced up when Nikki walked in. The cigarette dropped from her lips.

"You okay?" Nikki asked, and it came out thick and funny.

Smoke curled from the burning cigarette on the floor. Pushing away from the wall, Rachel took a step closer. She looked at Nikki with big-eyed shock.

"Nicole?"

"Uh. Yeah."

Rachel hastily retreated a step. "What are you doing here?"

Nikki stared at the floor drain. "Using the bathroom?"

A gap of silence, then Rachel exhaled loudly, equal parts sigh and huff. "If you've come here thinking you'll get to ride my horses, you're wasting your time."

"I'm not here to ride."

"No one'll believe you're my daughter."

"I've never told anyone before," Nikki said, braving eye

contact. "It's sort of embarrassing."

More silence. Hear-a-pin-drop silence. Shame streaked across Rachel's face like a fugitive emotion. She pursed her lips and made for the door.

"I'm sorry for not coming down from that tree," Nikki blurted.

Rachel stopped with a jerk of her shoulders, as though someone had lassoed her from behind. Slowly, she turned and stood staring with her mouth half open, as if she'd lost her voice. Outside, a horse nickered and hooves clopped past, clop-clop, clop-clop, clop-clop. Nikki frantically searched her mind for what next to say. Across the room Rachel thrust a finger at her.

"Don't you ever again lay into one of my jocks," she said, then was gone.

~

Rachel went directly to her barn, mounted her pony, and shouted for the next two trackers, an older bay gelding to two-minute lick a mile and a stud colt to work his first three-eighths. When Sam led out a pair of two-year old fillies to jog, she sighed and waited for the gallop boys to be legged-up. How could she think straight to be angry at her assistant for saddling the wrong horses with her head still reeling over the confrontation in the bathroom? Considering the circumstances surrounding her win in the Westover Meadows Derby, a visit from Nicole shouldn't have been unexpected; nonetheless, it had flattened Rachel. She felt strange inside. A scary strange that she now hastily attributed to angina or some other sort of chest discomfort associated with stress. Rachel removed a roll of antacids from a shirt pocket and popped three in her mouth, then accompanied the two-year olds to the main track. Her thoughts rode off in another direction.

Unexpectedly pleasant memories came to her first—a fleeting glimpse of early motherhood—before she was pitched into the realm of what might have been. The antacids were useless. After a few minutes, she took refuge in the black hole of her conscience, absolved by her old feelings of inadequacy and her obsessive need to be a success in the world. She recalled the times she'd returned to Beverly Hills for her daughter, only to drive away alone, crying. She remembered Nicole shrinking from her touch or sulking or hiding, unhappy to see her mother. Why would Nicole show up now, after twenty years?

Rachel waited along the outside fence for the two-year olds to trot a lap, her right arm extended stiffly and hand gripping the saddle horn, a tension relief appendage. A few months ago she had talked to Ginny and told her the entire story from cover to cover, with the exception of Nicole's name and profession. Ginny had summed up the matter from the rational perspective of a woman who had never had a child: events beyond Rachel's control had conspired to make her an inappropriate mother and she resolved the situation to the benefit of both parties. Rachel had always assumed that both parties *had* benefited. That she was cut out to be a horse trainer and not a mother. That Nicole was better off without her. After all, *she'd* managed just fine without a mother. Although *hers* had actually died, as opposed to having...figuratively died. Rachel made an effort to stop thinking about it and focus on business at hand.

Fourteen trackers later, right before the eight o'clock break for track renovation, she accompanied a set of two-year olds to the starting gate in the quarter-chute. Their third visit, the colts were loaded and the assistant starters opened the front doors manually. She watched the pair trot out and gallop away, then she loped to the paddock entrance, hung a right, and jogged her ponyhorse up the trench path and beneath the lip of the grandstand. She touched heels to him at the concrete stairs that abutted the paddock. Ever the faithful steed, he started up the south flight, steel shoes echoing throughout the deserted structure with each cautious step. At the top, she rode past parimutuel windows to the tiered seats overlooking the paddock. The heart of her world appeared lifeless minus the horses and trainers and crowd, so she closed her eyes until she heard the sounds and pictured the sights, reassured to see the place pulsating, if only in her head. When the tractors rumbled past, she rode back to the stairs, dismounted, and led her pony down. She remounted at the bottom and waited beside the track until it reopened, then started back toward the gap.

On a whim, Rachel gunned her pony. He burst ahead, eager to stretch out and run, and she flattened down and played jockey for fleeting seconds, the ground streaking past in a blur. After a furlong, she straightened in the saddle and eased to a lope and a trot, pulling up near the gap beside one of her gallopers. She instructed Clint to backtrack the gelding to the wire and give him a strong mile-and-a-half, then reined her pony right and walked along the outside fence to the half-mile pole to wait. As she rode past the trainer's stand something caught her eye, and she turned to see Nicole talking with Reno McAllister. This, Rachel thought, was why she'd had her tubes tied.

~

Nikki walked to the backside bleachers and sat unnoticed near the top, watching horses gallop. Rachel rode past several times, a flash of black-clad rider on black ponyhorse, the Zorro of Peninsula Park. Nikki hunched over and rested her chin on a palm and contemplated her next move. Her thoughts were being pulled in so many directions, she felt dizzy. All the things she'd planned to say had fallen into some sort of emotional crevasse, just beyond her reach. Things she wanted to scream and shout but couldn't even make herself whisper. Things that she could hardly even make herself think since the moment she had caught sight of her mother. Her chin sank deeper into her palm. The only thing she resolved with certainty was that she hadn't the slightest idea what she planned to do.

An hour went by, then a trainer walked over and introduced himself and asked if she was a jockey. She nodded and told him her name and his face registered something akin to reverence. She rolled her eyes after he had walked off. He joined the others on the trainer's stand at the base of the bleachers and soon heads were turning back to look. When Nikki scowled at them, everyone quit staring. During the break for track renovation, the bleachers and the stand emptied, and she sat alone watching the tractors, two abreast, harrow the track. They finished a lap and started a second. They chugged along, burying all evidence that horses had set foot on the track that morning, and exited the track at the quarter-chute.

People began filing back into the trainer's stand. The outrider opened the gate and the herd of horses waiting impatiently in the gap streamed onto the fresh surface, backtracking to warm up. When she turned her head in the other direction, she saw a man sitting beside her on the bench. He looked her over and started to smile, as if he knew her, as if she were a close friend, then he extended his right hand.

"Reno McAllister. Heard you're Nikki Summers."

She glanced at the track below. Rachel had reined her pony to a halt along the outside fence and sat frowning at the two of them.

Nikki shook his hand vigorously. "Pleasure to meet you, Mr. McAllister."

~

Reno McAllister knew of her troubles in the Westover Meadows Derby. He told her he had a horse he'd claimed several months ago that hadn't run in the money for him, much less won a race. He wanted to know if she was interested in riding it. Since she had come to California with no intentions of racing or even galloping, she asked sarcastically if he realized woman jockeys were as popular with horse owners as their training bills and pointed out that her height made her doubly disfavored, seeing as tall jockeys were subject to comparison with parachutes on top-fuel dragsters. McAllister smiled and said he appreciated people who could laugh at themselves. Then he told her that he'd claimed the horse from Rachel. Nikki decided it wouldn't hurt to ride one race.

After she paid for her jockey's license and had filled out the paperwork, he asked her to breeze the horse a half-mile. Nikki went to her car and dug her helmet from the trunk. In twenty minutes, she pulled up a smallish roan gelding and jogged back to where Reno McAllister was waiting on a buckskin pony.

"How'd he go?" Reno asked.

"Like driving a Rolls," she lied.

"You ever drive one?"

"Not exactly."

"I'm not one of those trainers who ask the question but don't want to hear the answer."

"Bobbed on his left front when he switched leads," she said. "I've felt worse."

"Still want to ride him?"

She thought a moment. "I do."

Reno dipped his chin in a nod. "You've got light hands. Nothing worse than a boy who's always hanging on a horse's mouth."

"I try."

"Anymore, the boys are about half-afraid to get on a horse if it isn't push-button gentle."

"If I were a top jock and making big bucks, I'd be hesitant to risk my butt on some two-bit, goofy, son-of-a-gun. But I'm not."

The trainer grinned. "Care to try a baddie?"

"Couldn't be any badder than some of the things I've gotten on at Westover Meadows," she said.

It wasn't. The horse was a head-tossing outlaw who grabbed the bit in his teeth and tried to run off, but Nikki was able to keep him under control — albeit just barely — while at the same time remembering to look in charge of the situation as she and her mount roared past the backstretch bleachers. Because she was a newcomer, many eyes were on her. This was a racetrack given. Reno had her gallop a third horse, then the track closed. He told her the one she'd worked would be entered for Friday, paid her for getting on the two gallopers, and asked her to catch another worker for him in the morning. This pleased her, for top jockeys spent mornings working horses, not galloping them.

She had no sooner walked out of his barn when an agent approached her. He wore his shirt partially unbuttoned to reveal four gold chains and a mat of chest hair. A fast talker, glib and opportunistic, he was everything a jockey's agent was expected to be and worse. He told her that trainers had heard she packed a mean stick and had almost outrun Nottingham's heavy favorite in a big race up north. She told him bluntly that she was a competent rider, no more, no less. He all but got down on his hands and knees and begged to hustle her book. She shook her head and walked away.

Nikki went to the kitchen, where three trainers asked her to breeze horses for them in the morning. She promised them nothing, bought a banana and an orange, and slipped outside to ponder her sudden popularity. A bouncing sound to the north of the kitchen drew her to the chaplain's office and a basketball hoop mounted on the outside wall. Five grooms were playing two-on-three. They were Mexicans and it was obvious from the way they chucked the ball at the hoop with both hands that they were new to the American sport. She stole the ball, dribbled through her legs, and showed them a jump shot. They caught on quickly. Her Spanish was limited but they understood her smile.

"Dr. Steele to Rachel Nottingham's barn," came over the backside PA system as Nikki was shooting. The ball fell short of the rim by several feet.

"Brick," she explained, waving good-bye.

Nikki started down the road to the parking lot. She walked along puzzling what she planned to do and the answer came to her like an epiphany of sorts. She would stay and ride. And win.

At a phone booth outside the main stable gate, she called the Wilcoxes and informed Matt and Susan. She called her apartment manager next. Back at her motel room, she stretched and did ballet barre exercises for about thirty minutes, then crouched and did five sets of 100 squat jumps each, keeping her chest tucked to her knees and pumping her arms forward in unison, elbows in and arms fully extended, hand-riding a make-believe mount to the wire. Between sets, she caught her breath and practiced cocking her whip, flipping it right handed and switching to her left while keeping taut an old set of reins she'd found in her truck and secured to one of the bed legs. Next, she did abdominal and back exercises, and push-ups until her muscles ached. After that, she crouched in a tuck at the end of the bed and practiced her whipping technique, working to keep her back flat and body still while perfecting a swing that was economical, swift, and powerful. When her right arm ached, she switched corners and practiced left handed, slashing the mattress again and again until the whacks elicited an answering thump from the room below.

Lastly, Nikki went outside and ran until her legs and lungs burned with fatigue, almost three miles, and half of it uphill, for there was no shortage of steep hills in the Bay Area. For dinner, she ate a small container of nonfat strawberry yogurt, two hard-boiled eggs, a whole-wheat bagel, and a carrot, then fell asleep studying the racing form.

~

From Nikki's perspective, the bleakness that permeated Westover Meadows seemed completely absent at Peninsula Park. Barns were newer, trainers spiffier, horses classier. She had gotten on nine head by the break the next morning. Twice she rode past Rachel and her black saddlehorse, but made a point of not looking, for fear of what she might see. When the main track closed for renovation, Nikki brushed dust off her leggings, tucked in her sleeveless shirt, and walked to barn 28 where she found Rachel in a stall, preparing to take the occupant's temperature.

She peeked inside. "Need any help this morning?"

Rachel held up the animal's tail and inserted the thermometer. "No."

"Let me try the gray," Nikki said.

Rachel turned toward the back wall.

Nikki clutched the metal stall gate to keep herself from running away. "I can ride her."

"Do us both a favor and go back to Oregon."

"You don't have to pay me or anything."

"Not if I ride you in the afternoon, right?"

Nikki shook her head. "I don't want you getting in the doghouse with clients on my account. I'll just gallop the filly to prove I can."

"So you're riding here after all?"

"Maybe I changed my mind."

"I'm not sticking you on that filly," Rachel said, still addressing the back wall. "I don't need any more goddamn insurance claims."

"Bullshit. You're afraid I'll ride her," Nikki said, before she could stop herself.

Rachel turned around. "Get the hell out of my barn."

But Nikki was already gone.

~

He walked bow legged and chewed snuff. Half his teeth were missing; the other half were stained yellow. His jeans were air-conditioned with numerous holes and only blue in name, and his chaps were so stiff, they could have stood up by themselves. He wore pointy-toed cowboy boots, a Western shirt with shiny snap buttons, and an old, flesh-colored helmet—minus a cover —that brought to mind a bad roller-derby player, a wooden salad bowl, or an extremely ugly bald head. A helmet that bore more dents and scratches than could be absorbed in a lifetime without losing numerous IQ points. The man was pure cowboy by Rachel's estimation.

He had come from Pleasanton to ride Lucifera. A former rodeo cowboy with a reputation for breaking the baddest of broncos, Rachel had offered him fifteen hundred dollars if he could cure her number one headache, but she held little hope that he'd succeed. She was ready to admit she couldn't afford to waste any more time or money on the gray. Reno McAllister's lead in the trainer standings had grown to four wins. She had more important things to worry about than outshining him with Lucifera. The cowboy was the filly's last chance.

"You're late," Rachel said to him. "I said nine. It's nearly nine-thirty."

"It's Wednesday, ain't it?" he said.

She nodded.

The cowboy tapped his helmet. "I get my days all messed up. Ever since that bull gored me at Pendleton, I can't remember shit."

"Fantastic."

"Huh?"

"Nothing. Listen, this filly can buck," Rachel said. "She can mop up the earth and break in two like the meanest bronco I've ever seen."

"Sweetheart, there ain't a horse been borned I can't ride."

"That's 'Ms. Nottingham,' and I got news, this filly wasn't borned. She hatched out of an egg like her cousin, Tyrannosaurus Rex."

"I rode that Rex feller at Calgary. He was nothing but a shit-eatin' crow hopper. Couldn't buck a lick."

Rachel gazed up at the sky and shook her head. She mounted her pony, then shouted at Sam to bring out Lucifera, but the cowboy insisted on being legged up in the stall and riding the filly to the track without accompaniment. Rachel frowned but didn't argue. His kind was independent and she needed him.

He proceeded to ride Lucifera round and round, both directions of her stall, then Sam held open the gate and the cowboy rode her across the shed row and onto the road. The filly walked toward the track like a well-trained saddlehorse until he put the reins in one hand and waved to a big-busted groom as she emptied a manure cart. A careless mistake not left unpunished.

Lucifera buried her head between her legs and kicked her

butt so high that she about somersaulted, then swapped ends and slammed the cowboy into the pavement where he lay in a heap, all arms and legs and not moving. Lucifera trotted a circle around him, a victory dance, tail up and streaming over her rump. A half-dozen people came running to his aid.

Rachel gunned her pony and took out after Lucifera, swooping in to snatch a rein, but she ducked away. At that point, Nicole appeared from nowhere and snagged the gray, running backward with her until the filly bumped into the side of a barn and was forced to stop. Lucifera blew out sharply. Clearly, she was not pleased at being robbed of an opportunity to terrorize the barn area.

After dismounting her pony, Rachel walked over to the gray filly and the girl. A sleepless night of sheet wrestling had convinced Rachel to regard Nicole as though she were somebody else's daughter. A self-assured, hard-headed young woman who just happened to somewhat look like Rachel. Although she felt confident Nicole more closely resembled her father, who'd been a ringer for a young Paul Newman. Or maybe Harrison Ford. Handsome, but beyond that general description, she'd no recollection. At any rate, she guessed that there were lots of young women in the world who bore a resemblance to her. Somewhat.

She took hold of Lucifera's reins. "I'll take her. Thanks."

Nicole tightened her grip. "I can ride this filly."

With a flick of her head, Rachel motioned toward the circle of people who were helping the cowboy rise groggily to his feet. "That's what he thought."

"Give me a chance."

"No." After prying the reins from Nicole's grasp, Rachel walked off leading the gray and her pony. She wished that she had choked down her pride, heeded common sense, and sold Lucifera long before the problem became so unsolvable.

"I ride well enough to suit *Reno McAllister,*" Nicole shouted from behind.

Rachel stopped and turned slowly back.

Nicole was staring at her. "Well?"

The words *Reno McAllister* repeated in Rachel's head, over and over and over, until she lost all perspective of good sense. "You don't last eight seconds, I'm not paying," she finally said.

Nicole fastened her helmet strap. "Deal."

She went to Lucifera and adjusted the stirrups and checked the girth. When Sam legged up Nicole, she eased her weight down, slipped her feet into the irons, gathered the reins. Sam then led the filly partway to the training track before inexplicably letting go of the bridle headstall and moving aside, as per Nicole's request, Rachel presumed and shouted at her assistant to lead the filly all the way to the track. Before Sam could comply, Lucifera bogged her head and did her thing.

~

Nikki remembered what Matt had taught her about riding a bucking horse. She sat way back and pretended her rear end was bonded to the saddle with Super Glue, gripped the knot at the end of the reins, and braced her feet near the gray filly's ears to keep from being jerked over and off. She cranked the filly's head to the left, since pulling up a bucking horse's head was next to impossible unless a rider could bench press significantly more than eighty pounds. Lucifera whipped her rump in the opposite direction, spun in a tight circle, and bucked like a Brahma bull. Nikki jerked the filly the other way, guiding her toward a huge pile of shed-row fill dirt dumped outside one end of a barn. With her head pulled tight to one side, Lucifera bucked straight into the mound, bobbled, and lost her balance. Nikki saw a dark eye with a darkly transparent cornea glaring back at her before she vanished beneath twelve-hundred pounds of horseflesh.

Lucifera fell swiftly. Nikki's stirrups were too long so she had no chance to spring clear. On solid ground, no telling how many bones she might have broken, but the dirt was deep and soft. When Lucifera leaped to her feet, Nikki scrambled to her own and lunged for the reins before the filly could run off. Rachel made a grab for the reins at the same time and the pair nearly collided.

"What in the hell were you trying to prove?" she cried out, exposing, however briefly, the possibility that her heart was not the world's largest diamond.

Nikki shrugged, feeling stupid. "Sorry."

They each drew back a step. Sam arrived on the scene to lead Lucifera toward the barn. Rachel turned and motioned to one of her gallop boys to see to her pony, which was standing ground-tied not far away. A crowd of twenty or more, who had gathered to watch the gray heifer misbehave, were now gawking at Rachel in expectation of an emotional outburst as opposed to her usual hardass yelling and cussing, although Nikki guessed that her mother intended to disappointment everyone. Sure enough, when Rachel turned back around, her face had regained its impervious veneer and her vulnerabilities returned to wherever she kept them hidden.

Now Nikki felt stupid *and* pathetic. A single sentence uttered with dubious concern had fueled her hopes that the second Sunday in May wouldn't find her buying a *World's Worst Mother* coffee mug. Then again, Nikki *was* a racetracker and racetrackers were irrationally optimistic by necessity. Fortunately, neither optimism nor short-term stupidity blinded her to the reality that her mother was never going to change. And so Nikki stood there expecting the worst.

Rachel pulled a wallet from her back pocket and took out a bill. "Well, congratulations. Filly's never done *that* before. This ought to cover your laundry tab." She held out a twenty.

Nikki shook her head. "I didn't ride her."

"You lasted eight seconds."

"Let me try her again."

"No."

"I know I can straighten her out."

"No."

"Give me a week," Nikki pleaded.

"She's shipping back to the farm this afternoon."

"I'll go there."

"No," Rachel said. "I'm selling the cow before she kills

someone."

Nikki thought fast. "This the filly you bought off Reno McAllister?"

Rachel moved to leave. "That won't work twice."

"Maybe you should just concede the trainer's race to *Reno,* seeing as you're such a quitter," Nikki said, to the back of her mother's head.

Rachel walked all the way to her barn before slowing, then stopping. She looked over her shoulder in Nikki's direction and sighed heavily. "You've got one week. Be at the farm by noon tomorrow."

Nikki fought off a smile, answered with a businesslike nod, and strode away before her mother changed her mind.

Oceanstead Farm, Half Moon Bay, California
April 1994

Thursday morning, Nikki made a wrong turn on the Pacific Coast Highway and took an hour instead of forty-five minutes to reach Oceanstead Farm. The Bay Area's premier off-track training facility consisted of eight forty-stall barns, a dozen grass paddocks, a five-eighths of a mile track, a starting gate, an equine swimming pool, and two treadmills. A quarter-mile trail provided beach access. There was an indoor arena and a round pen. Nikki found the farm foreman in a tack room and told him that she'd come to gallop Lucifera. Nikki did not tell him who she was for fear Rachel had changed her mind.

"You must be Nicole," the man said, looking up from a clipboard. Sacks of grain stacked waist high served as his desk and chair.

"That's *Nikki*," she said, with a measure of crossness to conceal her surprise that Rachel had actually told him her name.

He nodded and pointed to the far wall. "Feel free to use anything here, only put it back like you found it. Filly's in stall eighteen. Give a holler and someone will throw you on."

"Where's the round pen?"

"Out back, behind the last barn." The foreman lit a smoke and combed a hand through his thick dark hair. "You need any help from me?"

She smiled. "No, but thanks for asking."

"We've just been jogging the filly on the treadmill and swimming her. Hear she's the devil to gallop."

"She can buck some."

"Guess she can't go far in the round pen."

"Probably not."

"Well then, good luck and don't break a leg."

"Right."

Nikki gathered an armload of tack and headed to the gray's stall. Her plan was to tire Lucifera with ground work in the round pen, then lead her to the beach and do battle in the dry, deep sand there, a medium that would hobble the filly's wild-ass agility and perhaps fatigue her to the point of submission. Like sticking chaos into a vat of honey, Nikki thought, for lack of any other analogy.

Lucifera greeted her with a snort, curling back her upper lip to expose a registration tattoo in black letters and numbers, conspicuous against her pink skin. Figuring she'd just been given the finger, Nikki stuck out her tongue, then tacked the filly, led her to the round pen, and attempted to lunge her. Lucifera planted her feet and sulked. Rather than start a fight, Nikki unsnapped the long nylon line and let Lucifera race round and round on her own. Twice the big gray pinned her ears and charged. Nikki leaped aside and cracked the filly over the rump with a bull whip. Lucifera kicked at the walls but charged no more. When her gray coat shined darker gray and sweat ran off her neck and chest, Nikki caught Lucifera and snapped a shank onto the halter beneath her bridle. They exited the round pen and headed down the dirt road to the ocean.

An attractive but flimsy white wood fence enclosed the farm's outer reaches, more boundary marker than barrier, giving way to open fields of grass and scrubby bushes. A breeze blew off the Pacific, the salty air pleasantly cool. At first, Lucifera walked gingerly, extending each leg in the manner of a mechanical horse, lowering her hooves to the ground with much caution as though expecting to step on a land mine. Her nostrils widened and quivered, her long ears swiveled like radar dishes, alert to her new surroundings until, without warning, she leaped ahead, snorting and blowing and seeing horse-eating monsters everywhere. Nikki had her hands full.

The road went up a slight crest that blocked all view of the ocean and turned out to be the opposite bank of a wide sluggish creek. A trail of muddy hoof prints led into the greenish-brown water. Nikki judged the creek to be shallow and started across with the filly. Lucifera balked for an instant, then broke and ran with lunging leaps to the opposite shore while Nikki struggled to keep pace through knee-deep water and up a steep, greasy, ten-foot bank. By the top, she was clinging to the knot at the end of the leather shank but managed to plant her heels and stop the filly. They walked on.

After another hundred yards or so, the dirt road came to an end, t-boning a sand berm on the upper beach, about a hundred yards from the ocean. Nikki stopped in the deepest sand and tied the shank around Lucifera's neck, pulled down the stirrup irons, and freed the reins from where she had looped them under the back of the saddle, then kicked up her right leg and shimmied on. The instant her butt touched the saddle, Lucifera bolted. Just threw her head skyward and barreled toward the farm. Nikki's boot toes found the irons in seconds but the stirrups were too long to give her enough leverage to stop the runaway filly, whose hooves cut into the dry beach sand like knives into soft butter, then hammered down the dirt road while Nikki wrestled with the reins to no avail. Lucifera neared the creek in a dead gallop.

A few strides before sailing off the bank, she dug in her toes and slid to an abrupt halt. Nikki braced her feet, but the stop was too sudden. Launched airborne, she sailed into the water, somersaulted, and broke the surface sputtering and cussing. Lucifera watched from the top of the bank with her mulish ears cocked upright and curious, before she crept down and streaked past. Nikki dove for the reins and hung on tightly, splashing through the creek in pursuit until, halfway across, she tripped and fell and was towed to the opposite shore like a water skier hooked to a hydroplane. The mud and bushes convinced her to let go. Lucifera stopped on dry ground, cranking her head back to look. Nikki scrambled to her feet, kicked a rock and cussed.

"Here, Luci," she said, as sweetly as possible through gritted teeth.

Lucifera blew out with a rippling sigh and began walking

down the road toward the farm.

Nikki followed. "Easy, girl," she called.

The filly cocked one ear back and kept walking. Nikki burst forward and lunged for the reins, angling in from the side so as not to be kicked. Lucifera easily trotted out of reach, turned in a half-circle, and gazed back at Nikki, who figured her present strategy was hopeless and stood in the road, feeling like an imbecile. Then she remembered her lunch. She reached into her back pocket and extracted a soggy green granola bar wrapper, tore open the paper, and popped a piece in her mouth.

Munching loudly, she turned her back to the filly. After a moment, she heard the clomp of hooves moving nearer, felt hot breath and tickling whiskers on her neck. Lucifera reached over her shoulder and snatched what remained of the granola bar, paper and all. Nikki grabbed the reins. The filly was too busy chewing to notice. After prying the paper from Lucifera's mouth, Nikki let her eat the rest of the granola bar, then shortened her stirrups a few inches for better leverage and led the filly back to the beach.

This time, facing her toward the ocean, Nikki kicked up and swung on. Anticipating Lucifera's attempt to wheel right and bolt toward the farm again, Nikki pulled the filly's head to her left knee and drove heels into her ribcage until she bounded forward and skittishly sideways across the deep sand onto firmer wet sand near the water. Before Lucifera had a chance to balk, Nikki gunned her again. The filly bellowed like a bull and went to bucking straight ahead into the surf, blind to her surroundings until the bottom sheered off and horse and rider plunged into deep water.

Everything happened so fast, Nikki had no time to consider the rationality of taking Lucifera for a swim in the Pacific Ocean. Upon realizing the filly—who was accustomed to swimming in the farm's exercise pool—dog-paddled with authority, Nikki decided to coax her into swimming for about ten minutes before they headed in. Mission accomplished, Lucifera was leaping toward dry ground through chest-deep surf when a huge wave slammed her down. The current dragged horse and rider across the sandy bottom with the filly writhing and churning and Nikki's left leg pinned beneath. Seconds passed. The water grew colder as the undertow sucked them deeper. Nikki closed her eyes, held her breath, and wondered if her plan to teach the gray a lesson had been such a bright idea.

They burst to the surface with water cascading off their heads. Lucifera blew out like a whale and made for shore, while Nikki, choking and gasping, clung to her mane and worked her way back onto the saddle. The filly bounded through the waves and across the beach as if the ocean were liquid fire. She stopped only after reaching the dirt road then lowered her head and shook and water flew in all directions. Nikki about fell off again.

She stroked the filly's neck. "Hope you learned something."

Lucifera answered by walking across the creek and back to Oceanstead Farm, making her way calmly but directly to the concrete washrack outside barn A. Nikki gave the filly a warm, soapy bath. Soon thereafter, Rachel's foreman dashed around the corner, wanting to know where they had been for the past two hours. Nikki, for all appearances wetter than the horse, grinned and told him they'd gone on a picnic. When he requested a more detailed explanation, she replied that they had taken a short swim and he walked off muttering in Spanish. Nikki kept all optimism to herself. With her bad luck, she feared the filly would come down with pneumonia and die.

~

Back at Peninsula Park, Rachel exited the cafeteria at a brisk clip. Head down and sights fixed on the toes of her cobalt blue lace-up riding boots, she was recalculating the month's feed bill owing to a recent rise in the price of timothy hay, when someone extended an arm, forcing her to duck under or stop. She lurched to a halt and looked up.

Reno McAllister lowered his arm. "My assistant told me Lucifera fell on Nikki Summers yesterday morning."

Rachel studied her rival's face and saw he was not poking fun at her troubles.

"They landed on a big pile of dirt," she said. "Nicole...the girl didn't get hurt."

"A jockey's got no business on that gray. Stewards should've ruled the filly off months ago, but they trust your judgment. Wish you'd start using it."

Rachel flinched, bit her lip, then shook an index finger at him. "Yesterday I saw the girl galloping that goofball bay gelding of yours, and I see you're riding her on that sore roan sonofabitch you claimed from me," she calmly shouted, recalling *his* transgressions.

Reno took off his hat. Put it back on. "I don't plan on breaking the horse down. He was sore two months ago and he'll be sore two years from now. A trainer has to run a horse like that and you know it."

She grumbled in agreement.

"Why don't you give her a chance on something in the afternoon?" he said next. "The gal looks like she can horseback to me."

"I don't ride women," Rachel said, glancing at her wristwatch.

Reno made an eye-rolling face. "Everyone knows you're the biggest sexist on the backside."

Shock flashed across her own face like a lightning bolt, there and gone. "You know full well it's a losing proposition. She wins, the horse would've won by more under a man. She loses, it's her fault, which means it's my fault for riding her in the first place and eventually I'm saddled with a reputation as a woman trainer who rides woman jocks and half my clients go bye-bye."

"You could ride her on some of your own horses," he said.

"And if they run well, trainers will really be drooling to claim my horses, thinking they can move them up with a boy."

"A woman jock isn't quite as damned as you seem to think.

Didn't anyone ever give you a chance?"

"No," she said.

"Not ever?"

"Is this going where I think it's going?"

Reno gazed at her with calm intensity. "You bet."

The self-assurance in his voice laid her open like the stroke of a blade so sharp it felt painless, though she was acutely aware he intended to dissect her innermost stigma. She reached into her shirt pocket, took out a cigarette, and held the smoke between her fingers as though it were lit.

"Listen, I don't know what my aunt told your friend, but I'm sure I probably did it."

He opened his mouth. Closed it.

It was noon and they stood along the edge of the gap, the gates to the track locked, the gap deserted but for several by-passers who'd wandered over to eavesdrop. When she glanced in their direction, they hurried off, though she had no idea what they'd read in her expression. Across from her, Reno's mouth was doing a slow twitch. She found his reluctance to attack her strangely comforting.

"There was no *friend*," he said after a moment. "I hired a private detective."

Rachel just stared at him.

He exhaled heavily. "I lied."

She thought she should probably cuss him out, but instead reached over and briefly touched his shoulder. He shifted his arms into several positions before putting them behind his back. A minute passed.

"It's not like I've never lied," she finally said.

"You know, really, it's none of my business," he said. "But I am curious to know why you did what you did."

She absently tapped the unlit smoke against the side of her leg. "Sometimes things get so badly broken they can't be fixed."

"So you walked away?"

"Whoa," she said. "I'm confessing nothing to *you*."

"I'm not as big a bastard as you think."

"You're the competition."

"We're not talking horses, Rachel."

Her hand was now drumming the side of her leg. "What's the difference?"

"If I beat you, I'll beat you on the racetrack."

"Yeah, right. All those horses you bamboozled off me just walked out of my barn on their own."

"You got out hustled. I *didn't* badmouth you."

"Whatever," she said.

Reno removed his hat again, fiddled with the band. "Remember a few months ago, when I said you didn't have a conscience?"

Rachel tipped her head skyward and pretended not to recall. "Vaguely."

"I was wrong," he said. "You have a conscience. Trouble is, you don't always listen to it."

Her mouth wiggled at the corners. "Compliments are wasted on me."

"That wasn't exactly a compliment."

"From you it was." A smile burst onto her face, an embarrassingly huge smile—as though something inside her was blossoming like an exotic flower that had never grown for her before. The nervousness that she always felt in his presence took on new significance. A disturbing new significance, her mind and body at odds over the prudence of having a thing for the enemy.

Reno crammed on his hat and started away, glancing back over his shoulder to return her smile before he had taken a dozen steps. Halfway to her barn, she put the decidedly bent cigarette between her lips and smoked it. For the first time in her life, she thought about seeing a therapist.

~

Two hours later, Rachel headed out the door for a business lunch date with a potential client in Foster City. All that remained of her once formidable classy string was Redwood Comet, a potential two-year-old stakes colt she owned in partnership with J.K. Vanderford; Royal Master, the Oregon Derby winner; two older stakes mares; and five allowance horses. Besides the stock that Reno had claimed or bought outright from her clients, Rachel had lost eight solid claimers to other trainers since the meet had begun in October, not to mention the Seth Marten disaster. And during the past week, another of her clients shipped four of his best horses to southern California to race for bigger purses. All the numbers Rachel punched in yielded the same answer: she needed more money. More money to buy horses to win races to regain her clients' confidence to obtain more horses to win more races. Ever so briefly, she considered stepping off the merry-go-round. Then the ring flashed past, thoughts of winning rife in her head, the training title, bigger races, more races, more, more, more. To win races, she guessed that she'd subject herself to worse torture than hustling new clients.

The restaurant overlooked one of the many saltwater canals that crisscrossed the flat suburban sameness on the edge of San Francisco Bay. Her potential client showed up twenty-five minutes late without an apology or even a bad excuse. He owned a computer software company and Rachel estimated he could buy Rhode Island and not bounce the check, so she concealed her irritation and greeted him with a pleasant smile. Over drinks and sushi, they discussed the glories of owning and racing horses, then drove to her barn and discussed the technicalities before sealing their business relationship with a handshake. The man's forearms suggested he was used to wielding a pick and shovel. Barbells, she guessed, were closer to the truth. Their fingertips brushed, then he withdrew his hand.

"Almost forgot," he said. "I have one minor stipulation."

"Yes?"

"It's quite simple, really. I expect certain, shall we say, 'gratuities' from my female employees. I trust that won't be a problem?"

She eyed his gold wedding band, diamond big as a marble. Her hand fell to her side. "Is this a trick question?"

He smiled a perfunctory smile. "Every trainer at Peninsula Park would kill to land a client with my money. You've nothing to lose but your pride."

Rachel snapped her fingers, searching for polite words, finding none. Her five-win deficit in the trainers' standings flashed to mind. "That may be true, but I have to tell you to go fuck yourself."

"Temper, temper. It's not entirely about sex."

"Really?"

"In order to overcome my prejudice of women in racing, I need to know what sets you apart."

"That I'm easy?"

"That you're willing to do whatever it takes to stay on top." His expression said he was completely serious.

"You must think I'm desperate."

"I think you like to win."

"Get out of my barn."

He shrugged, the slightest flinching of his shoulders. The set of his mouth matched the downward curve of his thin mustache. "It's your loss."

"Won't be my first."

"Just your biggest."

"Get out, pal. Now."

She threw a condition book at her office door as it closed behind him.

Ginny showed up, approximately thirty seconds later. She knocked and poked her head inside, then quickly withdrew. "I'm not wearing my riot gear," she called out from the shed row.

Rachel lowered the coffee cup that she was aiming at the door. "Sorry. Come in."

A white tissue appeared first, followed by Ginny in a flowery pink smock and shorts. "This have anything to do with the unhappy man I passed, tromping out of your barn?"

"Unfortunately," Rachel said.

"A prospective owner?"

"Oh, naturally. He was convinced that it's a female trainer's duty to, you know, keep him extremely happy."

Ginny cocked her head and puzzled the matter. "Oh. What a disgusting jackass."

"Had a shitload of bucks, though. Damn. I can't remember the last time I was five wins down at Peninsula Park." Kicking off high-heeled sandals, Rachel sank into her desk chair, crossing her legs at the ankles. She consoled herself with the knowledge his money would more than likely not end up in Reno's barn.

"You have nearly four months to catch up, dear."

"Gets harder to win races near the end of the meet. Horses are tired. Trainers start taking their best shots."

"I can buy one more horse," Ginny said. "Providing he wins now and then."

"Thanks, but I think you could do with one *less* horse."

"I'm not catching your drift."

"I don't want you losing money you can't afford to lose."

Ginny sighed. "If only my husband hadn't gone on that gambling binge before he died."

"Good riddance, I'd say," Rachel said, without thinking.

Sitting down on the couch, Ginny clutched her hands in her lap. "I miss him terribly."

Her tone warranted a hug and kind words, but acting warm and fuzzy was a challenge for Rachel, even in a good mood. "I didn't mean to be insensitive," she said.

"Don't worry about it, dear."

Rachel stared at her feet. "Sorry you hurt," she said.

"Shame on me for whining. At least I enjoyed twenty-five years with a man I loved."

Now Rachel was the one who sighed. "If I develop a thing for a guy, I'm crazy about him the second we meet and for about an hour after that."

Ginny's eyebrows climbed her forehead.

"Okay, maybe a week," Rachel said. "Then I want him out of my sight before I kill him."

"You simply haven't found the right one."

"I'm beginning to think the right one doesn't exist." She

paused to consider her earlier encounter with Reno McAllister. "Think it's possible for me to do it backwards?"

"You want to run that past me again, dear?"

"Do you think I might hate someone, then not hate him, then kind of like him, then really like him, then, you know, the crazy part?"

Ginny leaned closer and sniffed. "How many drinks did you have with lunch?"

"One. Okay two, but they were weak."

"Too much booze makes you squirrelier than that gray filly of yours. How's Luci doing, by the way?"

"According to my farm assistant she went on a picnic today." Rachel walked over to the refrigerator, took out a beer, and waved the bottle at Ginny. "Make that three."

~

Nikki was well aware that nothing earned a rider a reputation for being a loser faster than finishing out of the money, horse after horse, race after race, no matter the odds. To improve her chances for success, the first thing she did when she reached Peninsula Park the next morning was hire a quality agent. Unfortunately, she knew nothing about any Peninsula Park agents, except for Kurt Kaiser, who in her opinion was mediocre at hustling book. And an immature jerk. The few Westover Meadows trainers at the track were unlikely to enlighten her on the subject, and she didn't know anyone local to ask other than her mother. Since Nikki wasn't going *there*, she made her selection based on presentability, selecting an agent that dressed classier than the pimpmeister who had accosted her the day before. Also, her new agent spoke English minus the racetrack refer-to-the-past-in-the-present-tense dialect that she found mildly annoying. A black man in his mid-thirties the size of an NFL offensive lineman, his name was Maltby Aurora.

"That your real name?" she asked.

"Is Nikki Summers yours?"

She stuck her hands on her hips. "Okay, we'll skip the personal stuff. Just don't be putting me on a bunch of dogs, please."

"And don't be telling me how to conduct my business."

"My tongue slipped."

The agent scrutinized her through the thick lenses of wire-rimmed glasses. A charcoal bowler atop his head accented a lighter gray three-piece suit. Nikki shifted her stance. The agent cleared his throat with a low rumble.

"I hustled for the leading rider before he broke his leg," he said. "Reno McAllister's stable jockey. Since you seem to have an in with Mr. McAllister, I'll take your book, but consider yourself extremely fortunate."

"Do I kiss your feet now?"

"I'm gay, so I'd appreciate it if you'd refrain from kissing any part of my anatomy."

She whistled. "A gay black agent and a girl jock. Don't we make a pair? Well, hear this, Maltby, I don't give a shit what color you are or who you're dating, long as you can get me on winners."

"I'll do my job. What remains to be seen is whether your horsebacking skills transcend your rudeness."

Nikki snapped her whip and it hissed through the air. "I can ride. And I'm sorry for being rude but the thing is, most successful people are jerks."

"No apology necessary," he said. "You're absolutely right. Courteous jockeys win fewer races."

A fact Nikki could vouch for with depressingly personal detail, but instead she just nodded.

"Now run over to Mr. McAllister's barn and offer to kiss *his* feet," the agent said. "He has two open horses on tomorrow afternoon's card."

Nikki got on four head for McAllister and he named her on one of his jockeyless horses for Saturday, then she worked five more for various trainers. Over the course of the morning, she saw her mother twice and each time, they eyeballed one another momentarily before Rachel made a point of turning away in a show of indifference. When their paths crossed again, Nikki swore to be the first to look in another direction. Her mother, she thought, could damn well make the effort to ask about Lucifera's progress.

Luckily, the filly had survived her underwater swimming lesson, Nikki was relieved to find when she arrived at Oceanstead Farm later that same morning. Lucifera yawned several times, but her nose was dry, her temperature normal, and her legs cold and sound. Nikki tacked and brushed the filly, then rode her to the ocean with two granola bars stuffed in a back pocket. Just in case.

~

The clerk of scales assigned Nikki a valet when she reported to Peninsula Park's Jockey Room at four that afternoon. He took her tack and showed her to the women's quarters, which seemed unbelievably plush to her, with a real bathroom, a large color television, thick carpeting, a new sofa, and two twin beds. Women jockeys with afternoon mounts were not in abundance at Peninsula Park, so Nikki had the area to herself that day. With an hour until post time, she changed into her riding clothes and returned to the main room to study the posted program for the third race. Her mount was listed at 17-1, though she suspected the odds would have been lower had the jock been one of the popular local boys. Rachel trained the favorite. Jockey Jim Bruner was scheduled to ride it as well as her entrants in the fifth and the eighth races.

"Hey, Brutus, quit eyeballing the new girl," said a squeaky male voice.

Nikki spun around. A rider with pockmarked cheeks and bedroom eyes was staring where her butt had been.

"Nice ass," he said.

"Brutus short for Bruner?" she asked.

"Smart, too. Smart broad with a nice ass." He laughed at her and traded rude comments with three other jockeys standing nearby.

"I say we stick her on the head end till the quarter pole. I like the view from behind."

"Looks mighty fine from here."

"Sort of scrawny, you ask me."

"I know a joke," Nikki said, interrupting their banter.

"Suspense is killing us," Bruner said.

She smiled sweetly. "What did the one shark say to the other after eating a Peninsula Park jockey?"

"What?"

"Tastes like pig."

The riders listening in the background muttered amongst themselves. Bruner unsnapped his pants and tucked in his silks with a show of arrogance.

"You're wasting your time gettin' on that crazy gray bitch. Nottingham don't ride no jocks without balls. That's guts *and* nuts."

"She rides *you*," Nikki said.

"Better keep your head picked up, little girl. This ain't Westover Meadows."

"I make a point of watching the road," she told him. "Especially around California drivers."

This time the laughter was not at her expense.

~

Reno McAllister waited for the horses in Wednesday evening's third race with his back to where Rachel stood on the other side of the paddock. At long last, he was on the verge of feeding her his personal recipe for humble pie, but instead, he longed to give her a hug, which made him think that he was in the clutches of a midlife crisis. Or that he had lost his mind. His rational side hoped that a hug represented the extent of his sympathy. Next, he'd be letting her win races.

These past few months, Reno had gotten a kick out of watching Rachel squirm when cornered with a truth that she'd rationalized to death or conveniently forgotten. The fact that she did squirm made him think she might actually have a heart. Rotten of him to be so judgmental, he thought, since he had no kids of his own and couldn't imagine what it'd feel like to pack one around inside of him for nine months, let alone knowing he would be the sole parent. Now he felt somewhat ashamed of himself for picking on her, though in all fairness, she'd gone for his throat without provocation on more than one occasion and was about as defenseless as a hydrogen bomb.

After saddling his horse, Reno waited for the jockeys. He was riding the newcomer, Nikki Summers. Nottingham's daughter, he presumed, an educated guess considering they looked similar, were both cursed with obnoxious confidence, and twice, he'd heard Rachel refer to Nikki as Nicole, the name rolling off her tongue like the truth. He shook her hand when Summers walked up. An attractive girl with a vise grip handshake for one so slight, the program listed her as twenty-eight, neither young nor old for a rider. He had spoken with two trainers from the small Westover Meadows' contingent that shipped down to race at Peninsula Park. Both claimed Nikki Summers was a competent if unspectacular jockey with a reputation for riding passively, although they said she had been a different jock in the Westover Meadows Derby. Nothing like a little childhood angst to turn a mediocre performer into a world-beater. Reno hated to think he was counting on it.

He may have held a slight lead in the trainer's race, but in his effort to beat Rachel, he'd gotten stuck with a number of dogs and in the end, clients hated claiming stinkers, no matter how much money they had. And Rachel had claimed two nice horses from *him* recently. Caution was in order. Her horses were training sharply and she would more than likely gain ground on him in upcoming weeks. Without his favorite jockey, he'd nothing to lose but a race he figured to lose anyway. And if Nikki Summers worked out? He could imagine classier ways to beat Rachel Nottingham than with her own daughter, but the fact that he might teach one or both of them a lesson bolstered Reno's resolve.

Across the paddock, Rachel was heading his way in a swank airman's style jean jumpsuit with the sleeves rolled above her elbows, looking tanned and fit but thinner than usual and less intimidating minus the black chaps, gloves, and hat of her basic morning attire. Her confident step contradicted her tentative face, a woman confronting unfamiliar territory who hadn't the slightest idea which way to go. Reno directed his full attention to Nikki Summers. Having spent more than two hours the previous night debating whether to tread into the moral gray zone that bordered on unscrupulous conduct, he forged ahead.

~

Rachel saddled her horse—the even money favorite in the third race—and stood waiting with sweaty palms for the jockeys. When Bruner arrived, she told him to go to the front and stay there, then headed seven stalls over to where Reno was greeting Nikki with a handshake and a smile. Rachel ran her own hands down the sides of her blue denim jumpsuit and stepped between them.

"I need to talk with your jock a second," she said, as though speaking to another trainer's rider in the paddock was the most natural thing in the world.

Reno looked her over. "Do you mind? I'd like to have a word with her myself."

"I promise this'll only take a minute."

"Rachel, don't make me call the paddock judge."

"Reno, please."

"If it'll speed your departure, be my guest."

"Thank you," she told him, then turned to Nikki. "Oregon State Racing Commission just informed me that my entrant in the Westover Meadows Derby was dropped to second. You won the race. Congratulations."

Nikki burst into a smile that she deftly counteracted by pursing her lips. "I would've won it a month ago," she said, matter-of-factly, "if the asshole who rode your horse hadn't rammed me into the rail."

Rachel, who was disposed neither to big gestures of good

will nor ducking verbal punches, twisted her mouth in a frown. She experienced a disturbing sensation of seeing a younger version of herself, while Reno grinned in the background. Changing topics seemed the wisest move.

"How's it going with Lucifera?"

"Fine."

"Fine?"

"Yesterday we went swimming, but this morning she behaved herself, so I just galloped her on the beach."

"Both of you went swimming? In the pool?"

"The ocean."

"The Pacific Ocean, for crissakes?"

"Yeah."

Reno butted in now. "Lady, can you have this conversation some other time, please?"

Rachel responded to his request by thrusting an index finger toward Nikki's face. "See me in the morning," she said, and wheeled to leave so fast she got dizzy.

Back at her saddling stall, she wobbled to catch her balance. Jim Bruner regarded her suspiciously and spat out a mouthful of chew.

"Never mind," she snapped.

"Didn't say nothin'."

"Don't."

~

The post parade rushed by in a blur, then the bell rang and Nikki was at the quarter-pole behind a wall of horses with nowhere to go. When a trickle of daylight appeared between rumps, she cut her mount, twice quickly, then twice more, oblivious to the hail of clods exploding like dirt grenades on her face and neck and arms. On she rode, harder, harder, until it was not Nikki Summers riding, but someone meaner, crueler, more ruthlessly successful. Win, she must win, a voice whispered in her head.

"How's the view, Jimmy?" she shouted to Bruner as her

mount swept past his at the eighth pole.

Nikki crossed under the wire, first by a nose, and popped up in the irons with a cowboy yeee-haaa and almost fell off. Her mount acted equally wired and pranced in place after galloping back, air shooting in and out his dilated nostrils, tied-tongue flopping dark purple from the side of his mouth. A groom led them into the winner's circle. Reno placed a hand on the horse's hip and maneuvered him into position for the photo. The horse leaped sideways and nearly trampled several people, who kept right on smiling as they scrambled to get out of the way. By the time the photographer snapped the picture, the winner's circle held more jubilant faces than Nikki could ever recall seeing at one time, a victory celebration that more than compensated for her belated win in the Oregon Derby.

Peninsula Park
April/May 1994

Nikki went directly to Reno McAllister's barn early the next morning and breezed four head, then reported to Maltby Aurora. The agent gave her a list of trainers to see. Having made up her mind to wait until the track closed to speak with her mother, Nikki hustled from barn to barn and caught fourteen head before the outrider shut the gate at ten o'clock. In between, she turned down no less than a dozen horses for lack of time. Much to her shock, the rejected trainers acted all the more eager to procure her services, a heretofore unprecedented phenomenon that boosted her confidence. Her bubble developed a slow leak as she came to find that her popularity emanated not from the public revelation of her talent but from a revenge factor—namely, every racetracker she encountered noted her first Peninsula Park win with obvious delight, none of them shy in expressing satisfaction that she had beaten Rachel Nottingham's favorite. By the end of the morning, Nikki got tired of hearing about it.

Dismounting her last horse in the gap, she handed the reins to a groom, then broke and ran for her mother's barn. The same tall blond kid who had saddled Rachel's entrant in the Westover Meadows Derby intercepted Nikki in the shed row. She watched as recognition erupted on his placid face. She stopped.

"You're that girl jock from Oregon who cost us the Westover Meadows Derby. You win on Reno's horse last night," he said.

Nikki planted her hands on her hips. "Yeah?"

He threw back his shoulders and attempted to puff up a chest flatter than an ironing board. "No offense, but you'd better beat it."

"Like you think I'm gonna scope out your horses or something? I've got way more class than that, pal."

"You ride for Reno McAllister."

"I'll be riding for all the top trainers before long."

"Not this barn," he said with authority.

"You want to bet?" she all but shouted. "I've been galloping that gray filly."

"The boss is just desperate to straighten out Luci. When she's ready to race she'll have a boy on her back."

Nikki rose up on her toes and looked him in the Adam's apple. "Do you know who I am? Do you have a clue?"

Sam rubbed his head. "Uh. Nikki Summers?"

She counted to ten and considered the consequences. "Oh, forget it. Your *boss* told me to see her this morning.

He pointed down the shed row. "Last door on the left, but you're wasting your time. Rachel'll never ride you."

"We'll see," Nikki said, sweeping past him.

She stopped at her mother's office and knocked.

"What," Rachel yelled.

"It's me."

Silence.

"It's me. Nikki."

Complete silence.

She raised a fist to knock again, then let the arm drop to her side. With butterflies contesting a dogfight in her stomach, she shifted from foot to foot and waited. After what seemed like minutes, her mother called out to come in and Nikki opened the door and stepped inside. Rachel sat at her desk, her face partially obscured by a layer of smoke that hung in the air like a smog bank.

"I hope you're smart enough not to smoke," she said, extinguishing a cigarette.

The insult, as Nikki heard it, tweaked a nerve between her pride and mouth, resulting in a temporary self-control malfunction. "I can smoke if I want."

Rachel cocked an eyebrow. "Bad habit."

"Maybe I like the taste," Nikki said next. "You're not the boss of me."

Rachel tossed a pack and matches. "Be my guest."

Nikki jammed a cigarette between her lips, fairly confident the filter end went in her mouth, then realized it was a mighty poor time to recall that she had always used a lighter on any candles or campfires. The first match fell apart from repeated inept striking. The second seared her finger. The third shot onto the carpet, and she nonchalantly stomped out the flame. She managed to light up on her fourth try but — after inhaling a puff — succumbed to a coughing fit.

Rachel, who sat watching with a grim expression, calmly snatched the cigarette and ground it into an ashtray. "I'm going out to see Lucifera gallop on Monday morning. No use both of us driving, so meet me by the barn gate at ten." She gestured toward the door with a flick of a hand, the conversation over.

But Nikki's capacity for rational thought remained at large. "I'm accustomed to a lighter, not matches," she said, determined to get in the last word. She then spun on her heel to leave and stomped straight into the wall, smacking her forehead on a beefcake calendar. The collision jump started her intellect. Thus embarrassed by her graceless exit and the confrontation in general, she slunk from the room to the sound of her mother's muffled laughter.

~

After Nikki left the office, Rachel focused on business, diving face first into her life's purpose as a horse trainer like someone who had forgotten to check the pool for water. She filled her mind with schemes to acquire more horses to win more races, until there was no room left for any doubts or the recollection of doubts. She drank enough coffee to wake a corpse. Smoked a pack of cigarettes, one after the other. Gave herself a mother of a headache.

That same evening, she dined in the Turf Club with a potential client, then they went to her grandstand box and talked business. The man was a bald, multi-chinned proprietor of a West Coast fitness chain. She soon discovered that he wanted to train his own horses and needed a licensed trainer to obtain stalls and saddle for him in the paddock, a puppet to take credit for his genius, nothing more. He would call the shots, all the shots, every last bullet. He'd pay half her usual day money per head, she would provide straw and feed, he'd hire his own exercise rider and grooms. When the guy had finished blabbing, she pointed to the door.

Based on her theory that trainers possessed a limited amount of patience for schmoozing rich people, Rachel decided she had exhausted her supply and turned her attention to winning races with her present resources. Taking her best shot, she had entered a solid $32,000 claimer for a $25,000 tag. The gelding was the odds-on favorite to win the evening's sixth race and a sure bet to be claimed, except that she had taken pains to leave his soundness in doubt.

In the two weeks since his last race, she had given him one five-eighths work and a quarter-mile blowout, in addition to his usual mile-and-a-half gallop every other day. On both occasions, unbeknownst to anyone, she drew a syringe of blood from the gelding, which she hid up her sleeve and squirted into his left nostril after she pulled him up with her pony on the backstretch. A clever trick from her repertoire of clever tricks that savvy trainers knew and used. Like most of the horses at the track, the gelding was a bleeder and already ran on the permitted drug Lasix, a diuretic, given to prevent hemorrhaging of the lungs due to hypertension or over exertion. Not wanting the clockers to see blood and report him to the state veterinarian—who would put him on the bleeder's list, making him ineligible to race until he completed a workout to the veterinarian's satisfaction—she had tucked a white rag into her pocket and made a show of discreetly wiping away the blood as she rode past the trainers' stand with the gelding. A bad bleeder was a horse to be leery of, an animal on the verge of a long lay-up.

Sure enough, the gelding had gone unclaimed and won the

race. Two days later, she entered a colt that was coming off a win for a $16,000 tag in a $10,000 claiming race, a double drop in class intended to make trainers think he had physical problems. This time, she had implemented the opposite strategy, going so far as to gallop the colt without polos or running bandages, giving trainers a clear look at his clean legs. Nothing bred suspicion faster than the truth. But Rachel hated to chance losing a sound colt and took an added precaution. Two races before the colt's, she left her box and went in search of fellow trainer and rule bender Opal O'Reilly.

Rachel marched past rows of parimutuel windows, past concession stands selling popcorn, pizza, prime rib sandwiches, nachos, egg rolls, sushi, tacos, the aromas blending into an unrecognizable stench that piqued her headache. In the bargain bleachers at the north end of the grandstand, she found Opal under a floppy sunbonnet, drinking beer and eating a hot dog smothered in pickled jalapeño peppers. Opal stuffed a bite of hot dog into her mouth and motioned to an empty spot beside her on the bench.

Rachel sat down. "Want to do me a favor?"

Opal took a swig of her beer. "Not particularly."

"Come on. I need your help."

"What's it worth?"

"A hundred cash."

"Do I look that hungry?"

Rachel blew a breath through her bangs. "Okay. A stall."

This perked Opal's interest. "A stall?"

"Till the end of the meet."

Opal made a pained face. "What do I have to do, kill someone?"

"No, smart ass. I'm running a horse in the seventh that I don't want to lose. Drop in a claim."

"Nottingham, protective claims are against the rules. I'm to risk my license, not to mention my sterling reputation for a crummy stall?"

"Two stalls," Rachel said, through clenched teeth.

Opal about fell off the bench. "What's the catch?"

"I'll need you to claim a few more before the meet ends."

"Oh, I get it. *My* two stalls are gonna be filled with *your* horses."

"*No*. To keep from arousing the stewards' suspicion you'll ship anything you claim to Oceanstead Farm. They'll train there for a month, then I'll pretend to legitimately buy them from you. Of course, in reality I'll pay you immediately."

"Stewards aren't completely blind."

"I'll have you run one and I'll claim it back to throw off the stews," Rachel said.

"Inside of a month that'd be for a higher price. Suppose I'd have to give you back the difference."

"*Yes*."

"You've fed Reno a bellyful of bad ones," O'Reilly said. "Man ought to be gettin' gun shy by now."

"He's not the only trainer with money. I can't afford to part with any more pay horses. My clients haven't been real eager to claim replacements."

"Well it's all fine and dandy, but I'm eating common grub with the poor folk. Ain't got twenty-five bucks let alone twenty-five thousand."

"You miserly old broad, I know for a fact you've got at least forty-grand in the office."

Opal's smile split the corners of her mouth with deep creases. "What makes you so sure I'll sell a horse back for the same price if it wins?"

Rachel smiled with equal aplomb. "What makes *you* so sure I'll reimburse you if it staggers home dead last?"

~

Nikki won another race for Reno McAllister on Saturday afternoon. The horse felt sore but she warmed it up thoroughly in the post parade, drove to the front at the break, rode and rode, and hung on by a whisker. Back in the Jockeys' Room, she shed her silks and went to the jock's kitchen, a stark, narrow room with three round tables and a counter where orders were

Munchkin,

placed. To celebrate the win, she treated herself to a nonfat frozen yogurt cone. Between all the horses she was breezing each morning and her intense workout program, Nikki had lost a few pounds and felt leanly fit. The cook doled out a smallish serving and teased her about getting fat. She directed a glance toward his potbelly, then proceeded to an empty table and sat licking her cone. At another table, two riders talked while they ate. She couldn't help but overhear.

"Nottingham'll catch McAllister before the meet's over," the one said.

"No way," the second replied. "Bitch's history. She's gettin' her ass whipped."

The first shook his head. "Don't hold your breath. She can train."

"You're just kissing up to her 'cause she sticks you on something if she's got a pair in the same race," the other said. "Notice she always sticks you on the one that barks."

"I win six races for her so far this meet."

"And she's win what, seventy races?"

"Bruner gets hurt, I'm her man."

"I'd rather ride the jock room couch. Cunt's a fucking bitch."

Nikki sprang to her feet. "Don't call her that."

The two riders turned to look.

"Don't call her that," she repeated.

"Don't call who what?" the one said.

Nikki ignored him, focusing on his buddy. "Take back what you called Nottingham."

"I'm not taking back shit," he said.

"Take it back." Nikki stepped closer, the yogurt cone clutched in her hand.

"Kiss off. Nottingham's a cunt."

Nikki crammed the frozen yogurt cone into his face. "Eat shit, you fucking elf."

The jockey jumped to his feet, cussing and wiping his eyes. He chucked his chili at her, bowl and all, while the other rider let loose with a large cola, followed by a dish of potato salad.

251

She dodged everything and lunged for an empty table that hadn't been cleared, launching a Styrofoam cup of lukewarm coffee and a half-eaten hamburger in retaliation. The two men fired salt and peppershakers and whatever else lay handy. A ketchup bottle bounced off her stomach and a plate sailed past her ear like a Frisbee. The cook was cursing the three of them. With nothing left to throw, she covered her head and ducked a flying chair, then sprinted for the door.

~

"Nice touch. Starting an altercation in the Jockeys' Room. Trainers like a rider with spunk," Maltby Aurora informed her, first thing the next morning. He removed his bowler, revealing a thin layer of neatly shaved hair the color of semi-sweet chocolate, then patted his forehead with a monogrammed hanky.

"Funny," Nikki said, with no trace of amusement.

"I'm completely serious. Another win didn't hurt either."

"Then how come I'm not riding any today?"

"Several trainers approached me about changing riders for this afternoon, but they were desperate trainers looking for miracles," he said. "Slow horses make even the best jockey look bad."

They stood along the edge of the gap while the sun rose in a cloudless sky over brown hills to the east. Horses and riders flowed past, an unpredictable river predisposed to flooding its banks. Nikki focused on Maltby Aurora's broad face with an intensity that so thoroughly blotted out the scenery, the two of them might have been stuffed into one of those old photo booths and the black curtain drawn.

"I can't win if I don't have any mounts," she said.

He took her by the arm and guided her clear of a fractious horse. "Patience is a virtue, in case you hadn't heard."

She brushed off his hand. "Virtue is for losers."

The agent cleared his throat with a low rumble. "You'll be riding five or six short-priced horses a card before the week's out. Trainers have watched you ride and like what they've seen."

Nikki studied his face, searching for deception, finding none. "You think?"

"I know."

"Five or six?" she asked, breaking into a smile.

"Or eight. Keep winning and I'll have you riding every race. Oh, and next time use your knuckles, not an ice cream cone. Give your competitors a big black shiner and I'll sell you faster than Microsoft."

She stopped smiling. "Mouthy bastard really ticked me off."

Maltby Aurora returned his hat to his head, careful to impart a distinct sideways cant. "So I gathered."

"Be sure and check with Nottingham. She might stick me on something."

"The definitive word is *thing*," Maltby said. "From the disturbing rumors I've been hearing, she already has."

"Lucifera can run and I'm going to ride her."

He laughed. "Silly girl. She won't ride you. No doubt she'll pay you. Nottingham pays. I'd even venture to say she'll give you a bonus for straightening out a desperado like that gray, but ride you, she won't."

"She will."

The agent rapped on her helmet with a fist. "Wake up. Nottingham's using you."

Nikki slapped his hand away. "She is not."

"Oh yes, Summers. This is the nineties. It's chic to rip people off."

~

True to Maltby Aurora's prediction, Nikki found herself named on six head for Wednesday's card. After the draw that Sunday morning, she drove out to Oceanstead Farm and spent the afternoon working with Lucifera. The filly let out a nicker when she spotted Nikki coming down the shed row with an armload of tack. She chalked up Lucifera's reaction to the expectation of a granola bar and tried to regard her like a thing whose light would be extinguished when economics deemed it profitable. The filly rotated her nose in vigorous circles over Nikki's head, a happy if eccentric greeting. Nikki responded with a pat on the neck and kind words, figuring her job would be easier if the filly liked her, figuring her job would be impossible if Lucifera didn't. A few minutes later, when led saddled from the stall, the filly stopped to stretch in the doorway, easing down until her belly was a foot from the ground and shutting her eyes with a yawn, just as Donnie used to do. Nikki looked the other way. She knew better than to get attached to a horse.

~

Having thought up a list of intelligent topics to discuss with her mother on the drive to Oceanstead Farm on Monday morning, Nikki found that she needn't have bothered. Rachel stuck a Led Zeppelin tape in the cassette deck and cranked the volume. Nikki could barely hear herself think. Her mother drummed her fingers along the steering wheel in beat to the music, locked her focus on the road, and roared past slower vehicles—namely, all vehicles—in what surely was an attempt to reach Oceanstead Farm in record time. Nikki swore the Ferrari was pulling G's on the turns. Talking was out. After ten minutes, she got carsick and spent the remainder of the drive trying not to throw up.

They went separate directions at Oceanstead Farm. Rachel rushed off to watch her other horses gallop, while Nikki brushed and tacked Lucifera. An hour later, it became apparent that Rachel had no intention of dealing with them anytime soon, so Nikki walked over to a vending machine in the farm's office and bought a package of jellybeans. Her upset stomach had calmed and she hadn't eaten anything for breakfast or lunch but an apple. She attempted to share her snack, but the concept of sharing did not appeal to Lucifera, who ended up hogging most of the candy. After an hour, Nikki grew antsy. To pass time, she brushed the filly, massaging her darkly dappled gray coat with a nubby rubber mitt, then wiping her sleek with a soft rag. Lucifera was one shiny horse when Rachel appeared in the doorway, some two hours later.

"Let's go," was all she said, before heading off to the other end of the barn like a creature whose livelihood depended on constant motion.

Chasing the image of a shark from her mind, Nikki led Lucifera outside. When the foreman piddled around with his cigarette and was slow to offer a leg-up, Nikki swung aboard herself and started down the dirt road to the ocean with Rachel leading the way at a safe distance. Every so often, Rachel glanced over her shoulder in expectation of disaster, if judged by her dour frown. Nikki kept any comments to herself.

"Get tied on tight," Rachel said, after they'd gone about fifty feet. "I don't feel like chasing that gray cow up and down some goddamn beach for miles and miles."

"I'm tied on," Nikki said.

"Good. Stay that way."

"I intend to."

"That's what everyone says."

They walked on to the clomp of hooves. At the creek, Nikki halted the filly.

"Where's the bridge?" Rachel asked, totally serious.

"It's not very deep," Nikki said. "I can hop off and lead you over on Luci."

Rachel waved off the suggestion with a "no thanks." She removed her boots and socks, rolled her pants to her knees, and started across in Lucifera's wake. The filly scampered up the muddy bank on the opposite shore without difficulty. She and Nikki waited at the top for Rachel.

"Careful, it's kinda slippery."

"I can see," Rachel said. "My vision hasn't deteriorated to the point of blindness yet."

"It's slipperier than it looks."

"I'm sure I'll manage."

Halfway up the bank, Rachel lost her balance and fell with a splat, sliding feet first to the bottom. Looking like a professional mud wrestler, she crawled to the top and rose with great dignity as if nothing had happened. Lucifera cocked one ear forward, one back, and exhaled with a snort. Nikki gazed on with the gravest of faces before bursting into laughter.

Rachel spit out a mouthful of grit and wiped mud from her face along with a splinter of a smile. "It's not funny."

"Sorry." Weaving a finger in and out of Lucifera's mane, Nikki squeezed her lips together till they ached.

"Don't you dare tell Reno."

"I won't."

"Promise?"

"I promise."

"Stop grinning."

"I'm trying."

On the beach, Nikki sent Lucifera into a trot to warm up before galloping away. After a half-mile, they turned around and raced back across the firm wet sand, gray on gray, to streak past Rachel. She was smiling.

~

Rachel lay in bed unable to sleep that night, so she turned on a lamp and read the racing form for an hour. She compared times and track ratings and speed indexes, but the numbers eluded her comprehension, a lost cause. Nervousness brewed in her gut, a compilation of every nasty thing she'd eaten the past month, an achy flutter that had nothing to do with food. After another twenty minutes, she tossed aside the form, got up and went to the closet of her spare bedroom. There, buried beneath chronologically ordered stacks of win photo albums, she dug out an old scrapbook and sat cross-legged on the floor, looking at the snapshots within. Nicole's baby pictures. Her first steps in a pink lace dress with ruffled panties and white patent leather shoes. Smiling toothless atop a tricycle. There were no pictures of Nicole beyond age six. Monica had never sent any and Rachel hadn't asked. Rachel skimmed over the remainder of the photos and read pages from the diary she had started after Nicole's birth.

Febuary '66 — Three Months

Babies are ugly (unlike foals) but Nicole is beautiful (light brown hair, blue eyes, long black lashes). She doesn't cry much. And a good thing because dad gets cranky when she cries. After three months of sloppy diapers and jabbing myself in the thumb, I'm still a klutz at folding and pinning.

December '66 — Age One

Nicole can walk fine, but just to be sure she always goes around so she can touch the wall or cupboards with one hand. While she does this there is always her happy little song. Jibber, jabber, jibber, jabber. Had to run out to the barn and check on a sick horse yesterday and while I was gone Nicole pulled a Christmas ball off the tree and ate it (one of those little round shiny ones). Thank goodness the thing went through her in one piece. Found it in her you-know-what the next day. Father made me wash it and hang it back on the tree. Yuck!

July '68 — Age Two-and-a-half

A couple months ago, I built Nicole a playhouse out back by the creek. She has a play stove. One day I saw what looked like chocolate in a pan. I said, "Nicole, what are you cooking?" and she looked up and said, "Shiten (chicken) poo." We had some chickens in the barns and that's exactly what she was cooking. I told her that shiten poo didn't sound very appetizing.

September '68

Nicole was napping, so I went outside to take the wash off the line, as it had started to rain. When I came in, this tiny voice said,

"How do I look, mommie?" There she was, stark naked with cold cream all over her body, finished off by a substantial layer of baby powder. "Like you need a bath," I told her.

Rachel closed the scrapbook and pushed it across the carpet as far as her arm would reach. The album made her feel like a stranger stealing a peek at someone else's life. She couldn't decide whether something she had once possessed was now missing, some maternal sensibility or instinct or desire long dis-remembered like all things even remotely maternal in her life. Or if the album had simply been a ruse meant to con her pragmatic side into believing that she could be a successful mother. Rachel sat on the floor for more than an hour worrying that the former was the truth and wondering if this missing part of her was irretrievable or if she just feared finding it again. She returned to bed with the racing form in hand. After studying Wednesday's card till well past midnight, she couldn't name a single horse but knew that Nikki was riding three for Reno McAllister.

~

The detention barn, the test barn, and the offices of the official veterinarians at Peninsula Park were located in the same building at the west end of the center stable row, adjacent to the gap. At approximately 8:20 p.m., a guard slid open the solid wood door to the detention barn and the fillies scheduled to run in Wednesday's sixth race, a $12,500 claiming contest, left walking or prancing alongside their grooms, single-file and in post parade order.

Rachel stood in the gap and watched them pass, making no attempt to hide her objective. Most had their legs concealed beneath polos or paddock boots, so she gauged their soundness from how they stepped, eliminating from consideration the two who walked as though stepping on nails and the one with a subtle limp. The second-to-last filly wore a blanket made out of an army camouflage material. Rachel gave the trainer credit for having a devious sense of humor. Her attention lingered on the last filly, a chubby testament to bad training.

"Find any runners?" Ginny asked, from behind.

Rachel turned. "Do you think I look fat?"

"You look slim and trim as ever, dear."

"I'm going to start working out."

"Better focus your energy on catching Reno McAllister."

"For crissakes, Ginny, I'd be better off catching the Ebola virus."

Ginny's eyebrows ascended her forehead. "I was referring to the trainer's race."

Rachel winced. "Oh."

"I see Reno's already won two races today." Ginny was still staring with raised-brows.

Rachel opened her mouth to relate the trick she'd pulled the other day—she won the race and had Opal claim the horse, having out-shaken Reno—then considered the odds of Ginny accidentally sharing the story with the biddies in the Turf Club. "I'm only five down. There's still three months left to run."

"Last week you seemed more concerned, that's all."

"I'm concerned as holy hell."

"Funny, I'm not sensing the same animosity between you and Reno."

"Okay, so maybe I don't hate him anymore."

Ginny's eyebrows climbed her forehead a little further, if that were possible. "You have the hots for Reno McAllister?"

"*No,*" Rachel said, wincing again. "I just don't hate him anymore."

All the same, she had been avoiding Reno, an easy enough thing not to speak to her rival, though she was finding it more difficult to eliminate him from her thoughts. But not impossible. She started across the infield at a brisk pace, her boots leaving deep footprints on the sand pathway. Up ahead, the horses in the sixth race were halfway to the paddock. Rachel followed their progress like a wolf stalking a herd of elk until she reached the other side, then she stopped and waited for Ginny to catch up. An attendant slid open the inside rail and the women walked across the racetrack and into the grandstand, past rows of mahogany red tables with white parasol canopies, past hanging baskets of red and white geraniums. Rachel stepped in line at an espresso stand and dug through her wallet for money.

"My treat. Want something?"

"An iced tea, please. That new girl, Nikki Summers, rode both of Reno's winners," Ginny said. "You might try giving her a chance on something."

"I have. Lucifera."

"A chance in a race."

Rachel paid the cashier and found a table. She sat and sucked the whipped cream from the top of her double mocha latte, the act requiring her complete visual attention. "You know how I feel about women jockeys."

"Looks to me like she can 'horseback,' as you're fond of putting it."

"She can ride some."

"People are saying that you're using her," Ginny said.

"I've been paying her good money to gallop Lucifera at the farm."

Rachel wasn't ready to tell Ginny or anyone else the truth about Nikki, and Nikki wasn't pressing the issue. All Nikki seemed to care about was riding. They hadn't spoken since last week at the beach, both going out of their way to snub each other if they happened to pass, though Rachel was disturbed to find that she always seemed to know where Nikki was when they were both on the racetrack. Her thoughts were interrupted by a light kick to the shin from Ginny.

"Yes?"

"You'd stand a much better chance of catching Reno, if you rode the hottest jockey at the track."

"That's debatable."

"You always ride the top jockey," Ginny said.

"*No.* Whoever rides for me ends up leading rider."

"You're being difficult, dear. Did you fall out of bed this morning?"

Rachel sighed. "I've already named her on a horse for Friday. Now can we drop it?"

Peninsula Park
June 1994

The outside world blurred, and for Nikki there was only winning and the process of winning. Unlike her previous life as a jockey, when she occasionally rode the fastest horse and won, she now also coaxed or coerced true long shots into the winner's circle. Having never imagined herself capable of such feats, her success was an addiction that locked her focus in a single direction. Straight ahead. She worked horses, kept fit, rode races. She watched the nightly Peninsula Park recap on television and read the racing form, watched and read nothing else. Her twice-weekly calls to Matt and Susan — who were in western Canada — became once weekly, then stopped altogether. By June, Nikki was the hottest jockey at Peninsula Park.

Soon thereafter, she came across a short article in the *Daily Racing Form* about an accident at Saguaro Downs in Phoenix, Arizona. A Westover Meadows jockey, Rita Marshall, had been killed in a Quarter Horse race when her mount broke both front legs and fell a length from the wire. Rita had fractured her neck and died instantly.

Closing her eyes, Nikki tried to picture Rita's face and hear her voice, but all she could manage was blackness with little spots and silence — augmented by the groan of water pipes from the neighboring room. Rita had become as one dimensional as a character in a book. Flat as a paper doll. After a few minutes, Nikki came to the conclusion that all her memories of Westover Meadows had taken on a surreal quality. Likewise, the past month and a half at Peninsula Park consisted of faces and names but little detail. Even Rachel had receded into the landscape. Mother's Day had been a memorable

Sunday for Nikki, only because she'd ridden two winners and Rachel had saddled losing favorites in both races.

Three weeks ago—and just an hour before post time—Rachel had scratched a horse that Nikki was named to ride. Supposedly, the colt had been colicky, though Nikki later heard via backside gossip that the colt hadn't really been sick, that Rachel had lied to obtain a late scratch. Rumor had it, Rachel feared the colt would be claimed. A more likely scenario, Nikki suspected, was that Rachel had changed her mind about riding *her.* Since winning kept Nikki on a keel that was far from even, yet disturbingly straight, she bided her time like someone who expected to come out on top in the long run. To that end, she won more races. And felt extra pleased each time she won one for Reno McAllister, a fact that she'd have proudly admitted had she any friends at Peninsula Park to tell.

~

Three weeks earlier, Rachel had, in a weak moment, named Nicole to ride one of her horses. Rachel didn't really know why she'd done it but convinced herself that she was doing what she had to do to win races. Her common sense side backed this theory one hundred percent. After all, McAllister was winning races riding her daughter. Any fool could see what was wrong with *that* picture. Rachel dismissed a sentiment that the world had conspired to make her feel guilty. Or, worse yet, that she was under the influence of anything the least bit maternal.

Later that evening, she had been attempting to unlock the door to her condominium when she heard crying. She looked across the street and spotted a small boy collapsed on the lawn in a wailing pile of skinny legs and baggy shorts. By the time a woman ran from the house to gather the child in her arms, Rachel was recalling the time Nicole had ridden right off her rocking horse...how she'd cried but only briefly, and more out of frustration than fright. The next morning, Rachel had scratched the horse that Nicole was named to ride. Afterward, Rachel wondered why she had yanked the colt from the race rather than simply change riders. The answer eluded her, but she'd managed to convince herself that it was *not* because changing riders would've reflected unfavorably upon Nicole.

Three weeks later, Rachel had come to the conclusion that she was losing her mind along with the trainer's race. She had fallen seven wins behind Reno McAllister, who was winning all too often with Nicole in the irons. Watching her daughter win race after race for Reno about tore Rachel in two. While half of her felt proud, the other half became furious whenever she spotted Nicole on one of Reno's horses. How dare she take sides against her mother, Rachel would think, then wince. From a logical standpoint, she couldn't justify her decision to ignore a jockey who was routinely winning on horses that had no business winning, but her emotions were in charge, leaving her about as rational as the weather. When clients Larry and Natasha Parker insisted that Nikki ride one of their horses, Rachel gave in to their demand without an argument.

Their filly was making her first start but was fit and had been training sharply, so Rachel expected her to run well, if not win. Jockeys would lick Rachel's boots to ride such a live mount, but Nikki had made no effort to stop by the barn, as was customary, the morning of the race. She had nothing to say in the paddock either, her weight slouched onto one hip with her arms folded and her whip tucked beneath and an expression of cocky disinterest on her face. Rachel recited her instructions, only to find them greeted with silence. The slightest of nods revealed that Nikki had heard. Her reaction or lack thereof caused something to bubble inside Rachel. She thought she might yet grab Nikki by the wrist and tow her aside and give her an ass chewing on the finer points of jockey/trainer etiquette.

But the paddock judge shouted for riders up.

After the trainer in the preceding stall gave his jockey a leg up, Nikki looked at Rachel and said, "If this thing's fit enough to win, I'll see you in the winner's circle."

There was no time for Rachel to reply. The groom led the filly off and Nikki jogged alongside, hopping on her right foot in expectation of a boost that was late in coming. When Rachel caught up, she grabbed hold of Nikki's boot and about launched her over the other side. A handful of mane was all that kept Nikki from falling off. After the horses had filed from the paddock, Rachel kicked the wooden partition between stalls so hard that she limped the whole way to her box. She studied the racing form rather than watch the post parade, glad that Ginny was out of town, glad that the filly's owners were watching the race from their own private box. At the announcer's call, "They're all in the gate," Rachel looked up. She raised her binoculars as the bell rang.

By unlucky coincidence, her stable jockey, Jim Bruner, was riding a long shot in the same race and had drawn the adjacent outside post position. When Rachel's filly broke slowly, not an uncommon occurrence with first-time starters, Bruner veered toward the inside rail and shut off Nikki. Her mount clipped heels and fell. The riderless filly jumped up and galloped after the field, leaving Nikki behind—a purple and gold and white splat on the track.

Rachel dropped the binoculars and threw herself in the direction of the door. Down the stairwell she ran with the announcer's call blaring incomprehensibly and her heart pounding as if it might break, then she was on the ground level, charging through the crowd. She reached the Jockeys' Room as the horses were galloping back.

The two-story, white-and-red compound that housed the riders during the races was strictly off limits to trainers, so she paced outside near the entrance, wondering if she'd ever felt as frightened in her entire life. She thought about why she felt so afraid and scared herself even more. The track ambulance pulled away from the starting gate, drove clockwise around the first turn, then off the track at the Jockeys' Room, which meant Nikki would not be going to the hospital. Rachel was there when the door opened. Nikki climbed out and lowered a towel from her face. Fresh blood trickled from her nose and down the front of her silks.

Rachel opened her mouth and was relieved to hear

something practical come out. "You okay?"

"Five horse dropped me...sorry," Nikki said, groggily — like someone who'd just fallen on her head going thirty-five miles per hour.

"Anything broken?"

Nikki wiped her nose and spit out a piece of chipped molar. "Long as I land on my head I never get hurt."

"I think you should take off the rest of your mounts."

"I'm fine." Nikki took a wobbly step and almost fell.

Rachel lunged forward to help, except her feet refused to move. She watched as the medics who drove the ambulance steadied Nikki. She assured the two men that she was unhurt and shooed them away, swatted at them with the back of her hand until they backed off. The taller one shrugged at his shorter companion, who sternly shook his head. He told Nikki that they would have to check her out more thoroughly if she intended to ride her remaining mounts on the card, then explained that they would wait for her inside the Jockeys' Room.

"You're done riding for the day," Rachel said.

Nikki tottered as though she might blow over. "Say again?"

"You're going to the hospital for a complete check-up, and you're definitely not riding tomorrow, either."

Like a tin girl in need of oil, Nikki nodded in rapid succession with each nod coming slower than the previous one until the motion ceased altogether. Her face went blank as fresh snow.

"Screw you," she said. "I'm on some live horses."

~

More certain than ever that something inside her was about to blow if she didn't let off some steam, Rachel had requested to speak with Jim Bruner after Nikki disappeared inside the Jockeys' Room. The clerk of scales shook his head. When she gave him a murderous look, he relented and called out for her stable jockey. A moment later, Bruner emerged sheepishly, like a dog with his tail tucked between his legs. Rachel locked her hands together behind her back, then informed him that he had ridden his last horse for her. He swung his head to one side and spit. She fired the dirtiest look in her arsenal and walked away to the pleasant sound of his pleading for her to reconsider.

"Never thought I'd hear Jim Bruner grovel," Rachel said, recounting the tale to Ginny, a few weeks later.

In light of her mental state at the time, Rachel had left out certain parts of the story, such as how she'd gone directly to the nearest bar and gotten drunk, and how she completely forgot to check on the filly, who, luckily for Rachel, survived the fall uninjured. And how she had explained her nonappearance at the barn after the race to clients Larry and Natasha Parker, by admitting that she'd tied one on. Then saying it was their fault because they insisted that she ride a girl jockey when she never rode girl jockeys, who were far more fragile than the boys and caused her excessive anxiety in the event of an accident, which was exactly what had happened. Her clients would have been hard pressed to find more bullshit at a feedlot.

Ginny was waiting patiently for the conversation to resume. She sat on the couch in Rachel's office and picked at a Caesar salad. Rachel finished the last of a chocolate milkshake, then swept aside a pile of bills, gripped the edge of her desk, and commenced doing forward leg lifts.

Ginny stopped chewing.

"What?" Rachel said.

"Nothing." Ginny hastily swallowed.

"You think I'm goofy, worrying about my weight, don't you?"

"Actually, I was thinking you should be more concerned with figures, not your figure." Making no effort to be diplomatic, Ginny stared directly at the slips of paper burying a full quarter of the desk.

Rachel's leg lifts became increasingly forceful until she might have been punting an imaginary football. She'd always paid her debts on time but had recently decided to disregard her M.O., along with any bills—seeing as she was ever so slightly broke. She muttered the word ten and switched legs.

"Ignoring the problem isn't going to make it go away," Ginny said.

Rachel made a face like someone entering an outhouse. She had a sudden revelation that there were positive aspects to not having a mother.

"Ginny, I plan on paying."

"I keep hoping so."

"I'm going to pay. Eventually."

"I've only mentioned it because I care."

"Thanks. Now can we talk about something else?"

"Of course, dear."

"Fine."

It took roughly ten seconds, by Rachel's estimation, for Ginny to bring up another happy subject.

"How's Lucifera doing?" she asked.

"Lucifera worked a half from the gate in forty-seven flat under a strangle hold and couldn't have blown out a match afterwards," Rachel said, without pause or inflection.

"When will she be ready to run?"

"There's a maiden allowance race next week."

"Is she that good?"

"Who *knows*. But after all I've gone through to get the filly to a race, I'd have to kill myself if someone claimed her first time out."

"Will you be riding Summers?"

Rachel kicked her foot high above her head, groaning from the effort and a sharp pain in her upper hamstring. "I *don't* know."

"Without her, Luci would never have come this far." Ginny reached for a tapestry handbag and removed a small sack with a thick sterling silver chain and a polished turquoise pendant the size of a quarter. "I brought you a little present. My nephew sent me this, but blue isn't my color."

Relieved to talk about something else—anything else, for that matter—Rachel smiled and put on the necklace. "Thanks. It's almost identical to my stable colors."

"Well, I suppose, but actually I was told it has protective powers. In case you fall off your pony or get kicked or whatnot."

"Yeah, that would be bad."

"We women have to stick up for one another, if you catch my drift."

"I caught it," Rachel said, in a sinking tone.

"On the chin?"

"In the teeth."

"I was aiming for your chin, dear."

"Listen, Ginny, I honestly can't decide who to ride on Lucifera. I may just flip a coin."

And that was the truth.

~

Nikki got even with Jim Bruner the following week. The old Nikki would have beaten herself up over all the things she might have done differently in the gate to get the filly to break faster. She would have second-guessed herself into taking a guilt trip for two weeks, maybe a month. She would have claimed full responsibility for falling in a race on her mother's horse, even though the head-on replay of the accident clearly showed Jim Bruner to be at fault. The new Nikki dumped all the blame on Bruner without a second thought.

Since the stewards suspended him for seven days over the incident, she had a week to plot her revenge. Rather than retaliate in a race and risk a suspension of her own, she opted for a sneak attack—an hour of phone calls yielding a business that sold a potent itching powder. Located in Chinatown, the tiny shop was a maze of cramped aisles with merchandise stacked to the ceiling: rice noodles, bamboo mats, porcelain dolls, bird cages, dried mushrooms, cans of exotic fruits, delicately painted dishes—a place of cluttered order that required vigilance not to break something. For fifty dollars cash, she received a small plastic bag of whitish powder. Before she left, the cashier warned her that the stuff would produce a serious red rash along the order of poison oak and was not suitable for party gags. Nikki promised to exercise caution. With that in mind, she was extremely careful not to spill the itching powder on anyone else's clothing but Jim Bruner's.

On the morning of the day Bruner was due to resume riding, Nikki hurried to the backside parking lot during the break for track renovation and made the short drive to the Jockeys' Room. The janitor, a former jockey of little note who was a favorite target of Bruner's cruel wisecracks, let her in. Just past eight, none of the valets or jockeys had arrived, so she was able to slip into the men's dressing area and access Jim Bruner's box and a neatly folded pile of four riding pants, five T-shirts, six briefs, and ten socks, all marked with his name. The janitor watched in silence as she slipped on latex gloves and went to work.

"Ain't seen nothing," he said, and walked off chuckling to himself.

By the last race of the day, Jim Bruner had scratched his body into an angry red rash from the neck down. The medics diagnosed his condition as an allergic reaction. Slow to heal, the rash kept breaking out anew for almost a week—until he had worn all the clothes that Nikki had dusted with the itching powder. Over the course of his "allergic reaction," Bruner lost on eleven even money favorites and had only two wins in thirty-four tries. Counting the three races that she'd won on the day of her fall, *after* Rachel ordered her to take off the rest of her mounts, Nikki had amassed thirteen victories. She kept track every night, scribbling statistics in a notebook before going to bed.

Several pages were dedicated to Lucifera's progress, as well, noting when she worked, the times, gate schooling, etc. Based on Nikki's training know-how, she estimated that Lucifera had outgrown Oceanstead Farm's bullring of a track and piss ant starting gate. Therefore, she wasn't surprised when Rachel found a stall for the big gray at Peninsula Park. Lucifera adjusted to the mile oval and the full-sized starting gate like a seasoned racehorse, while Nikki was happy to eliminate the drive to Oceanstead Farm from her weekday schedule. After six gallops, Lucifera worked from the gate with a pair of three-year-old geldings, the filly shifting gears of her own accord at the quarter-pole to leave the competition twenty lengths behind. Nikki might have been a 110-pound sack of shit, for all the success she had in slowing the filly.

Par for the course, Rachel's post-workout dialogue consisted of three or four fragmented questions that could be answered by a yes or a no, such as "Filly go good?" or "She fit enough to run?" Nikki either nodded or shook her head. The question of why Nikki hadn't been given another mount since the spill went undiscussed as well. With an excess of horses to ride for trainers who *wanted* to employ her, she didn't need her mother's business, so Nikki stockpiled Rachel's disrespect with her other injustices and continued to exercise Lucifera, confident that no other jockey could handle the gray. Nikki was counting on her indispensability to result in a win that would mean more than all her other wins combined. The Peninsula Park Derby. She had recently begun to think of it as her mother's comeuppance, although Nikki wasn't quite ready to admit that training the winner of a Grade 1, half-million-dollar stakes race was debatable punishment.

"Think she'd tolerate another jock?" Rachel asked, after Nikki dismounted at the barn following Lucifera's next work, a five-eighths breeze that she had completed in less than a minute to gallop out the six furlongs faster than some races were run. Nikki pretended she hadn't heard the question and walked away. Near the end of the week, she was paying for a potato, egg, and cheese burrito at a vendor's truck after the track had closed for training, when Maltby Aurora leaned over her shoulder.

"Careful," he said, speaking directly into her ear. "You have to tack twelve tomorrow."

Nikki stuffed change into her jeans and moved aside with her agent. "Maybe I'm gonna throw it up," she said.

"It's my understanding you don't utilize that particular weight loss procedure."

"Maybe I'll start."

"You work hard. I suppose one fattening treat probably won't hurt."

"It's for a horse," Nikki said, no longer tempted to rankle her agent by eating the burrito.

"A horse?"

"Lucifera."

"Nottingham's nightmare. I hope you smothered it with jalapeños."

"She likes them plain."

"You do know you won't be riding the filly?"

Nikki looked at Maltby. "I will too be riding her."

"I'm afraid not," he said.

"Who then?"

"Amanda Vasquez. An apprentice from Hollywood Park. Brunette, ivory complexion, freckles, comes up to about here on you." He pointed to her waist.

Nikki shook her head with confidence. "Rachel won't ride a bug girl."

Maltby cleared his throat with obvious deliberation. "Your mistake, as I've pointed out numerous times, was volunteering to work with the filly in the first place. Top jockeys do not gallop horses and they especially do not gallop certifiably crazy horses."

"I do my own thing," Nikki said.

"Let me repeat myself." The agent removed an antique style Swiss pocket watch and checked the time. "Top jockeys aren't exercise riders. They breeze workers and they ride races."

"Rachel won't ride another girl. I know she won't."

"Oh yes, Summers. Lucifera and Vasquez just drew the three hole in Saturday's second race."

A brief pause ensued from Nikki, after which she wiped the bewilderment from her face with the back of her hand, then punched a clenched fist into her open palm with a crisp clap. "I have to win more races," she said, and hurried away.

~

She went directly to the race office, took a freshly printed overnight of Saturday's entries from the stack on the counter, and discovered that A. Vasquez *was* named on Lucifera. Nikki stared at the paper in disbelief. Her insides went all achy and hollow. She wavered near tears. Then she stiffened and crumpled the paper, hurtled it into a trash barrel, and sprinted to her mother's barn. She found Rachel in the main tack room, mixing batches of leg paint. Nikki burst inside.

"You put Amanda Vasquez on Luci instead of me?"

Rachel poured rubbing alcohol from a gallon jug into a smaller plastic bottle, then added a pungent smelling liniment without looking up from her work. "I paid you for galloping the filly."

"I didn't do it for the money."

"I don't owe you any explanation."

Nikki flinched. "You used me?"

Rachel screwed a lid on the liniment and put it aside. She reached for an unmarked brown glass bottle. "I'm not obligated to ride you."

"My own mother used me."

Rachel stopped what she was doing and turned to look. "I'm not your goddamn mother."

Nikki stared back. "That's for sure. *She* wasn't a bitch."

A gasp, followed by the sharp report of breaking glass as the brown bottle slipped from Rachel's fingers, hit the floor, and shattered in a puddle of clear liquid capped by a faint rising mist evocative of dry ice. "You're fired," she said.

Nikki stomped from the room, pausing in the doorway. "You can't fire someone who's already quit," she said, without looking back, then slammed the door.

Down the shed row she went, her anger deflating like a popped balloon. She stopped at Lucifera's stall and looked around, half expecting to be confronted by Rachel's assistant, but it was lunch time and the barn appeared deserted except for the horses. Stepping inside, Nikki re-latched the full-screen gate and fed Lucifera the burrito, piece by piece, which she promptly devoured. Afterward, Nikki lay her face against Lucifera's neck and stroked her mane and the filly fell asleep where she stood. A horse in the next stall rustled a hay bag hung in its doorway. In the distance, a tractor emptied manure bins. Nikki searched her mind for childhood memories of her mother's warmth and kindness but couldn't find them. She kept expecting to hear Rachel emerge from the tack room but never did.

~

The next morning, Nikki awoke in a foul mood that grew fouler as the day progressed. First off, the *Daily Racing Form* had made a rude comment about her in its handicapping of Friday's third race. She was named on the 2-1 consensus favorite. She had ridden the same horse his last out as the favorite and accidentally dropped her whip for the first time in more than a year. The horse was fading badly at the time, having struggled the entire race over a muddy track surface. The trainer had blamed himself for not shoeing the horse in stickers.

"Mondo Dancer will be right there if Summers can hang onto her whip this time," was the *Form's* assessment, a harsh remark from a publication that reserved the majority of its criticism for the horses.

Secondly, a local television station had interviewed her during the eight o'clock break. The temperature had risen to seventy-five degrees by seven-thirty and she had worked nine head before the outrider closed the gate for track renovation. When she took off her helmet, her hair was wet with sweat and plastered to her head wherever it wasn't sticking straight up. The old Nikki wouldn't have worried about something as trivial as her appearance, but the new Nikki had taken to wearing make-up and dressing neater, in deference to the attention that came with success. And because she had been asked on dates by approximately one hundred men and a dozen women since becoming the hottest jockey in northern California and liked to look sharp when she told people no. And because she wasn't beautiful like Rachel and feared embarrassing her if people discovered they were mother and daughter.

Nevertheless, in spite of her helmet head hairdo, things went well until the reporter, a clean-cut slimeball with a smile like a piano keyboard, said, "An attractive woman jockey must have a real advantage over the male riders, considering ninety-percent of the trainers are men."

Since the interview was a live broadcast, she was debating whether to use the word screw in her answer, when the reporter waggled his eyebrows at her in a suggestive manner.

"It doesn't matter who you fuck, if you can't ride," she said, with a big smile.

That had ended the interview. The reporter relayed frantic hand signals to the grinning cameraman, who swung the camera away from her face.

"Nice," was all the reporter had said to her before leaving.

"My pleasure, dickslut," she had replied.

Later, Nikki was heading to her motel room for a nap when Maltby Aurora intercepted her in the parking lot. First off, he complimented her on her fine interview on the Channel 5 morning news, highlighted by her classy and intelligent choice of verbs, which had garnered a beep and a humorous remark from the sportscaster. Everyone in the kitchen—and there were no empty chairs in the cafeteria during the break—had laughed at her on the big screen television there. Maltby hadn't endured such an intense barrage of wisecracks since he'd taken violin lessons as a teenager. He went on to say that she was riding a short-priced horse in the feature race that evening, the Menlo Park Stakes, for trainer Opal O'Reilly, who was somewhat displeased about having to ride a *girl* jockey.

"O'Reilly partook in a quarrel with the horse's owners that was heard three barns away," Maltby said. "You were distinctly referred to as 'that damn chick.' Be sure and win."

Lastly, he informed her that Lucifera had ponied kindly on the main track with another rider up.

Nikki absorbed her agent's news without comment, then got in her car and drove to a nearby department store and bought something special to wear in the eighth race. Something to enlighten the old lady trainer who obviously had no respect for women jockeys. Afterward, Nikki went to her motel room and ate a small packet of trail mix while studying the racing form. She took an hour nap, stretched and did light exercises, showered, and arrived at the Jockeys' Room by five that evening. At nine-fifteen, she walked into the paddock for the $50,000 Menlo Park Stakes wearing heavy eyeliner, candy red lipstick, and two balloons stuffed inside a 42 D cup beneath her silks, her slightly cautious step indicative of someone who was accustomed to seeing where her feet went. Opal O'Reilly was too busy staring to shake the hand that Nikki extended.

"What the hell you pulling," O'Reilly said.

"What is it with women trainers snubbing women jocks?" Nikki said.

"Girls are too damn emotional. Always acting like silly boobs." O'Reilly pointed at Nikki's falsies. "I rest my case."

"I knew it was a boob thing."

"Cut the crap, honey."

"It's pretty crappy, all right. After all the races I've been winning, *some* trainers still won't ride me because I'm a woman."

"You'd score more points with a jock strap."

"That's my point. I don't need one."

"Don't go getting your dander up with me, honey. I'd yank you off this horse here and now, but my clients would throw a shit fit."

Nikki glanced toward the center of the paddock, where two older gentlemen in matching polo shirts the color of her silks were watching in amusement. "You mean the pair laughing on the owner's stand?"

O'Reilly gave her a sharp look. "Horse lays just off the pace and he's got one move. Don't you dare ask him before the quarter pole. And lose them damn jugs."

Nikki opened her silks with a rip of Velcro as the paddock judge and his assistants arrived on the scene. They confiscated the bra and balloons, imparting grave looks while straining not to smile. O'Reilly muttered a good luck and something unintelligible but for several profanities, before giving Nikki a leg up. From Nikki's higher vantage point atop the horse, she spotted Rachel standing by the entrance to the paddock though her mother had nothing in the race. Rachel waited there until the field was led past, conveying her displeasure with Nikki's stunt, by all appearances a woman in need of an exorcism. The only part of the evening that Nikki relished more was winning.

~

In the morning, her high spirits evaporated faster than ground fog. Her first thought upon waking was that she would not be riding Lucifera in her maiden race, a reality that defined her mood like a sucker punch. A sullen Nikki went about business with her usual competence and got through the ordeal without insulting any trainers. Nobody but Maltby Aurora seemed to notice a difference from her normal disposition. Before she could haul herself from the stable area and go hide, he cornered her outside a barn. He advised her to concentrate on the seven mounts she was riding and forget about Lucifera, who, in all likelihood, would end up killing her unfortunate apprentice jockey.

By the stable gate, Nikki was walking along with her head down, immersed in gloomy thoughts, when a familiar voice called her name. She looked up and there was Susan Wilcox. They hugged politely, then Nikki stepped away. She knew she should have felt pleased to see Susan but wasn't sure she did.

"Why aren't you in Canada?" Nikki asked.

"I'm in town for my brother's wedding," Susan said. "I've been kind of worried, since you haven't called lately."

"Never been better."

"So I hear. Read an article about you in *California Now*

magazine."

Nikki burst into a smile. "Can you believe they put me on the cover?"

Susan's smile faded. "Your new nickname was what really grabbed my attention. The blonde assassin."

"Nobody calls me that to my face," Nikki said.

"I don't imagine. The big question is how did you earn a nickname like *that?*"

"I didn't read the article."

"*Nikki.*"

She tossed her head back and stared at the sky. "I don't know. Maybe because I don't act like a bimbo, so the guys think I'm cold-blooded? Or maybe because I shoved an ice cream cone in some punk's face and now I'm the scariest broad since Lizzie Borden."

Susan was definitely frowning now. "Wouldn't be because you beat the piss out of horses, would it?"

"Only if they're not trying." Because *that* was what trainers and horse owners wanted to see, Nikki thought, but knew better than to admit to Susan or anyone else that she usually whipped more air than horse, a technique she'd so mastered it was difficult if not impossible to detect, even on the head-on replay of a race.

"What in the hell happened to you?" Susan asked next.

"I'm winning a lot more races."

"At what cost?"

Nikki stared through Susan. "I'll survive a bit of moral degradation. Everybody does."

"This isn't you, Nikki."

"I'm making a ton of money. Enough to pay for college and then some."

Susan's expression lightened. "I guess that's one good thing. Now if you'd just come home and *go* to school."

They had slowly made their way to the parking lot and were standing in the middle of it when Rachel drove toward them, her eyes hidden beneath mirrored sunglasses that had been added to her wardrobe over the past week. She laid on the horn. Susan darted out of the way of the speeding car, but Nikki stood her ground, forcing her mother to brake hard. She revved the engine. Nikki raised a fist and extended a middle finger at the windshield. Her impromptu salute completed, she stepped aside and the Ferrari sped past, tires spitting gravel.

Susan was watching with big eyes.

"That," Nikki said, "was mother."

~

Lucifera circled the paddock on the muscle Friday night, switching her tail, bouncing in place, and kicking up her heels, much to Rachel's displeasure and the groom's dismay. Rachel waved him into the stall after two rounds and had him stand the filly with her big gray rump facing out of the stall so she couldn't kick the walls while being saddled. With the steward's permission, Rachel ran Lucifera without a whip and instructed her apprentice jockey not to slap the temperamental filly on the neck or anywhere else lest they part company. Rachel hoped for the best but expected the worst. Earlier in the day, she had thanked Maltby Aurora for not hustling a mount for Nikki in the race.

"Lucifera may prove herself a runner, but her trainer exhibits the class of a cheap claimer," he had said, and tipped his bowling ball of a hat.

Words that kept Rachel solidly grounded when the filly won the maiden allowance race by four lengths in a pull. For a woman who knew that using people was best accomplished without second thoughts, she was having third and fourth ones. Never in her lifetime could she have anticipated using her own offspring. And so, she set out to celebrate Lucifera's win with low expectations.

At the Blue Bayou, an upscale bar in nearby Redwood City, Rachel finished her first screwdriver in a dark corner of the room. Like all such places, lighting was not a high priority. Nor privacy. A jazz band began to play as she finished her second drink. The small dance floor soon filled, but she declined two offers, then no one else asked. Halfway through her third drink, Reno McAllister sat down at her table. This was not the first time she'd seen him there.

She glanced around. "I'm sure there's another empty chair somewhere."

He rose and took the one right next to hers, sliding a beer across the table in his hand. "You're awful unhappy for someone who just won a race with the horse from hell."

"It's a side effect of euphoria," she said. "What goes up, comes down." With the aid of a napkin, she flagged a waiter and ordered a Bloody Mary, then searched her purse for a cigarette but decided to visit the ladies' room instead. When she returned Reno was still sitting there.

Rachel ran her tongue over her teeth and gave him a look.

"You didn't have to come back," he said, with a shadow of a smile.

She scooted her chair clear of his and drained her drink while eying him over the rim.

He shrugged. "Guess it took some heavy-duty sweet talking to get a nut case like Lucifera into the winner's circle."

"Hired good help."

"That Nikki Summers does have a way with horses."

Rachel fished a lemon wedge from her empty glass, squeezed the slice dry, and drank the sour watery result. The band went into a song, loud and fast, the walls vibrating, the bass guitar pounding deep in her chest. She sensed that Reno was leading her somewhere she'd rather not go but felt too dispirited to throw her weight against the rope. Reno bought her another screwdriver.

"Thanks," she said, and inhaled the fresh drink without pause for air, having decided inebriation was her best defense.

"Feeling better?" he asked, moving closer.

"Well, I'm not thirsty anymore."

"Can't believe you haven't rubbed my nose in her win."

"I'm saving it for the mob that gathers at the draw."

"I might've guessed."

He smelled of beer, spearmint gum, and men's cologne. She

didn't think he could sit any closer unless he climbed onto her lap, but he *had* taken care not to touch her, either accidentally or accidentally-on-purpose. The alcohol had bypassed her head and saturated her body with heaviness. She felt like a sitting duck but couldn't say whether he had her in the sights of his rifle or camera. The darkness seemed at once a blessing, one thing in her favor.

"You got something to say, say it," she said. "You're making me nervous."

He studied her face. "I don't think you're drunk enough yet."

"I'm drunk enough."

"I'll get you another." He started to rise.

"I've had nothing to eat since lunch," she said. "I think four screwdrivers and a Blood Mary did the trick."

He eased back down. "Where do you get off riding that Vasquez girl on Lucifera after Summers busted her butt getting the filly to a race?"

"Bug girl rode okay."

"It'd been bad enough if you'd ridden a boy."

"I can't ride Summers."

"I forgot," he said, snapping his fingers. "You don't ride women."

"Can't ride *her.*"

"Amanda Vasquez isn't half as good."

Rachel held up her hands. "It's the jockey police. Hallelujah."

He smiled and drank from his beer. "Pretty tough watching your own daughter fall in a race, wasn't it?"

"She's *not* mine."

"We've already established that she is."

"My ass."

"Last month, as I recall. That time when you were acting like you didn't hate me?"

"I never told you shit. I've never told anyone Nicole's mine," Rachel snapped, then a mortified look froze on her face.

"Booze," Reno said, "makes a person say the damnedest

things."

She closed her eyes. "Okay. Maybe I had her, but I'm not her mother."

"Keep telling yourself that."

Rachel opened her eyes. "Nobody wants to hear other people's shit. What's wrong with you?"

"Lady, I wish I knew."

"I think you're trying to mess with me. Get me so discombobulated that I can't train. Either that, or you're using the worst come-on lines I've ever heard." She crossed her eyes and saw two of him.

He laughed, leaning back in his chair to balance on the rear legs. "I knew you weren't drunk enough."

"I suppose you'll tell everyone."

"Haven't yet, have I?"

"You didn't know for sure."

"I knew," he said. "You made it pretty obvious."

"I did?"

"That time you stormed over to my stall in the paddock and had a word with her sure opened my eyes."

"I did that?"

"I believe you're drunk now."

"Oh, really."

After a while, he drove her home. They traded small talk and at some point, he offered her a breath mint from a tin on the dash and took one for himself. She felt drawn to the warmth of his truck, content to ride around all night, but he proceeded directly to her condominium and stopped in front. He left the engine running, got out, and walked around to open her door. He took her hand and steadied her as she stepped down. When he said goodnight, she fell into him and pressed her lips to his until he kissed her back and kissed her back hard, his tongue finding hers. Abruptly he pushed her away.

"Not tonight," he said.

"That bad?" she asked.

He retreated a step. "No."

"What then?"

"Not when you've been drinking."

"Tomorrow?"

"You need to think this over better."

"I know what I feel." She began to wonder if the alcohol had caused her to imagine that he'd returned her kiss.

He stared off into the night. A car passed, then another.

"I'm not sure *I* do," he finally said.

"I see."

"It's not how it sounds."

"I'm drunk, not stupid, Reno."

"I need some time," he said, his voice trailing off.

"Look at me, please."

He wouldn't.

She slapped him across the face. "Thanks for the ride, bastard."

Her Last Race

Peninsula Park
June/July 1994

The alcohol zeroed in on Rachel's stomach during the night, a merciless assault, wave upon wave of nausea preceding the tsunami. She was late for work the next morning. After silencing her assistant with a scowl, she put on her chaps, hat, and gloves, and swung aboard her pony to accompany the first set of gallopers to the track. She rode past the crowded trainers' stand in a trot, in a Jones New York tank-top that fit like a latex glove. The leers and wisecracks alerted her to the minor detail that she had forgotten to wear a bra.

And so the morning went. Somehow, all the right horses were galloped or worked. By a quarter to ten, Rachel waited on her pony in the shade of the outside fence while her last tracker galloped two miles. The main track was almost empty. A cup of coffee fermented in her stomach like vinegar. She thought about how Reno had made an ass of her the night before, then searched for that place in her mind where nothing could hurt her but losing races. Yawning, she closed her eyes for a few seconds, then nodded off and slowly tipped to one side.

The ground woke her.

Rachel hit shoulder first with a thud and a shriek of surprise, while her pony leaped straight in the air and cowered over her, trembling as though certain he was to blame. She scrambled to her feet, crammed on her hat, and hurried to brush off the dirt before someone saw. The fast approaching hoof beats told her that she was too late. She stroked her pony's neck until his tensed muscles relaxed, then remounted from the off side, her butt finding the saddle as Reno McAllister loped over from the direction of the gap. He halted his pony head-on to hers and sat staring.

"I was trying to adjust a stirrup and lost my balance," she spat.

"I see the only thing hurt's your considerable pride," he said, and touched a finger to the brim of a high-crowned black Stetson, reined hard right, and galloped away.

Rachel watched him go through narrowed eyes. She clutched the saddle horn and squeezed it tightly until her hands stopped shaking.

~

The day after Lucifera broke her maiden, Nikki rode two winners. She was not scheduled to ride the seventh or ninth races and went to the Newmarket Pub to watch the remainder of the card after her mount in the eighth came up sick and was scratched. In a short sleeveless summer dress and high-heeled sandals, she lacked neither company nor cocktails. The four empty seats at her table were quickly filled, others pulling up chairs from around the room, men in sport coats and ties, sport shirts and slacks, and one gentleman in a Giants T-shirt and Bermuda shorts, black socks and Oxfords. Soon she had six strawberry daiquiris lined up in a pink row. After finishing her fourth, she ended up in the lap of a slickly handsome playboy of a lawyer. He wrapped his arms around her waist as she sang her flat, off-key interpretation of the chorus from a popular hit.

"I've got friends in loooooooow places, where the whiskey's brown and the beer chases the flu away, I think I'll pray."

The occupants of the table whooped and whistled and joined in to sing the chorus as a group. The bartenders gave them the evil eye. Three women at an adjacent table collectively plugged their ears. The room erupted in applause when they finished singing, more a show of relief than appreciation. When the applause died, Nikki spotted Rachel watching from the bar with both hands wrapped around what appeared to be a cup of coffee. Nikki grabbed another daiquiri and toasted her new friends, then crossed her legs and kicked a foot onto the table. A few minutes later, she thought to look again but Rachel had gone.

Maltby Aurora was towering overhead when Nikki twisted back around.

"What?" she said.

"Time for you to go home," he said.

"You're worse than my real big brother, who's not really my big brother either."

"Do I look as though I could ever be mistaken for your sibling?"

She gazed up at him. "Naw, you're too damn big."

"I'm constantly amazed at your perception."

"Kiss off, Maltby."

"The liquor's incapacitated your head faster than success."

"My head's not indecapitated. It's right where it always is."

"Up your ass?"

"Take a hike."

"I intend to," her agent said. "Let's go."

Nikki held her breath and didn't move.

"You're riding seven tomorrow," he said.

Her body jerked with a silent hiccup. She exhaled. "Like, am I on parole and you're my parole officer?"

"Seven short-priced horses. I'll drive you home."

"Trevor's taking me in his Porsche." She glanced over her shoulder to the face of the man on whose lap she was sitting. He smiled at her agent.

"Splendid," Maltby said, frowning deeply at them both.

"You're just jealous 'cause you're not sitting on his lap," she said.

"I *will* see you in the morning."

"Unfortunately."

Before her agent could respond, the occupants of the table launched an onslaught of rude comments addressing the slimy nature of agents in general and the ulterior motives of Maltby in particular. He walked away with his chin held high and his gait stiffly upright, like a knight in full armor. Nikki watched him go, feeling no more in need of rescue than a small army.

Three daiquiris later, she left arm in arm with the lawyer,

who was quite sober. After stopping first at a drug store, they went to her motel. In her drunken blur, she recalled only how good it felt to be held by another human being.

~

In the morning, Nikki awoke alone with a wicked headache that mercifully helped her forget the previous night. She crawled from bed and took a hot bath followed by a cold shower, dressed, and managed to stumble through the stable gate by eight. Maltby accosted her before she could find a place to hide. He kept trainers at bay and lined up only three horses for her to get on after the break, which she worked without throwing up or falling off, much to her relief. She was about to leave, when she received a page to Opal O'Reilly's barn. The trainer was talking to Rachel in the shed row. The two of them were eating something. Upon spotting Nikki, Rachel broke into a smug grin and started away. Nikki had no idea what the smugness or the grin was all about but didn't think it had anything to do with *her*, considering the whole Lucifera saga had gone in Rachel's favor. About then, the throbbing of Nikki's head joined forces with her queasy stomach to waylay her thoughts on the matter.

"Thanks for the snack, Nottingham," O'Reilly called out, and turned to Nikki and stuck a burrito sold by one of the backside's Mexican vendors under her nose. Rice and peas and stringy chicken coated with a lumpy orange-colored chili sauce. "Want one?"

Nikki swallowed hard. "Not particularly."

"Backside pigeon population's practically gone extinct. Rumor has it the grooms are setting traps on the roofs." O'Reilly took a big bite of the burrito. "Well, whadaya know. Tastes just like crow."

With a hand crammed over her mouth, Nikki sprinted for the restroom. If eating crow was Opal O'Reilly's way of saying she'd been wrong about woman jockeys, Nikki wondered why *she* was the one on the verge of barfing.

"Don't dilly-dally around," O'Reilly shouted after her. "I got a horse needs tracked."

Nikki returned in a few minutes, pale and shaky, and the trainer had her jog a two-year-old stud colt four laps on the training track. Now she *got* the smug grin. Nikki had four laps to contemplate whether the pot was trying to teach the kettle a lesson or if her mother was just plain cruel, because the colt bounced and bucked every foot of the way.

~

Late Monday morning, a semi-truck of timothy hay and wheat straw pulled up and parked beside Rachel's barn. When she instructed two stocky workers wielding hay hooks where to stack what, they both shook their heads and pointed at the driver, a John Deere billboard in his bright green and yellow shirt and cap. He walked over to Rachel and handed her an invoice.

Slapping the paper in half, she stuffed it into a back pocket of her jeans. "I'll pay you next week."

"Sorry," he said, "but I can't unload a bale unless I get paid now."

She lit a cigarette. Eyed the dull green hay and yellow straw on his truck. "I'm a damn good customer."

"I've been lettin' you slide for two months, Rachel."

"I'll pay you tomorrow for sure."

His mouth twitched purposefully, as if adding up pros and cons. "You don't, I'll have to come pick it all up. Every last bale."

"You'll get your money," she said.

That afternoon, she went to the bank and took out a second mortgage, borrowing $200,000 against her half-million dollar condominium. Her banker, ever smiling, politely, warmly, disingenuously, shook her calloused hand with his clammy soft one, then passed her a fancy ink pen. The loan would be due in one lump sum in six months, which seemed like six years in Rachel-time, as engrossed as she was with the battle at hand.

Her signature on several pages sealed the transaction.

After paying the pile of bills on her desk, she set out to buy horses. With six weeks left in the current race meet and trailing Reno by seven wins, she could either buy horses privately from other trainers—and pay through the nose for anything competitive—or chance that her present stable would win enough races to catch Reno, providing she haltered a few of his claimers. She would be unlikely to gain an immediate advantage with such horses. They would have to compete in tougher races—running for a twenty-five percent higher tag than they had been claimed for—until figuratively getting out of jail after a month, but neither would they do Reno any good from her barn. And she'd have them to freshen for the new meet come October. Profit figured into her equation like arithmetic done by smoke and mirrors.

She planned to beat Reno at his own game, win the training title, and assuage a smoldering heart that had been burned beyond recognition for the first time since her first time. This strategy took over her thoughts from morning till night. For a week, she awoke with screaming headaches, trembling and sick to her stomach. She survived on caffeine and nicotine and aspirin. She claimed eight of Reno McAllister's horses and drew two wins closer, winning three races on Sunday, the ninth day since he had shunned her kiss.

One of those wins came in the feature race as Royal Master, the disqualified winner of the Oregon Derby, captured a $75,000 stakes by four lengths. The colt had fared poorly in the shorter races of late spring and early summer at Peninsula Park. He'd recently begun to shine again when the distances stretched out beyond a mile, and he appeared to have a legitimate chance of winning the Peninsula Park Derby. With nearly $500,000 to the victor—and her owning half of the colt—she envisioned her loan paid-off and Reno cut down to size, as his best three-year old had been lucky to catch Royal Master's dirt clods at the finish.

Besides the local competition, there was the likelihood that the Derby would attract some fast colts from southern

California, but she was inclined to think that the fastest, Speedmeister Slew, the top three-year old on the West Coast, would opt for bigger races. Speedmeister Slew, the colt that she had picked out and developed for client J.K. Vanderford, the colt that Reno had stolen out of her grasp, ended up in the barn of a trainer at Santa Anita. Speedmeister Slew never even started a race for McAllister. Small consolation in Rachel's eyes, but one she treasured. She celebrated the day's victories and future prospects with her first alcohol in more than a week, a beer, followed by a vodka tonic, then another. She thought she might yet live.

~

Reno bought a black Stetson when he saw that the trainer's title would be decided by a shootout, but Rachel's kiss had pitched him into a quandary of sorts. The hat remained in a box on his dresser. Seeking to defend her, he listed his own imperfections and bad habits until he ran out of paper in his head, then listed her good qualities aloud to his empty house. No matter how much slack he cut her, she always managed to hang herself. After a week, he started wearing the hat. He felt like a thug.

The claiming war that they had started last fall and conducted along typical lines, with well-planned maneuvers and wily tactics, had deteriorated into a crude exchange of horses bereft of anything remotely crafty or wise. Lose a horse, halter a horse, hope it was the better, pray it was an equal. Whatever claimer one of them saddled in the paddock was certain to be led away afterward by the other. Reno thought he'd be apt to lose his pony if he entered him in a race.

Since her initial move a week ago to buy every decent horse in his barn, his lead in the trainer's standings had shrunk to five, although he saw the events as unrelated. He figured that both of them would be hard-pressed to win or even light the board with most of their new horses before the meet ended in a month. He presumed her intent was to force him to run horses over their heads to protect them, but he would sooner lose his favorite claimers than let her dictate his strategy and cost him wins. The good news was that he trained more allowance and stakes runners. Horses Rachel couldn't touch. And his trump card guaranteed him a win, barring extremely bad luck. Hence, the black hat. He wasn't feeling too shiny about his trump card.

A year ago, he had set out to land a client who would buy the track's top two-year old, Speedmeister Slew. Naturally, he'd wanted to train the colt himself at Peninsula Park, but no one he approached was willing to race such a valuable animal for less than top purse money, so Reno worked a deal to purchase him for a client in southern California and took satisfaction in seeing Nottingham lose the best horse that she had ever trained. His actual compensation? Speedmeister Slew would be vanned north to run in the Peninsula Park Derby with Reno to saddle the colt as his trainer of record. His program trainer.

A year ago, he would have relished seeing the look on Nottingham's face when she heard who his Derby entrant would be. Now, he planned to be anywhere but the race office on the morning that entries were drawn for the Peninsula Park Derby.

~

Royal Master grabbed a quarter and strained a tendon on his first gallop, four days after winning the stakes race. Rachel cleaned and disinfected the wound to his front right heel — where he had clipped himself with a hind toe grab — then treated it with a topical antibacterial ointment. The heat she detected in his deep flexor tendon of the same leg required a veterinarian's equipment to determine the extent of the injury. Sam held the colt in the shed row, while Dr. Steele and Rachel huddled over an ultrasound machine. An internal view of the injured tendon was frozen on the view screen.

Steele printed the picture. "Damage is minimal. Give him some time and the leg will heal strong as new."

Rachel unplugged the ultrasound machine and wound up

an extension chord running from the feed room. She handed Steele the coiled chord.

"Derby's in three weeks."

"Colt won't win on three legs," he said.

"You think I haven't bowed a tendon before?" she said.

An hour later, Rachel noticed that Sam had applied the wrong brand of medicated poultice on Royal Master's injured leg after icing it. When she yelled for her assistant, horses five stalls down jumped about skittishly. Sam came running. He removed the bandage and hosed off the poultice, all the while receiving a furious lecture. Did he know how much the colt was worth? Did he realize how important it was to keep the swelling down to prevent further damage to the tendon fibers? Was he purposely screwing up? Rachel kept finding one more reason to be irritated. In the midst of her tirade, Ginny showed up unexpectedly and took a seat on a bale of hay in the background.

"Well?" Rachel asked her assistant, after she was finished.

"That girl jockey's feeding the filly granola bars," Sam said.

Rachel pursed her lips and stared down the shed row in the direction of Lucifera's stall. "Did you hear a word I just said?"

"But..."

"The filly likes her. Leave her be."

"You're the boss," Sam said.

"Are you questioning my authority?"

He stared at his sneakers. "No."

"Do up the colt's leg—right this time—and stay clear of me the rest of the morning. Can you manage that?"

Nodding, Sam led the colt off the washrack and to his stall, trailed by Rachel, arms swinging stiffly at her sides.

"You've been working too hard," Ginny said from behind. "Those circles under your eyes get any darker, people will think you're part raccoon."

Rachel stopped abruptly and turned around. "You know I hate it when clients show up without calling."

"I called yesterday."

"I'm not in a very good mood."

"Yes, I've noticed," Ginny said.

Something about her tone or her expression or her uncharacteristically somber black outfit kept Rachel on edge. She took a deep breath and exhaled loudly.

"Sorry to be a bitch," she said, "but I really need to win the Derby."

"How much do you owe?"

"Never mind."

"Perhaps your obsession with beating Reno has gotten out of hand, dear."

"What's *that* suppose to mean?"

"You've been drinking too much lately."

"For your information, I've had no alcohol for almost ten days. Except for yesterday and the day before. Not that it's anyone's business."

"I'm worried about you."

"Can we not discuss this?"

"You see, I've heard things."

"If I had a buck for every rumor about me...."

"You wouldn't have any money troubles."

Rachel put a hand on her hip. "I guess you would know, Ginny, being a betting fool. You think I haven't noticed?"

"Sometimes I don't know why I bother."

"Don't be polite on my account. You got something to say, say it."

Ginny gazed back without blinking, her cheeks flushed reddish pink. "The biddies in the Turf Club are claiming Nikki Summers is your daughter."

A gelding in the nearest stall pricked his ears toward the sound of their voices as though he were eavesdropping, a little old man in a horse suit. For a minute Rachel imagined that the entire barn area had paused to look and listen and pass judgment, her subconscious blocking out the background noise until there were no sounds. Nothing. Then a pony trotted past on the road, the clap of hooves on pavement like a slap to her face.

"The relationship was severed years ago to the benefit of

both parties," she said. "I told you that."

"You told me your daughter was raised by wealthy relatives who could provide for her better than you at the time, which all sounded perfectly reasonable," Ginny said. "You forgot to mention she's a jockey."

"It slipped my mind."

"Like hell."

"I didn't want you playing the good fairy and trying to make everything right."

"People are saying you used her."

"You know damn well I paid her for galloping Lucifera."

"She worked a miracle."

"She did a good job."

"Then why won't you let her ride the filly?"

"Has it occurred to you that maybe she came here to get even? That she planned to lure me into feeling all motherly, then walk away?"

Ginny folded her arms. "Why won't you ride her?"

"The bug-girl's tougher."

"Dear, you're a very poor liar."

Rachel wheeled and took a swat at a horse that was nibbling at her belt. He leaped backward and out of reach. She spent the next minute preoccupied with coaxing the frightened animal to the front of his stall, but he repeatedly pinned his ears flat to his head and would have none of it. From behind, a hand brushed over her shoulder blade. Footsteps crossed onto the pavement. When she turned around, Ginny was a distant and darkly unrecognizable figure, some three barns down. Rachel watched, her insides tightening and hardening as she found that place in her mind where nothing could hurt her but losing.

~

"I certainly hope you don't plan on punishing yourself every time Lucifera wins a race," Maltby Aurora said as he guided Nikki onto the passenger seat of a sporty gold Lexus.

"Can we go dancing?" she said. "Gay guys are really good dancers."

"I don't do bars and I *don't* dance."

"My aunt made me take ballet till I was seventeen."

"I'm sure you do a mean pirouette," he said.

"I did four turns a couple times. Triples easy."

"Intoxication makes one disposed to exaggeration."

"Say what?"

"I think you're drunk." He fastened her seat belt. Closed the door.

"You don't know my aunt," she said, after he got in. "I did serious ballet."

"Where was your mother in this pas de deux?"

"Gone."

"She died when you were a child?"

Nikki cocked her head and thought. "You might say that. Yeah, that works."

"No wonder you're so...abnormal."

"I guess you would know," she said.

Maltby grumbled to himself and left it at that. He acted more real than her last agent, but she was not foolish enough, even drunk, to believe he cared about her beyond the dollars and cents of his paycheck. With the alcohol to dim her senses, she had no trouble pretending he wasn't there for the ten minutes it took to reach her motel. When he stopped the car, she stumbled out the door, blowing off the help he failed to offer, plugging her ears at his demand that she show up for work no later than seven.

Inside her claustrophobic hole of a room, she flopped onto her bed and stared at the ceiling. After a few minutes, she sprang dizzily to her feet and wrenched open the lone window. Sometimes, she thought about finding an apartment but could never decide how long she planned to stay. Susan had wanted her to return to Oregon and finish college, but Nikki was too enamored of her growing fame. They had argued, Susan candidly pointing out that she was turning into her mother, Rachel Nottingham, the win-at-any-cost bitch, which Nikki, at this point, considered a compliment. Susan had left in a snit. Now Nikki lay back down and tried to sleep but when she closed her eyes, Lucifera galloped under the wire, again and again, as if seeing her win from the vantage point of fifteen lengths back hadn't sufficed.

Earlier that day, Lucifera had won the feature race, a mile allowance contest for fillies and mares three-years old and up. Luci had dusted the field handily despite almost losing her jockey at the break. From a motivational standpoint, the outcome ignited Nikki. Right handed, left handed, she flagged her long shot mount in the last race everywhere but over the head and compelled an underachiever to victory, Nikki's fourth win of the night. When she returned to the women's room, Lucifera's apprentice jockey, Amanda Vasquez, who had also ridden the last race, was hurrying to undress for the explicit purpose of hogging the shower. She glanced up long enough to convey triumph, then ducked into the bathroom and slammed the door.

In another place and time, Nikki might have liked the apprentice, but not here, not now. Vasquez was a pretty girl with hair and eyes as dark as coffee beans—the former Amanda Peterson, whose classic-jockey Mexican surname was a gift via marriage. From Nikki's perspective, Vasquez had been similarly dependent on charity to acquire the mount on Lucifera.

As if Nikki's thoughts had been read, Vasquez shouted from behind the bathroom door that she had ordered Nikki copies of Lucifera's win pictures. Nikki told the apprentice that she ought to try hanging onto the filly's mane out of the gate, as opposed to her mouth. When Vasquez replied that she didn't need any pointers from Lucifera's ex-gallop girl, Nikki punched the wall, just drew back her fist and let fly, raising a purple welt the size and shape of a small plum on the back of her hand. Then she shut off the access valve on the hot water heater, which effectively shortened her wait for the bathroom. After a hot shower and a change of clothes, Nikki went straight to the Clubhouse bar and medicated her injured pride, sitting alone with a former Stanford offensive lineman turned computer software programmer from Menlo Park, whose immense size discouraged a larger gathering. This time, she had let herself be rescued by her agent.

At quarter-to-ten, four days later, she exited the backside cafeteria with a bottle of orange juice and headed home for the morning. She had won her third stakes over the weekend and was making big money. As her success evolved from novelty to expectation, the high of winning big races made her impatient for bigger wins, and she regretted having wasted some of her most productive years at an ass pit like Westover Meadows. In her mind, it was time to pack her bags and hit the road for Del Mar in August, then Santa Anita in the fall, but every time she attempted to set a definitive departure date, her resolve scattered like smoke in a stiff breeze. The tie that held her was fraying, swiftly and surely, and when it tore she anticipated departing without so much as a glance over her shoulder, free at last. In the meantime, it burned her, this fraying of ties that never were, this procession of her life that she was powerless to alter. All in all, she thought happiness was relative to one's mastery of detachment.

Rachel's quiet, silky smooth gallop boy handled Lucifera with the ease of a dressage horse, a sight that Nikki had thus far seldom managed to avoid since the large number of horses she worked most mornings put her on the racetrack or in the vicinity of the gap much of the time. Not that she would enjoy seeing Lucifera misbehave; although, if it came to pass, Nikki didn't intend to cry any tears for Rachel. Nikki's latest vengeful vision had her becoming a top jockey down south at Santa Anita, Hollywood Park, Del Mar, pinnacles of the West Coast racing world, then telling the media that her mother trained horses at some bush-track in northern California. How does it feel to feel like nothing, mother? To be denigrated by your own daughter?

A week later, Nikki entered the paddock to ride a race in which Rachel was running a horse. Not an uncommon occurrence, but on this occasion, Nikki made a spur of the moment decision to take a detour through her mother's saddling stall. She marched up to her and stopped.

"The bug-girl will ruin Lucifera," she said. "Is that what you want?"

Rachel's eyes were hidden beneath mirrored wrap-around sunglasses, the kind worn by skiers and other vainglorious speed junkies. Nikki saw her own reflection in the lenses and felt as though she were standing before a one-way window, where it was impossible to tell if anyone was on the other side.

"Filly can win the Derby if you'd let me ride her," she went on to say.

Rachel had, of course, not replied. But a few days later, she entered Lucifera in a three-year old stakes against the colts, a mile-and-an-eighth tune-up for the Peninsula Park Derby. Amanda Vasquez lost the mount. A boy had been named up in her place, Rachel's new regular rider, and he was waiting to greet Nikki when she walked into the Jockeys' Room that afternoon. In choosing Jim Bruner's replacement, Rachel had gone to the opposite extreme and selected a jockey who was a competent, dependable sort, about as ballsy as a neutered tom cat. Dirk Cassel wanted to know all about Lucifera, her infamous quirks in particular. He was concerned that she might blow up and dump him in the race, hurt him and cost him money, make him look bad. Don't ever piss off the filly, she told him, truthful advice that, judging from his scowl, seemed to dismay him worse than if she had lied.

After that, Nikki thought she would definitely stick around for a few more days, on the off chance that she might be called upon to ride Lucifera at the last moment, despite the technicality that she was already named on an inferior mount in the same stakes. Since the race fell on Nikki's birthday, she indulged in a bit of false hope, the illusion of a fairy tale ending. What she expected was a mouthful of grit from the rear of the pack, atop a horse *not* Lucifera.

On the Sunday morning of the race, there were no rider changes at scratch time. Nikki turned twenty-nine without fanfare and expected none. She was on her way to the Jockeys'

Room, when her agent handed her a small package wrapped in tin foil with a tiny blue bow. Her mouth fell open as though her jawbone had snapped.

"Thanks, Maltby."

"It's not from me," he said.

"Who then?"

"It was left anonymously on the counter in the race office."

Nikki opened the package, expecting to find a corny gift from a secret admirer, a heart-shaped locket, a zirconium diamond ring, an imitation gold horse trinket, but what she found was an oval cut, smoothly polished black veined turquoise pendant on a sterling silver chain. She put it on.

~

Lucifera had tweaked a suspensory ligament in her most recent race when apprentice Amanda Vasquez broke on the filly's mouth. Whether Vasquez took too short a rein hold leaving the gate or simply lost her fingerful of mane and her balance, the result was the same to Rachel. Lucifera had thrown her head skyward and taken several climbing, lunging, awkward strides. The next morning, the filly had walked from her stall sound, but Rachel detected a small amount of heat in her right foreleg. To determine if Lucifera was favoring the leg, Rachel had Sam lead the filly at a trot over the hard-packed ground between the sand walking ring and the hot walker behind the barn, then had him turn her in tight circles for the same purpose. She stepped right out, never once limping or stumbling.

Even so, Rachel was wary when it came to injuries and had the leg treated with electromagnetic therapy, a newfangled gizmo reputed to speed healing, though she reserved her trust for the familiar remedies such as the turbulator of ice water that Lucifera's leg was submerged in for thirty minutes that morning, and again at noon, and in the evening for four days in a row. In between, her forelegs were done up in a secret leg paint whose primary ingredient was DMSO. She was given bute to keep any inflammation down, to dull any pain. On the fifth day, she resumed training.

In Rachel's book, suspensory ligament injuries, no matter how minor, never fully healed. She pictured the suspensory in simplistic anatomical terms, a thick band of fibrous tissue that extended from the back of the knee to the fetlock joint. Just above the fetlock, the ligament split into two major branches that attached to the sesamoid bones to form the suspensory apparatus, the main supporting structure of the lower leg, which was under constant tension when a horse stood. As a result, Rachel knew from experience that lay-ups yielded dubious results and were best utilized as a last resort, when an animal was too lame to race. Time off guaranteed nothing but an unfit horse, typically fat to boot. For an overweight horse with an iffy leg to endure months of training before racing again, required a sizable measure of luck. Luck was not something Rachel liked to depend upon.

As Lucifera's sole owner, Rachel had already made twenty-five grand with the filly and figured to race her twice more in the next few weeks. With money and wins vying for Rachel's attention, the end of the meet closed in. Though she recognized that the outcome was not exclusively hers to control, she was determined to take her best shot. And so, Lucifera got a new rider for her third race, Dirk Cassel, and was entered in a stakes against the colts.

Rachel had contemplated a change immediately after the filly's second race, when Vasquez broke on Lucifera's mouth at the start, but the apprentice got along well with the enigmatic gray and switching to a boy seemed a dicey move. Why mess with a winning combination? The answer became apparent when Rachel had Vasquez give Lucifera a half-mile blow out four days before the stakes race, and the filly ran off after the wire. Rachel and her black pony were all-out to catch Lucifera on the backstretch by the five-eighths pole. The apprentice had contributed nothing to the effort, unless not falling off counted for anything.

"Filly grabbed the bit," was all Vasquez had to say, her face whiter than a cadaver's.

Rachel had never been one to abide a coward and had no plans to start. Because it had taken a woman to tame the filly's independent streak, the natural assumption was that Lucifera bore a deep-seeded grudge against men. Now that the filly galloped kindly for both of Rachel's male exercise riders, Rachel decided she was wrong. Two races convinced her that she had a runner on her hands. One of those rare Thoroughbreds who needed neither encouragement nor stimulation to win. She figured her new stable jockey, Cassel, would fit the filly just fine.

On the last Sunday in July, two weeks before the close of Peninsula Park's current race meeting after ten long months, Lucifera finished fifth in the Golden Gate Stakes. Under a sanitary ride. Apparently, Dirk Cassel had been more concerned with making the course than winning. He took the filly back at the start and went into the first turn so wide that she appeared to have bolted. When Lucifera exited the turn for home she was still ten wide, but her head was clearly being cocked toward the outside fence by the pull of a rein. Rachel remained in her box until the horses were led away after being unsaddled. She smoked a cigarette and let her anger simmer and cook.

"Filly was off in her right front," Cassel told her early the next morning.

"We'll talk in my office," Rachel said, pointing the way like a thrust from a foil. She slammed the door behind them.

He retreated to the corner and faced her, all five-foot two-inches of him. A matchstick in a hurricane.

"You might've loosened your death grip on the reins and allowed her to win instead of finishing fifth. You cost me over forty grand," Rachel shouted, as the enormity of owing a bank $200,000 had begun to dominate her thoughts.

"I was afraid she'd snap a leg off if I let her run," he shouted back.

"You'd have won anyway, if you hadn't wasted so much ground. In case you haven't noticed, the inside rail's a shorter route than the outside fence."

"I didn't wanna be trampled if she fell."

"Ninety-percent of the horses at this track are sore," she said. "Are you a vet?"

"I know sore," he said.

"You ball-less bastard."

"I don't have no suicide wish, that's for sure."

Rachel paused to study his reaction, but was struck by the details of a face that she had previously failed to notice, his badly scarred cheek and off-kilter nose, a jagged gash under his chin, a chipped front tooth. The battle scars that made for a cautious warrior. Never mind, she told him. Just forget it. He and Lucifera had been a poor fit. The trainer's fault and she would rectify the situation.

From there on out, the morning soured. She stepped in a pile of fresh shit and gummed up her favorite boots. She gave her black pony the day off and rode her bay pony, and he made it his personal mission to annoy her by loping on his stiff lead with a brazen ass-pounding exuberance, then breaking into the damnedest springy trot, hooves reaching up and out, a teeth rattling ride. She lasted two hours, then took to foot, cussing whoever had fed the bay pony too much grain. Shortly, she broke the screen door to the race office by slamming it on her way out, was later tattooed on the forearm by the teeth of the formerly sweetest two-year-old filly in the barn, and then was so intent on pretending not to see Reno McAllister as she climbed the steps to the trainers' stand that she tripped and almost fell.

Rachel was convinced that the worst of a rotten morning had passed, when Murphy's Law kicked in and a horse that was cooling out on the hot walker began to nicker frantically. She happened to be close at hand and shouted for Sam to call the vet. She led the gelding to his stall, stroked his head, and spoke to him gently, but he continued to nicker and tremble and she watched helplessly as he dropped dead. An autopsy revealed he had burst a major artery and bled to death. There was nothing anyone could have done.

The horse lay where he had fallen, a stiffened heap on

blood-soaked straw with his belly slit and his eyes glazed and the air reeking of a sickly-sweet stench. Every fly in miles appeared to have converged on the scene. Rachel closed the stall's bottom and top doors until the backside maintenance crew arrived to haul away the carcass. She bit her lip and clenched her jaw shut and the tears inside her surged like waves against a bulkhead, but never wet her face.

That night, she went home and thought about the futility of trying to predict the limits of tendons and ligaments, bone and muscle, to foresee when a seemingly healthy horse might drop dead after an easy gallop. She poured herself a glass of brandy and sat in the dark, watching Sunday's Peninsula Park recap show recorded on her VCR from the night before. The bottle of brandy went slowly south. She recalled all the horses she had seen win on only three sound legs and recalled the distance of the suspensory ligament from the heart. She watched the races, the horses, and the riders. The riders in particular. Before the night was over, Rachel had picked out a new stable jockey. Nikki Summers.

Peninsula Park
August 1994

Nikki sat tall in the saddle and smiled for the photo, the sixth winner that she had ridden for her mother. A flash, then she hopped off. An unsmiling Rachel had already moved to depart the winner's circle, her eyes hidden behind her mirrored sunglasses. In an effort not to sweat the small stuff, Nikki had previously decided to pretend she was someone else's daughter.

Eleven days ago, Rachel had asked Nikki to ride her stable and take first call on all her horses. Nikki wasn't sure what to make of this move. There was no mention of the money Rachel owed her bank, which was the hottest buzz on the backside. Nor later, any warm kudos for the seven wins that had enabled her to tie Reno McAllister in the trainer's race with one day left in the meet. Not that Nikki had expected a hug or a handshake or at the very least a sincere thank you. If the rules of winning and losing were to be believed, the respect she had won from her mother exacted a corresponding degree of loss. Rachel, poor loser that she was, figured to be a bitch. But Nikki was too busy winning to be bothered with hypothetical bullshit. As she closed in on her goals, every race had become her last race, a life and death ordeal where in a state of controlled panic, she willed horses to victory. By her calculations, a win in the Peninsula Park Derby would entitle her to walk away in the black.

Nikki jogged Lucifera a mile the morning before the Derby. The filly wore blue support bandages with the outline of rundown patches beneath each of her four fetlocks. She kicked up her heels and squealed walking onto the main track, then strode out like a Standardbred trotter, forcing Rachel to press her pony into a lope to keep pace. When Nikki mentioned that Lucifera felt sharp and sound, Rachel adjusted her sunglasses and looked the other way. Content to let the best trainer at the track do the training, Nikki didn't dwell on Lucifera's rumored suspensory problem.

One subject that proved harder to dismiss was Reno McAllister. While Rachel had been winning races daily, Reno had gone 0-11 over the same period. Nikki felt like an ingrate for spinning the trainer who'd initially given her a shot at Peninsula Park, though lately she had begun to see loyalty as a bad habit. She wished that he would've thrown a tizzy-fit like a normal trainer after she informed him that she'd given first-call to Rachel for the final week-and-a-half of the meet. Instead, McAllister had burst into a fat grin. She stared at him while her brain added up two and two, then said, "You know she's my mother." He nodded, and told Nikki that he still trusted her to ride his horses whenever she was able. For McAllister's sake, she hoped the rumors were untrue and that he didn't really have a thing for Rachel. Nikki considered sending him a sympathy card all the same.

~

Three days before the Derby, Rachel had almost cleared the gap on her pony when a horse jogged up from behind, slowed, and fell in beside her. Without turning to look, she caught a glimpse of the black mane and tan hide of a buckskin. Recognizing Reno McAllister's pony, she kept her sights focused straight ahead and would have ignored him completely had he not ridden too close and bumped her knee. This action was interpreted as a calculated violation of her space. She responded immediately and reined her mount sharply into the buckskin, who sidestepped clear but continued to walk alongside with a half-length between them.

"That was one helluva kiss, if it makes you feel any better," Reno said.

"*Bastard*," she said, and swore not to look at him.

"Glad to see you can handle a compliment."

"What do you want?"

"Speedmeister Slew's shipping up for the Derby."

She slapped her hip with the end of the reins. "Shit."

"I tried to talk the owners out of it, but they think he'll gallop."

"Shit," she said again and felt a little sick in her stomach.

"I pointed out that there's a stakes for the colt at Santa Anita next weekend," he said, "but the purse isn't quite as big."

Rachel pulled up sharply and reined her pony around to face him. "You did *what?*"

"I told them to get someone else to saddle the colt," Reno said. "I'm feeling like an asshole over the whole Speedmeister deal, especially with us running neck and neck."

"Pride is for fools."

"Pretty hard for a man to shave without seeing his face in the mirror every morning," he said.

"Yeah," she said, "mirrors are hell."

They exchanged what Rachel would only let herself believe were looks of a polite conciliatory nature and rode away in opposite directions. She spent most of the rest of the day wondering why Reno would turn down an opportunity to stick it to her with Speedmeister Slew.

~

On Derby morning, Nikki ate breakfast at a restaurant across the street from the track. The hostess and the wait staff greeted her with the overblown awe and warmth reserved for successful athletes who competed in sports that normal people wisely avoided. Silks, blinkers, bridles, and other racing paraphernalia adorned walls papered in win photos. Nikki eyed the room in a daze. She tried to pump herself up with thoughts of further triumph but was sobered by the difficulty of what lay ahead. Two races for Reno, three for Rachel, the pair tied, and Nikki with the unenviable job of riding all five horses. And then there was the Derby with a purse of more than a half-million.

She was finishing her oatmeal when Maltby Aurora sat down in the chair across the table.

"It's not too late to change your mind," her agent said.

"I'm riding Lucifera," she said.

"McAllister's colt isn't a world beater, but it does have four legs."

"You can't switch horses in the same race after scratch time."

"Never underestimate me," he said.

"I'm riding Lucifera," she repeated.

Maltby clasped his hands like a man praying and mumbled something to himself. He ordered a cup of tea, two soft-boiled eggs, and dry wheat toast. "Inherently, jockeys have no common sense or they wouldn't do what they do, but most learn to differentiate between bad horse..." — he gestured to his left— "and good horse." Then to his right. "I'm going to give you the benefit of the doubt and assume you've fallen on your head once too often."

"Lucifera *will* win."

"On three legs?"

"Big deal. So the filly strained her suspensory," Nikki said. "It's a long way from her heart."

"Nottingham will have her so pumped full of goodies, you won't be able to tell," Maltby said.

"She wouldn't run the filly if she didn't think she could win."

"I heard she's in debt. The woman's desperate."

"She wouldn't put the horse at risk."

"Desperate people use bad judgment. Even if Lucifera were sound, she couldn't outrun Speedmeister Slew."

"How would you know? I bet you've never even ridden one of those horses outside grocery stores that you stick a quarter in."

Maltby laughed, a baritone rumble that gave way to a wistful smile. "Oh, yes," he said. "I once broke down a palomino outside a Safeway. I was somewhat larger than the average seven-year old."

Nikki leaned into the table and got right in his face. "Don't expect me to cover for you on the morality train. I've been that route. I couldn't even save one stupid horse."

Maltby pushed his glasses up the bridge of his nose as if seeing her anew. "And here I thought you possessed the depth of a mud puddle."

She took a deep breath and let it out slowly. "You don't know me."

"It would appear not."

"I've gone to college."

"As have I."

At once, she was struck with a sense of waking from a bad dream only to find the dream was her reality, that the glaciation of her moral core had turned her into a cold-blooded, cutthroat competitor. She glanced around at the enlarged win photos of her mother's horses with Rachel smiling the same adrenalin smile in each, like an addict who'd just gotten a fix.

"What are we doing here, Maltby?" Nikki's voice caught in her throat. She thought she might cry, then the feeling vanished.

"Absolutely annihilating the traditional stereotype of an agent and a jockey," he said.

They traded palm slaps.

"Swell," she said.

He sipped at his tea, put the cup down. "I'd rather another jockey win the silly race than see you hurt. I can assure you the world's not going to end if you don't ride Lucifera in the Derby."

She looked out the window at the cloudless sky. "Maltby?"

"Yes?"

"Rachel Nottingham is my mother. I *have* to ride Lucifera."

~

Sunday's eighth race, the Peninsula Park Derby, went to post with ten entrants, four of the nine colts having shipped up from southern California to run in the prestigious Grade 1 stakes race for three-year olds. Lucifera was the lone filly.

The back of Rachel's hand was still numbly cold where earlier she had splashed leg freeze. It was not a thing she liked to do, freezing a horse's leg. Ice was bad enough, but the deadening effect of ice, even in conjunction with a simple leg paint such as menthol crystals and DMSO, tended to wear off before the animal reached the starting gate. The chemical freeze that she had scrubbed over Lucifera's sore right foreleg was significantly stronger. For a split-second each stride, the filly's entire weight would be supported on a single foreleg with little or no feeling.

Rachel envisioned the physics of the matter. The pounds per square inch hitting the ground in the form of bones, ligament, tendons, muscle. At racing speeds, the slightest deviation on impact could throw an animal's stride off balance, causing the foot to strike the ground at the wrong angle, the leg to twist under the strain. And, on occasion, to give way. She saw ghosts of horses dead before their time. Bloody bones protruding from bloody legs, bloody stumps of fetlocks, a fallen animal crawling frantically on two broken knees with his lower forelegs flopping like a scarecrow's. Rachel reached for her cigarettes.

Lucifera had worn paddock boots over her running bandages, and the foam on the inside of one had been soaked with water and frozen beforehand. When the paddock judge called for riders up and Sam removed the boots, the filly's right fore racing bandage was frosted with ice. White on white, the frost hardly showed. Rachel had inconspicuously wiped it off with a rub rag after the paddock judge turned the other way. She had gone upstairs to watch the race in the privacy of her box, an air-conditioned refuge from the late afternoon heat, yet she continued to cook in black slacks, a suit vest, and tie. She loosened the collar of her blue silk shirt and tossed a black fedora onto an empty chair. Current odds were listed on the video monitor. Speedmeister Slew was the 3-1 second choice, while Lucifera was 42-1. Three minutes remained until post time. The parimutuels were clogged with patrons eager to part with their money and the post parade dragged on.

On the walk upstairs, Rachel had spotted Ginny at a table with her lady friends in the Turf Club. Their chatter, which could be heard across the room, had thrown another loop in Rachel's already knotted stomach, although Ginny appeared to want no part of the conversation and sat reading her program, a reluctant flower among the social butterflies. Rachel now wished she'd said hello or something. She drew on an unlit cigarette, then kneaded a piece of nicotine gum with her tongue and attempted to blow a bubble, but it was not bubble gum. She tried to think of a worse week to quit smoking. She had won a race, Reno had won a race, and neither was running a horse in the last, so they would remain tied for the season with 87 wins apiece, unless one of them won the Derby. The picture on the video monitor split horizontally to display the odds on the upper half, the post parade on the lower. The announcer called two minutes. She reached for her binoculars to see how Lucifera was warming up. The insides of her hindquarters were lathered foamy white, the kidney sweat a sign of extreme nervousness, a sign of dread.

Rachel tossed the binoculars aside and grabbed the in-house phone. She punched the three digit number for the steward's box atop the grandstand, intending to scratch Lucifera. No one answered. She dialed again and a woman put her on hold. The announcer called one minute. Rachel waited. The money came to her then, in a rush of anxiety more powerful than a narcotic drug or her repressed maternal instincts, and the cool composure that allowed her to do what she did without the burden of regret settled back over her like a warm familiar blanket. It occurred to her that winning had ceased being glorious at some indistinct point, yet she pursued winning like arrow to bull's-eye because winning was what she did.

The head steward's voice droned in her ear. Wrong number, she told him, and hung up the phone.

~

Nikki focused on the starting gate doors. Dead center, where the steel bars met and formed a V, not on the racetrack beyond, nor on Lucifera's long gray ears, nor on the crowd of 42,000, an undulating patchwork of color and sound. Only on the doors. Around her the gate crew hurried to load the rest of the field. The tailgate slammed behind the last horse. She slipped her right index finger into gray mane, took a hold, and sat calmly molded to her two-pound jockey saddle while inside she tightened like a feral animal about to spring. Her heart was pounding when the bell rang.

Lucifera broke on top and Nikki settled into fourth and let the speed go on. The leader's hooves fired baseball-sized clods that crusted the sleeves of her blue-and-black silks. She pulled down a pair of goggles. Beneath her, Lucifera switched to her left lead and rounded the first turn without trouble, then switched to her right and rolled down the backstretch, smooth and powerful, hooves skimming the earth like the soundest three-year old at the track. Nikki stopped thinking about the frosted bandage she had seen in the paddock. Win, they must win, said a voice in her head.

The second turn came quickly, the three-eighths pole flashing past like a giant green-and-white striped candy cane, a blur in the corner of her eye. She folded her body over Lucifera's withers and clucked. The filly changed gears and shot past a tiring colt, overtook a second horse at the quarter pole, and straightened for home with one to catch, one chestnut rump. Speedmeister Slew.

But Lucifera would not switch back onto her right lead. Nikki decided the filly knew best and melted into her ground-eating stride, pumping her arms in smooth rhythm until a silhouette of horse and rider would hardly show where one ended and the other began. They drew within a length of the leader. A half-length. A neck. Then Lucifera began to tire, her long stride slowing, shortening. Nikki hollered encouragement, pleaded, begged, but the filly continued to struggle and Speedmeister Slew opened up two lengths. A colt on the outside loomed like a dark starboard shadow. Win, they must win, shouted the voice in Nikki's head.

She cocked her stick and slashed Lucifera. Startled at feeling the sting of a whip for the first time, the filly leaped ahead and put away the outside challenger, then closed in on Speedmeister Slew. The sixteenth pole flashed past, a giant black-and-white stripped candy cane. Win, they must win screamed the voice, and Nikki hit the filly twice more and the two horses bore down on the finish, neck and neck, head and head, nose and nose, the pounding of their hooves muted by the roar of the crowd.

Lucifera stumbled abruptly.

A sharp jerk, like stepping in a hole and the ground giving way, before she sprawled to the track and under the wire, the loser by a leg.

~

The cheering wavered briefly, then resumed at subdued pitch before fading. People crowded the outside fence by the finish wire and watched the tragedy in stunned silence, while others muttered profanities and ripped up losing tickets. The photo finish sign flashed on the tote board.

By the time Rachel dashed onto to racetrack, Lucifera had struggled to her feet on three legs with Sam at her head and surrounded by the gate crew. Her right foreleg hung limp at the ankle, her fetlock drooping. Rachel ran past the filly and drew a hand to her mouth. Nikki lay on her back, very still, her face a mixture of blood and dirt. Paramedics had stabilized her neck with a C collar, slid her onto a flat wooden board, then lifted her onto a stretcher and into an ambulance. They offered no opinions about her condition but assured Rachel that Nikki was in capable hands and drove away with lights flashing, joined by the siren's wail as they cleared the track.

Someone called her name. Rachel turned.

"Filly's either broken one or both sesamoids and blown her suspensory," the state veterinarian said. "Doesn't look promising."

"Take her to my barn," she told him.

He ignored her. "On the plus side, the leg isn't compound fractured so you won't have infection to contend with. If she was mine, though, I'd put her down."

"No."

"Save yourself having to do it later."

"No," she repeated.

He regarded her curiously, then turned to his assistants. "You heard the lady. Let's get an inflatable cast on that leg."

Someone retrieved one from the starter's car. The horse ambulance arrived on the scene shortly, the tractor rumbling at idle while a hydraulic lift lowered the trailer floor to the ground. After the cast was in place Sam led the filly inside the trailer, assisted by one of the huskier valets, who supported her injured leg, then the floor was raised and the door closed. The tractor inched slowly forward and the rig started away.

A cheer erupted from the crowd when Speedmeister Slew was announced the winner and the race declared official. Rachel heard it as she ran to her car.

~

Nikki's world had been reduced to a two-dimensional flatness incomprehensible to her three dimensional eyes. Blurred faces and hands, reaching, touching, then pain, stabbing pain that started in her chest and exploded outward as though something dank and ruthless had reached inside her and torn out a vital organ, then left her adrift in blackness too dark for anything but her darkest nightmare to penetrate.

She lay on the racetrack circled by a wall of sober faces. They were staring at her leg. She lifted her head with much effort and saw that the leg in question was no longer facing in an anatomically feasible direction. When she tried to rise farther, two men squatted at her shoulders and held her down and stroked her head and told her they were sorry. Very, very sorry. She kept expecting to hear the scream of sirens but no sirens sounded and no ambulance came, and there were only the sober faces and a man with a syringe and needle in his hand. And her mother. Her serenely pragmatic mother, whose words to the man with the syringe pierced Nikki from the inside out.

"Put her down."

~

Rachel dashed inside the emergency room and up to the information desk at Bayview Hospital approximately one minute ahead of Ginny. Rachel saw her and started. She searched her friend's face for signs of criticism, but saw only a reflection of her own guilty conscience. A tightness rose in her throat, her mouth opened, and out fell a single word.

"Sorry."

Ginny rushed over and hugged her. When they finished embracing, a nurse accompanied them to a private waiting room. They were seated on a couch amid a jungle of indoor plants and tropical fish. While Ginny rattled on about the wonders of modern medicine, Rachel got up and started to pace with an unlit cigarette clenched in her teeth. Visions of jockeys crippled or dead materialized to haunt her thoughts.

"It's wonderful you've stopped smoking," Ginny said. "I hope you haven't resorted to eating them."

Tossing the cigarette in a wastebasket, Rachel removed two pieces of nicotine gum from her purse. "What's taking so long? Why won't they tell us what's going on?"

"I'm sure the doctor will be in shortly," Ginny said, in a soothing voice.

Rachel chewed furiously on her gum. "You're a good friend, by the way," she said.

"I was too judgmental."

"I should've told you the whole truth."

"And have me sticking my nose where it didn't belong?"

"We might not be here if I'd let you," Rachel said.

She was still pacing, when the door opened and a white-coated doctor entered. The jockey had sustained two broken ribs, some facial lacerations, and a concussion, he informed them, glancing up from his clipboard. She had regained consciousness in the ambulance, but would be kept overnight for observation. He paused in the doorway before leaving to say that they were free to see the patient.

Rachel sat down on the couch and closed her eyes, opened them. The fluorescent lights hummed overhead. Air bubbled in a fish tank. She twiddled with her fingers and thumbs and tried to envision herself as a mother again.

"I'm not any good at this, Ginny."

"She's all grown up, dear. How difficult could it be?"

"I almost killed her."

"But you didn't."

"What if she hates me?"

"She won't."

"But what if she's as hard-hearted as me?"

"You're not hard-hearted."

"Sometimes I am."

Ginny patted Rachel on the back. "Would it help if I talked to her first?"

Rachel nodded.

Together, the women left the waiting room and discovered Nikki's whereabouts. Ginny went in alone, leaving the door open and Rachel hunched outside, eavesdropping.

The clicking of Ginny's heels stopped. "I'm your mother's friend, Virginia."

"She has a friend?" Nikki's voice, labored, as though something ponderous had sat down on her chest.

In the hallway Rachel frowned, partly out of concern for Nikki and partly because of her comment.

"How are you feeling?" Ginny asked next.

"Fine."

"I heard a rumor that you plan on becoming a veterinary doctor." Ginny again. "I bet you'll make an excellent racetrack vet."

"And patch together horses so they can break down another day? No thanks."

"You could invent new techniques to spare them that fate."

"Nobody cares about saving horses," Nikki said.

A jaded remark that prompted an entrance from Rachel. She swept into the room with the resolve of a spokesperson for the Humane Society, heart surging with good intentions—until she recalled having once destroyed a horse for the insurance money.

"I care about saving horses," she said, in a small voice.

Nikki lay on a bed in her sport bra, dirty riding pants, and boots, staring blankly at the ceiling. A cut on her chin had formed a bloody scab. Dirt crusted the back of her hands and her face in places, her lip was fat and swollen with fresh stitches, and her languid spread eagle position hinted of uncertain mobility. Rachel walked up to the bed and reached out a hand.

Nikki drew away.

Rachel retracted her hand. Fussed with her cuticles. "I'm sorry I haven't been much of a mother."

"You're not my mother."

"I want to be."

"Now that I've proven myself useful, you think you might keep me around?"

"No—I mean, of course I want to keep you around."

"You're *not* my mother. She wasn't like you."

Rachel felt herself trembling. She feared saying the wrong words, feared herself incapable of the right ones. Out of desperation, she blurted the simplest of truths.

"I'm sorry. I'm sorry for everything."

Nikki stared at the ceiling with no expression but for a watery glaze to her eyes.

"Go away," she said, then closed her eyes and held them closed.

Rachel felt tears coming and stumbled backward from the room as if she'd had the wind knocked out of her. She made her way to the stairwell where she smoked a cigarette, then another, while Ginny doled out tissues and searched for the bright side of the catastrophe that included a rambling sermon on the behavioral idiosyncrasies of children and how they always made up with their parents in the end. The blind were leading the blind, was all Rachel could think. When she walked out the Emergency Room's double-glass doors, reporters swarmed her like flies to a fresh kill, wanting to know if Nikki was her daughter. Rachel hastily wiped her eyes, but the tears kept coming. After ditching the reporters, she accompanied Ginny to McDonald's. Rachel drank three cups of coffee and picked at a French fry. When Ginny mentioned something about needing to eat to stay healthy, Rachel started to cry again.

"Oh hell," she said, daubing her eyes with a napkin, "for years I couldn't cry. Now I can't stop."

"Leaving her must have been awful," Ginny said.

Rachel sat wringing her hands for a moment, then removed a thick-banded black watch and pointed at the scar on her wrist.

~

Afterward, she drove straight to her barn. Along the way, she phoned Dr. Steele, and he updated her on Lucifera's condition. Since the filly had finished second in the Derby, he had been unable to give her a shot of tranquilizer or bute until after blood and urine samples were drawn for testing. The blood sample had been an easy matter, but an official from the test barn—armed with a bottle on a stick—had waited in the corner of her stall for over an hour before she urinated. Rachel thanked Sam for giving Lucifera only a swallow of lukewarm water every ten minutes, relieved to find that some of her expertise had rubbed off on him, because were the filly to founder, there would be no hope of saving her.

Rachel had seen two grotesquely foundered horses during her childhood. With that in mind—and it *was* memorable— very few horses under her care had even contracted laminitis, a complex and potentially crippling inflammatory disease that preceded founder and was unique to hooved animals. She'd always detected laminitis early and immediately iced the afflicted hooves and called a vet, thus preventing degeneration of the sensitive laminae that held the main bone of the horse's foot—the pedal/coffin bone—in place. Laminitis could be triggered by numerous causes, although she had dealt with just three: excess grain, colic, and ingestion of cold water by an overheated horse. In Lucifera's case, Rachel was also extremely concerned with a fourth cause: excessive weight bearing on one leg due to the injury of another leg. Of course, laminitis was only one of several complications that might sabotage Lucifera's recovery.

X-rays had revealed a base fracture of the inside sesamoid, a fracture that didn't heal well and wasn't availed by surgery. In conjunction with the damage to her suspensory ligament, Dr. Steele hadn't seen much hope but yielded to Rachel's request to save Lucifera. He set the filly's leg with her foot bent back so that she would be standing on the toe of the hoof wall if not for the tip of a metal splint called a Kimzey splint, which was shaped like a backward J. The cannon bone would bear the majority of her weight, taking the pressure off her suspensory ligament, sesamoids, and fetlock. Steele recommended leaving the splint on for a month, then removing it and having her shod with a wedge shoe and pads to raise her heel to an angle of approximately forty-five degrees. Her shoer would gradually reduce the angle once a week. Lastly, he agreed with Rachel's plan to take Lucifera off bute in a few days, after the inflammation in her leg had a chance to subside. The more the filly hurt, the less likely she would be to jump around and injure herself further.

It was eight-thirty, three hours since the accident. Dr. Steele and Sam were waiting in the shed row when Rachel pulled up in her Ferrari. She thanked her assistant and sent him home for the night, then she and Dr. Steele walked to the other side of the barn. Lucifera was lying down, resting, with the Kimzey splint on her lower right foreleg. Her stall had been bedded with an extra bale of straw. Her full screen had been replaced by a half-gate, as there was no longer any danger of her escaping. At the sound of their voices, she lifted her head and nickered softly.

"Filly's thanking you," Steele said.

"For what? Killing her?"

"Saving her. Though you'll be damn lucky if she doesn't founder or colic."

"Let's face it, Doc, she's as good as dead and I'm to blame."

"You ruin fewer horses than any major player at this track," he said. "Horses break down."

"So I'm not the biggest butcher on the grounds. Why does that compliment make me feel like shit?"

"I work for several trainers who almost never break down horses, but they don't get any run out of them either. Hypothetically speaking, every horse with any ability is capable of X number of wins. The trainer who can extract those wins at the highest performance level in the shortest amount of time is the best trainer in my book."

"You make it sound so cold-blooded."

"I'd ten-to-one rather be a racehorse than a steer," he said.

"Better to end up glue than a steak?"

"Worst case scenario."

"I don't imagine you've ever noticed the look in their eyes when they're standing there on three legs, knowing their number's up?"

"Not really."

"I don't think I can pretend not to see anymore," Rachel said.

"It's kinder to put them down."

"Says who?"

He smiled sheepishly. "The owner's pocketbook?"

Rachel paused. And perceived the issue from the horses' vantage point, looking out from the stalls of creatures with no voice or choice. Oh, how she'd exploited their docility and betrayed their naive expectations of a benevolent master, all for the sake of winning. And money. Self-disgust and shame creased her face, though she figured to be damn grateful if the worst that came of her misdeeds was *her* needing a face lift. The whatifs came next, but she was already looking ahead. "I realize some injuries are unfixable, but if we're going to use these horses, maybe we owe them a better effort."

"In a perfect world."

"I can make *my* world more perfect."

"Good luck."

"I probably need my head examined."

"I'm not touching that one," he said. "I'm just a vet."

~

Besides the pills that Nikki only pretended to swallow, the nurses at Bayview Hospital dispensed derogatory comments about Peninsula Park being an endless source of broken bodies. Clearly, they were unappreciative of the fact that carnage from the track was good for business. Nurses did not get paid by the patient, Nikki decided. She lay in bed in a stark hospital room and a clock on the wall marked the seconds with slowly sweeping indifference, an instrument of mental torture. She had no company but her thoughts, and they were dark company bent on self-contempt, malevolent parasites with an appetite for optimism that consumed her fortitude and fight. The night passed more slowly than a bad meal. By morning, Nikki felt clinically depressed and wanted to return to Oregon as soon as possible.

Consequently, she took it upon herself to depart the hospital. Maltby Aurora had driven her to the motel and helped her to load her things and now she was going home. Nikki thanked Maltby for everything and confessed that she would miss him. He hugged her gingerly, so as not to crush her broken ribs, then she eased into her car and drove away with the sun aglow on the eastern horizon.

Halfway across the Golden Gate Bridge, Rachel's apology screamed through Nikki's thoughts. Her only reaction was to turn up the radio. She wanted to forget her attachments to horses and racing. She longed to disappear and welcomed the morning fog that shrouded the bridge. For this reason, she took the coastal route and wound her way north through scuddy gray landscape, invisible until Cresent City, beyond which her car burst into the sunshine and she hid beneath a floppy rain hat and her darkest shades. By Portland, she had come to terms with the fact that she finished second in her last race. It seemed like small punishment for what she had done to Lucifera.

~

Trainers had surely committed greater acts of foolishness than trying to save a doomed horse, although Rachel couldn't recall any such incidents off hand. One of the keys to success, she believed, was the ability to forge ahead with blind determination, undeterred by the prospect of failure because failure was not an option. She added a footnote: more difficult in matters of life and death.

Before Dr. Steele left, they discussed the possibility of rigging up a sling on the grounds for Lucifera, as Rachel wanted to personally supervise the filly's recuperation. There was no racing at Peninsula Park for the next three months, but the track remained open for training and most stables stayed put, including Rachel's, vanning the occasional horse or horses to race at the county fair meets or in southern California. The racing secretary had already left word that Lucifera would be allowed to convalesce for a few months. Rachel slept on the couch in her office that night and rose to check the filly every hour. Later the next day, she obtained permission to erect a sling in her stall.

The backside maintenance crew volunteered to do the job. They fixed a block and a pully to a roof beam near the front of the stall, a half-inch steel cable serving as the tackle, which ran to a come-along winch outside the door. The workmen had suggested an electric winch, but Rachel envisioned Lucifera dangling from the rafters and nixed the idea. The sling went under the filly's girth and belly, buckling on top, with chest and rump pads/straps to keep her from sliding forward or backward. She seemed to appreciate the load off her forelegs and stood quietly for part of each day—tied in the doorway to keep her from swiveling around the block and tackle—her feet on the ground but just barely.

A week passed without incident. Rachel spent much of the time untangling herself from the financial mess she had woven. When all the pluses and minuses were added up, the bank took a piece of property that she owned at Lake Tahoe, but between the horses she sold, her Ferrari, and the money her horses had recently earned, she managed to pay off most of her debt outright rather than be burdened by monthly payments inflated with astronomical interest rates. Throughout the week everyone from the feed man to the shoer, the tack shop, the vet called her asking to be paid. Rachel was ready to throw the phone at the wall, yet she desperately wanted it to ring—too desperately for comfort. She took to hiding the phone in her desk drawers, out of sight, out of mind. The one call she was hoping for never came.

On the morning after the Derby, Rachel had returned to the hospital to see Nikki. But too late. Nikki had left an hour before, simply walked off without being released according to an irate nurse. Later the same day, Rachel learned from Maltby Aurora that Nikki was already on the road to Oregon. After pleading with him for a telephone number, Rachel called Nikki's apartment in Portland exactly fifteen times over the next week. Seven times Nikki hung up on her, then Nikki stopped answering the phone.

Serious pain plagued Rachel, pain immune to sleeping pills and cigarettes and alcohol. She remembered the rejection she'd dished out, the phone calls that *she* had rejected in New York, the messages from her daughter unanswered, the letters from her daughter thrown away. And, for the first time in a long time, twenty-five or thirty years or more, Rachel recalled how badly she'd hurt, missing *her* mother. From her own pain, Rachel was finally able to see that her selfish behavior had been devastating to Nicole.

And the memories kept right on rolling, a Hallmark Hall of Fame home movie of Rachel's life shown in reverse, which she watched with a repentant and damaged heart in the hopes of someday becoming whole. She saw herself as a woman who'd fled to the East Coast to hide from her maternal failings and start anew with a different last name and no child. The same woman who'd made poor choices and bailed when things had gone bad in northern California. She watched herself raising someone else's infant daughter, the child of a nonexistent deceased relative. Heard her father's voice, his shame of his illegitimate granddaughter. Heard herself telling Nicole to call her Rachel, not mother. Saw a bottle of red wine, hidden beneath her mattress. A bottle of vodka concealed behind the dirty diaper hamper in the laundry room. Saw herself late one night with a buzz on stumbling numbly after Nicole, who'd just learned to walk and had wandered outside alone.

The movie stopped suddenly, the lights thrown on. Nicole had given Rachel a dose of her own medicine and it tasted just like chicken. Chicken Marsala.

Rachel sprung to her feet, sending her desk chair over backward. Everything unfolded before her as clearly as words in a book she had authored but neglected to read. The gist of it was: she had let her father's shame become her own and, like a coward, had used alcohol to deal with her shame and rationalize the abandonment of her daughter.

As easy as it would have been to blame her father, Rachel realized that her father was no longer the one to blame. She cussed aloud, calling herself a bitch preceded by every humiliating, abject adjective she could think to shout until her voice went hoarse. She righted her chair and sat back down and fat tears streamed down her cheeks and onto her paperwork. The room blurred, but her vision grew in clarity. Whether figuratively blindfolded or shit-faced drunk, she felt it was no longer possible for her to circumvent the moral of the story, nor did she wish to. In the process of winning that had wholly consumed her over the years, nothing that she'd won, not the glory, not the money, the respect, the fame, the infamy, none of it could ever make up for what she had lost.

Rachel sat at her desk in her blue-carpeted barn office mourning the past for over an hour. It had occurred to her after the first ten minutes that she could grieve for the rest of her life without altering history, and it took fifteen more minutes for her to realize that she really did have the power to change the future. And another fifty-five, to admit she had a drinking problem. She laid her head on her arms on the desk and had a long hard cry.

~

A month into Lucifera's recuperation, Rachel's help got into a rush at feed time and accidentally gave the filly the two-and-a-half gallons of grain intended for the colt in the neighboring stall, instead of her own reduced ration. When Rachel returned from Stockton that evening, she found the filly lying in the middle of her stall with her head cranked around, staring at her belly like a horse with a painful stomach ache. A sure sign of colic.

Sam had already taken away her hay bag and called Dr. Steele. His associate, Dr. Reese, was en route. While they waited, Rachel and Sam gently coaxed Lucifera to her feet and into the sling in order to keep her from rolling in pain and twisting her intestine or further damaging her injured leg. Rachel searched the stall for manure to determine whether or not the filly was compacted. Three piles of hefty green turds suggested otherwise. Her assistant explained about the mix-up, how the colt had devoured Lucifera's half-gallon of rolled oats, then banged his tub against the wall nonstop for thirty minutes, alerting his groom to the mistake. By that time, the filly had almost fully consumed the colt's huge mash.

"*Thirty minutes?*" Rachel had commented, while taking deep breaths through her nose.

A rectal examination by Dr. Reese indicated that the filly had no blockage, which was confirmed when the vet pressed his stethoscope to her belly and heard gut sounds. Gastric dilation was his verdict. Horses couldn't vomit, so he passed a large tube into the filly's stomach and attempted to siphon the accumulated contents, but the mass was too pasty to flow through the tube. He then pumped Lucifera full of mineral oil, activated charcoal — to absorb toxins — and water, and gave her a shot of painkiller and a dose of intravenous fluids. Rachel had dealt with hundreds of colicky horses before and knew that every horse suffered the ailment uniquely. Death was neither uncommon nor predictable. They could do nothing more for the filly but keep her out of pain and wait.

Rachel spent the night in the shed row, sitting in a metal folding chair outside Lucifera's stall. Dr. Reese returned twice to check on the filly and to administer more IV fluids. Rachel dozed intermittently. By morning, Lucifera was no better, so throughout the day, Dr. Reese or Dr. Steele treated her with fluids and painkillers, plus another dose of mineral oil, along with an antibiotic solution to kill gas-forming bacteria. By early evening, Rachel smelled ranker than Limburger cheese and took her disheveled self home for a shower and a change of clothes before returning to the barn. She was preparing to spend another night outside the filly's stall with a stack of self-help books, a six-pack of cola, and a bag of corn chips, when Reno McAllister showed up.

"Heard the filly was sick," he said. "Thought you might need some help."

She lowered a book on alcoholism, laying it opened facedown in her lap, so as not to lose her place. Eye-level to the zipper on his blue jeans, she glanced up, gesturing with a hand to the ground beside her. "Have a seat," she said.

He hung his hat over a halter on the nearest stall door, grabbed a set of hay hooks, and pulled down three bales of timothy, stacking two behind and one in front to form a makeshift couch. She closed her book, more uncertain than ever what to make of him.

He sat on the hay. "Why thank you, lady, I think I'll take that seat."

"Suit yourself."

"How long she been colicky?"

"Yesterday afternoon."

"Feed her a bucket of prunes," he said. "Nature's little roto-rooters."

Rachel gave him a look. "Someone's full of shit, all right."

"Listen, I respect you for trying to save the filly. Can't honestly say I would."

"Yeah, I'm a real hero," she told him.

"I'm supposed to be on a plane to Hawaii right now."

"Should I be jealous?"

"I'm going alone," he said.

"That's not what I meant."

He slapped the hay beside him. "Sit over here."

She shook her head. "I don't think so."

"I won't bite."

"Oh, really?"

He was chewing on a piece of gum, his broad jaw lazily sawing. "You're starting to sound like I actually got to you."

She tossed the book in her lap onto the ground beside her chair. "How come you're not on that plane, anyway?"

"Unfinished business." His face erupted in a devilish smile.

She feared misreading his smile and turned away. "I think you should go finish your business."

"I'm trying to."

She sighed and looked at him. "So you've heard I'm broke and want to buy horses."

"I'm not here on *business* business."

"You're too late," she said. "I've already settled up with my bank and sold all I'm selling."

"I don't want any of your damn horses, lady."

"You won the trainer's title, mister. Okay?"

"We tied."

"You would've won if you hadn't taken pity on me and turned down saddling Speedmeister Slew."

"I didn't deserve to be rewarded for orchestrating his sale, especially since you were the one who made him into a champion. I couldn't beat you that way."

"A win's a win."

"Since you're not listening," he said, "I'll cut straight to the point."

"Which is?"

He sprang toward her bullet quick, a blur of motion. Before she could think to protest, he had yanked her onto her feet and kissed her, a head-on collision of lips and teeth and tongues. They parted gasping for breath. Rachel would have been hard pressed to say who was smiling the biggest smile.

"I'm still not selling you any horses," she said.

"Forget the horses."

Their eyes met briefly, as if to confirm mutual yearnings, then they lunged into another kiss. Afterwards, he traced a finger over the outline of her lips. She pulled away.

"I'm temperamental as hell," she said

"Tranquility's boring," he said.

"No expectations?"

"None."

"I definitely need my head examined."

"I'd like to think your heart's finally calling the shots."

"For what it's worth, it's hammering like Woody Woodpecker."

He grinned. "Too many cigarettes."

She leaned into him and put her lips to his ear. "I'd like at least a week of bliss before I start to hate you."

They kissed again, reluctantly stepping back from one another, blushing and breathless, saving the moment for later. She returned to her chair and he to his hay couch. Physical separation seemed best for the present time, lest Lucifera's condition worsen and they—having succumbed to animalistic lustings or some love/hate infatuation that, in either case, Rachel dared not categorize as passion—be elsewhere.

"My luck, if we walked to the kitchen for coffee she'd go and croak."

"Knowing horses, I wouldn't be surprised," he said. "Anyway, won't hurt us to talk some."

"Right," she said. "Talking's good."

"So." He folded his hands, unfolded them, tapped a boot toe. "Heard from Nikki?"

"No."

"She'll come around in time."

"Probably help if I'd stop training, but I can't quit the racetrack any more than the horses can."

"I take it she's a little down on racing after what happened."

Rachel tossed up her hands. "I don't know. I imagine. One of these days, I'll get the whole mess sorted out. Right now, I'm just trying to take better care of myself and the horses."

"Come to think of it, I didn't taste any cigarettes on your breath, did I?" he said, slapping his knee.

"Nope," she said. "Quit drinking, too. Figured I wasn't setting a great example, even if she is an adult."

"Does Nikki know Lucifera's alive?"

"No. Never got the chance to tell her, she left in such a rush."

"Probably better you didn't," Reno said. "Between the leg and the colic, things aren't looking real hopeful."

~

By midnight, Lucifera's condition began to deteriorate. Her temperature had dropped and her pulse was rising, both signs of shock. She groaned repeatedly and broke into a sweat. Dr. Steele came and pumped more fluids into the filly, but her blood pressure kept falling. He suggested a parasympathetic stimulant to increase the contractions in her gas-filled and distended intestines, a risky move, guaranteed to worsen her pain, but he saw no alternative. Rachel agreed.

A short time after receiving the injection, Lucifera began to paw and grab at her belly, insofar as the rubber-tie that secured her to the doorway would allow. She writhed in the sling, her cries of pain answered by anxious nickers from up and down the line. Rachel, Reno, and Dr. Steele watched from the shed row like witnesses to an unfolding disaster they were powerless to halt. The vet shook his head.

"We've done everything humanly possible to save her," he said.

"What about operating?"

"She'd probably tear herself up on the ride to the clinic. I'd consider putting her down."

"Filly dies, she dies on her own terms," Rachel said.

"Hate to see her suffer."

"Then don't look, Doc."

"You're serious about this."

"I am."

"Another shot of bute's probably her best bet."

"Do it."

Rachel held Lucifera, twisting the filly's upper lip to keep her head still until Dr. Steele had given the intravenous injection. They waited outside the stall, Reno pacing, the vet slumped on the hay, Rachel staring at Lucifera as though forbidding her to die. Seconds turned to minutes turned to more minutes. Sweat darkened the filly's coat along her neck, chest, and flanks, wetting the canvas sling with a dark yellowish stain. Lucifera flung her head and fought to break free. The painkiller seemed to have no effect, so Rachel cranked the winch until the filly's front feet were no longer touching the ground and she hung kicking and screaming and savaging the air. When kindly spoken words failed to soothe her, Rachel ducked into the stall and stroked Lucifera's wet neck, but the filly was crazed with pain and struck out with her good foreleg, missing Rachel's face by mere inches.

"You better not die goddammit," she shouted, right before Reno grabbed her from behind and dragged her from the stall.

She struggled against him the entire way with his calm voice in her ears, an incomprehensible lull. In the shed row she threw herself forward and strained to break his hold and go to the filly, but he wrapped his arms around her like a straitjacket. Swearing at everyone and no one, she tasted salt from the tears streaking her cheeks and fell quiet. The frantic motion of her breathing eased. The thud of her heartbeat slowed. With Reno standing behind her and his hands planted gently but firmly on her shoulders, Rachel watched the tragedy play out.

Epilogue

Nikki lost track of time.

August became September became October and November then December. The days grew shorter and colder. Blustery winds rode the Columbia River. Leaves turned yellow and orange and red, the sky favoring gray. After she returned to Portland, she worked at a landscape business, mowing lawns, trimming, raking, and weeding. She hid her veterinary medicine books under her bed and forgot about school, her dream having turned into a nightmare of dead and mangled ghost horses that haunted both conscious and unconscious hours. Matt and Susan had called her almost every day during those first few weeks. Susan wanted Nikki to have dinner with them, while Matt wanted her to show up at his barn wearing a helmet. Nikki had no desire to talk about her stay in California or the infamous horse trainer who happened to be her relative and refused to contemplate working at the racetrack again, so she packed her things and headed farther north. Since fog seemed to suit her, she bought a cabin on an island in southern Puget Sound.

Harstine Island, a somewhat remote and sparsely populated evergreen forest speckled with homes and summer cabins, was connected to the mainland by a short bridge on its western shore. Shelton, the nearest small town of any distinction, was roughly eleven miles to the southwest. Tacoma, the nearest urban city, was a circuitous hour's drive to the northeast. Employment, therefore, proved limited. Nikki didn't know what she wanted to spend the rest of her life doing—the future had dropped off her map—but purchasing the cabin wiped out most of her Peninsula Park earnings. She needed some sort of work to make ends meet. With that in mind, she took a part-time job at the Olympic Mountain Oyster Company.

The term, company, seemed to her a laughable overstatement for a business that had two employees besides herself and the owner, an elderly fellow who claimed to be sixty-eight but looked ninety. The old man leased tidelands at the western end of the Sound, in Totten and Little Skookum Inlets, a hundred feet here, two hundred there, a dozen or more parcels, none of them abutting. At her job interview, he had popped open a large oyster using a blunt edged shucking knife and handed her a half-shell containing a blob the size of her fist. He advised her to chew it thoroughly. She politely gagged down a creature that looked like various genitals, possessed the texture of a booger, and smelled and tasted like fish guts, then told him that she was thinking of becoming a vegetarian. He had hired her on the spot, the ideal applicant for a job whose only perk was free oysters.

Her primary duty was to gather the shellfish. To that end, she accompanied him in a much dented aluminum skiff with mismatched twin outboard motors of indeterminate power— since she had programmed her brain to tune-out the word horse. They anchored in shallow water and waded onto the exposed tidelands wearing hip-waders and thick rubber gloves. Armed with tubs that—full—took all her strength to lift back onto the skiff, they harvested clumps of oysters that she broke apart with a short stout crowbar. Other days were dedicated to spreading mesh bags of yearlings over acres of empty beds. Or collecting predators such as starfish or Japanese oyster drill snails. Periodically, they checked bags of spat growing on clutch shells that were stacked on pallets to keep them from being buried or swept away by the swift currents. Fall and winter saw the lowest tides at night, which meant working in darkness by headlamp or kerosene lantern. She had already been introduced to cold in her former career and now came to know it intimately, the skiff pounding over whitecaps, the wind and spray in her face while she clung to the deck as tenaciously as a barnacle. Gray sky reflected onto gray-green water reflected onto green-gray trees. On the gloomiest days, windless, when the clouds hung thick and low or the fog blotted out the sky without reprieve, the surface shimmered black like some wicked sorcerer's mirror. Nikki stared into the water and saw nothing staring back.

The cabin that she had purchased was tucked among twenty acres of western red cedar, Douglas fir, big leaf maple, red alder, madrona, hemlock, dogwood, huckleberry, salal, Oregon grape, and sword fern. A graveled dirt driveway cut through the trees from the two-lane blacktop road that crisscrossed the island. The cabin was small but cozy, her favorite feature being a clawfoot standing tub that she would soak in—sore ribs and all—after a hard, cold day at work. She had phone service but no cable, and her television picked up one channel when the wind was calm. A previous owner had raised llamas and there was a fenced pasture with a loafing shed, the grass overgrown, the longest blades dried and brown above a carpet of yellowish green. Nikki didn't see herself ever wanting or needing a pasture and envisioned the area as a potential garden site. A dog or a cat seemed the sort of pet to suit her, animals that were unlikely to break any legs and for whom, in the event they did, a genuine effort was actually made to mend their damaged limbs with euthanasia a last resort.

The first heavy rain came in late September and after that, she roamed the woods hunting for huckleberries and mushrooms in her spare time. Huckleberries grew everywhere. The attractive, shiny-leaved, head-high bushes were covered with clumps of blackish-blue or dusty-blue berries that looked and tasted similar to blueberries, only smaller and tarter. Mushrooms presented a less common delicacy. With a Swiss army knife, a mesh canvas bag, and a guide to western mushrooms, she combed through moss, salal, and ferns, the forest a refuge to her, a place of quiet beauty that captured her attention and held it safe. She soon learned to identify a few edible species and picked pounds of white and orange chanterelles, bright orange-red lobster mushrooms, and one humongous cauliflower mushroom growing from a rotted stump. She sauteed her first batch in olive oil and didn't get sick or die. After that, she ate mushrooms and huckleberries for dinner on a regular basis.

Sometimes, they were all she ate. She was plagued by a nervous achy stomach, a sort of perpetual case of indigestion triggered by the act of breathing or eating. Most everything gave her heartburn. Nothing sounded appetizing. A lack of bathroom essentials was the only shortfall that would drive her to the grocery store, where there were people to contend with who might initiate a conversation that led to personal questions. Since she couldn't think of anything nice to say about herself, she'd just as soon say nothing. In order to expedite the ordeal, she took to purchasing the same items: boxes of macaroni and cheese, bananas, apples, carrots, non-fat milk, and corn flakes. By December, her once snug size six blue jeans fit baggily.

Christmas arrived all sunshine and blue skies. With the day off, she had big plans to stay home and sleep in until noon, but by ten she was wide awake and drew a hot bath. She soaked in the tub for more than an hour. Her fingers and toes went wrinkly. She closed her eyes and felt the smoothely rounded edge of her turquoise necklace, the mystery gift for a birthday that had gone otherwise unacknowledged. The fact that only one person at Peninsula Park really knew her birth date was not lost on her, just purposely misplaced. She thought about sharks next. Of how she almost envied their remorseless existence, their immunity to sadness in a world bent on swallowing with impunity each and every living thing. Life, she saw, was a compilation of unhappy episodes separated by brief periods of tranquility meant to lull people into marching bravely onward. She got out of the tub and dried herself. She brushed her teeth and dressed, then headed outside to wander the woods in search of mushrooms.

Three hours later, dew soaked the front of her jeans, her socks were sodden inside her hiking boots, and her hair was tangled with dead fir needles and various leaves and twigs. She had found no mushrooms worth keeping. A recent cold spell followed by rain had turned the chanterelles into slimy mush.

She made her way home on a moss-covered trail, pausing in the backyard beneath an old cedar, broader of girth than she was tall. The cedar rose up a hundred-and-fifty feet or more. Compared to a tree that might live a thousand years, her life span seemed a pittance measurable in dog years. She gazed up at the thick branches, the majority of the lower third broken with the ends protruding like uneven rungs on a ladder to nowhere. Thus dully abstracted, she heard nothing, not the measured beat of a pileated woodpecker, not the snap of a branch, not the approaching footsteps.

"Hello," said a familiar voice.

Nikki wheeled around. She took a step back. Never once, neither in dreams nor nightmares nor wistful thinking, had she imagined this scenario.

There stood Rachel buried under a puffy down parka.

She forced a smile. "Feeling better?"

Nikki just stared at the ground.

"You look a little thin."

"I'm fine."

"That was a hard fall."

"I guess."

A dead maple leaf the size of a paper plate crunched underfoot. Rachel had taken a step closer and stood blinking in the sunlight.

Nikki looked up. Rachel was gazing at her with uncharacteristic warmth, which Nikki interpreted as a misinterpretation and wondered if she'd accidentally consumed a hallucinogenic mushroom. For the first time, she noticed the lines around her mother's eyes and mouth, the face of regret if regret had a representative face.

Rachel turned away, gesturing at the forest with the sweep of an arm. "This place's gorgeous, but I think Alaska's closer."

"It's not," Nikki said.

"Your friends, the Wilcoxes, gave me your address. Get much snow here?"

Nikki shook her head. "How come you're not racing?"

"Sam's covering for me. With Reno's help."

"Reno?"

Rachel turned back around and smiled for real now. "We're sort of dating."

"You and Reno?"

"We bought each other earplugs."

"Oh." Nikki wanted to smile, too, but her mouth wouldn't cooperate.

"First man I haven't felt like killing after a week," Rachel said. "Had my head examined and the shrink says I'm not completely hopeless. Been going twice a month. I always thought that my personal troubles were nobody's business, but it's actually kind of relaxing to talk to someone who's objective and not a friend."

"You're in therapy?"

"Well, no, not really. Yes. We should go sometime."

"You and me?"

"I think it would help."

Nikki felt as though she had fallen into a hole deeper than light or sound could penetrate. She dug at the soft earth with a boot toe and stared at the treetops on the horizon.

Rachel wrung her hands then clapped them together. "I spoke with the dean of the veterinary school at Cal State Davis and he says you shouldn't have any trouble getting in, soon as you get your degree."

The news drew another blank from Nikki.

"It's less than two hours from Peninsula Park," Rachel added.

"Aunt Monica sent me when I was in high school," Nikki said, in a raspy whisper.

"To *vet* school?"

"Therapy."

"*Oh.*" A pause from Rachel. "That must have been a real treat."

"No one listens to you when you're a kid."

"Ain't that the truth." Rachel exhaled a long breath, like someone blowing on a fresh cut to an old wound.

Nikki stuffed her hands in her pockets and confronted a

reality that had mercifully never occurred to her before. "You wanted an abortion, didn't you?"

"I don't remember," Rachel said, too quickly.

"I don't blame you."

Rachel shivered. "It was a long time ago. I was young and scared."

"We'd have both been better off."

"That's *not* true."

"You didn't have to come," Nikki said. "You don't owe me or anything."

"I wanted to come," Rachel said.

"I don't need a mother."

"Is that so?"

"Yeah." Nikki stood her ground, less securely planted than she might have been a year or even six months ago but determined to remain wind firm despite a future that promised more storms than sunshine.

Rachel stuck her hands on her hips like a woman who meant business. It was the passion of her reply as much as her message that penetrated the walls of autonomy that imprisoned them both.

"Well, tough shit," she said, "because you've got one."

The calm of the forest resonated like a sounding board for the crippled of heart. Nikki stood as still as death. A layer of detachment fell away, only to reveal more layers beneath, but she caught a glimpse of hope and the sight intoxicated her subconscious and spread. She felt herself breathing again, the barest rise and fall of her chest.

Rachel wiped a hand across her eyes, smearing black eyeliner above and beneath her lids and down her wet cheeks. There would be no hugging now. The first step had overwhelmed them with the realities of what lay ahead, the commitments and constraints and wonders of family. A shrill thumb-and-finger whistle from Rachel punctured the silence.

Shortly, from the direction of the cabin there came the drumming of hooves down a trailer ramp, followed by the high-pitched cry of a horse. Something about the sound caused

Nikki's heart to beat faster. She froze in place with her head cocked, listening as the whinny came again to ring out in the clear air like a miracle proclaimed. A lump of incredulity wedged in her throat. She looked at her mother. Rachel motioned toward the cabin with a shooing flick of her wrist and a smile that said everything. Nikki took a tentative step, then another. She was running by the time a man led a blanketed, bandaged, free-spirited dappled gray filly with a silver mane and tail into sight, Lucifera's racehorse days over but not her life.